Give me wings, he whispered to himself.
Give me life again.

Golden light flared so brightly he went blind, and he threw back his head, gasping. Fire burned against his tongue.

Until, abruptly, he could see again, and the night was warm and lush, and his skin shimmered with heat and glimmers of gold. Everything around him seemed small and very far away.

"Karr," Soria called urgently. He found her standing close, her hand raised to touch one of his claws. She was pale, and a tremor raced through her that was so violent she swayed. He caught her, and she was small in his grip, his long fingers easily encircling her waist.

"If I frighten you," he rumbled, "close your eyes."

———

By Marjorie M. Liu

In the Dark of Dreams
The Fire King
The Wild Road
The Last Twilight
Soul Song
Eye of Heaven
Dark Dreamers (anthology)
The Red Heart of Jade
Shadow Touch
2 A Taste of Crimson (Crimson City Series)
Tiger Eye

Coming Soon

Within the Flames

[handwritten:] 1 Crimson City
4 Darker Crimson
3

ATTENTION: ORGANIZATIONS AND CORPORATIONS
Most Avon Books are available at special quantity discounts for
bulk purchases for sales promotions, premiums, or fund-raising.
For information, please call or write:

**Special Markets Department, HarperCollins Publishers,
10 East 53rd Street, New York, New York 10022-5299.
Telephone: (212) 207-7528.   Fax: (212) 207-7222.**

Marjorie M. Liu

The Fire King

A DIRK & STEELE NOVEL

AVON

An Imprint of HarperCollinsPublishers

This is a work of fiction. Names, characters, places, and incidents are products of the author's imagination or are used fictitiously and are not to be construed as real. Any resemblance to actual events, locales, organizations, or persons, living or dead, is entirely coincidental.

AVON BOOKS
An Imprint of HarperCollins*Publishers*
10 East 53rd Street
New York, New York 10022-5299

Copyright © 2009 by Marjorie M. Liu
ISBN 978-0-06-201986-8
www.avonromance.com

First Avon Books mass market printing: August 2011

Avon Trademark Reg. U.S. Pat. Off. and in Other Countries, Marca Registrada, Hecho en U.S.A.
HarperCollins® is a registered trademark of HarperCollins Publishers.

Printed in the U.S.A.

10 9 8 7 6 5 4 3 2 1

ACKNOWLEDGMENTS

My thanks, as always, to my editor Chris Keeslar and all the people at Dorchester Publishing. And to Lucienne Diver, as well—my spunky, spitfire, extraordinary agent.

For more information about the Disk & Steele series, please visit my Web site at www.marjoriemliu.com.

. . . a thing of immortal make . . .

HOMER, *The Iliad*

This is the after-hell: I see the light.

SYLVIA PLATH, from "The Stones"

PROLOGUE

THE humans allowed Karr to wake up, which was their first mistake.

He opened his eyes inside a small, tight space where the walls were made of a heavy billowing cloth that flapped against a sharp wind. A tent. Except, the tent was rocking and bouncing like a wagon in motion, and the human men he glimpsed were seated around him on short benches. *Eastern-bred*, he thought. Dark hair, golden skin. Holding oddly shaped black sticks in their laps.

Weapons, whispered his instincts, reading danger in all the little details that had nothing do with the objects the men held. It was their cold, bored gazes, the uniformity of their youth, and their odd clothing. Karr knew soldiers when he saw them.

It took only seconds for him to make his evaluation, and less than that to realize he was strapped to a hard wooden plank too small for his body. The backs of his shoulders rubbed against a cold floor that felt like stone or metal, and thin leather restraints bound his chest, arms, and legs. He was nearly naked, and smelled like urine and dry bones. None of which was as disturbing to Karr as the fact that he was still alive. He had been quite clear about the matter. His friends had promised to murder him.

And so they had. He remembered.

Yet, here he was, breathing and conscious. Karr snarled, golden light swallowing his vision, burning him up from the inside until he felt as though the sun were exploding inside his chest. He heard shouts, but they sounded very far away, and he snarled as scales burst from his skin, his bones shifting, melting, his chest and limbs expanding painfully against their restraints. His fingers lengthened into long serrated claws.

The men hit him with the blunt ends of their black weapons. Karr ignored the pain. He twisted violently, throwing himself upward, and the plank he lay on crashed down hard against the floor. He did it again, and the wood splintered as his body continued to shift. He cut himself on the leather restraints. Blood trickled down his chest and arms. He howled with rage, and hearing his own voice again was a terrible, sickening thing.

The plank broke. Karr's arms swung free. A small blunt object slammed into the side of his head, but he had already begun to turn, and in that small space his long reach and claws arced across soft, startled faces and throats. Blood sprayed. Men screamed, falling backward against the wagon's cloth walls. Karr glimpsed sunlight.

He leaped wildly against the wagon walls, tearing at the heavy cloth with his claws. Hands tried to pull him back, but he could taste the heat of the wind and desert,

and the need to feel the sun on his skin was so powerful, so terrible, he thought he might choke on his own
heart if he did not break free.

He managed to burst through, and was momentarily
blinded by the sun and a sky so blue his throat ached
with nameless longing. He glimpsed large moving objects, glittering and shining, and then jumped away from
the wagon with one powerful lunge.

Karr hit the ground hard and rolled. Loud bleating
sounds filled his ears, and he sensed something large
roaring toward him He threw himself sideways again,
and great dark wheels passed him in a blur, moving faster
than anything he had ever witnessed. Everything was
fast, he realized, struggling to stand, dazed by the assault
on his eyes as he stared at squat square wagons, fully
enclosed, moving without the aid of horses or men. Inside,
faces. Men and women, staring out at him, wide-eyed and
startled. He stared back, just as surprised. Beyond, as far
as the eye could see, rose a metropolis, golden brown and
white, shimmering in the sun. It stunned him breathless.

And then the wind shifted and he smelled her: a shape-
shifter, pure-blooded and wild.

Too late. Pain exploded against his shoulder, and he
turned, staggering, reaching back to find a long smooth
object jutting from his body. Not a knife. More slender,
rounded.

Karr's vision blurred. He saw the shape-shifter, but
not her face—just a glimpse of short blonde hair as
she darted around him. He tried to follow but his knees
buckled. Darkness fluttered. Voices shouted, but he

understood nothing that was said. He tried to fight. He tried with all his power, staring down at his clawed hands, skin rippling with golden scales.

The shape-shifter's scent made him sick. She said something to him, but it was nothing but a buzz in his ears. Karr collapsed on his side and closed his eyes, hoping for just a moment that he would not open them again.

CHAPTER ONE

It had been a long time since Soria had found herself in a crowd, and so she supposed she could be forgiven for having a case of the jitters, even when something as harmless as a staring child proved enough to make her hand shake.

She was in the Minneapolis airport, leaning against the counter of a small island Starbucks. It was early, not quite seven in the morning. She had paid for orange juice and happened to glance sideways, to her right, just as the cashier was carefully placing change into her palm. A child was tugging on his mother's hand. Staring at Soria. A tousled, sweet-looking boy, maybe four or five. Nothing wrong with what he was doing. Kids were always curious.

But it took her off guard, and her hand trembled—so much so that the change slid and clattered to the counter, bouncing down on the floor around her feet. It should have been a small thing—it *was* a small thing—but it was also loud and awkward, and drew unwanted attention.

Soria was very much tempted to grab her drink, leave the scattered nickels and dimes, and run.

She bent, her face hot, and glimpsed from the corner of her eye the long line of men and women fidgeting impatiently behind her. For one moment as her purse swung awkwardly from her left shoulder to hit the floor, she felt herself trying to reach out with her missing right arm to pick the change off the tile. All she got for her trouble was excruciating pain, a phantom echo where her limb should be, and another dose of humiliation. Bitter loneliness smashed through her heart like a fist. Her ghost fist, maybe, as stubborn about dying as she had been.

Beside her, someone knelt. Large, sinewy fingers enclosed her hand, and loose change was carefully deposited into her palm. The contact was brief but fiercely warm, and it sent a tingle through her. She had not been touched by anyone in a long time.

Soria poured the change into her purse, grabbed the juice from the cashier, and stepped away from the counter to make room for the next woman in line. Flustered, sweating, she finally gazed into the face of the man who had helped her. He was handsome, which was just her luck. His face was paler than his hands, but just as sinewy and spare. Light green eyes glinted with sharp intelligence, and his neatly trimmed dark red hair appeared skimmed with golden threads under the overhead lights. He was tall, with broad shoulders straining against a forest green cashmere sweater that hugged the lean muscles of his chest. A silver chain glinted around his neck, disappearing beneath his clothing.

"Thanks," Soria said, feeling rather numb and scatter-brained.

"You're welcome," replied the man smoothly, and held out a thin folded airline envelope. "This dropped out of your purse when you bent down."

It was her plane ticket. Soria wanted to kick herself. Again, she felt her brain tell her missing right arm to reach out—such a hateful sensation—and the pain that echoed through her head was nauseating and dull.

Soria awkwardly dumped her juice bottle into her purse and took the ticket from his outstretched hand. "Good thing you saw that."

"Yes," he agreed, not letting go of the ticket.

Soria hesitated, staring into his eyes, and all his attractive features faded into a blur. Uneasiness rolled through her stomach, into her lungs, into the lurch of her heart. Not simply because of his reluctance to release the ticket, and not just because the glint in his gaze suddenly seemed irredeemably cold. The man had switched languages on her. English to Welsh, she realized. And not just any Welsh, but an old dialect, practically medieval, and most certainly dead. And she—like an idiot—had responded without thinking. In the same tongue.

The man stepped back, still holding her plane ticket. Soria licked her lips, and in very careful modern English said, "Who are you?"

"Roland sent me," he replied, still speaking ancient Welsh. "He needs you to come home, Soria."

Home. Not just a place. Home was people. Home was old dreams.

Soria turned and walked in the opposite direction. Never mind her plane ticket; she could buy another. Never mind the job interview in New York with the U.N. If she missed that, there would be others.

She felt the ghost of her missing arm swinging from her body, that phantom limb, replete with an itch where her wrist should have been. She ignored the discomfort, wished she had some chewing gum to take the bad taste out of her mouth. Airport crowds passed in a blur, but she felt gazes flicker to her empty sleeve and then dart away. She did not know what was worse: those brief embarrassed glances or the people who pretended her disfigurement did not exist. That *she* did not exist.

You exist for someone now, she thought grimly, quickening her pace. *Damn it, Roland.*

Ahead, an impossibly slender girl stepped into her path, facing her. She was Asian, clad in a pink plaid miniskirt so short that if she had not been wearing cropped gray tights underneath, she might very well have been arrested for indecent exposure. A pink hooded sweatshirt clung to her torso, and her glossy black hair, streaked pink, was pulled up in pigtails decorated with plastic Hello Kitty beads that clacked when her head tilted. She wore a mockery of tennis shoes: hot pink and silver, raised up on an inch-thick sole. A messenger bag covered in yet more Hello Kitties slung loose over her flat chest.

Men stared. Women looked away. Soria stopped walking, light-headed. The girl's age was impossible to determine—anywhere from thirteen to twenty, though her dark eyes were old as dirt and the set of her mouth was lethal. Soria herself was thirty years old, but she felt ancient and used when she looked at the girl, old eyes or not. She was no better than some grizzled gunslinger, too long alive in the world.

Heat settled in her chest, old instincts, raw and battered. She was not ready. She had retired. Everyone had agreed.

Soria turned her head, slightly. The red-haired man was behind her, close enough to touch. His gaze was assessing and cold. Like ice.

"We should talk," he said, in perfect Gaelic; and then, in a Persian dialect that was just as old as his Welsh, he added: "If you please."

Fear tingled through her. Intrigue, as well. Curiosity, she admitted, was what had gotten her into trouble in the first place, and here it was again, that same intellectual itch that was as dangerous as a gun to her head. A puzzle. A linguistic riddle.

"What," she asked slowly, "does Roland want?"

"Your time," the man replied in English, as a sea of travelers passed around them. The terminal was a long, winding hall of upscale shops surrounded by golden wood and the occasional elaborate sculpture—no doubt meant to imitate the warmth of some lodge, easy and comfortable. A good scream would draw hundreds of eyes.

But that old curiosity kept her silent, as well as nostalgia . . . and loneliness. She sensed that slip of a teen girl swaying closer, and stepped sideways so that she could keep both her and the man in sight. Cold amusement flickered through his eyes.

"My name is Robert," he said. "My associate is Ku-Ku."

"Bitter," Soria replied, translating the girl's name from Mandarin. "Appropriate, I assume."

"In so many ways," replied the man.

Soria did not want to know. "How can I be certain Roland sent you?"

Robert reached into his pocket and pulled out a battered silver bracelet: thick, scarred, and tarnished with age. A chunk of turquoise, like an eye, had been embedded in the cuff. Soria's breath caught when she saw it.

He held out the bracelet. "He thought you would stay long enough for him to return this. Or at least, that's what he told me."

It was not proof, exactly, but Soria had no doubt that the piece of antique jewelry had come from her former boss. She took it from Robert, half expecting him to pull back at the last moment. The bracelet was cool in her left palm, and the old habit of slipping it over her right wrist was so strong that for a moment she felt the echo of silver sliding over her ghost skin.

"Roland can have my time," Soria said hoarsely. "But he better make it good."

"That's up to you," Robert replied, tearing her plane ticket in half. "But you know it will be interesting."

Indeed, thought Soria, ignoring the phantom ache of her missing arm. With Roland and the other agents of Dirk & Steele, life was always a bit *too* interesting.

ROLAND HAD CHARTERED A PRIVATE PLANE TO SAN Francisco. Soria spent the four-hour flight nursing her orange juice, which soon turned warm and tasteless. She did not care, just wet her tongue on the drink here and there.

Asking Robert questions was useless. She gave up after the first thirty minutes. He stayed at the back of the plane, reading an archaeology magazine and occasionally shaking his head. Ku-Ku sat beside him, gigantic headphones jammed over her ears, seat back, eyes closed.

Soria, after some careful maneuvering, managed to slide the bracelet over her left wrist. The silver felt cold and uncomfortable. She had not worn jewelry in a long time, but she did not remove it. She stared at the turquoise rock embedded in silver, swallowed some ibuprofen to dull the first tingle of a headache, and spent the flight trying not to think of much at all.

It had been over a year. San Francisco had not changed. It was early summer and still cold. Crooked streets, steep hills, crowded sidewalks. Business suits were mixed with chains and Mohawks; Victorian architecture crammed between modern office buildings and Art Deco landmarks. Soria had always thought that Bay Area neighborhoods felt like people: unique, constantly evolving, but with certain essential personalities that at all times stayed the same. She missed that—but not enough to move back. She liked her small condo in downtown Stillwater, with her view of the St. Croix River, even if she was considering jobs in New York City. Quiet had served her well for the past year, but she wanted to be useful again.

Robert drove a red Audi. Ku-Ku sat in the backseat.

Soria glanced over her shoulder, and found the girl still listening to her headphones and cleaning under her nails with a rather large knife that looked better suited for a military commando than some kid.

Soria said, "Roland's recruiting them kind of young, don't you think?"

Robert glanced at her. "I never said we worked for Dirk and Steele."

He spoke in Russian. Soria gripped her seat belt as he accelerated around a tight corner. "Roland wouldn't send an outsider."

A faint smile touched his mouth. "You assume too much."

The edge of a cool blade grazed the side of her throat. Soria twisted, heart hammering, but Ku-Ku was still cleaning her nails. Looking like a bored teen, glued to her seat. She glanced up, though—just for a split second— and her eyes were cold and dead.

"Here we are." Robert pulled off the road, parking in front of a familiar stout office building constructed from dark stone blocks and decorated with modernized elements of a Grecian and Gothic flair: stone pillars and rounded corners, smooth carved faces perched on top of the pedestals, gazing down at the street. Nine stories tall. Restaurants lined the first floor: a Starbucks, a small Italian deli and pizzeria, a little café specializing in gourmet chocolates.

Soria scrambled out, almost falling on her knees. She half expected to get stabbed or shot in the back, and hopped a few feet from the car before turning to gaze at Robert. He tossed her purse at her, and then leaned out to dump her carry-on suitcase onto the sidewalk. She paid no attention to her belongings, but instead watched him. Hands back on the wheel. No visible weapons. Cold green eyes.

Ku-Ku slithered from the rear, coiling sinuously in the passenger seat like a pink snake tattooed with white cats. Graceful, flexible. No sign of knives or headphones. The girl braced her pink tennis shoes against the dashboard, and smacked her chewing gum. Robert peered around her at Soria.

"Some advice," he said, in Icelandic. "Don't think about the arm so much."

It took a moment for Soria's mind to translate, which meant that—unlike the other languages Robert had spoken earlier—he was not fluent in this one. Not that it mattered.

"It's none of your business," she replied.

"Not yet," he said enigmatically—and Ku-Ku, with a knowing smile, slammed shut the door. Soria watched the Audi accelerate back into traffic, cutting off several other cars that braked hard, blaring their horns. She stood there until its taillights disappeared at the intersection, feeling a bit like an alien marooned in a strange world, and then shook herself, clenched her teeth, and stooped to pick up her belongings.

The restaurants were the only public areas of the office building. No alleyway doors, no kitchen entrances. Concrete embedded with steel and lead sheeting lined the walls dividing the public from private, which was accessible only from one narrow street-side door lined with old-fashioned copper and leaded glass.

Soria stepped inside the alcove and pulled free her key. Despite removing herself from the agency, it had never occurred to her to cut all ties. Certainly not this key. Which, now that she was standing here, told Soria a lot about how much she had missed the place and its people. Enough to drop everything and follow a stranger.

This better be good, she thought, irritated at herself. *Better be damn good.*

Soria jammed the key into a copper faceplate set in the stone blocks of the alcove, unlocking the small compartment. A keypad and biometrics scanner was inside. She pressed her thumb to the screen, and then typed in the six-digit code. The front door unlocked. She kicked through her carry-on bag, and shut everything tightly behind her.

The lobby was quiet, the marble floors dark and shining. Only one elevator. Soria keyed in another code, and rode all the way up to the ninth floor.

She heard screams before she reached the penthouse. A man's voice cut straight through the elevator shaft into her bones. Doors opened. Soria ran into a warm foyer, across scuffed and battered oak floors. Screams continued to fill the air, and then cut off into abrupt, terrible silence. Soria hesitated, heart pounding—and then continued down the long hall, slower now, more careful, blinded by a floor-to-ceiling wall of windows through which the afternoon sun was shining. She glimpsed low tables sagging with books, and soft overstuffed sofas piled high with papers. Nothing she could use as a weapon.

She entered the living room and immediately sensed

movement on her left. A hand shot out and grabbed her arm.

"Soria," Roland growled, holding her steady as she stumbled. It had been a long time since she had heard his voice, and it cut through her, more painfully than she could have imagined. For a moment she could not look at him; she could just stare at his feet, in socks, with those familiar holes in the toes.

But that hurt, too, and she forced her chin up, thinking, *Brave girl. Be brave.*

Little had changed. Roland was still a big man, scruffy and unshaved, with a hard-knocks face and brown hair that needed a cut. But a year had deepened the lines in his brow, and his blue eyes squinted at her with weariness. He looked terrible.

"So, you came," he said gruffly, after a long moment of tense silence.

"You asked," she replied, pulling away. "Who did I hear dying?"

Roland's jaw tightened, and without a word he turned and walked across the room toward a flight of stairs that disappeared downward. Except for the first level, which was owned but not used by Dirk & Steele, all the floors of the building were part of the penthouse, but the only entrance was on the ninth. Soria jogged after him.

For as long as she could remember, the eighth floor had been part of a massive kitchen and dining area, large enough to accommodate a small army of loud and messy eaters. But the dining tables and couches had been removed, and now a thick glass wall blocked off the entire right side of the room. Smooth polished concrete covered what had been a hardwood floor, and concrete blocks covered the walls and windows. Clothing had been tossed on the floor outside the glass.

Inside, on the floor, curled a naked young man. All Soria could see was his long, lean back and dark hair, but she would have known him anywhere. The air around his body shimmered with heat.

"Eddie," Soria breathed, and might have fallen on her knees in front of the glass had Roland not grabbed her arm and hauled her toward the stairs.

"Go," he whispered roughly. "The kid'll be embarrassed for you to see him like this." *Weak. Exposed. Helpless.*

Soria stumbled backward, staring through the glass at Eddie. She thought she must be losing her mind. Lights danced in her vision. Roland shoved her again, and she scrambled up the stairs.

He joined her, moments later. They stood together, shoulder to shoulder, staring out the tinted windows. Soria glimpsed the blue edge of the bay, but it meant nothing to her. All she could see was the young man behind the glass, and then her own reflection: long black hair framing an olive-toned face and brown serious eyes.

"There was an accident," Roland said quietly, his voice little more than a growl. "Happened in Africa. Kid got sick. Affected his control. Been like this for a little under six months. He'll be fine for a while, then . . . fire. Fuck-load of fire."

You should have called me, she almost said, before

remembering that she had no telephone. "So you keep him in a cage?"

Roland shot her an angry look. "He can come out whenever the hell he wants. Eddie knows when he's losing it. That's the only safe room in this goddamn place."

Soria closed her eyes. Her head ached, and a tingle ran down the ghost of her missing arm, a feeling so real and substantial she could almost believe, truly, that she was still whole. "If you're not careful, Roland, he'll never leave this building. He'll become just like you."

Or me, she thought at him, knowing he could hear her thoughts if she wanted him to.

Roland stiffened. "You know it's different. A missing arm doesn't kill people."

Soria turned on him, and shoved her finger hard against his chest. "Eddie is only twenty years old. You let him start down this road, and he'll spend his entire life too afraid to do anything meaningful. You'll *kill* him."

Roland grabbed her wrist, squeezing hard. "I didn't bring you here for this."

"Well, you got it," she snapped, trying to remain unmoved by the anger and grief in his eyes. "Do his mom and grandmother know?"

"They think he's overseas. He calls them every week. Writes postcards, and I have the others send them." Roland released her slowly, almost wistfully; then he turned and threw himself down on the nearest couch, covering his eyes with one raw-knuckled hand. His stomach bulged slightly against his shirt. "He's a good kid."

Soria forced herself to breathe. Eddie was more than good. He was *sweet*, a genuine golden heart. And, it just so happened, a pyrokinetic. Able to start fires with his mind.

Dirk & Steele. To the public it was nothing but an elite, internationally respected detective agency—and that was the truth. But it was just one truth. Because the men and women who were part of the agency, Soria included, were not entirely human.

Psychics, shape-shifters, creatures out of legend. The world was a strange place. Got stranger every day. Soria's personal library was filled with books on evolution, mutation, mythology—anything that could shed light on the how and why of those differences that separated the men and women of the agency from other humans. Soria still had no answers. But being part of Dirk & Steele allowed its employees the most basic opportunities to hide and work in plain sight, to do good under the auspices and protection of a legitimate, respected organization. Because even though almost no one in this world believed in magic—like, that a man could start fires with his mind, or read thoughts—such things were real, and did happen.

And, it was good to be useful. It was good not to be alone. To have friends who knew the truth.

We are family, she thought to herself, plucking at the wrist of her empty sleeve. *One crazy, messed-up family*.

Soria looked up and found Roland watching her. Reading her mind, perhaps. Or not. He had some morals. Soft heart, rough exterior. Like a big grizzly bear. Boss of them all, even though he was not the ultimate last word at the agency. That was a privilege retained by its elderly founders.

"I'm sorry," he said finally, his voice little more than a quiet rumble. "About everything. I don't think I ever told you that."

"You wouldn't leave this building to come to the hospital," she reminded him.

Roland's gaze hardened. "That's not why you left the agency."

Soria sat down on the couch, opposite him. "So why am I here now? Why did you send a stranger to track me down?"

Below them, at the bottom of the stairs, she heard clicking sounds, glass rattling. Roland rubbed his face, grimacing. "There's a situation. We . . . found someone. He doesn't speak English, or anything else that's comprehensible. In fact, we don't even think his language exists anymore."

"That's impossible."

"Cocky woman. Trust me, it's possible."

She made a rude gesture. "In remote areas where native tongues are going extinct, outside influences are almost always to blame. But that does create some kind of universal commonality. Are you saying that this . . . person . . . has been so totally isolated that there's *nothing* he understands? Not in any language?"

"Yes," Roland replied, covering his eyes again. "Fuck, yes."

Soria leaned backward, staring. "Is he a child?"

Roland shook his head, still not looking at her. Uneasiness made her stomach ache, and she twisted her empty sleeve in her fist. "Then who is this man?"

"We don't know. But he's not human. Not quite. And not being able to talk to him has limited some of what we can do. I need you to go and . . . speak his language. Evaluate whether he's a danger to us."

"To the agency," she asked slowly, "or everyone?"

"Both," Roland replied. "I wouldn't have interrupted your new life if it wasn't important. You're the only one who can do this. The only one who can do it right. I promise . . . I promise it'll be safe."

"I'm not worried about safe," she muttered, still fussing with her sleeve. "I'm just not certain I want to do this anymore."

"Your mind works, doesn't it?" he shot back. "You can still speak any language in the world, can't you?"

Soria gave him a sharp look. "That's not the point. I killed a person. I murdered a man in cold blood."

Roland laughed bitterly, a familiar reaction that angered her now as much as it had a year ago. "Yeah. But he deserved it."

CHAPTER TWO

Death offered no respite from Karr's nightmares, and resurrection was little better. Not that he had expected tranquility—not while alive, and certainly not while dead. Actions made echoes, from birth into eternity, and he had known very little peace in his life.

Karr was in a small room. Not a tent, not a wagon. Four solid walls and stone beneath him. He had been here for a long time, and while he had no clear recollection of how he had arrived, the presence of a pure-blooded shape-shifter did not bode well. He had not yet seen her face, but he could smell her. Every time the door to the room opened, her scent lingered.

Close. She was very close. Which only made Karr wonder why she had not yet cut his throat. It was no less than he expected. No less than what had been done to others of his kind. No less than what his own hands had done.

A single white light burned overhead with an uncannily steady flame. It was not fire but something different, perhaps born of magic or some arcane tinkering, such as those fast-moving wagons. This was a new world, he had decided, and one he was ill prepared to confront. Though if shape-shifters were still declaring war on the chimeras, then some things had stayed the same.

We must kill them first, Tau had told him often. *We must destroy them.*

And Karr still remembered, so clearly, what he had always said in return. *They fear us. For good reason. So we will kill, but we will not destroy. We will have mercy. We will not be like them.*

But he had, in the end. His worst fears had come true.

And he was alive again. Despite his friends burying him, despite bleeding to death in the catacomb.

The wound was fatal, Karr thought, feeling his side itch as it had, unmercifully, for what felt like days.

He could not move to scratch himself, or to feel for a scar. He could not move at all, not one inch. Iron surrounded his body. His arms and legs were pinned in place by a series of cold, thick bars, and his hands and feet had been wrapped in a heavy cloth made of linked iron ribbons. An iron collar bound his throat to the stone floor he lay upon, and every time he breathed, his chest expanded against yet more cold metal.

A soft sheet covered his loins, but nothing else. Sores were forming on his hips, but the pain was no worse than the boredom. There was very little to look at but the shining light and smooth stone walls. Nothing else was visible beyond the confines of the iron hood that had been placed over his head.

Clever, thought Karr coldly, forcing himself to be

careful as he breathed. A small hole had been left for his nose and mouth, but the hood was already moist from his sweat, and hot. He could shape-shift, but his body would be too large for the restraints—he'd be risking impalement or a crushed skull. He had been lucky in that wagon; wood and leather could be broken or snapped, and nothing had covered his face. Here, now, a full shift would surely kill him.

Probably. Maybe. Death, apparently, was not so easy to come by. Karr wanted to know why.

So, patience, he told himself. Waiting, in utter stillness, for just the right opportunity. Little different than hunting, really. Less painful than his other brief incarcerations before and during the war.

But always, *always*, he felt the shape-shifter close by. That female. She stirred all kinds of unpleasant memories the longer he remained confined.

Until finally, again, something changed.

HE HAD JUST BEEN FED. LIKE A BABY, FED, SWALLOWING the mashed, tasteless food placed in his mouth, careful not to let any dribble past his lips because he knew his face would not be cleaned, his itches not scratched, his tears not wiped away when he slept, briefly, and dreamed.

Karr heard the door open and a tingle rode over his skin. With it, a familiar scent. Shape-shifter.

She moved slowly into the room. Quiet. He imagined the lashing of her tail, though he knew she walked on two feet. He could taste the feline in her scent, wild and musky.

Something else, too. Sunlight. Heat. She had been outside recently, or near someone who had. The new scent tasted sweeter than water, and he drank it in with restrained, careful greed.

The shape-shifter spoke to him. Her language was sly like her voice, and he understood none of her words. He did not need to. Karr found nothing reassuring in her tone, and when she finally stepped into view, allowing him to see her for the first time—and blocking out the light—her face was just as he had imagined: sharp and bony, and hard with a cold beauty that Karr suspected might frighten weaker men into instant obedience. Her hair was short and blonde, and a black patch covered one of her eyes. The other iris was golden but disfigured: the pupil was a slit, like a cat.

Caught between skins in a bad shift. Karr had suffered several of those himself, but had healed, in time. Time healed all, he had been told.

But not the heart, he thought. *Not that.*

The shape-shifter was not young . . . but not old, either. *Well aged*, Tau might have said. Karr watched her carefully, tension finally pushing through his tight control. She reminded him too much of the old queens of the southern clans—unpredictable in their rage and disdain, and pleased to have a chimera as their slave and plaything.

Her clothes were odd. That she wore anything at all was strange enough, but she was covered from neck to ankle in tight black cloth, the weave so fine it could hardly have been made by human fingers. Her feet were bare.

She stood above him, and for one brief moment he saw raw flickering tension in her eyes. *Fear.* She hid it well, but he knew what to look for. He had seen it often enough in her kind.

Her right hand flared with golden light. Spotted fur rippled over her skin, her fingers lengthening into claws. Razor sharp. She flexed each one of them, slowly. Watching him. Tension still twisting through her.

Karr braced himself, but instead of attacking him she said another word. Somewhere on his left the door opened. He smelled that fresh scent again, stronger now, as though a slice of the sun and wind had been cut for him and braided into flesh. Human flesh. He could taste that, too, now. A woman.

Her footsteps were slow but almost as light as the shape-shifter's. Careful movements. Cautious. Or just curious. He had suffered idle eyes enough in his life. Anger curled through him, but he swallowed it down. Not yet. Now was not the moment to lose himself. He had done that in the wagon and failed to escape. Strategy was the key now. Strategy and deception.

Karr's gaze ticked sideways as the human woman finally entered his line of sight. The hole in the iron hood framed her face for him, as did two long black braids, frayed and unkempt. A similar rugged wildness was in her eyes, which only enhanced the delicate beauty of her features. High cheekbones, a small mouth, long throat. She wore a man's clothes, as all the women did in this place: black leggings, skintight, and a long, shapeless tunic made of blazing white cloth. Around her neck hung loops of lapis chunks, resting heavily against her olive-toned skin, a color that marked her as a woman of the desert or sea.

The desert, he decided, staring into her dark eyes, drawing in her scent until his chest pressed hard against the restraints—holding her within him, holding her until he thought he might choke without air. He exhaled slowly, still trying to possess that sunlit scent, and her mouth tensed, as if in pain.

The shape-shifter spoke, a melodic one-sided conversation that was soft and cold, and infinitely menacing. The human flashed her a hard, angry look; brazen, defiant, without a shred of fear. Startling, utterly unexpected. Karr had never seen a human look at a shape-shifter as an equal. Not with such confidence, or disregard.

The human muttered several sharp words filled with scathing disdain, and the shape-shifter tilted her head, a dangerous smile touching the corner of her mouth. Karr tensed, certain he was about to bear witness to death, and pain, and humiliation. No shape-shifter would tolerate such boldness from a human. The woman would not be suffered to live.

Do not, whispered the cold part of his mind. *Do not care. Do not involve yourself.* But the shape-shifter's hand flexed, and he remembered screams—screams in the darkness where he had hidden the cubs, and the blood glistening on claws, on the mouths of the soldiers standing over him—and he tugged hard on his restraints. So hard the iron bit into his flesh.

The human woman gave him a sharp look, anger still bright in her eyes. No fear. Not even in her scent. He could not tear his gaze from her, not until he felt the shape-shifter throw him a cold, careless glance. It was a fleeting look that lingered and then sharpened. She gazed between him and the human woman, and her smile grew even deadlier.

It was too much. Karr threw himself against his bonds, fighting them in silence. The iron did not yield. Golden light spilled over his skin. Soft scales rippled, edged with fur, and the tender flesh of his wounds, incurred while breaking the leather restraints in the wagon, split open.

It hurt, but he did not stop. Not when the shape-shifter growled, baring her sharp teeth, dropping into a half crouch. Her musky scent grew stronger, bitter. Golden light trickled from her single eye.

The human woman stepped between them. She moved fast, with determination, and stood with her back to Karr, facing the shape-shifter. She did not say a word, but instead placed one hand against the shifter-woman's shoulder, pushing her back. Firm, unflinching. Karr stopped straining against his bonds. Caught in the moment. Staring.

No one spoke. The human did not back down. Not even when the shifter-woman dragged one claw down her slender arm, looking past her, directly into Karr's eyes. Karr kept himself very still, though the tension that rode through him could not be hidden; scales continued rippling over his skin and his muscles bunched against the iron. It felt good. So good he did not want to stop, even if it killed him.

The human glanced over her shoulder, meeting his

gaze, and something wild fluttered through her expression: a fracture, small and pained. Without a word, she began shoving the shape-shifter toward the door. With urgency, determination. Anger.

He expected the shifter-woman to strike back, but instead she yielded gracefully, casting Karr a cold look that made his hackles burn. Whatever this was—this human, this shifter, this power struggle between them—he was still a prisoner. He was still *her* prisoner. And she wanted him to know it.

The shape-shifter stepped backward, followed by the human. Karr watched as much as he could, but the hood limited his peripheral vision. He heard the door open and close. Silence followed, though he could still smell warm sunlight. He strained for that scent. He listened painfully as feet scuffed the floor.

The human woman moved back into sight. Her cheeks were red, her dark eyes narrowed, her breathing just slightly rushed. But when she looked into his eyes again, there was still no fear.

Bold, striking. Few had ever fascinated Karr, but this woman did. He wanted to know what made her strong enough to compel a shape-shifter's deference—and how she could look him in the eye without hesitation. When no one else ever had.

"Hello," she said.

Karr blinked, staring.

"Hello," said the woman again. It was not his imagination. Since his resurrection, he had not heard one word he understood. Not one. His brief attempts to communicate had brought him nothing but confused looks. Captivity was bad enough, but to be isolated in language was a burden he had wondered seriously whether he would be able to bear. Pain could be controlled. So could fear. But words, even the hostile words of an enemy, were still an anchor, a connection—the only thing, at times, that separated an animal from a man.

"Hello," he said, his voice muffled by the mask. His throat hurt. So did his heart.

The woman drew in a slow, deep breath and nodded to herself, her gaze solemn and thoughtful. She began to crouch, must have realized that would take her from his line of sight, and moved even closer, up his body, until she stood by his shoulder. Karr could see her better there. He looked straight up at her—and realized, stunned, that she was missing her right arm. He had not noticed before. She had kept that side of her body turned from him. But it was clear now; her sleeve was empty.

Karr looked back at the woman's face, and found her staring at him with a steely directness that sent a thrill of unease and confusion down his spine. Her scent altered, too. He tasted more of her anger.

"I would like to know your name," she said, each word spoken slowly, carefully, her accent unlike any he had ever heard.

He almost told her. He came so close. It shocked him, the ease with which she made him want to talk. He had never given in so easily. Never.

A trick, he told himself. *Mind games. They have known*

how to speak to you all this time, and now they put on a performance. They give you a woman who is no threat, who fascinates you. Who can talk to you. Lull you.

Bitter disappointment crawled up his throat. It was true. It had to be. It had been tried before in the first years of the war, but the human women tossed at his feet had been frail, timid creatures, shivering in his presence like newborn cubs. There was no fire in them. No strength and intelligence blazing in their eyes. Not a shred of defiance. They were nothing like this woman who stood above him.

She is not false, whispered his instincts. *Look into her eyes. She has never been broken.*

Neither had Karr. But he found himself close, in that moment. He wanted to be lulled. He wanted to be spoken to, so badly he could taste it. He was tired of fighting, then and now. He had been so disturbed by his own insanity that he had sought relief at the end of a sword; he had allowed himself to be buried alive for little more than the knowledge that he would never again be allowed to hurt the people he loved.

Karr said nothing. The woman tilted her head, frowning, and sat beside him, so close that he felt the heat of her body against his shoulder. Her scent, so full of sunlight, filled him with another kind of warmth that he refused to dwell on.

And yet . . . She rubbed her chin, silver and turquoise flashing along her wrist, and he found it impossible to look away from her face. He told himself it was for his own good, that he had to study her—divine her weaknesses, if he could—but the simple truth was that she intrigued him. And if he was going to die in this place, then at least it would be from torture and not boredom.

"My name is Soria," she said.

And the rest was silence.

THE NEXT TIME YOU SEE ROLAND, SORIA TOLD HERSELF, ten minutes later, *you are going to kick his ass.*

She already had it planned—a knee to his nuts and, once he was down, another good stomp. She was going to dance a goddamn jig on his testicles. Followed by a verbal browbeating that she hoped made his ears bleed.

Soria managed to hold it together until she left the holding cell. For years she had been good at compartmentalizing her emotions, staying cool and calm, focused under any condition: bullets, fire, stampede. The past year had frayed her edges, but seeing that man— that giant of a man strapped inside something that resembled a medieval torture device—sent her back to fundamentals.

Get the job done. Be calm. Focus.

Then freak.

Serena McGillis waited in the hall. She had already slipped her sunglasses back on, which so far seemed to be her only weakness: a reluctance to show her eyes. One eye was missing, the other golden and inhuman. Soria understood, but that was the only thing about Serena that made sense.

The shape-shifter was tall and sinewy, a cold blonde beauty who had to be in her fifties, though she hardly looked it. Her daughter, Iris, was married to one of Soria's friends and colleagues. Everything else was a mystery.

Soria had never met Serena before this morning. She was not a member of Dirk & Steele; she belonged to another organization, one that until recently had gone unknown, unnoticed, and well under the radar. Serena was not one of the bad guys, so the others said, but she was not so good, either. Unnamed, relegated to shadows, she and her group took a pragmatic approach to problems—and they were particularly handy for fighting and undermining yet another organization that *was*, in fact, evil.

The Consortium: a criminal network made up of psychics engaging in everything from organized crime to human slavery and genetic experimentation. Because of them, Soria's friends had been kidnapped and tortured. A lab in the Congo had recently been discovered full of human women impregnated with the sperm of captured shape-shifters. Serena's own daughter had been targeted for capture and to become one of their breeders. Soria found the whole situation horrifying.

But this . . . this was right up there. Worse, it was her own people involved.

"You are so full of shit," she said to Serena, who had seemed more bothered by the lamb chop served at breakfast than the wounded man imprisoned in the room behind her. Even now the shape-shifter showed nothing except a faint smile, more bitter than amused.

Serena replied, "If you think I overstated the danger,

you are mistaken. He has already killed ten of my men. He would kill you, given the chance. Those restraints are the only thing that can contain him."

"Funny you had them," Soria replied. "You do this often?"

Serena's mouth tightened. "This, or death. For one such as him, there is nothing between."

Soria twisted her empty sleeve. Those golden eyes glimpsed inside that iron hood continued to burn through her; the entire memory of the man's presence filled her with both unease and curiosity. She had felt something in his brain, felt his language move through her as though it could be held and tasted. It had taken her longer than usual to process that slow, steady feed, made her feel like a kid again, her brain thick with words, full and turgid as a water balloon just waiting to pop.

Ghost fingers tingled. Soria gritted her teeth. "Then why am I here? Why bring me all this way to talk to a shape-shifter you think is too dangerous to live?"

"What did Roland tell you?"

"Not enough. Certainly not why we would partner up with people like you."

"And yet, you came."

Like a fool, thought Soria, hearing the rich layer of contempt in Serena's voice.

She let it slide, kept her gaze steady and cool. For ten years she had stood toe-to-toe with kidnappers, hostage-takers, murderers, presidents, military commanders, every manner of man or woman, good, bad, and down-right disgusting. All of them had thought they were more dangerous than Soria, and all of them were absolutely correct. She had few skills as a fighter.

Yet, she controlled words. She was a link that bound strangers. She was the one who communicated needs and desires between parties. And that was a power all its own.

Soria stared at her reflection in Serena's sunglasses. "I came because a friend said I was needed."

"You are a convenience," the shape-shifter replied dismissively, and brushed past to walk down the hall.

Soria followed, dogging the woman's heels, refusing to be intimidated by the lethal flex of the woman's right hand, which remained more leopard than human. Dark curved claws extended from the tips of Serena's fingers, and she moved like a cat—aggressively graceful, hips rolling. Soria wanted to plant a boot up her ass.

The hall was short and poorly lit. Part of a maze. Soria had gotten off the plane in Beijing, China, only to be swept up by a portly little man who shuttled her north out of the city, driving through the entire night. Big, comfortable backseat, with a pillow and blanket. Soria had fallen asleep. Late this morning she had opened her eyes and found herself in a dusty village surrounded by the remains of an ancient crumbling wall. The streets were twisting, narrow, made of dirt; and the homes, built seamlessly together, had been crafted of stone and wood and clay. It looked remote, felt remote, and the children who lingered around the car when she stumbled out, bleary-eyed, squealed with delight when she spoke to them in their native language.

Khalkha dialect. Mongolian. Not quite to the border

between that country and China, but close enough to taste grit in the air from the Gobi Desert. One of the boys, no older than eight, had asked immediately if she'd come about the bleeding soldiers. This question invited a hard shove from one of the older girls, who called him stupid and said that Soria *surely* had arrived to see the giant white man who had been hauled away from the military truck, ass first, unconscious.

Well, Soria had just seen the giant white man—nearly seven feet of him, if she had to guess. All muscle, all frustration, and definitely not human. She could believe that he had killed ten men. She would have believed he had killed twenty, with his bare hands, if Serena had said so.

Hello, he had rasped, from behind his mask. *Hello*, in a language that was utterly unfamiliar to Soria, in a voice that sounded like the very definition of pain.

It had been so startling to hear him. Soria still felt chills, though she was not certain why the memory of his voice haunted her. Perhaps because it was so very human. Perhaps because hearing him speak made him real to her in ways that merely looking at him had not.

He was real to you before, she chided herself. *He was real.*

Yet it was different, hearing him. Without a face to be an anchor, a body was only a fragment, an echo of a person's existence. A body said too little about personality, or character. And the shape-shifter's eyes had barely been visible inside the shadows of the hood. But his voice . . .

Soria tugged at her empty sleeve, breathing through

gritted teeth. *Enough*, she thought angrily. *Voices mean nothing. You have to go deeper.*

If she was allowed to. This whole operation stank.

The shape-shifter led Soria up a narrow flight of stairs, directly into another small room made of stone. Unlike the cell, this was aboveground. A sliver of light pushed through a small window set near the ceiling. The air smelled musty, and everything was covered in a thin layer of dust. Northern China suffered from sandstorms blown in from the Gobi Desert. Years ago, Soria had spent time in Beijing, helping another agent investigate a kidnapping. She still remembered how impossible it had been to keep things clean inside the little apartment they shared.

A slender young Chinese man sat at a long wooden table watching a row of security monitors. Soria saw the door of the room she had just left, and on another screen, the captive shape-shifter. She leaned in, studying him, seeing him remotely—bound and hooded in iron which made him seem even more alien and strange. Far more so than she had felt sitting beside him on the floor, wondering what the hell she was supposed to do.

Serena's hand was human again. The shape-shifter placed it on the young Chinese man's shoulder as she bent to whisper in his ear. His expression never changed, but a faint flush stained his cheeks as he dragged a laptop close and typed on the keyboard. The screen darkened, revealing a frozen image from what appeared to be another security tape.

Not security, Soria realized, noting the eye-level angle of the picture, and the presence of color. *A handheld camera.*

"Watch carefully," Serena said, as the young man hit another key.

No sound. Just film. Scattered men were holding flashlights, moving slowly down a long, rocky tunnel that gave the impression of being underground. It was hard to make out details. Images kept jumping. Soria felt as though she were watching some amateurish indie flick, a *Blair Witch* wannabe. It nauseated her, and she leaned back, putting some distance between herself and the screen.

The men entered a cavern. There was not much to see, except far on the right she glimpsed a pillar. The camera jerked in that direction and then steadied long enough to see that there were two pillars, rough and squat, framing what might have been a door—but that was now a cracked heap of large rock. Beyond, lights flashed.

The camera bounced closer. Soria glimpsed Serena in the shadows, leaning over an enormous stone structure, long and waist-high. There was nothing fancy about it. To Soria, it appeared as though it had been hacked straight from the earth.

A tomb, she thought. *A coffin.*

"More than a year ago there was a major earthquake in Chengdu," said Serena softly, as on the screen she and several other men pushed and pulled at a flat slab of stone resting atop the carved mound. "I think you might have heard about it."

Almost seventy thousand people had died. Soria had

heard a great deal about the earthquake from her hospital bed in San Francisco. Cartoons, soap operas, and death had been her televised companions. She'd had her friends there, too, and family. But not Roland. Hardly even a phone call.

"The ground opened in the mountains," Serena continued. "Some locals found artifacts. When our archaeologists went in, they discovered a great deal more than that."

Soria gave her a sharp look. "*Your* archaeologists?"

Serena's mouth tilted coldly. "You would think, given the diversity of your agency, that there would be more interest in relics of the past, in the reality behind myths and legends. Instead, you people focus on small things."

"Like saving lives," Soria replied, crumpling her empty sleeve. "You make it your business to investigate all major archaeological finds?"

"Before anyone else does."

"So you're grave robbers."

"One must respect the past."

"For profit?"

"Money is irrelevant. Money can be earned or stolen." Serena tapped the screen. "Knowledge is quite different."

Soria wanted to argue, but instead she looked at the screen as the video suddenly jumped—violently enough to make her light-headed. The image steadied just as the stone slab was pushed aside. The person holding the camera moved closer, revealing the interior of the mound, which indeed had been hollowed out to form a coffin.

Even without much light, Soria could see the outline

of a massive body crammed inside. Not a skeleton. Certainly not some desiccated mummy. She saw bulky muscle, which looked firm and very much alive.

Serena wore sunglasses even while underground. In the video, she leaned in for a closer look, staring at the corpse. Quite abruptly, her entire body stiffened, as if in pain or shock. Even now, watching the video, Soria felt the shape-shifter tense, ever so subtly.

Bad memories, she thought. And moments later, she understood why.

The body moved. Soria jumped, startled, as did everyone else on the screen. The camera jerked sideways and then steadied. Golden light seemed to shimmer in the air above the body, and over Serena as well, who in the video stood closest of all to the coffin.

More movement, a rocking motion. A man sat up.

Soria could not see much of his face, but his body was unmistakable. He was also very clearly dazed, swaying within the coffin, hands pressed to his head. His mouth moved.

"I need to hear him," she told Serena.

The shape-shifter, frowning, tapped a button on the laptop. Crackling sounds immediately filled the air, layers of sound that in real life would have been hardly noticeable but on tape were each as loud as breaking glass. Soria could hear the rush of deep breaths, the scuff of rock underfoot, and gears creaking. She could hear the silence surrounding those sounds, and in that silence a man's voice floated, his words flowing softly together.

To anyone unfamiliar with his language it would have sounded as though he were growling, rumbling, even snarling. On its own this was a threatening sound, even hair-raising. Soria knew better, though it was difficult to piece together anything coherent. However it was that her mind absorbed the languages of others, proximity was required, and time. Without being in his presence, Soria could not hold on to the meanings of each sound.

But some things lingered more than she expected.

No, she heard him whisper. *No. Impossible.*

He looked miserable and ill, as though he hardly had the strength to lift his head. Soria waited for him to realize that he was not alone.

When he did, it was a breathless moment. A profound stillness fell over him, a tremendous quiet—and the way he sat, staring, made her think of every time in the past year she had awakened in the night to a strange sound, pulled from one nightmare into the possibility of another. Vulnerable, frightened. Ready to fight.

He began speaking again, but the only words Soria understood were "who" and "here." His tone was firm yet reasonable, and there was an undercurrent of strength that she recognized.

Do not fuck with him, thought Soria, at the men and women in the video. *Do not move.*

But one of them did.

It was Serena, stepping from behind, sunglasses pushed up. A faint light was in her eyes. The man twisted inside the coffin to look at her, and a tremor raced through him, his voice snarling into a jumble of words.

You, Soria heard, understanding only fragments. *You. Here. Dare you.* He sounded furious. Soria watched the video version of Serena hiss, golden light streaming from her good eye, teeth dropping into fangs. Fingers lengthening into claws.

The man moved. Soria did not see him leave the coffin—the camera image jumped too much for that—but bodies scrambled, and between them she glimpsed a blur. Heard shouts, screams. Other men moved in, wielding the pickaxes and shovels they had been digging with.

When the camera steadied again, the shifter-man was on the other side of the tomb. He did not attack, but studied those around him with pure disdain twisting at his mouth. He was huge compared to everyone else, his size and presence filling the small dark space until Soria began to feel claustrophobic simply watching.

Give you. Mercy, he rumbled dangerously. *Leave now*, But no one understood.

Ripples of light surged over his limbs. Soria glimpsed scales, and flinched as one of the men lunged with a shout, swinging a shovel. He never got close. The shifter knocked the shovel away and caught the man across the face with a blow so strong his head whipped around a full one hundred eighty degrees. Neck broken. Head crushed. The camera jerked backward, picture tumbling wildly, until suddenly it stopped. It was still filming, but all Soria could see was feet and falling bodies.

Serena reached out and shut the laptop screen. "We were unprepared for him. Then, and later."

Soria wet her lips, trying to steady herself. The group had been at a serious disadvantage, being unable to communicate. "He could have been reasoned with. He gave you chances not to fight."

"Only because he was in a weakened state," the shape-shifter replied. "He killed several before we subdued him. And then later, during transport to this place."

It was a miracle they had stopped him at all, given his size and fury. Soria asked, "Had that coffin been tampered with?"

"No." Serena touched the young Chinese man's shoulder, and without a word he stood and left the room. When he was gone the shape-shifter added, "You saw the rubble between the pillars? That was a seal. A door. We spent almost six months studying it before another aftershock brought it down. We learned enough, though. By our estimates, it was set in place several thousand years ago."

"Several thousand?" Soria echoed, jaw aching. "Really."

Serena's long finger tapped idly against the laptop. "Perhaps three, to be exact. You think I lie?"

Something cold and hard settled in Soria's chest. "I heard you lied to your own daughter for years. I don't expect much from you, Serena McGillis, except falsehoods and meanness."

The shape-shifter went utterly still. Soria braced herself.

Serena said, "I could say there was an accident, you know."

"Yes." Soria crumpled her empty sleeve. "And luckily for you, there would be less of me to hide."

Nothing. And then an unpleasant smile ticked at the corner of Serena's mouth. "I asked how you lost your arm. Roland would not tell me. So I dug. And discovered an unexpected story."

It was Soria's turn to go still and quiet.

Serena leaned in, close. "I will not turn my back on you," she whispered. "I know what you did, to yourself and to that man. He was family, if I understand correctly."

Pain throbbed, radiating from Soria's stump up through her neck. "I'm certain you might have done the same, in my situation," she remarked.

"Indeed," replied Serena. "But I would not turn my back on *me*, either."

CHAPTER THREE

THE human woman returned while Karr was being cleaned. Naked, exposed, his genitals and hindquarters wiped down by warm washcloths. It was humiliating, though the old woman responsible for the task was efficient and quiet. Her strong, wrinkled hands did not hurt him.

The old woman had been tending his needs for days. Karr marked time by her arrival and departure. He supposed he looked forward to her presence, in some small fashion. Solitude had never disturbed him, but seeing her took his mind away from the torture of forced stillness.

Where are your wings? whispered a familiar voice inside his mind, memories so keen that Karr could close his eyes and imagine his friends were with him again. Althea with her snow-spotted pelt, or gruff Delko, more crow than fox.

Tau, especially, lingered in his mind; too much a wolf to ever be mistaken for a man, whose own wings were

born of an eagle skin. *Where are your wings*, Tau would
tease, when Karr was very young and desperate to fly.
Little brother, where are your wings?

Here, thought Karr, as his shoulder blades itched
against the cold, hard stone. *Ready to be free.*

He heard the door to his cell open, followed by a
sharp breath. The old woman, who had been bundling
up the soiled clothes placed beneath him, paused and
looked up. Karr heard a familiar voice say several quiet
words in a musical, rolling tongue.

Soria, he thought.

He could not see her through the slit in the iron hood,
just the old woman, who tossed a clean sheet over his
hips and then squatted to finish her routine. He smelled
his liquid meal, bland and warm, and beneath that his
nurse's scent, rich with meat, pepper. She had been eating well, and recently.

Soria's footsteps sounded light on the stone floor. She
said another soft word, but the old woman ignored her,
reaching out with that odd, hollow glass spoon she always
fed Karr with. Long as a branch, and filled with liquid.
Despair filled him when he saw it. Terrible fury. He was
sick of this. Sick to death.

Soria's pale hand grabbed the old woman's arm, pre-
venting her from feeding him. Her fingers were long, her
wrist delicate. Not much strength. So small and frail, he
could snap those bones with two fingers. Her hand was
weak, soft.

Her voice was another matter. Low and compelling,
it was a melody of words. He did not understand what

she was saying, but he understood her tone: furious, demanding. Her anger intrigued Karr. It meant something to him.

The old woman, who had been utterly emotionless throughout the feedings and cleanings—and his occasional bouts of rage—began muttering to herself. She set down the bowl so hard he thought it might break, got up with a grunt and then, with great deliberation, spat on the floor.

Soria remained silent. The old woman walked away, her shoes loud against the stone. She slammed the door behind her. The room felt very quiet without her, cut only by sounds of soft breathing. After a moment, Soria stepped into view, holding a small cloth bag. She was frowning, her cheeks pink, and when she glanced down at Karr, he imagined loneliness in her gaze, lost behind intelligence and pain.

"She thinks I am taking her place," Soria said to him, as though he were free and standing at her side; as if he would care. Which he did, but only because listening to her stumble over his language was a dangerous pleasure. He watched, as best he could, as Soria crouched and upended her bag. He could not see its contents, which rattled against the floor. "I do not want her work. I tried telling her that."

She spoke softly, carefully, with a formality that was somewhat old-fashioned. Karr listened to her words, but there was nothing but a distracted breathlessness to her tone, as though she were simply trying to fill the air with words. Words that he would understand, despite her accent.

"She did not clean your wounds," continued Soria. "I brought something for that." And then, very quietly, "I do not want to hurt you."

Then release me, he almost said, despite his promise to himself that he would not break silence with this woman.

Instead he bit his tongue and closed his eyes, thinking perhaps that being given this opportunity to communicate was a worse torture than the bonds surrounding his chafed, aching body. Torture, because he could not trust it. He could not engage this chance to be heard, to be a man again. To be something more than a lump of flesh chained to the floor.

He made a small sound, surprised when he felt her delicate fingers graze his chest. Her slender hand reached between the iron bands and spread a creamy balm over his lacerated skin. Soria did this carefully, tending every inch of his body that touched cold iron, binding his wounds with gauze. She occasionally made little hissing sounds between her teeth, as though pained, and he found himself hungry for those noises.

She worked on his throat last of all. Bent over him, her long braids brushing his skin. For the first time Karr could see her face clearly: every soft line, from the curve of her cheeks to the sweep of her dark brow. Her scent remained strong—wild sunlight and sand—and beneath, fading, the dull, bitter presence of the shape-shifter.

Despite the scent of his enemy—this woman *was* the enemy—every time she touched his body, warmth tingled through him, followed by a roaring ache in his heart. He had been touched frequently for untold days, and felt nothing; nothing but emptiness, disgust, and humiliation. He did not know why this woman was different. Why she made him . . . *feel*.

Soria finished tending his wounds, and she sat back, studying him. She stayed like that for a long time, until her gaze ticked downward. She held up the hollow glass stem.

"They feed you with this." It was not a question. Soria turned the glass over in her hand, a drop of brown liquid squeezing from the tip. She suddenly looked ill.

Karr felt little better. Nausea pooled in his throat, and he could feel the stickiness of his face beneath the hood from sweat and dirt, and from those remnants of food that he had not been careful to swallow.

Soria gave him a sharp look. "How do you stand it? All of this? Being tied down, hooded." And then, seconds later: "Stupid question. Forget that."

She put down the glass stem and leaned forward, studying him with unrelenting straightforwardness. He studied her in turn. Odd, strange woman. Still so bold. Not as lean, or as aged, as the humans to which he was accustomed. He would have thought her very young had it not been for the glint in her eyes, which were ancient and tired, fraught with suffering. Eyes never lied.

"I have been told you are a killer," she said.

Karr's jaw tightened with displeasure. Of course she had been told that. And it was true, he supposed. He was a killer. He had killed. He would kill again, if given the chance.

"You have been judged," Soria continued quietly, still staring into his eyes. "But I think you know that."

She leaned back out of sight—he thought, perhaps, to leave—but then he heard scuffing sounds behind him and felt the hood move over his head. Karr held his breath, not quite willing to believe. Not until the iron was pulled away. Cool air swept over his sweat-soaked face, delicious and soft, and his lungs seemed to yawn open and force his jaws apart. He took deep, shuddering breaths—gasped—and realized with some horror that he had been suffocating, slowly, inside the hood.

Soria stood a safe distance from him, holding the iron. It looked monstrous in her hand, shaped like a drum, with slits for his eyes, nose, and mouth. Fitting for a beast and not a man, though Karr wondered if there was much difference between the two.

She stepped toward him, then stopped. For the first time she seemed uncertain, her knuckles white around the edge of the iron hood. Karr looked past her, briefly, now able to see more of the room. He found it smaller and duller than he had imagined. Scents were stronger, too, not so mixed with the dead air trapped inside the hood.

Foul, he thought. The air had been foul and he had not realized it. He'd become too used to the scent.

Again, Soria moved closer. Karr studied her empty sleeve, noting the slight awkwardness of her grip as she carefully set the iron hood upon the floor. Her left hand was clearly not dominant, and not one she was completely accustomed to using—which meant she had lost her arm somewhat recently. Karr had enough experience treating similar injuries to know the signs.

Accident or punishment, he wondered. If it was punishment, then she remained unbowed.

Soria knelt beside his head, lightly, as though ready to spring away if he blinked at her wrong. Her left hand fumbled against the floor, and he saw a parcel made of slick, shiny material. She placed the corner in her mouth and ripped it open. Inside was a small white cloth, rolled up tight. It smelled odd.

She touched his face with the cloth. It was surprisingly cold and wet, and up close the scent was even more bitter. But Karr did not say a word, or move, as she wiped around his mouth and chin. He watched her eyes, transfixed and suspicious, searching for some kind of truth—truth about who she was and what she wanted. Or why her hand was so gentle when nothing else about this place was.

Talk to her, he told himself. *It does not mean you are weak.*

Just vulnerable. But better to confront that now. The woman had power here. A human, in a position of control. He did not understand that—not unless she was royalty—but he could accept it and learn. She seemed willing enough to talk. Forming connections while imprisoned could be a valuable thing. But only if one remembered that such bonds were not real.

You led armies. You were tortured at the hands of queens. You can speak to one human woman. You can do this.

His mouth was dry, his lips cracked. Karr tried to

speak but could not make a sound. Soria twitched, her hand going utterly still.

"Thank you," he finally managed to whisper.

She stared. "You are welcome."

Karr hesitated, but could think of nothing else to say—not to this woman, who was both captor and enigma. He had made his move, though. Opened himself.

After a moment's hesitation, Soria began wiping his face again. Her touch was light and warm, and dangerously soothing. Karr turned his head, just slightly, to stop her.

It worked. Her hand hovered, very still, and she studied him thoughtfully. "Tell me. Was it self-defense?"

Karr blinked, for a moment, confused, until he remembered waking from death bewildered, surrounded, the air thick with the scent of that pure-blooded shapeshifter. He recalled the wagon with its young soldiers, and his desperation. Blood splashed through his memories. He heard screams, screams that flowed into older remembrances: children screaming, crying out for him, but despite his size and skill he could not fight his way to their sides. He remembered claws flashing, and swords, and the silence that followed. He remembered losing his mind.

"It is war," Karr rasped softly.

She frowned. "What war?"

"You must know."

"No." Soria sat back, frowning. "I do not."

"You lie," he accused.

"I have no reason to." Her gaze had hardened.

Karr strained against his bonds. "A reason was never

required for what was done to my kind. Lies would be no different. You ally yourself with the shifter, and for that you are the enemy, too."

Soria shook her head, tossing aside her small white rag—but not before he saw real anger flash through her eyes. It was quick, though, and became something far worse: pity. She looked at him as though he was a sad fool, and for a moment he felt like one. Something was not right here. Something had been *not right* since he had opened his eyes in the catacomb, but the way this woman looked at him suddenly made it all too real.

"Maybe you are right about some things," she said quietly. "But if there was a war, it ended long ago. You are not . . . where you think."

"Then why am I imprisoned?" Karr tried to flex his hands inside the iron cloth. "I am an animal in this place."

"You are feared."

"Am I?" he asked coldly. "And the shape-shifter? You should fear *her*, and yet you do not. She defers to you, I think. I wonder what that makes you."

Soria's eyelids twitched but she did not answer the implication. "You hate her without knowing who she is."

"I know *what* she is." Karr briefly closed his eyes, hearing sobs inside his mind—echoes of young voices, cut with screams. "Nothing has changed."

Soria leaned back, fingers tapping her thigh. "I saw you begin to change your shape. Are you telling me you are not like her?" She sounded surprised.

Cold laughter escaped Karr, cutting his throat. "You can ask that?"

"I just did," was the human's grim response. "And I am awaiting the answer."

Fury choked him. He could not believe such ignorance—almost accused Soria of more lies—but he stopped himself just before he spoke, caught by her eyes and scent. Brittle, both. Angry and weary. But not sly. There was no hint of guile.

Karr blew out his breath, frustrated. Talking to this woman was impossible. She reminded him too much of his initiation through the old canyon core: confusing, dangerous, with no guide but instinct. No wings. No claws. Just his own fragile human flesh to see him through.

He was still searching for words when he heard an odd popping sound outside the room, sharp sputters, a *rat-tat-tat*. Soria stiffened, staring at the door, and all the color drained from her face. Fear had entered her eyes. *Fear.* The shape-shifter had not frightened her, and neither had Karr, but this sound, whatever it was, was enough. And if it was enough for her, it was enough for him.

Soria rose to her feet, flinching as she heard the sound again. It was louder this time. Much closer. Karr strained upward, his iron restraints pushing into his wounds. "What is it?"

She shook her head and moved around him to the door. "I will return."

He had heard such promises before, in battle. Few had ever been kept. Karr bared his teeth and hissed, "Stay." The woman ignored him and he growled, furious, "You are a cripple. You cannot defend yourself."

She shot him a startled look, but then the door to the room rattled. Soria slid two steps to the left, putting herself between him and it. Her spine was straight, chin raised. Her left hand was curled into a fist.

"Release me," Karr hissed—just as the door opened.

Men crowded into the room. There were only three, but even one would have been too many. They wore dark, tight clothing made of a fine weave, and their heads were covered with black hoods that molded to their faces. Only the eyes and mouths had been cut out. It was a startling sight, yet too familiar, though the accompanying circumstances had changed. These men carried oddly shaped black sticks similar to what he had seen the soldiers in the wagon wield, and they were pointing them at the woman. They shouted deep guttural words that Karr would have understood in any language.

Soria did not yield. The knuckles of her left hand were white and straining, her fist clenched so tight it shook. Karr had a fine view. Soria spoke quietly to the men, her voice far calmer than the tremble of her hand.

One of the men aimed his weapon at Karr. Soria moved to block him, and another man lunged forward to grab her arm, yanking her close. He was fast but she was quicker. Even as she slammed against his body, her left hand came up in a blur and her thumb dug deep into his eye. Blood spurted and the man holding Soria screamed, jerking backward. He threw her away from him and Soria lost her footing, landing hard against Karr's chest.

The impact—and Soria's elbow—knocked the breath out of his lungs, but he recovered quickly, meeting her gaze for one brief moment. Her face was very close to his. Karr could taste her scent, could feel the heat of her breath on his face. She was soft and warm, and very much alive. He realized, with some surprise, that he wanted her to stay that way. He was not done with her.

"Free me," he rasped angrily.

"Too late," she replied—and hissed in pain as the man she had attacked grabbed one of her braids and hauled backward.

The man's left eye was little more than pulp, his mask soaked with blood. Holding tightly to her hair, he kicked her in the ribs and then the stomach. Soria gasped, trying to curl into a ball, but he yanked at her again and began dragging her across the floor toward the exit. The sight broke something in Karr. Rage filled him—pure, striking bloodlust—and golden light clouded his vision until he felt blind. Muscles rippled beneath the iron bars, scales pouring upward through his skin. His shoulder blades tickled. His jaw began to lengthen, sharp teeth pressing against his lower lip. He snapped at the air, restraints cutting painfully into his body. Much more and he would impale himself. More than that, and he would slice himself into pieces.

He was not certain he cared.

The men froze, staring. Soria was still on the ground, trying to gain her footing, raw determination in her eyes. Her left hand was covered in blood. She leaned to her right, swaying unsteadily, and it seemed to Karr that she forgot, in that moment, about her missing arm. More pain flickered over her face.

Karr heard another loud popping sound, similar to

the sputtering that had presaged this entire encounter. One of the men jerked back, staggering. His companions began to turn, but more sharp raps rattled the air and Karr saw blood spray from small impacts in their masked heads. The men fell, one by one. Soria managed to roll sideways, barely avoiding them. She was staring at the doorway, where another man suddenly appeared.

The newcomer was tall and fair, his hair a rare shade of red. He dressed in loose clothing the color of wheat, and silver flashed at his throat. He held in one hand a smaller version of the black sticks, pointed down at the fresh twitching corpses. He did not look at the bodies. He studied Karr. Then he considered Soria. He spoke to her quietly, and held out his hand.

She ignored his help, standing on her own, swaying just slightly, enough that she placed her palm against her head. She was very pale. Somewhere close Karr heard more sharp pops, followed by screams. The redheaded man spoke again and Soria gave a curt reply before she glanced down at Karr. Conflict filled her eyes. Unease.

"I came here to see if you could be trusted," she told him.

"Words are a poor substitute for action," Karr replied. "Release me."

Soria hesitated. The redheaded man edged toward the door, where a young girl appeared, holding a very large knife. She wore startlingly few clothes.

The man spoke to Soria, sharply. Karr did not like his tone, or him. Too cold. There was something ancient in his eyes.

Soria ignored him and dropped down on her knees beside Karr. "Your name."

He did not want to tell her, but he remembered her standing between him and the men with their weapons, attacking with nothing but her bare hand, and a swell of dangerous admiration filled him. "Karr," he said.

"Karr." Soria held his gaze a moment longer, then fumbled for the bolts binding his iron restraints. "You show me what you are made of. Good or bad."

I will show you both, he thought wearily. *And hope I do not kill you.*

CHAPTER FOUR

I T was hard to breathe. Hard to think, hard to sit up. Hard to undo the bolts in the iron restraints. Soria worked fast, phantom pain shooting up her ghost arm, making her shoulder and head throb. They hurt like hell. So did her ribs.

Having an eyeful of bleeding corpses did not help, either. Feeling her hand sticky with some of that same blood was worse. That she had been attacked at all, with a gunfight still going on—

"Fuck," she muttered, encountering a particularly stubborn bolt. It was the restraint that bound Karr's wrist. She had managed to undo the ones holding down his throat, chest, and waist. It would have made more sense to start first with his hands so that he could help her, but she had put those off until now, part of her still wondering if this was a good idea. Giving herself time to change her mind.

She had seen the videos—this man had practically taken off heads with his bare hands—and here she was, undoing his restraints. She had come here to judge him, to discover if he was a danger. And he was. He most certainly was. But the question remained whether or not he was a danger to *everyone*.

There was no easy distinction between a "right" killing and a "wrong" one. Death was death; only the circumstances and intent made it different. Was Soria qualified to judge? Maybe. But the reason for that was not something Soria wanted to think about. Not with fresh blood on her hand, which was far more disturbing and revolting than she could afford to let on. It brought back bad memories. If there had been any more blood on her body, she was quite certain she would not still be conscious.

She struggled with the bolt again, and felt Karr watching her. She could see his golden eyes beneath her lashes; steady, unflinching, restless. His was a dangerous gaze, utterly inhuman. Just like the rest of him, still covered in rippling patches of golden scales, each one the size of her palm, and iridescent as some sun-riddled desert pearl. His skin resembled metal or shell more than flesh.

His face, too, had not yet regained its humanity: his jaw was long and pointed, his upper teeth sharp. This was less affecting to Soria than seeing him free of the mask for the first time, filthy, sweating, startled. So human. He had been fed with an eyedropper, but the food had clearly missed his mouth for part of the time, and a crusty film still remained on his face. All this only made him appear wilder, even more unpredictable.

You're risking lives on a theory, Soria told herself

angrily. But she had run out of time to talk with this man. Nor was she going to leave him here to die or be experimented on. Even if it killed her.

She bit her bottom lip as her left hand—still weak after all this time—refused to turn the bolt. "Robert," she called over her shoulder. "I need help."

Robert. In his fine linen suit, looking as though he had stepped directly from the cover of *GQ*, straight into the firefight. Cool, calm, utterly unbothered by the violence. And Ku-Ku, standing guard in the hall, wearing minishorts and a pink tank top, chewing gum, holding a knife and semiautomatic in her hands.

Soria was going to kick Roland's ass. Oh, God, was she going to throttle him.

"You should leave the shifter," said Robert smoothly. But a moment later he appeared at her side, dropping gracefully to one knee. Soria made room for him, stepping over Karr to work on freeing his other hand. He was a big man, nothing but sinew and hard, lean muscle. She felt small beside him, practically Lilliputian.

Thousands of years old, she thought. *Impossible*.

Just as shape-shifters were impossible. Or mermen, gargoyles, psychics, and magic spells. Or women who could speak any language in the world.

"Why are you here?" she asked Robert, flinching as more gunshots rang out down the hall. "Serena said nothing about you."

"And my contract said nothing about her. I was paid to be here, just as I was paid to intercept you at the airport."

Soria stared. "I told you, Roland wouldn't do that."

"Not when he has an agency full of able-bodied men and women at his disposal? Interesting quandary, isn't it. Maybe you should ask your esteemed boss what he's so afraid of the others knowing." Robert undid the bolt on Karr's wrist, tossed it away, and then quickly reached behind his back, beneath his suit jacket. He pulled out a small pistol and slid it across the floor to Soria. "For you, fully loaded. Roland said you're trained."

"Roland's quickly becoming a jackass," Soria replied, staring at the gun like it was poison. "I'm not touching that."

"I told you not to think too much about the arm." Robert left the gun on the floor and backed toward the door. Ku-Ku glanced inside, pigtails bouncing, then disappeared again. "A gun is a gun. Not a reflection."

Soria remembered what it felt like to hold a gun in her hand. The weight, the smooth slide of the trigger beneath her finger. The kick and roar.

"Who are those men?" she muttered.

"Mercenaries. Well trained, expensive. Good equipment. They came by car, probably from Beijing."

"You think the Consortium sent them?"

Robert said nothing, and pulled the mask off one of the dead. Soria did not want to look, but found herself staring into the face of a middle-aged man of indeterminate race; perhaps Asian, maybe Latino. A bit like herself: a mixture of different things. His features had not softened in death, but retained a coarse harshness; the brow lines were deep, the mouth twisted in a grimace.

"No," Robert finally replied, staring thoughtfully at

the corpse. "I don't think these men belong to them. Someone different is running this show."

"How can you tell?"

A brief, sardonic smile touched his mouth. "Professionalism precedes itself. These men were not psychotic enough to be Consortium."

Nausea climbed Soria's throat. She looked away, and focused on the bolt beneath her fingers. Karr, watching both her and Robert through narrowed eyes, worked loose his other hand, shaking off the chain mail wrapped around his fist. Soria held her breath as his immense hand flexed—and then forced herself to start breathing again as he sat up and reached over to where she was fumbling with the other bolt.

Their fingers brushed. Karr rumbled, "Who is that man?"

It was easy for her to understand him, his language crystalline in her mind, rich with nuance, though it was still difficult for her mouth to form the right words to reply. Different muscles made unique sounds, and the rolling growl of some vowels made her feel as if she were imitating Eartha Kitt's Catwoman.

"He is no one," she told him.

"More a wish than the truth, I think," he replied, and then, "How did you loosen the others?"

"Turn it, like this." Soria showed him how to handle the bolt, still taken aback every time he spoke with calm and thoughtfulness similar to the restraint he had initially shown in the video, so at odds with his bursts of rage.

She looked up and found Robert watching them,

smiling faintly. "I'll be close," he said, and stepped out of sight into the hall.

Close, my ass. Soria gritted her teeth and started working on Karr's ankle restraints.

He freed his other hand, and sat up quickly, spine cracking, gauze sliding off the long lines of sores and wounds she had treated. In the few moments she had looked away, his face had regained its humanity, as had his flesh. The scales were gone, jaw normal, teeth no longer razor sharp. Only his eyes still shimmered with magic, lost behind a rough mane of golden hair.

He helped her free his ankles, fumbling at the last moment as a faint tremor raced through his body. When the last shackle was loosened, he stood, swaying, his joints still popping. The sheet fell away. Soria ducked her head, trying not to look, but Karr reached down and grabbed her hand. He pulled her up, fast, and then bent to pick up the gun.

He held it awkwardly on his palm, the barrel pointed at her. Instinct took over. She reached out without thinking, plucking it deftly from his grip. He let her, though his eyes narrowed.

"I did not free you to hurt you," she said, remembering the video of the catacomb, and how a simple reassurance would have probably prevented the deaths that followed. Maybe. Except for Serena.

Karr's jaw tightened. "That means nothing to me."

"Mercy," she whispered, struggling to pronounce the soft growl. "I think *that* means something to you."

He went very still. Soria tore her gaze from him, looking down at the gun. The safety was off, and the weapon felt odd in her left hand, unnatural. Holding it frightened her, but Soria could not bring herself to put it down. A crazy woman. She was crazy for doing this.

It won't make the dark place go away inside you, whispered a small, hard voice in her head. *It won't make it easier to sleep at night. You were reckless the last time you got hurt.*

And before *that* she had been reckless, too; in that free-spirited, love-of-life way that had taken her on long journeys down unfamiliar roads, into the most remote regions of the world, with only luck, brains, and a gift for languages to keep her safe. She had considered the consequences and danger but never let herself be ruled by fear. She'd never imagined that what could go wrong actually would. She had trusted people as much as her instincts would let her.

Now, here, she felt that same drive in her gut, that old intuition. She had thought it dead inside her; trust, gone forever. Maybe it should have stayed dead.

Karr glanced sharply at the open door. Soria heard nothing, but in two smooth movements the shape-shifter crossed the room and pressed himself against the wall. She followed, but was several steps away when he lunged through the door into the hall, golden light streaking across his skin. Soria heard a muffled snarl—and watched in horror as Karr stumbled back into view, a leopard clawing at his shimmering body.

Soria ran forward, but there was nothing she could do as Karr slammed his arm into the leopard's mouth, trying to push her away. Robert and Ku-Ku were nowhere in sight. The gun was useless in Soria's hand.

"*Serena!*" she screamed, shoving the weapon into the elastic waistband of her leggings. She lunged and grabbed the leopard's slashing tail, hauling backward as hard as she could.

The shape-shifter twisted violently and her body began to shift, a transformation of light and flesh that lengthened her legs and straightened her spine. She did not stop fighting, though. She struggled harder, with terrifying desperation. Karr pivoted on one foot and slammed Serena so hard against the wall it cracked. Merciless, enraged.

Soria heard a scuffing sound behind her, and she turned. One of the masked gunmen had appeared, was raising a weapon. His eyes widened when he saw Karr and Serena, and he stared with a horror that seemed to melt through his ski mask. Soria was afraid he would piss himself. She had a feeling her own bladder might empty, were their positions reversed: the sounds that Serena and Karr were making as they tore into each other were hair-raising, and the spectacle of their desperate inhuman bodies was something out of a fantasy movie.

To be honest, Soria later thought, she might have been fine if she had stayed perfectly still. But she did not, and the movement caught his attention. The man's gaze fell on her with almost desperate relief.

His mouth moved. Soria could not hear him. She realized she was holding the gun again. She had no idea how it had gotten back into her hand, but it was pointed at the man. Her arm trembled violently.

Shoot him, she told herself. *Him or you.*

But her finger was frozen, and she could not focus enough to aim. When she looked at the man in front of her, she saw another face instead: pale and fleshy, covered in thick glasses perched on the tip of a bulbous nose speckled with greasy pores. She could smell the memory, smell *him*, like old kitty litter and moldy broccoli.

Ghost fingers twitched. Pain rocketed through her head. She heard another shout, but it sounded very far away.

And then strong arms grabbed her around the waist and yanked her backward. Shots boomed out. The gun was wrested from her hand, and her vision cleared enough to see Serena—barely human, covered in spotted fur—returning fire. She was bleeding from deep cuts and scratches; and her eye patch was gone, revealing a gaping hole.

"Are you hurt?" rumbled Karr, the tremendous heat of his body soaking through Soria's clothing into her skin. For one moment she sagged against him, limp and numb, hungry for someone else to be strong—these arms holding her were the strongest she had ever felt—but reality set in, and she shook her head in response, struggling to break free.

Karr did not release her. He held on even more tightly as Serena finally lowered the gun. The masked soldier was dead, and two other bodies that Soria had been too distracted to notice lay sprawled in the hall nearby. *Robert and Ku-Ku's work*, she decided, wondering where they were.

Serena stared at the piles of corpses, at the blood

spreading toward her clawed feet. She was human only in her bipedal form; everything else belonged to a cat. The shape-shifter's face made her look so much like Egyptian statues of Isis that Soria suspected the gods of the Nile had sprung into existence because of inter-actions between shape-shifters and humans.

Serena herself was certainly imperious enough to frighten mere mortals. She looked at Soria, her single eye cold and furious and more disturbing than the hole in her leopardess head. But her voice was worse: full of pain and dread, and edged with unease. "You released him," she said.

"I did what I had to. Those men wanted Karr alive."

"Karr," Serena echoed, staring. "Everyone who knew about his existence is beyond reproach."

A low growl rumbled from Karr's chest. "Speak so I can understand you," he commanded. "Or I will think you are planning how to capture me again."

"Maybe we should be," Soria retorted. "We were discussing the attack. We don't know who sent these men, but they came for you."

And me, she did not add. The men now dead in the cell had told her, in no uncertain terms, that she would be traveling with them. She knew quite well it was the only reason she hadn't taken an immediate bullet to the brain.

"Let go," she said to Karr.

He growled again, softly. "Will she use that weapon on you?" He was talking about Serena.

"To stop you, maybe, so don't bother using me as a shield."

"I am no coward," he snapped, pushing Soria away—but with a gentleness completely at odds with his harsh voice and demeanor. Then Karr stepped in front of her, facing Serena with his arms held loosely at his sides. Scales rippled over his massive muscles, and a ruff of golden fur spread down his spine. His fingers lengthened into long black claws. "Tell her we will finish this," he whispered.

"Serena," Soria said quietly, but the shifter-woman was already shaking her head.

"I am no fool." Serena stood very still, her gaze locked on Karr. "I might not speak his language, but I know what he wants."

"Then let him go," Soria replied. "Or kill him now. I think he would prefer that to the cage you had him in."

"What are you saying to each other?" Karr demanded. "Tell me!"

Soria ignored him.

A bitter smile flitted at the corner of Serena's feline mouth. "Look at his anger," the shape-shifter warned. "You think you know him so well? He'll murder you for that naivete."

"You have bigger problems," Soria replied. She moved in front of Karr, felt him reach for her—and knocked aside his hand without thinking. He went very still, and so did Serena, tensing. Soria pretended not to notice, but inside her body, her heart hammered so hard she thought she might pass out.

"Give him a chance," she whispered, unable to speak any louder; not without the risk of her voice breaking on the words. "Give me a chance to do my job and find out whether or not he can be trusted."

Serena stared, golden light trickling from her eye. "You're a fool."

"You could have killed him already," Soria replied quietly. "Or drugged him. But your people want him alive, conscious. Someone else does, too. Why?"

"Because they are all idiots," Serena whispered. "You can never trust him. It is in his blood. His kind are broken from the inside."

Chills rode down Soria's spine. "How do you know?"

"He is a chimera. All they are good for is war."

Serena spat on the ground at his feet. Karr snarled. Again, Soria acted without thinking and grabbed his arm. Deep scratches covered his skin, which was slick and hot with blood. She expected him to pull away, even to strike her, but instead he quivered beneath her grip, rooted in one spot. She risked a look at him, unwilling to let go no matter how much she wanted. Touching Karr felt the same as being burned, and his gaze was no different. He stared at her with wild intensity, dangerously thoughtful.

"We are leaving," she told him, and then looked at Serena and said, "Watch your back. You have a leak."

"Or you do," replied the shifter-woman; but she seemed distracted, staring as she was at Soria's hand on Karr's arm, and then his face, her expression inscrutable.

The half leopardess retreated down the hall, still facing them but stepping lightly over the corpses with a grace and ease that made Soria think that she had eyes in the back of her skull. "Go. I'll give you a head start, and then I'm coming. Maybe you'll be alive when I catch up. Or perhaps I'll finally have enough proof to kill him."

Soria suspected the second option was far more appealing to Serena. "The man came alive after being in a coffin for thousands of years. You think it'll be that easy?"

Serena said nothing, but stooped to pick up another gun from one of their fallen enemies. Karr moved sideways, so smoothly that Soria hardly noticed until she suddenly found herself partially hidden behind him. The protective gesture startled her, but not enough to distract from the guns held loosely in Serena's clawed hands, weapons aimed directly at their heads. Soria could almost hear the shots, imagined the bullets slamming into both her and Karr.

It'd be easy to hide, she thought. *Easy to blame on these dead men.*

But Serena did not shoot. "Go," she whispered, and disappeared around the bend in the hall.

Soria stared after the shape-shifter, breathless. Karr shook off her hand and strode down the hall, watching where Serena had disappeared. Tense, coiled, still begging for a fight. Utterly alien. Lethal.

And he was *her* responsibility now. If he hurt anyone it would be her fault for letting him go, for trusting in nothing but faith and instinct. A tremendous risk, and the enormity of it slammed into Soria so hard that she held her stomach, bent over with nausea. She *was* a fool. Certifiably insane.

Karr's back was still turned. "What is this?"

"You have your freedom," Soria said through gritted teeth. "For now. Prove you deserve it."

"No shifter would agree to such a thing." He gave her a sharp look, which darkened instantly into a frown. "Are you certain you are not hurt?"

"Yes," she muttered, and turned from him to walk unsteadily down the hall, trying in vain not to look at the bodies on the ground. Listening hard for the living. No way to know how many gunmen were left, and Serena's own men might not react well to seeing Karr loose.

She glanced over her shoulder and found him standing very still, this giant of a man, inhuman and bleeding. Watching her with that same frown.

"You prefer to stay?" she asked.

"It is a trick," Karr said. "Why are you helping me?"

Soria set her jaw, suffering a trembling weakness in her knees. Her stump throbbed. All she could smell was blood: her hand was sticky with it. She wanted to go home and hide for another year, in shadows, away from the world and its nightmares.

"No one else can," Soria told him, and started walking again, not waiting to see if he followed.

But he did, moments later.

CHAPTER FIVE

No one stopped them. The halls were silent. Karr did not trust the quiet. During his days of captivity there had been voices, footsteps, the clink of metal and glass. Always, someone nearby.

Now, nothing. Everything felt emptied, broken, like the remains of a village after an army's sweeping pillage. Even the small white lights burning cold and bright from the ceiling held a hint of death about them; there was no spirit in their odd, unwavering flames. He wondered if his elderly caretaker was safe.

Soria walked in front of him, quick on her feet, almost running. She was his guide through the labyrinth of rough-hewn corridors, the walls little more than dirt and stone. He was led by her, defended, perhaps manipulated—but it was all done in such a manner that Karr found himself unable to turn her away, to shed himself of her presence. She was, he thought, indispensable. And that, in his view, was almost as strange as coming back from the dead.

"You are unwell," he said, as Soria stumbled. Three

times now she had almost gone down, and she had begun clutching her empty sleeve, twisting it in her hand,
her knuckles white.

"I am fine," she told him.

Another dead man lay in their path, the seventh that
Karr had seen since the first encounter in his cell. Blood
seeped from a massive head wound, pooling along a
slant in the floor away from the body. His bowels had
voided, and the scent triggered memories: battlefields
churned to mud and ravaged flesh; shape-shifters and
chimeras, lost forever in death, bodies halfway between
animal and human. His vision darkened, as though the
sun were setting again in his mind. Sunset had always
brought out the scavengers.

Soria stopped, staring at the body. "You need
clothing."

"I think not," Karr replied.

He was finding it difficult to speak. His voice sounded
wet, thick, as though made of mud; and he swallowed
hard, struggling to remain impassive when all he wanted
was to charge ahead, quickly, and be free of this place.
His body ached to shift as well, but the hall was narrow
and small, and he could not say what would happen. His
control had always been limited to what skins his instincts made him wear.

Soria frowned. "I was not suggesting *his* clothes."

"You misunderstand," he replied.

"Then tell me."

Karr struggled for words. "It is another cage."

A peculiar expression passed over Soria's face, and
he pushed past her to take the dead man's weapon. It

was heavier than it looked, and he tried to hold it as he had seen the others do. Soria gasped. He found her staring at him with alarm.

"You should put that down," she said.

"You fear it?"

"I do." Soria held out her hand. "Please. Give it to me."

His fingers tightened, but her unease was infectious. He wondered if it was wise to hold something so dangerous, a weapon he knew so little about. Perhaps it was magic, as the lights seemed to be, or another manifestation of human tinkering. Certainly it was nothing as straightforward as good sharp steel or his own claws.

"I require a weapon," he said.

"You can kill a friend just as easily as an enemy with one of those. They are difficult to control, and you have no training."

"But you do."

Her expression hardened. "I know enough."

Karr studied the weapon, its long dark lines. It was hammered from some odd metal, he thought, a construction both clunky and elegant, depending on the angle from which one studied it.

He reluctantly held out the weapon. Soria released her breath and took it from him, gingerly, with distaste, kneeling quickly to set it down. She lingered, though, studying the weapon, and squeezed part of it with her fingers. Karr heard a click, and watched as the base slid free. Soria held it up to him, turning it sideways so that he could see the small objects tucked inside: made of metal, pointed on one end.

"Bullets," she said, pronouncing the word carefully. "And this is a gun."

"Gun," he echoed.

She tossed aside the bullets and stood. Karr gave the gun another long look, then started moving again down the hall, stealing the lead from her. Such weapons caused great damage from a distance, and though he and Soria could just as likely be attacked from the rear, it bothered him that she should be so exposed by going first. It bothered him more than he cared to admit. She was the enemy. She was allied with a shape-shifter.

Shades of gray, whispered a small voice in his mind. *You do not know where the lines are drawn in this place. Make no assumptions. Just watch and learn.*

He could see the human woman in his mind, standing in front of the masked soldier, pale, sick, her weapon unsteadily raised, her dark eyes lost. But not with fear. Just memory. Karr knew the signs.

Not that it helped explain anything about her. Or about why seeing her in danger so utterly stopped him. Suddenly, killing the shape-shifter had no longer seemed so important. Suddenly, breathing was impossible. Suddenly, despite his strength, he could not move fast enough to reach her.

But he had. And the shape-shifter, rather than continuing her attack, had acted to save the woman, too.

You are living in a mystery, Karr told himself. In war, as in life, he had become accustomed to finding himself in situations where he had no control. Even over himself. But this was wholly different.

Perhaps *he* was different.

He touched his side and felt the thin line of a scar. Behind him, Soria made a small, irritated sound.

"About the clothes. If you want to survive outside this place, you need to follow basic rules. Covering up is one of them."

"Do not patronize me," said Karr mildly, listening hard for anyone else who might be close. He continued to finger the scar in his side, remembering the blade that had slid into his body, twisting. "I understand survival."

"Not like this," Soria replied, with an intensity and gentleness that cut him so deeply he could do no less than stop again and look at her.

"I do not trust your interest in helping me," he said.

"I do not care," she replied. "Trust is irrelevant when committing oneself to an honorable action."

It was an old proverb. Her mouth had trouble pronouncing the low, formal tones, but the meaning encapsulated in those few short words was perfectly clear. Karr had heard it often while growing up, and it startled him to hear her repeat an adage known to few outsiders. He thought she looked surprised, as well.

"Where," he asked slowly, "did you learn my language?"

She ducked her head, braids swinging. "We have to keep moving."

Suspicion filled him, then a thought, a theory that made his chest tighten with unease. "Were you held captive by my kind? Was that how you lost your arm?"

She flinched, then met his gaze. "No."

He felt little relief at her answer. "But you were among us. For some time, I think."

Soria shook her head, knuckles white as she twisted her empty sleeve. "You are wasting time."

"Were you a slave?" he persisted. "I forbade the practice, but I do not know how long I have been gone. Someone else—"

"Stop," she commanded, her hand flying up to touch him but pausing just at the last moment. His skin prickled, suffering the heat of her nearness. He wanted to feel her touch, and gritted his teeth until his jaw ached. "I was not a slave," she told him quietly. "Now, please. Move."

"Perhaps there was another before me," Karr went on in his coldest voice, furious at himself for wanting this woman. "Did you learn my language through interrogating *him*? Gaining *his* trust?"

She blew out her breath and shoved past—or tried to. Karr grabbed her arm and she twisted, shoving her knee up into his groin. No human had ever struck him, and he was unprepared for the attack. Pain exploded, rocking him forward as he stifled a throat-cutting gasp. Tears squeezed from his eyes. He was dimly aware of the woman standing beside him, still and silent as a grave.

"I am sorry," she said. "Reflex."

Both were lies. He could hear it in her voice. But he felt no anger, none except for himself. The woman was a fighter—in spirit, certainly—and he had cornered her. Underestimated her.

Karr wanted to vomit, but there was nothing in his

stomach. He fought for breath, sparks dancing in his vision, keenly aware that the woman stayed by his side. When he finally managed to steal a glance at her face, she was pale but resolute. No fear filled her gaze. Just a question: *What is he going to do?*

Karr looked down, found himself staring at a dead man. The air was thick with the scent of blood. Memories rose, swimming inside his mind with devastating clarity. With them, fear. With them, heartache.

Enough. Karr closed his eyes, placed his hands on his knees and, after a careful negotiation with all the disparate, aching parts of his body, finally managed to straighten. He loomed over the woman. She had to crane her neck to look into his eyes—which she did, unflinching.

"How is your arm?" he asked.

Her gaze finally wavered. "Fine. Your balls?"

"Still attached," he rumbled. "Shall we go?"

A wry smile touched the corner of her mouth, and for one moment—defying sanity—he almost smiled back. But his groin still ached, it was difficult to stand, and he was still a prisoner, even though Soria had assured him otherwise. He would be a prisoner in his own ignorance until he learned about this new land he had found himself in. And why he was still alive.

Gritting his teeth, he began walking down the hall, struggling not to hobble. Soria murmured, "Ahead, turn left," and when the corridor split, Karr did as she suggested, pausing briefly to test the air.

He smelled the shape-shifter, as well as the red-haired

man who had entered his cell and killed the soldiers. The man's scent was strong here, twined with another—perhaps the young woman Karr had glimpsed, dark and long-legged. And then, quite abruptly, cool air touched him. He saw no door but smelled the desert, and the rush of relief that poured through him was both agonizing and sweet.

He looked over his shoulder at Soria. "You need not follow. I can go the rest of the way alone."

"I suppose we all tell ourselves that."

Karr deliberately settled his gaze on her empty sleeve. "And how long have you been alone?"

Anger sparked inside her eyes. Karr grunted, turning quickly before regret could shadow his face. He had never been good at hiding his emotions. Of course, he had never felt so compelled to speak so freely as he did with this woman.

Small heart, he chastised himself. *Using words to hurt her.*

Cool air caressed his shoulders and chest. Karr walked faster, straining his senses for any hint of danger. He heard nothing, and when he rounded the bend he finally saw a door, standing ajar. Beyond, the night. No guards. None he could see.

"A trap," he murmured.

Soria peered around him. "We could have been stopped long before this."

He edged forward, lured by the fresh promise of night. "There were many people here, but the only bodies I have seen belonged to the men in black."

"I cannot explain that," she replied, in a voice hushed and wary. "Perhaps Serena called them away. Or they escaped."

"Serena." Karr shot her a quick look. "Is that the shape-shifter's name?"

Soria ignored him, staring at the door, her empty sleeve twisted in her hand. Karr padded forward on light feet, testing the air. He smelled nothing, heard no one breathing, heard no creak of clothing or weapons. He nudged open the door. No one attacked.

Karr stepped outside, suffering a brief moment of utter, devastating loss. He could not explain it. He had spent most of life beneath the open sky, but when his toes dug into the dirt, a shock riddled his bones, and when he craned his neck to stare at a clear sky full of stars, his heart ached so fiercely he forgot to breathe.

You were dead, and now you are alive, he told himself, pressing his fist over his heart. *This is the first time you have seen stars. It is your first time breathing in the night without the stink of stone and sweat.*

He heard distant voices: women speaking, children laughing, men breaking into loud shouts that quieted instantly. Music thrummed, peculiar and shrill, interspersed with crashing notes and tumbling squeals that somehow carried a melody. He had never heard such songs.

Soria joined him, turning in a slow circle. He followed her gaze, and made out the lines of low, slanted roofs and walls that surrounded them on all four sides except for a narrow gate just opposite them.

"This is an old village," she murmured, moving quickly

to the gate. "Out of the way. A foreign presence inspires gossip but little else. If they think the government is involved, most mind their own business, too afraid to get involved."

"It is a common story," Karr replied, following her as she slipped past the gate. There were still no guards, but he smelled men and his eyes adjusted quickly to the darkness, allowing him to see fresh footprints in the dirt.

"Allowed to escape," Karr murmured, almost to himself. "Granted the ability to run—all the better for a good long hunt." He glanced at Soria, wondering what mysterious truths lingered behind her unflinching dark eyes. "It has happened to others of my kind but never me. I have always escaped before it came to that. Escaped, and killed my captors so that no one might follow."

"You still can," she said. "You have made no secret that you consider me one of them."

Karr tested the air, his shoulder blades itching with the promise of wings. "You have not tried to hide your allegiance. And yet you help me. You are a human who defies a shape-shifter. You defy *me*. You speak my language."

"Ah," she said. "So as long as I pique your interest, you will keep me alive."

He gave her a disdainful look. "I am not so fickle with lives. You will keep yours until I decide you have betrayed me."

"No, not fickle at all," she replied dryly, and walked away from him up a narrow street crowded with shadows and high dirt walls.

He watched her: slender, spine straight, empty sleeve flapping behind her in the breeze. *Let her go*, he thought. *Better to pretend she might have been true, rather than learn she was false. You do not want to kill her.*

No, he did not. No matter what her allegiances, he did not want the stain of hurting her on his soul. He had enough regrets, and she was brave. Brave, when too few were.

He caught up with her. "Where are you leading me?"

"Out of here," she said, her eyes scanning the shadows. "We need to find you clothes, and transportation."

It was very dark. Clear sky, soft winds. A pulse throbbed through his heart, into his shoulders. "Are there archers along the walls?"

Soria blinked hard, staring at him. "No."

"How odd," he murmured, and dug his fingers into his thighs. Golden light filled his vision, pouring through him in throbbing waves, each one crashing down as scales and fur rippled across his skin, cascading from scalp to the soles of his feet. No iron bars held him, no cages. He dropped to his knees as his limbs lengthened, muscles shimmering. His spine cracked as his shoulders shifted, bones pushing outward, stretching until he gasped in both pain and pleasure.

He felt Soria watching, heard her speaking to him in low, urgent tones, but nothing she said made sense. He could not hear her past the roar of blood in his ears, and the thunder of his heart. Heat poured up his throat.

Give me wings, he whispered to himself. *Give me life again.*

Golden light flared so brightly he went blind, and he

threw back his head, gasping. Fire burned against his tongue.

Until, abruptly, he could see again, and the night was warm and lush, and his skin shimmered with heat and glimmers of gold. Everything around seemed small and very far away, and he sat back on his haunches, studying himself as if for the first time.

His shifts had always been unpredictable, and this was no different. Below his waist he wore the skin of a lion, thickly muscled and silken with golden fur. His tail lashed wildly against the dirt road. Everything else was scales and ridges, his neck long as a sword, the claws of his hands obsidian black and razor sharp. Wings arched behind him, and he stretched them until he hurt—and then stretched them even more, hungry for that pain.

Shouts filled the air. Karr craned his long neck, peering over his shoulder, and glimpsed humans standing in the street, others running toward him. Men and children, and women holding babies. Staring with shock, and wonder. Staring, as if they had never seen a dragon.

"Karr," Soria called urgently. He found her standing close, her hand raised to touch one of his claws. She was pale, and a tremor raced through her that was so violent she swayed. He caught her, and she was small in his grip, his long, scaled fingers easily encircling her waist.

"If I frighten you," he rumbled, "close your eyes."

Soria did not. She stared at him with such intensity he almost forgot himself. But he heard more shouts behind him, even a scream, and he clutched the human woman to his chest with as much care as he could. She let out a muffled gasp, but did not try to free herself.

The street was too narrow to beat his wings. Karr launched himself upward, landing gracefully on the walled edge of the courtyard they had just left. He could see the open door. Still no guards. No sign of the shape-shifting female from below.

Destroy it, whispered a small voice. *Make certain.*

He thought of the old woman who had tended him, and the red-haired man who had saved Soria's life. He considered, too, the other humans inside that place who might be slaves. Enemies all, most likely.

Enemies like the woman in his arms.

Frustration burned through him, and anger—at himself, for his indecision and memories, which were still raging, full of death. He had died for those memories. Died to end them, and to protect his people. What few were left.

Anger filled his throat, bubbling from his heart. He swallowed it down and beat his wings against the air. His muscles ached from disuse. Karr wondered how far he would be able to fly.

He leaped into the air, catching the wind, and within moments glided above rooftops and then past them over an ancient wall into flat, vast grassland. He was surprised to see such a landscape; the desert scent was strong. In the distance, odd paired lights moved, and beyond that, even farther away, he glimpsed a glow against the horizon that was not dawn but something closer to fire. More lights, burning.

The air was deliriously sweet, and the stars crumpled across the sky in a ribbon of dusty light. Not as clear or vibrant as he remembered, but it was enough to make him heartsick, homesick, until he wondered briefly if it had been a terrible mistake to ask the others to kill him. Not simply because it had failed. Nor because it had needed to be done. It was good to be alive.

The woman clung to him, very small and still. He cradled her closer, listening to her heart pound.

Enemy mine, thought Karr, as her scent mixed with the night. He tried to orient himself, searching for the North Star. He found it almost immediately, but the comfort that brought him was short-lived. Violent shivers suddenly stole through him—sharp, painful yanks on his innards that made him lurch in the sky. Strength bled from his wings. He felt as though someone was stabbing him through the old scar in his side.

He tumbled, losing altitude. Soria squirmed, gasping, and he clutched her closer. Her extra weight should not have been a burden, but he was not at his best. It was a struggle to hold her safe. He managed, though, regaining altitude as his wings beat furiously. Yet, the feeling lingered, as though someone had reached past his healed wound, digging into his body to twiddle fingers and knives and snarl at his guts. He imagined a presence around him, like the cold cling of morning mist, and the chill that rode down his spine felt like the teeth of ghosts nibbling at his bones.

"Are you sick?" Soria shouted, her voice nearly stolen by the wind. She was trembling in his clawed hands, shivering.

He could have ignored her. He almost did. He was under no obligation to speak truth, or even to speak at all. But he felt compelled, nonetheless, to answer, and craned his long neck to place his head near her ear. "I do not know. I feel . . . odd."

"There is a city near here, to the northwest." She turned her head, peering up into his eyes. "I might be able to contact someone who can help us."

"No," he said. "My people would not be found in cities. I must go to them."

Something passed through her gaze—pity, he thought, or pain. It twisted at Karr, made him unaccountably afraid. She had that power over him, he realized. Just one look from her said more than entire nights made of words.

"You have been gone a long time," she said.

It was suddenly hard to breathe. His wings faltered again. Karr tumbled, cursing, and managed to glide a short distance before finding his rhythm. "What are you saying? Are they dead?"

"I do not know." Soria stared into his eyes, and this time he was certain it was pity he saw; pity and compassion. "I know nothing about who you are, or what you are. Or who your people might be. Do you understand? If your people are alive, almost no one remembers them."

"You know my language. Someone must have taught you."

She shook her head. "Not one of yours."

"Then how—" Karr stopped, his heart aching, and decided to ask another question, one that frightened him almost as much as learning that his people might be gone. "How long was I in the darkness?"

Soria wet her lips, her lone hand clutching his arm even more tightly. "I'm not sure. Thousands of years."

"No," he breathed.

"Karr—"

"You lie!"

Her mouth snapped shut. Karr straightened out his neck so that he would not have to look at her. His hands, though, might as well have been full of eyes; he could see her through touch, and she was still trembling. Maybe with fear. Perhaps with anger.

He had called her a liar, but that was his own lie. Soria had told him the truth as she knew it; Karr could taste that much in her scent, could see it in her eyes. He could not deny his instincts, no matter how much he wished otherwise. But he did not wholly believe her— not truly—until he saw the city.

CHAPTER SIX

*E*RENHOT—known for little more than being a border town, a required stop for motorists and trains,
as well as rich fossil territory. Soria had seen photographs of the giant dinosaur statues that lined the road.
She wondered what Karr would say about those. Some
of them probably looked like relatives.

She was being carried through the air, almost a thousand feet above the ground. Her childhood fantasy, flying, was less thrilling in the flesh. Soria was afraid to
look beyond Karr's chest, but every now and then she
glimpsed the spur of a wing as it swept up and down,
thrusting them through the air. Maybe she was halluci-
nating. This felt like a dream. She had suffered delusions
after losing her arm and crawling through the woods;
she had seen strange things in the hospital, lost between
consciousness and death.

Yet, she was not imagining the winds that stole her
breath away, or that buffeted her dangling legs with
perilous strength. She tried to tuck them closer to her
body, but she was in bad shape and that required more

strength than her stomach muscles possessed. Her lower back ached with the effort, as did her ribs from the beating she had received. Enormous hands cradled her, lengthwise; skinny fingers, triple-jointed, covered in scales. Tipped in claws sharp enough to cut her to the bone if she twitched wrong.

And Karr might just cut her. He was a man, after all, subject to the same emotional frailties. He was a man who had transformed within a veil of light, melting from human into a creature out of dreams: part lion, part serpent, close enough to a dragon to be one and the same. He had scales iridescent as sun-warmed pearls, and the bones of his face shifted into an elegantly inhuman mask that was fine-boned and deadly. A long snout, sharp teeth, high cheekbones . . . and those same golden eyes, intelligent and thoughtful. If Soria had not witnessed similar transformations from other shape-shifters—cheetah, crow, leopard; men and women who could shed one body for another, quick as thought—she would have doubted her sanity.

"We cannot let you be seen," she shouted to him, when the first lights of Erenhot—and Zamyn-Uud, a little farther across the border between Mongolia and China—flickered into view. "No one would understand!"

He did not respond, but moments later began a slow descent. Soria forced herself to watch, trying to memorize what it felt like to be carried through the air: floating, spinning, gliding with shakes and trembles as Karr battled the hard wind. Fear churned, turning over her stomach, but she gritted her teeth and suffered through it.

At the last moment, just as the ground loomed, she

realized she had forgotten completely about her missing right arm: no ghost pains, no discomfort from her stump. Just peace.

Karr landed hard, jarring Soria. She clung to him, dizzy, afraid to let go, but his claws loosened, and when she slid free of his grip, her feet touched hard earth. Her knees were weak. He continued holding her. She found herself gripping one of his claws, her fingers wrapped around a long, dark hook that reminded her of some museum piece on predators. The tip very nearly cut her hand.

"Take care," he rumbled, as golden light again shimmered. His claws receded, replaced by human hands, the transformation rolling down over the rest of his body. Soria watched as a creature almost fourteen feet tall— long necked, alien, covered in fur and scales, with a serpentine head that bore a close resemblance to a horse's skull—shrank well in half until a humanoid man stood before her, and then just a human. A human in appearance only, but that was enough.

Soria forced herself to breathe. Behind Karr, perhaps less than a mile away, Erenhot glittered. Grassland surrounded them, though the ground beneath her feet was very hard and dry. She heard the clack and rumble of trains, and then the rumble of her stomach. Karr turned to scan the horizon, lights reflected softly against his face, though it was still too dark for her to gauge his reaction. His nudity embarrassed her, but his own unselfconsciousness lessened the strain of keeping her gaze above his waist. Soria started walking toward the city.

"What will you do here?" Karr called out.

Soria stopped, hit suddenly by the enormity of her responsibility. It was dangerous, assuming he wouldn't hurt anyone. Unwise, naive. Roland would have a heart attack when he found out she had let Karr go and run off with him.

Stupid, he would say. *After everything you've gone through. You've got nothing to prove.*

Nothing at all. Except her own faith and instincts, which had been borne out so far. Karr had not hurt her. That had to mean something.

Right. Because every killer has a timetable. What a genius.

Okay, so she was stupid. And crazy. Maybe she did have something to prove, after all. That didn't mean she was wrong, though. She'd had a feeling from the first moment she laid eyes on him, a feeling that had only gotten stronger the longer she remained in his presence.

The tape had helped, too. Watching him wake up from death, surrounded, trying to reason with strangers . . .

No, he was not just a killer. Not a psychopath as Serena had implied. But she would never have discovered that while he remained locked up. Questions were a weak substitute to testing character in the field. Words could be twisted, manipulated. Lies were holy to a good manipulator. Masks, however, could only be worn for so long.

"I will try to find us help," she said, struggling to pronounce the words. "If you want it."

Karr hesitated, staring past her at the city. "Those lights are not fire."

There was no word in his language for electricity. "They are made from . . . small bolts of captured lightning. Very small, very controlled."

He did not argue or show surprise; he just approached her, slowly, his gaze still locked on the city until at the last moment he focused on her. Bearing the brunt of that scrutiny was like being lifted up, tossed about, caressed, and placed before a firing squad all at the same time. Soria had never felt so much from so little, but she set her jaw, forced herself to meet his gaze and wrestled her emotions into a neat little bundle.

"Are there many of these cities?" he asked.

"Not here. Elsewhere, there are many. Much larger than this. Erenhot is practically a village, in comparison."

"Populated only by humans?"

"If there are others like you, they hide. Perhaps mixed in with humans. I have seen it done. Most humans do not even contemplate the existence of what you are. No one thinks to look."

Karr frowned, again staring past her at the city. "It was not so when I died. Humans knew of us. Served us. Some even . . . worshipped."

"Did they worship *you*?" Soria asked bluntly, wondering if that was what he had expected of her: to fall down in awe and subservience.

He gave her a sharp look. "I stayed well away from humans, when I could. Most feared me."

"Because of your ability to change shape."

"Because I was dangerous." He took another step toward her, drawing so near that Soria had two choices: either step back, or be touched.

She dug in her heels, stubborn. Karr's eyes narrowed, and he slowly, carefully, raised his hand. Giving her time to move. She did not, holding her breath as he touched her cheek with the tips of his large fingers. She fought not to show anything on her face—not fear, and not the tingling warmth that melted into her bones.

"I cannot tell if your bravery is born from ignorance," Karr whispered, searching her gaze, "or if it is true from the heart."

His other hand unexpectedly touched her empty sleeve. Soria recoiled: caressing her breast would have felt less intimate.

Karr stared, and with great care, lifted his hand from her face. He did not give her space, though. Neither did she back away. Heat spread wildly into her cheeks, her heart thundering, aching with shame and embarrassment. Irrational feelings. But every time Soria thought she had overcome her loss it always managed to hit her again, in unexpected ways. She was not healed; not now, maybe not ever.

Just a sleeve, she told herself, angry. *Just a motherfucking sleeve.*

"True from the heart," he murmured. "Who hurt you?"

"Why—" Soria had to stop and clear her throat. "Why do you think it was a person? It could have been an accident."

"But it was not." Karr leaned in, studying her with what might have been compassion. "I can see it in your eyes."

Soria set her jaw. "Mind your own business."

Karr tilted his head and then stepped around her,

grazing her shoulder with his. He stopped, looking down at her. "You feel it, do you not? Your arm. As though it is always there."

"Yes," she whispered, compelled to answer, unable to look away from him.

"And you think," he murmured, "that it is bad enough that you lost your arm, but that it is so much worse having it linger. Until you almost wish you could cut it off again, if only the sensation would go away."

Tears burned her eyes. She opened her mouth but could not speak.

Karr leaned against her, briefly, just a faint nudge, their shoulders pressed together. "It will pass, in time. But it will take time. Memory clings longer than flesh."

Again, Soria tried to speak, but Karr moved past her, and the loss of his heat and presence cut almost as deeply as his words. *Get a grip*, she told herself, wiping her eyes.

"You want me to enter that place," Karr said. She turned, and found him staring at the city. "Why?"

"Because I need to go there," she said truthfully, "and I do not want to leave you on your own."

"You think I cannot care for myself?"

"I think you might be surprised at how much this world has changed." Soria joined him, staring at the lights of Erenhot. "Would you rather learn from me, or on your own?"

"If I chose the latter? Would you accept that?"

"Yes. I would call you stupid, but everyone has a right to be an idiot."

His mouth twitched. "Do you ever *not* speak your mind?"

"Words are reflections. What we speak comes back to us. I prefer being told the truth, so I tell the truth. Within reason."

"Within reason," he echoed. "So you do lie."

Soria gave him a hard look. "Are you coming?"

"I think," he said slowly, "that you might be the most dangerous woman I have ever met."

"That is no answer."

"But it is the truth," he replied, and pointed to the city. "So teach me, while you can. Until the hunters find us again."

A chill touched her. "That is what I am trying to prevent. If I can find out who sent those men after you—"

"You do not blame your shape-shifter ally?"

"No," Soria said firmly.

"She imprisoned me."

"She thought she had a reason. She still does. She will be coming, too, before long."

Karr shook his head, giving her a look that was both contemplative and disbelieving, as if he still could not figure out what side she was on. Soria was not entirely sure of the answer, either.

"It does not matter who wants me," he said coldly. "The result is the same. The only way to stop a hunt is to kill the hunters."

"No questions asked?" Soria peered up into his face, trying to read his eyes. "Are you not curious about *why* they want you?"

"I know why," he said, and began walking away from the city.

She frowned and ran after him. "Karr!"

He stopped, golden light trickling from his eyes, spreading over his skin. Fur erupted along his throat and chest, rippling down his arms. His face took on a feline cast that was a far cry from the serpentine visage he had worn so recently.

"Go," he whispered. "Go without me. I changed my mind. I will leave this place and search for my people."

Soria stared. "I do not—"

"Will you go back on your word? Or do you think you can force me?"

Karr stalked toward her, circling, his body continuing to transform until Soria felt as though she was staring more at a lion than a man. He stood on two feet, but just barely, and his body was tense, coiled. Almost shaking. Not with anger but something else. Grief, perhaps. No way to know for certain—just a feeling, an instinct. Soria knew about pain.

"I doubt anyone could force you," she said softly.

Karr's chest heaved with a deep, rumbling growl. "Try."

I won't give you the satisfaction. But Soria found herself walking toward him anyway. She stopped, shoulder to shoulder, as he had done to her, and leaned against him ever so slightly. He was huge beside her, muscles lean and rippling, hard as rock. A force of nature.

He had his back turned to the city, but she gazed at the lights, at the modern human sprawl, and could not think of two more ill-fitting pieces than Karr and Erenhot.

Man out of time, she thought, grieving for him just a little.

"Stay or go," she said, not looking at him, not needing to as he quivered in silence. "But I will return to this spot as soon as I can."

"Do not bother," he replied. "You are one of them."

"We are all 'one of something.'" Soria smiled sadly. "But I was looking for more."

And without another word, she left Karr behind and walked toward the city.

ERENHOT WAS LIKE MOST OTHER MODERN CHINESE CITIES: it looked better at night, when the shadows could hide the rough-and-tumble sprawl of squat buildings that were more concrete than glass. Soria felt cold looking at them as she walked down the sidewalk, skirting parked cars and old bicycles. Green taxis whizzed by, dinosaurs glued on top of cab lights. She had caught a ride in one near the outskirts of the city, after a long, stumbling walk that made her feel like a refugee, years lost in war and wilderness.

Her ribs throbbed, and a headache was building. She'd had the cabdriver drop her off in the area where foreign businessmen liked to spend time—which also happened to be the sleazy side of town. No real surprise. Music thumped from inside nightclubs, neon nights flickering wildly in the shape of a rainbow. Several other bars lined the road, as well as closed shops bearing advertisements written in both Cyrillic and English.

Foreigners were everywhere, mostly white men, walking with beer bottles and cigarettes in hand. Some of them gave her curious looks, but most were too drunk to see straight. Soria kept her head down, walking quickly. She heard Russian spoken, French, some English— all three were easy to understand. Long-term exposure tended to make some languages permanent in her mind. She had spent several months in France and Quebec, and one of Dirk & Steele's agents was Russian.

But the words felt empty, the speech patterns dull. Her mouth wanted to coil vowels and purr rumbling growls, and so she let it, speaking to herself, trying to hold on to a dialect that was already fading from her mind a mere hour from Karr's presence. It made her angry. Linguistically, she wanted more. Speaking his language was like eating cheesecake after a life spent dieting on oatmeal. Both were soft, both comforting; but she was used to oats, and had never realized she was tired of them until now.

You shouldn't have left him, she berated herself. *He doesn't know anything about this world.*

Though, she supposed Karr was smart enough to figure some things out. Like, how to stay out of sight. She had no doubt he was a man who could survive quite easily in the most remote regions of the world, invisible unless he wanted to be seen. Perhaps it was better this way. He was being hunted.

And now, so are you.

Soria needed a telephone. She thought about scamming a call from one of the foreigners walking the street—most of them probably had cell phones that would call out of the country—but bloodstains had spattered her white shirt, and a red crust remained on her left hand.

She did not want to risk the chance of anyone asking too many questions, or contacting local police for help.

A hotel was the best place to make an international call, but her passport would be required, along with other travel documents. She had most of that in her vest, along with cash, but given the circumstances, a paper trail seemed like a rather poor idea, right along with using a credit card, or writing her name across the sky with big giant arrows pointed down at her ass. No newspaper stands were around, either, which usually sold phone cards for cash. Local pay phones would be useless.

Limited options, and no time. Soria went looking for a whorehouse.

Finding one was easy. Along with dinosaurs and trains, Erenhot was also known for its sex trade. Women from Inner Mongolia and Russia were often brought through the city by organizations engaged in human trafficking. It was an easy scam, preying on girls desperate for work and who were willing to believe nicely dressed older women who promised respectable jobs in hair salons or restaurants. Until they arrived in cities far from home, and those sly older ladies sold their girls to men for the same amount of money that Soria had used to spend on a nice dress.

Brothels were an easy place to get lost, too: no one ever remembered anything.

Following the Russians led her to the right neighborhood. Large windows lined the buildings along the street, lit red from within. Girls stared out, some of them dancing, while others just looked small, shoulders slumped.

Prostitution was illegal in Mongolia and China, but Soria would never have guessed.

Only one of the buildings seemed to be doubling as a nightclub. Music pounded, neon lights throbbing over the doorway. It looked like it was doing well, with foreigners and Chinese in nice suits going in and out. Money demanded some civility in places like that, even for one-armed women in bloodstained clothes. She was certain they would have a phone capable of making an international call. In a place like that, there would have to be.

She felt incredibly uncomfortable approaching the club. A very large Mongolian man stood beside the front door, watching her. His hair was slicked back, and he wore a white T-shirt and black slacks. A cigarette dangled from his mouth. He held out his hand when Soria drew near, his gaze flickering down to her empty sleeve and then over the rest of her.

Yes, she told him silently. *I look like shit. Get over it.*

"Not for you," he said in badly accented English. "This naughty place."

Soria raised her brow, not amused. Words and nuance floated from his mind into hers, faster now than this morning when she had encountered the village children for the first time. Her mind had already been broken in. In perfect Khalkha she replied, "I need to make an international call."

The man blinked, startled. "You speak very well."

She shoved a small wad of cash into his hand. "A phone, please."

He tilted his head. "You a journalist?"

"I am a girl having a bad night," Soria replied firmly. "I am not here to cause you trouble."

A cold smile touched his mouth. "And all you want is a phone? Nothing else?"

Soria gave him her best *do-not-fuck-with-me* stare. "One call. Right now. I will pay the charges, and I want a private room."

The man shrugged and tossed his cigarette to the ground. The cash disappeared into his pocket. He held open the door for Soria and ushered her inside.

The lobby was small but well lit, the walls and floors tiled in glossy black marble. Gilt-framed oil paintings of naked Mongolian horsewomen hung on the walls, and below, like the waiting room of a dentist's office, deep leather chairs were lined in a row. A man was seated in each, a mix of white and Asian, most looked like business types, texting messages on their smartphones while girls in miniskirts served them bottles of beer. They were waiting in line, killing time before sex.

The men stared at Soria when she walked in, one after the other, glancing up and then doing a double take. Some of them smiled—smarmy, slick, but a smile nonetheless—until they saw her empty sleeve. Then the same look crossed their faces that she had seen a million times back home, at the grocery store or gas station, or in the airport: a flinch in their eyes, a faint twist of their mouths, and then nothing, a mask wiping their expressions clean away. As if she were no longer a woman. Just air. A thing taking up space.

The mass scrutiny only lasted seconds before the

men ducked their heads and began busying themselves on their phones; but seconds was all it took to cut Soria. Sometimes a person didn't want to be caught staring, so they went out of their way to do the opposite, while others were frightened, disgusted, unable to handle the reality of a missing limb and capable only of seeing its absence, not the person. *I'm still me*, Soria told herself, glancing down at the silver bracelet on her wrist, turquoise glinting. It was the wrong wrist but the same body. The same heart.

The front desk was staffed by a pretty young woman in a cheap gray suit, who wore a red ribbon at her throat. A faint bruise was healing around her eye. To the left a sheer curtain shimmered, hiding a room full of shadows. Music pulsed, mixed with rough laughter. Soria glimpsed a stage, and the dancing silhouettes of lithe bodies.

"She needs to make an overseas call," her escort said to the receptionist, with a hint of amusement. "What rooms are free?"

"You sure a call is all she wants?" The woman gave Soria a once-over that ended at her empty sleeve, and a smile of both disdain and bitterness crossed her tired face. "Pay someone to poke her. No one else will."

The man shook his head, still smiling. Soria leaned over the counter, staring into the woman's bruised eyes. "Save the commentary. All I want is a phone."

Her Mongolian was still flawless, the words settling comfortably on her tongue. Surprise flickered over the woman's face. She looked from Soria to the man, and then back again. "Why do you need it?"

Soria set her jaw and pulled out a one-hundred-dollar

Chinese bill. More than enough to pay for a prostitute's services in this place. She slid the money across the counter toward the receptionist, but the man intercepted and smoothly folded the crisp bill into his pocket. He gave the girl a hard look. "She can use the phone. And a room."

Not even Soria wanted to tangle with that glint in his eye. The receptionist fumbled inside a drawer. She pulled out a battered cell phone, and then stood.

"Follow me," she said.

The building was larger on the inside than it had first appeared. Soria followed the girl up three flights of stairs, and on each floor she heard echoes of tears and laughter, smacking sounds and rough grunts. Her skin crawled, and she found herself twisting her empty sleeve into knots. She hated it here—but she'd been in worse places, other brothels, acting as translator for the various trafficking cases in which Dirk & Steele involved themselves. It never felt as though they made a dent. The wheel kept spinning, and girls and boys were always getting hurt.

The receptionist led Soria to a room near the top of the stairs. It was plain inside, with a neatly made bed, a window, and a small bathroom that smelled like a mix of perfume and old urine. Soria dragged money from her pocket, and pushed it into the other woman's hand.

"For you," she said, and then gave her another, smaller, bill. "And for him, when he asks."

The woman narrowed her eyes but said nothing. She merely hitched up her skirt, revealing pale skin and bruises. She stuffed most of the cash into her underwear.

The rest, she placed inside her bra. Soria watched in silence, and then held out her hand for the cell phone.

The receptionist hesitated. "Businessmen sometimes lose their money here, or passports. He gives them this phone when they are desperate to make a call home to families. But it does not work. Just makes them owe more money."

"Ah," Soria said, not entirely surprised. "My options?"

The woman reached inside her suit for a small pink phone covered in glittering trinkets. "This works."

"He will know."

She shrugged. "Give me a little more money."

Soria smiled. Maybe this was part of the scam, too. But she would rather be scammed like this than by the greased-up man downstairs. "I want to test the phone and see if the call goes through."

The woman gave the cell to her, and Soria—awkwardly, one-handed—began to dial home and then stopped, realizing that it might not be safe. Someone could be tracing calls to her home. She cleared the screen, and then punched in the number of a local pizza delivery place in Stillwater that she knew by heart. She had been living off ham-and-pineapple specials for a year now. Easier than leaving the house.

Soria started breathing again only when their voice mail came on. It sounded remarkably mundane. Homesickness razored through her heart.

"Do not take long," said the receptionist, pocketing more cash. Her gaze drifted over Soria's empty sleeve. "This is not a good place."

She left. Clutching the cell phone in her sweaty palm, Soria closed the door with her shoulder. No locks. She leaned against the battered wood and slid to the floor. Took a deep breath, finally allowing her tight control to slip. Shudders wracked her. She had spent the past year as a recluse. Being thrown so hard back into the game, without support, was not how she had imagined returning to Dirk & Steele.

Scratch that. She had not intended on returning at all.

Her hand trembled so badly she almost dropped the phone. Ghost fingers wanted to reach up and dial. She could feel them, straining at the end of an arm that had been cremated, and shut her eyes, banging her head gently against the door.

It will pass, in time, she heard Karr rumble. Other people had said the same thing to her, but none with that same sincerity and calm, as though they truly believed it.

Soria gritted her teeth, and used her thumb to carefully, awkwardly, dial the number to Roland's private line. He would have to change it after this was all finished— not soon, but eventually. No way he would want a place like this having his digits. His fault, though, for not providing a three-band phone before she left San Francisco. He had promised that one would be waiting for her in Beijing, but that hadn't happened, and Soria had never gotten around to asking Serena.

The phone rang twice before it was answered, but the breathless, slightly frantic voice on the other end did not belong to Roland.

"Eddie," Soria said. "It's me."

He exhaled, sharply. "Are you all right?"

"No. Is Roland there?"

"Hold on." Eddie began shouting, his voice and footsteps fading. Moments later, she heard another click.

"I'm here," Roland growled. "What the fuck happened?"

"You tell me," she snapped, wishing she still had her other hand so that she could give him the finger. "There was an attack on the facility. I had to free the shapeshifter they'd locked up, and run."

"You *freed* him?" Roland dragged in his breath. "Goddamn it, Soria. Where are you now? All I can see is the ass end of some hotel room."

Mind reader, remote viewer. Roland was capable of seeing the surroundings of anyone he had a connection with—and a telephone conversation was good enough for a complex viewing. All he needed was something to focus on.

"Erenhot." She heard sharp laughter in the hall, and her heart lurched. "Border city between Mongolia and China. I'm borrowing a phone to call you."

"Serena's not there?"

Soria wanted to strangle him. "Do you have any idea what you sent me into?"

"A controlled situation," he replied tightly. "That's what I was promised."

"Bullshit." She dug her heels into the floor, pushing back harder against the door, suddenly afraid someone would try and open it. "If you had thought it was so controlled, you wouldn't have *paid someone outside the agency* to watch my back. Why did you do that, Roland?

What were you so afraid of the others finding out, that you couldn't send them with me?"

Silence fell, and very softly, Eddie said, "Roland."

Soria had not known he was still on the line. Roland whispered, "Eddie. Hang up. Now."

"No," replied the young man. "First Long Nu, then this—"

Soria heard a loud click. Moments later, more shouting. Eddie was still holding his receiver because his voice was loud and clear when he suddenly said, "How could you expect me not to notice? You should have seen the look on your face after she—"

His voice broke off, followed by a faint grunt and a scuffling sound. The next time Eddie spoke he sounded very far away and muffled. Angry, too, which took Soria by surprise. Eddie rarely lost his temper.

Roland breathed like he had been running a marathon. "You still there?"

"I'm sitting in a Mongolian whorehouse because I have nowhere else to go," Soria snapped. "And what does Long Nu have to do with anything?"

Long Nu. An enigmatic old woman, a shape-shifter, described by the others of her kind in terms usually reserved for royalty, sex addicts, and the villain of every bad Hong Kong movie ever made. Soria had never met her, but she'd heard plenty. The old shape-shifter had made it her mission to preserve her kind from extinction, and had allied herself with Dirk & Steele's elderly founders in order to do just that. It was hardly coincidence that she was sniffing around Roland, especially now.

A bad feeling trickled into Soria's gut. Shape-shifter reaction to Karr, if Serena was any kind of example, was radically unpleasant. And vice versa. Whatever the history, it went deep—but the hate seemed irrational, based more on a network of stereotypes than any attempt for real truth. *You know they're all like this* was not a good foundation.

Roland sighed. "She's a troublemaker, that's all. Worry more about that man you freed. You called him a shape-shifter?"

Again, anger stirred. "You should know."

"No," he said coldly. "I do not."

Soria was not entirely certain she believed him. "His name is Karr, and he can definitely change his shape. He doesn't consider himself to be a shape-shifter, though—not like Serena. Who, by the way, wants him dead."

"That, I *did* know," he muttered. "Is he a threat?"

"Why don't you come here and find out?" Soria replied harshly. "Oh, but no. I forgot. You're too scared to leave the house."

Roland made a hissing sound. "You know if I could change things—"

"You wouldn't," she interrupted coldly. "If there was ever a chance and opportunity to actually . . . be there when I needed you, when it wasn't on your terms, you had it. You had it for a month while I was in that hospital. And you never—"

She stopped, swallowing hard. "We need help, Roland. Now. I don't know who broke into the facility, but they meant business. They wanted him—and me—alive."

He was silent a moment. "Robert?"

"Gone now. Certainly not here."

Soria heard more drunken laughter in the hall. Roland muttered, "Can you get to Beijing?"

"That's the best you're offering?"

"Can you do it?"

"By train, maybe." She hesitated. "You're hiding things from me."

Roland made a small, frustrated sound. "Where's the shifter now?"

Soria closed her eyes, utterly weary and just a little heartbroken. "Go to hell, Roland. And thanks for nothing. I'll contact you when I reach Beijing."

She ended the call, and clutched the cell phone to her chest.

Son of a bitch.

Roland Dirk had thrown her to the wolves.

CHAPTER SEVEN

K ARR did not move for a long time after the woman
left him. He tried, but the vastness of the sky suddenly seemed less like freedom and closer to a cage,
and the lights of the city, as if they were the stars themselves, acted as an anchor, a chain. He stared at the spot
where the woman had finally, distantly disappeared, and
could not shake himself loose, no matter how much he
wished.

Thousands of years. *Thousands.*

The woman had said the words to him, and he had
not believed her—and even arriving here, seeing this
city glowing in the night, had not immediately proven
anything. Karr had ventured into cities during the war:
human settlements carved with beauty and violence from
river valleys and mountainsides, the world re-created
in fire and stone. Humans could do such things, and he
had lost himself in those places; but never for long. His
size and golden eyes had always made him a target—
of those who thought him gods-sent or, more often, a

monster. Either way, he'd always ended up feared and alone.

But not alone like this. If the woman's words were true, if such a vastness of time had passed, then there was nothing left of the world Karr knew. Nothing of the people he had left behind. Not Tau and Althea, or all the others he had seen just before being buried in the tomb. Losing Tau hurt the worst, though. His brother— not in blood—but in friendship. A friendship that Karr had betrayed.

You had them kill you. You gave up. You left them *behind. And now you grieve?*

Yes, he grieved. It was a fool's grief; he knew that. He grieved because he was still alive, and no matter how compelling his reasons for taking his own life the first time, it seemed like a coward's choice now. He could have chosen exile. He could have walked into the wilderness and never returned to his people. But he had asked for death. And now he was the one who had been left behind.

There are ways to know for certain, whispered an insidious voice. *Ways you can search beyond yourself to see if any of your kind exist.*

So tempting. All it would require was meditation, a trance. Blood magic. Small words for a dangerous act. But even now, desperate, he was not ready to take the risk of losing his mind. He was so close to losing it already.

Karr knelt in the grass, his fists pushing against his chest, rocking forward until his brow touched the ground.

He stayed like that, struggling to breathe as if the night and the stars and the entire world were sagging, collapsing, falling inward to crush his heart. He had seen ruins during the war, lumps and fragments of civilizations living only in legend. He had walked upon the bones of temples, had killed in those places and bled. But now . . . *You are the fragment. You are the relic.*

Perhaps. But he had a choice now. A similar choice to the one he had been given before: die or live.

Death is not an option, whispered a voice inside his heart. *Get up. Get up and do something. Find your people, if they still exist. Learn what you must. Learn why you are still alive. If it is a gift, then do not let it go to waste. Follow the woman.*

Karr lifted his head, staring at the city. Soria's scent burned through him. She was everywhere: on his skin, in the grass, carried by the wind. He could taste her on his tongue.

Follow the woman, though she might be your enemy. She can harm you no worse than you have already harmed yourself. Learn what you can from her. Even if there are others of your kind still alive, you cannot find them without knowledge of this world. You must know how things stand.

As always, information was vital to survival. Karr staggered to his feet—and winced as the scar in his side throbbed, sharply. It happened again, the pain more powerfully centered in his gut, and it was so like being stabbed that Karr bent over, clutching at his side, half expecting to feel a blade embedded there. But, nothing. Just air.

He closed his eyes, lost in memories that pressed tight and cold: his friends—*Tau, especially*—tight-lipped and shaking.

Do it, Karr mouthed, feeling the words move through him again. *Before I hurt anyone else. Kill me, as I killed your wife.* He remembered baring his throat to Tau, expecting claws, teeth, a ravaging. But a sword had slipped quietly into his stomach and that was enough. He had let himself be thrown into the tomb, locked inside the coffin. Bleeding out, alone in darkness. Drifting into nightmare.

The pain eased. Karr kept his eyes closed, becoming aware again of Soria's scent. A good distraction. He pictured her in his mind, heard again her voice. His name, on her tongue. He had not yet tried to say her name. It felt too personal to do so, though she was free enough with his. Hearing her speak his name was what had stopped Karr from entering the city with her.

Again, he was a fool. For one brief moment, hearing Soria call out to him had filled Karr with an unexpected sense of belonging, as if it was natural to travel with her, to be in the here and now with her. Never mind the rest. He had forgotten all of it, lost in the simple fleeting pleasure of being himself . . . with Soria.

The connection he felt to her frightened him, and he had given in to that fear. He had battled and overcome so many weaknesses—only to be unnerved now, by a human woman?

You cannot trust her, he told himself. *No matter how much you want to.*

But he needed her. Either way, he was damned.

Clutching his side, Karr followed her trail into the city.

HE KEPT TO THE SHADOWS AS MUCH AS HE COULD. He wore his father's skin, the skin of a lion, though his tail was long and serpentine, edged in a razor spine of golden scales. No wings. He did not need them, and for once his body had obeyed.

Scents crowded his nose, bitter and strange: human, but mixed with something else that scalded the roof of his mouth, especially when those odd enclosed wagons of varying shapes and colors roared past the shadows where he hid. He watched them all, unable to determine what propelled their wheels. Perhaps the wind set them in motion, or mere thought. He took nothing for granted—especially not when he saw men and women perched atop impossibly delicate rods made of iron and air, with two slim wheels spinning underneath. And there were similar, bulkier transports that also traveled on two wheels only much faster, releasing the same acrid scent as the wagon. He saw horses once: at the side of the road, hauling carts. They seemed out of place, as much relics as himself. He did not linger. The horses started screaming when they smelled him, trying to bolt.

The wagons—all those humans on wheels—sped down streets made of smooth, flawless stone, bordered by monoliths that blocked the sky—so many, of such height and size that Karr could not imagine the lives surely lost to build them. Lights burned everywhere. Cold light, shimmering bursts of silver shining from tall posts that bordered the road. Some were filled with color, glowing and twinkling with a brilliance he had never witnessed beyond jewels, or the petals of flowers.

Lightning, Soria had said. *Harnessed and controlled.*

There are places of light and thunder, Karr recalled his father saying. *Above the clouds where your mother soars. You will see them one day. You will steal fire from the sun.*

Or fire from another world, he thought, struggling to follow Soria's scent.

He lost the trail on the outskirts of the city, and found in its place the acrid bitterness of a wagon's exhaust. He considered this, briefly, imagining that she must have entered one to ride, as he had seen other humans do. It was a problem. All the wagons smelled the same to him, with only minor differences, and tasting those incremental distinctions required time. It was difficult to linger over the scent when there was so much activity along the road. He was not small, not in any form, and it was hard enough hiding with so many lights. Holding very still behind bushes and in the nooks between buildings was tiresome. And ineffective. Karr suspected he had already been seen.

Be wise, go back. If she returns and finds you gone, she will think you have left for good.

But he dismissed the idea. He could not quell the urgency growing stronger within him, perhaps nothing more than his grief becoming desperation. Or something more. He had suffered similar instincts during the war, and Soria had been attacked this night as well. He could picture every detail, every grimace and fall of light on her sweat-soaked brow. He could recall with perfect clarity the scent of her fear.

We share a common enemy. An enemy that might be here, searching for them both. He could not take the risk. She was his only connection to this world, for good or ill.

Giving up on subtlety, he crouched in the open with his nose pressed to stone. He chose a rare moment when the road was nearly empty of wagons—twin lights shining at him from a distance—but there were still humans out, perched on their strange wheel-machines, and they stopped, staring at him in horror and shock. None were armed. Karr closed his eyes, inhaling deeply.

At the side of the road, at the exact spot where Soria's scent disappeared, he detected a trace of burned metal, like the inside of a blacksmith's stall. It was a corrosive smell, and beneath, in the stone, was something earthier: the manure of a pack animal, horse or donkey. The wheels had rolled through shit. He could taste it.

Karr heard shouts behind him, and a strange whooping noise. He glanced over his shoulder and watched a compact white wagon roar toward him, blue and red lights flickering wildly upon its roof. Humans hurried off the road, staring and pointing, some with small, square objects that flashed tiny lights, leaving stars in his eyes.

He thought about staying, shifting shape in front of these humans to gauge their reaction, to see if it was true that his kind were unknown. But he took another look at the faces around him—mixed with fear and awe—and thought better of it. He had enough problems.

Karr leaped away from the road and raced into the shadows.

HE USED SIDE STREETS, CUTTING BACK AROUND TO THE road when he could, to test the stone for the wheel scent of Soria's wagon, to study his surroundings and memorize landmarks that would be useful from both the ground and the sky. The most fascinating things he found were statues of creatures that reminded him vaguely of his other skin: long-necked, long-tailed, reptilian. Not dragons, but something close. They were obviously revered—worshipped, perhaps, as he could see no other reason for creating such monuments.

He lost the trail several times, was forced to backtrack—but humans would shout and point, and within minutes flashing lights would appear, forcing him to run, intensifying his frustration. Time was running out, the streets becoming more tangled, scents crashing together. He was losing Soria. He thought, perhaps, he had lost her already.

Until, quite abruptly, Karr caught the scent of a shape-shifter.

He was cutting down a narrow street, traveling silently behind a human woman pulling a cart laden with bizarre-looking objects that looked dirty and used. She was utterly oblivious to the presence of the lion, and seemed quite old and tired. Karr did not want to frighten her. But the shape-shifter's scent made him stop dead, and a growl ripped free of his throat.

The human began to turn, but Karr slipped away. Not far, just behind a wall that smelled like urine, crammed with delicate-wheeled transports chained to a metal rod in the ground. Karr stood very still, his face upturned, inhaling deeply, listening as wailing music filled the night, accompanied by drums that sounded like the clash of fists on stone and metal. The scent, however, did not belong to the leopardess. This was the smell of someone new, though that was all Karr could determine. He could not even say for certain whether it was male or female, or what skin the shifter wore. Simply, there was a spice in the air, a current of power that made his hackles rise. Somewhere, in this city, was a shifter. And it stood to reason that where it was, Soria would be as well.

She has betrayed you, came the unbidden thought.

But he did not want to believe. Despite everything—all that he knew and understood to be true—he did not want to believe that Soria had entered this city with the intention to harm him.

So, find out the truth. If it means that much.

It did, Karr was surprised to realize. It meant a great deal.

And it meant even more, moments later, when he heard a woman cry out in the night, distant, almost lost beneath the odd drumbeat that was sparking a rhythm through the city streets. The sound tore right through him. He knew that voice.

Karr ran—fast, as though the human streets were little more than the canyons of home, twisting and riddled with false ends and loose rock. His feet barely touched stone as he raced through the maze, listening for that familiar voice. He heard it once again, closer, mixed with fear and anger, and burst onto a street full of color, daz-

zling sheets of flickering lights blazing from the fronts
of buildings, sparkling and thrumming in time to the
drumbeats roaring from within.

They blinded him for a moment. There was too much
to see and hear, including human women in windows,
barely dressed, posed in such a manner that he thought
of the priestesses who inhabited the temples in the desert near the warm Phoenician sea—women who used
their bodies to worship the goddess they believed lived
beneath their skins.

Movement caught his attention. Soria.

Karr's breath caught when he saw her—though from
relief or concern, he could not say. She stood almost in
the road, two men in front of her. Both wore dark pants,
but one was dressed in a flimsy white shirt and the other
wore black, his hair short and spiked, his frame soft with
fat bulging over the cinched waist of his tight pants.
His nose was bleeding. He was holding Soria's arm in a
tight grip, angling her arm so far up that she was forced
to stand on her toes. Words were being tossed back and
forth: heated, vicious. Soria's face was pinched and pale
but utterly defiant.

Other humans watched from a distance: men and
scantily clad women emerging from doorways, curious
and idle. Most turned away and did not go to help her.
Several stood on the sidelines, shouting at the men holding Soria. Waving their hands in agitation.

Karr hardly noticed. A growl rumbled loose, his
vision blurring behind a golden haze as his claws dug
into the stone, muscles coiled so tight his entire body
quivered. Rage choked him—more than was appropriate,

he thought dimly—but he could not control the terrible fury that swept over him while watching those men surround her, touch her, scream at her.

You were never a fool before, whispered an urgent voice inside his mind. *Not with anyone. Do not start now.*

Too late. Karr could not control himself. He lunged from the shadows, streaking across the road—and at the last moment, the man in the white shirt glanced up and saw him. His eyes widened, mouth contorting with shock and horror.

Karr barreled into him, pulling back his claws so that all he did was batter the human into a wall. Screams filled the night, but he ignored them, whirling to face the man still holding Soria, who dragged her in front of him to use as a shield.

Soria stared at Karr, her expression shaken—and then something warm entered her eyes, a warmth that cut through his rage, twisted at his heart. She began to laugh. The man holding her arm stared at her like she was insane, but she hardly seemed to notice. She bit her bottom lip, shaking her head at Karr with a fierce, dangerous smile.

Karr stalked forward, staring at the human whose white-knuckled grip on Soria began to loosen. Until, with very little fanfare, he shoved her toward Karr and ran away down the road. It was an unsurprising response, though not nearly as satisfying as planting his claws in the man's already bloody face would have been.

Soria stumbled against him, her fingers briefly digging into his mane. She smelled tense, frightened—far more so than her face revealed. His larynx was just human enough to rumble, "Are you hurt?"

"Seems like you are always asking me that," she replied, and then, "No. But we need to get out of here, now. I had help coming before you showed up."

"Really," Karr remarked, hearing the distant whoop of those flashing white wagons that had hounded him for the past hour. "It looked to me as if you only had an audience."

Soria made a low, noncommittal sound. "Come on."

Karr glanced at the humans around them, staring as if they had been confronted with a ghost, a monster, some apparition of tooth and thunder. He had seen such dazzled gazes often enough, but this time there was no awe, no wonder in their faces. Just fear.

His tail lashed angrily. Soria began running down the street. Karr followed, knowing full well that it would look as though he was chasing her, hunting for the kill. Such misconceptions had always plagued him among humankind—and among shape-shifters, as well. He heard more cries behind him, shouts, but the voices faded into a meaningless din.

He caught up with Soria as she rounded the corner and entered a dark, quiet street lined with wagons and small, scrubby bushes. All the buildings were squat and barren in appearance, but there were doors set in regular intervals, along with barred windows, and he heard children crying, raised voices, trills of music, and other loud sounds that seemed out of place. Urine and grease scents filled his nose, as did the same bitter odor that plagued the entire city and that he associated with the wagons.

Nonetheless, it did not take much imagination to find the similarities between this and any other human settlement he had ventured into. Places where people crowded always smelled dirty and thick, with sounds crushed upon each other.

He did not scent the shape-shifter, though. Not on Soria, not near her, not anywhere close. Which only meant that they had not yet made contact.

"Did you find the help you came for?" Karr asked, slinking through the shadows.

"Not quite." Soria glanced at him—and then behind, scanning the street with tense, thoughtful eyes. "We need to leave this city for another, in the south."

"Why?"

"Good question," she muttered. "I was not given a reason."

He stopped, tail lashing. "There is a shape-shifter in this city."

"Serena?"

"Someone else." Karr studied her face, finding it somewhat disconcerting that she was taller than he at this angle. "Were you expecting anyone?"

"No. But that was not what you were asking, was it?"

Have you betrayed me? Karr wanted to say, but he had spoken the words so often, in so many different ways— to her and within himself—that to say them out loud again suddenly seemed . . . tiresome. She had betrayed him or not. She was an ally or not. She was truly as compassionate as she seemed or not. He had no straight answers, and could hope for none; he could simply watch, and observe, and calculate strategies and possibilities based on words and actions, and all the myriad things that could describe a person's true character. And why it mattered to him—why, when he was alone, with no one else to anchor him to this unknown world but this woman—was the one thing he did not want to contemplate.

"Those men," he rumbled, walking again, ducking behind a wagon as a man on a wheeled contraption rolled by. "Why were they hurting you?"

Soria matched his pace, walking backward for a moment to look behind them again. "I had to contact someone who lives far from here. There were safer places for me to do so, but they would have kept a record of my presence, and I did not think that was wise. So I went to a place of . . . ill repute." Her mouth had trouble forming the word in his language, her accent raw and unsteady. "Unfortunately, they were not content with the price I paid."

"You bloodied a man's nose."

"He deserved it."

"I am sure he did," Karr replied mildly, which caused her to give him another sharp look. "You said you had help coming?"

"*Po-lice.*" Soria pronounced the word in her own language, slowly. "Soldiers, you might call them. They keep the peace. One of the men watching our fight . . . summoned them for me."

Karr's ears twitched. "Are they trustworthy?"

"Sometimes." Soria frowned. "Thank you for helping me. I was not . . . expecting to see you."

"You thought I left."

"Why did you change your mind?"

He hesitated, unsure what to say, suddenly finding it difficult to speak in the skin he wore. It was not that his mouth had trouble forming the words, though that was true. Instead, some ideas were easier to express when wearing a different kind of mask: human, lion, or dragon. Same heart, but the spirit felt altered.

Besides, he thought he was rather conspicuous as a lion.

Golden light flowed over his body, but he made the shift brief, pushing himself to the point of pain to transform as quickly as he could into his human body. Scales flared over his fur and skin, and then receded. His spine crackled, terrible pressure gathering around his jaw and nose, so much that for a moment he could not breathe.

The discomfort passed, though. Within moments he was a man again, and Soria grabbed his hand, pulling him into a crack between buildings where potted plants lined the ground and the air smelled stuffy. The space was so narrow, his shoulders brushed the walls on either side of him. Cold stone, clammy against his skin.

Soria blocked the exit, her back to the street, and craned her neck to stare at him. A faint blush stained her cheeks. "If you were going for subtlety," she said tightly, "then you failed."

"I believe I failed the moment I entered this place," he replied, the tight space making him uncomfortable. "I have never been accepted, save by my own people."

"*Your* people. Who have golden eyes and can change shape, but are not shape-shifters. There is no logic in that. Not for me."

"There is a difference between race and mere ability," he told her, exasperated, the cramped space still making his skin crawl. "What I am—" He stopped as a breeze shot down the alley, revealing fresh scents—fresh and familiar. A growl rumbled up his throat.

Soria reached for her empty sleeve. Not thinking, he caught her hand before she twisted herself into knots. She froze. So did he. Her hand was small and warm inside his, her bones delicate.

"I smell the shape-shifter," he said, wishing his voice did not sound so strained.

"Could be a coincidence."

"And are they still as numerous as humans?"

She hesitated. "No."

"I find that hard to believe." When Soria began to protest, he shook his head and added, "I was not calling you a liar."

"For once."

His jaw tightened. "When I . . . was killed, there were many shape-shifters of various clans, though they kept themselves apart from humans. What happened?"

"Time," she said. "Time or people. I do not know."

Karr leaned against the wall, trying to ease his claustrophobia. "Justice, perhaps. Why are you aware of such things if others are not?"

She broke eye contact, looking down at her feet, their joined hands, anywhere but at him. "We should keep moving. Find you clothes."

"Answer the question."

Irritation flashed through her eyes. "How is it you think I speak your language?"

"You refuse to tell me how you learned, so I cannot say. But it argues for the continued existence of my people."

"I wish that were the case." Soria stood on her toes, peering into his eyes. "I am not like other humans. My brain functions differently. I can speak many languages. *Any* language."

Karr stared. "That is . . . unlikely."

"I can speak your language because I am in your presence," she persisted. "The moment I leave you, that knowledge begins to fade. I cannot tell you how or why; it just does. I never learned from your kind, or from anyone who has been among your people. I simply knew how to talk to you from the first moment I stepped into that cell."

She was playing him for a fool—or telling the truth. Unfortunately, he suspected it was the latter, which complicated things even more. "You are a witch?"

Soria gave him a dirty look. "Are you?"

"I am what I am," he replied, then paused. "Are there others like you?"

"Not exactly . . . but similar." She drew a deep, shaky breath, as if it had taken something from her to tell him this. And he supposed, perhaps, it had. "*That* is how I know about shape-shifters. Some of us who are different found each other."

"Different," he echoed. "And the interest in me? Is it because I am also . . . different?"

"I truly do not know. I was sent to speak to you because no one else could. I was told to find out if you are a danger to others. But there are . . . competing agendas at work here. I can see that now."

Karr briefly closed his eyes, unsure how to react. All of this was too much. "I *am* a danger to others," he admitted.

"You are dangerous," she agreed quietly. "But that is not the same thing as being a threat."

A careful distinction—one that very few had made in his life. "And if you learned otherwise? What would have been done to me?"

Soria's expression turned impossibly grim. "I have been asking myself that same question ever since I saw you."

They would have killed me, he wanted to tell her. *And I would have done the same in their place.*

Karr glanced up and down the narrow alley, tasting the lingering scent of the shape-shifter. No doubt his own scent was drifting in the wind. "You were told to journey south?"

"Yes." Soria tried to loosen her hand from his, and he let go, startled to discover that he had still been holding on. He had rarely held the hand of anyone in his life, except for the children entrusted to his care. But this made him uneasy. He did not care for the way he kept responding to her, seemingly without thought. Perhaps the woman was a witch, after all.

"You do not sound enthusiastic," Karr rumbled.

"Something is wrong. In more ways than the obvious." Soria began to lean against the wall alongside him, braced against her arm. She stopped, though, wincing.

Karr remembered the exact spot where the man had held her, squeezing very tightly, white-knuckled. Perhaps bruising her to the bone. No telling what other damage had been done before he arrived. Rage flashed through him.

Soria glanced up. "Your eyes are glowing."

"Are they?" he asked sharply, and looked away, over his shoulder and down the alley. "What makes you uneasy?"

His companion was silent a long moment. "My friend, the man who sent me here, is withholding information."

"Then he does not trust you," Karr replied. "Or he does not have enough information to share—not without causing more harm than good."

Bitterness passed over her face; so much that he wondered who this man was, and what he meant to the woman. "You sound sure of yourself."

"From experience." Karr peered up the wall, noting the smooth stone surface. The windows were spaced at regular intervals, and the bars covering the glass looked useful. "Will you journey south?"

"Will you?"

He hesitated. "I do not know what I should do. I understand nothing of what happened to me. I should not be alive. And now you tell me that . . . years have passed, and everything I know is gone. And yet"—his voice dropped to a whisper—"they still want me in chains, and dead."

Her eyes narrowed. "Why?"

Such a simple question. Deceptively so. It was one that Karr had not asked since childhood, when he had first learned that there were those who would murder him simply for being born. He had not understood the answer then—not him, or Tau, or any of them—and he suspected this woman would do little better. It was not an easy thing to say or hear.

"We are their unwanted children," Karr told Soria, suffering a hard, throbbing ache in his side. "We are their mistakes."

And then, as if his words were a blade, his pain intensified. He doubled over, hissing, clutching his side, feeling with breathtaking clarity the sensation of steel entering his body. Something warm and wet touched his hand. Blood. His scar was bleeding. Quite a lot, really.

Karr stared at his hand, which was glistening red. His knees buckled and he fell hard, dimly heard Soria call out his name as another rush of pain rippled through him. It was difficult to breathe.

He was dying again. Only, this time, he was not ready.

CHAPTER EIGHT

THERE was blood on her tennis shoes. It was so dark in the alley, she hardly noticed—not when Karr bent over, hissing in pain. But she heard the drips, and felt them, and looked down.

Blood. On the concrete, on her shoes, forming a puddle between herself and Karr.

"No," she whispered, stunned. "Karr."

His knees buckled and she grabbed his arm. It was like trying to hold up a mountain. He went down and she followed him, hitting the ground so awkwardly the breath was knocked out of her. Her eyes kept working, though, and she got an eyeful of his stomach; there was enough light from the windows lining the alley to see the dark gaping slash in his gut that had not been there only moments before.

Wrong, she told herself. There had been a scar. She had a vague recollection of it: on his side, near his abdomen—which was too close to parts of his body she had been trying desperately *not* to look at.

There was no choice about the matter now. Soria crouched on her hands and knees, trying to see what she could of the bleeding wound. It looked fresh, which should have been impossible.

"Shit," she muttered in English, looking around for anything that could be pressed against his stomach. She was ready to yank off her own shirt, when down at the end of the alley she saw fluttering. Laundry.

Soria ran—quietly as she could, low to the ground, as if that would help keep her unseen, though most windows she passed had shades. She stopped at the alley edge, and found herself in a small courtyard filled with potted plants and bikes, as well as a small tree growing from a patch of dirt and grass. Some cars were parked around it. The courtyard angled out of sight around another apartment building, presumably with proper street access.

Sheets fluttered from several lines pinned to the hooks, just below the first-floor windows. Easy access. Easier, if she had another arm. She missed that the most—the ability to do some things with a little more ease. The doctors had suggested prosthetics, but with her stump up near her shoulder and bionics still so experimental, she had decided to make do.

Her arm ached as she tried to drag down a sheet. She still felt the grip of that man's hard fingers, digging in, his other hand grabbing her sleeve and stump, fondling it with a grin. He had been in the brothel lobby when she had come down the stairs, a drunk and stupid man who had followed her outside while the Mongolian muscle tried negotiating for more money.

Half a woman, she could still hear the man in black saying. *Half of a good hump, but I'm willing to do you a favor.*

Well, fuck that—and fuck him.

The sheet came down. There was another clothesline nearby, with jogging pants and a large T-shirt. She hesitated, not even certain they would fit, quite certain she was pushing her luck, but the temptation was too great. She tossed the sheet over her shoulder, grabbed a dangling pant leg, and yanked hard.

The line twanged loudly. Soria heard a creak from inside the apartment, a low voice. The jogging pants came loose and she ran like hell, back into the alley, feeling like a ghost with the sheet piled loose, flowing down her back.

Karr was still on his knees, hunched over. Blood pooled around him. Soria tried to move his hands to push the sheet over the wound. It was hard to breathe, difficult to think; her heart was hammering so hard she wanted to vomit. It had been a while since she'd seen so much blood. The last time, it had been her own.

There was a bleeding rip in his flesh that looked like a stab wound. Soria made Karr lie back, and gathered layers of cotton over his gut. She pressed down, and his slick red hand covered hers. His palm and fingers were huge, his touch firm.

"The scent is stronger," he rasped. "Close."

She understood. Nothing to do about it, though. If a shape-shifter found them, so be it. This was all she could handle. It was hard enough to breathe as blood began soaking through the sheet.

"How did this happen?" Soria muttered. "You were fine."

Karr said nothing, jaw clenched tight, eyes squeezed shut, golden light trickling from beneath his lids like spectral tears. She touched his brow, which was slick with sweat, and then his throat, searching for a pulse. What she got instead was a sharp pain in her head, a wicked throb that radiated from her brow—and deeper, like a worm was wiggling its way into the center of her skull. She rocked forward, gasping. Suffering, briefly, a flood of images and sounds that rolled into her head like a wave of hot water.

None of it made sense, just impressions of fur and sunlight, red rock and grasslands spread across an aching sky-kissed distance. She saw blood and heard screams, caught a flash of golden-eyed children laughing, swung into the air by two strong hands—and a sword, glinting in the darkness, held by a man with the face of a wolf.

Tau, she heard. *Forgive me.*

The whispered words echoed painfully through her head. Soria fought them. It had been a lifetime since she had suffered someone else's memories, but she dug deep, searching for an anchor—the blood on her fingers, hot and wet—and focused on that to ground herself.

She wrenched free of Karr's mind, fell forward, slumped over his warm body . . . and felt as though parts of *her* body were very distant. A large hand touched the back of her head.

Breathe, she told herself. *Deep breaths.*

It was difficult. Not since she was six years old had she suffered a reaction this strong, and that last episode had been the final one until now. Being around people had made her sick as a child, because she would see things in their lives that she did not understand. This caused her headaches, periods of unconsciousness that doctors blamed on some rare brain disease.

Brain disease? Close enough. Her father had been in the military. They had moved a lot. Soria had been called a freak by bullies in ten different countries, and survival in new schools and foreign environments required certain skills. One day, language had become one of those, to the exclusion of everything else her mind had previously tried to do.

She had been declared a prodigy at the age of seven. There were still articles about her on the Internet, which her parents liked to dig up and send every now and then. Little universal translator, some had called her. Able to hold a conversation in any language, no matter how rare, just as long as she spent time listening to that foreign tongue. Time spent with an actual native speaker, together, in person.

Of course, only a small part of language had to do with words. The rest was culture, time, experience. Language was a thing of constant change, with only some root variables remaining the same. After all these years, Soria still did not understand *how* she did what she did, or why her gift focused merely on languages, but she supposed mind reading was still part of it. At least the headaches and blackouts had stopped.

She held herself very still, as if that would keep her conscious. Beneath her cheek, Karr shifted ever so slightly, and this time she became more fully aware of his fingers buried in her hair. She glanced sideways but his eyes were still closed.

Several cars passed the alley, one after the other. She heard the distant wail of sirens, but those faded. There was no way to know how much time they had before someone found them. It was a miracle they had gone this long without interruption, though that was no guarantee that one of the windows along the alley didn't have a pair of eyes watching their every move.

Soria pushed herself up until she swayed on her knees, dizzy. The sheet covering Karr's wound was a bloody mess. He needed a hospital—but he was not going to get one. Some things had to stay secret. All it would take was a blood test, one single transformation, the goddamn glow in his eyes, and it would be done. Everyone—all the shape-shifters hiding now, in careful anonymity—would be fucked.

Or not. There was no way to know how the cards would fall, just probabilities. Soria was no precog, and even they could be lousy at telling the future.

You have to do something.

Contacting Roland was out of the question. All the help he had provided her—like Robert and Serena—was suspect. She was on her own.

So. Hospital. Maybe it *was* worth the risk. If she could get Karr to one.

She pressed her palm on his chest, and then his cheek. "Karr. Wake up. I cannot move you on my own."

He stirred, but not enough to do her any good. She stood, staggering, and was just about to raise a ruckus for help—God help them both—when his hand shot out and grabbed her ankle. "Wait," he breathed, so softly she could barely hear.

"I am going to get you help," she said, wishing her voice sounded stronger. "Let go."

"No." He drew in a deep breath, tilting back his head. "The pain is gone."

Yeah, she had seen movies where the dying talked all kinds of shit about pain being gone . . . just before croaking. She was not comforted.

Karr, however, began tugging at the sheet packed down on his wound. She knelt, trying to stop him. His hands outnumbered hers, though, and he yanked the sheet away. Soria winced. But Karr's fingers danced over the spot and he whispered, "Look."

She did, eyes wide. The hole in his side was gone. All that remained was a thin white scar, sticky with blood. Touching it provided proof; the wholeness of the flesh was not merely her imagination.

Karr grabbed her wrist. His eyes glinted golden in the shadows. "You saw it, too."

"I saw you dying," she whispered. *And other things in your mind.*

"It felt as though I was being murdered all over again," he replied hoarsely, struggling to sit up. Soria lost precious stunned seconds watching him before trying to help. He did not need it. Every moment he moved seemed to make him stronger, which was something she envied. Her own guts felt like jelly, and if her heart beat any harder it would burst.

"No one cut you," she said. "No one else was here."

Karr touched the white scar in his side, probing and

teasing the flesh. It was bloodstained but healthy. No gaping hole, which Soria remembered so clearly.

"Magic," he murmured, sending a chill down her spine.

She glanced down, and focused on the jogging pants, remembering how much of a risk-taker she had felt while stealing them. Some pitiful irony.

She bent unsteadily to pick them up, and thrust them at Karr, her hand shaking. She felt a similar tremor race down her missing limb, then lifted the sheet as well, unwilling to leave so much bloody evidence. There was nothing she could do about the concrete, but someone would definitely notice a gore-soaked sheet, and perhaps send it to the police.

Karr stared at the pants in his hands before passing them back to her. "Hold these a moment longer."

Or just toss them aside, she thought, trying to clutch everything against her chest.

Karr turned, and stared up the side of the building, which was more than ten stories high and covered in pipes, windows, air-conditioning units, and all manner of vents and hooks. His hands flexed, claws pushing through his nails as his arms lengthened, muscles bunching tight beneath his glowing skin. Soria checked both ends of the alley, afraid he would be seen. But no one was there, and she glanced back in time to see scales ripple over his limbs.

He looked even taller, stronger, a faintly leonine cast to his face that matched the tangled mane of blond hair covering his eyes. He met her gaze, solemn and thoughtful. "Put your arm around my neck," he said.

"Jesus," she replied in English; and then: "You are *not* going to climb that building."

A grim smile touched his mouth. "Do it."

"I do not take orders from you," she muttered. "I am not your human servant."

"No," he agreed quietly. "But this city is not safe, and this is the fastest way to leave it."

She gritted her teeth, running through options . . . but her brain was fried, and this was the best she could do: to climb walls, to be carried by a man who was probably going to sprout wings or bleed to death. Hopefully not at the same time.

You could have been in New York for your interview at the U.N., she told herself. Translators were always welcome—there, or in any corporate setting. Big money for easy work. But no. She was here. Living a life less ordinary.

Soria stepped close, slinging the sheet and jogging pants over her shoulder. Karr had to bend down so that she could reach around his neck. He was very warm and bloody, but beneath that strong metallic odor she caught a whiff of something sweet, like rain.

It was surreal, being so close to him. He had held her before, but as a dragon, a monster. Now he was a man, and it was far more discomfiting, partially because he was naked. But also because being near him, crushed close by the hard strength of his arm around her back, made her heart do a funny little twist that was wholly unexpected and more than a little unnerving.

His cheek brushed against hers, his breath purring and warm on her neck. "Put your legs around my waist."

Soria cleared her throat. "Are you sure this is necessary?"

His hands clamped down on her hips, lifting her off the ground. She gasped in shock, just hanging there, expecting him to drop her one hundred thirty pounds of dead weight. But he held on, giving her a steady, patient, and somewhat wry look.

"I tracked you through this city," he rumbled, eyes glinting. "Shouted and pointed at by humans, and followed by your . . . *po-lice*. I will not go through that again."

She did not have the strength to argue. Hoping he couldn't hear how quickly her heart was beating, Soria hooked her legs over his hips, tightened her grip around the back of his neck, and stuck herself as close to his body as humanly possible. He was large, broad, made of nothing but bone and sinew—not a man who had ever slept in a soft bed or eaten a meal that he had not fought for.

You can never trust him, she remembered Serena saying. *It is in his blood. His kind are broken from the inside. All they are good for is war.*

Yet his strength was gentle, and his voice soft and deep when he murmured, "Hold tight. This will be awkward."

It was already awkward, but she nodded, tight-lipped, and held on with all her strength as he let go of her hips and reached over their heads. She heard his claws scrape metal, imagined him grabbing the iron bars over the first-floor windows—and then he surged upward, hoisting them off the ground. Her back scraped the wall. She could not see what Karr was holding on to, or using as toeholds, but his process was careful and inexorable, and took them on a zigzagging path that reminded her more of an ascent across a rock face than a building.

Her arm ached. So did her stump. She focused on breathing, and struggled to tighten her legs, trying not to think about how useful a fire escape would be about now.

Karr murmured, "We are almost there."

"Good," she muttered. "Maybe you should have put me on your back."

"If you slipped, I might not be able to catch you."

Soria said nothing. She was already slipping, just a little each time he moved. The pain in her left arm was growing by the second, making it hard to breathe.

Halfway up, Karr paused by a window and grabbed the edge of a sill with one hand, digging in his toes along the edge of a narrow pipe she glimpsed at the corner of her eye. With his other hand, he reached around her waist and hoisted her a little higher up his body. Soria buried her face against his neck.

"Are you scared of heights?" he murmured.

I am now. "Just keep going, Tarzan."

He was silent a moment. "Tar-zan?"

"A . . . mythical person. Raised by monkeys, lives in the jungle, swings on vines."

"Ah." Karr began climbing again. "He sounds like my cousin."

Soria started to laugh—then realized he might be serious.

They reached the roof. It felt like a lifetime. Karr released her gently, and she staggered away from him, bending over with her hand braced against her knee. The sheet and jogging pants tumbled off her shoulder. She wanted to kick them, but settled for staring at bloodstains splashed on white, blood on her hand, blood on her shirt. She was sticky with it and started gagging, covering her mouth, choking with the effort to not be sick.

Karr drew near. She turned her back on him and forced herself to straighten, breathing deep, wiping her eyes. Winds shifted, blowing cool and sweet against her face. She tried to savor the sensation, but the silence of the man behind her burned.

"Go ahead," she said. "Ask."

"I think it would be cruel to do so," Karr rumbled, which made her turn to look at him.

"I do not understand you," she said.

"You do not know me," he replied. He rubbed his hands, golden light trickling up his forearms. "Perhaps it is better that way."

"You had your chance to go. You still do."

"And you? Will you journey south?"

Good question. Erenhot glittered beneath them, spread like a web of jewels. She wanted to rub her aching arm, and ghost fingers tugged—but without the usual accompanying pain.

Soria glanced at Karr again: coiled and lean, golden light sparking over his chest and face, leaving behind a bloom of scales. He was a haunting, alien sight, filling her with both fear and wonder. "If I do, will you come with me?"

Karr gazed out at the city. "Thousands of years. Those are numbers I cannot comprehend. And yet I stand here and can almost believe it is true. I died, and time moved on. But that still leaves me with nothing. And no one."

Soria could not imagine his loss. "Others of your kind could still exist. A new generation. It is a big world."

"Never big enough," he whispered. "When I died . . . there were not many of us, but there were enough. We had only each other. But they are dead now. Even if time has not passed as you said, my friends must be dead."

Whoever his people were, whatever he had meant when he called them the mistaken children of the shape-shifters, he was right: everyone he knew was dead. His world was gone. And the enormity of that—imagining herself in his situation, waking from death into a world wholly unfamiliar, alone—was enough to make her ill in an entirely different way.

Karr turned in a slow circle, surveying the roof, and yet more of the city, finally tilting his head to watch the stars. "We had a homeland in the north, a place that was ours. I want to go there and see what I find. Even if it is nothing but dust, I want to see. Perhaps I will be surprised.

"But," he added, finally looking at her. "If I go with you to the south, I am afraid that I will never know for certain what was lost—or what might still be found. And yet, if I do not go with you, and discover nothing . . . I will have lost my only anchor in this new world."

Soria went very still. Light trickled from Karr's eyes, washing his face in gold, as though he wore a mask made of the sun. But his silence was strong and thoughtful, and she knew he was waiting for her, because she was an anchor, because words always were and she was the only one in this world who could speak to him. Words could humanize or brutalize. She had already seen what resulted from not being able to communicate with Karr.

If you convince him to travel south, what will you expose him to? More of Serena and her cage? Or something worse?

What can you live with?

Soria had been asking herself that question for the past year, and she still had no answer. "And if I go with you?"

"You have no reason to."

"Does that matter?"

He was silent a long time. Winds buffeted them. The cold night. Soria remembered other windy nights, standing on rooftops, with Roland and others from the agency, drinking beer and eating pizza, listening to the mixed tapes that people always brought, where ribbing about the song choices was as much part of the entertainment as the music itself. All of them shrugging off the strangeness of their lives, and just being themselves: human, shape-shifter, gargoyle; male, female. Friends.

Magical times. Perfect, floating nights. Soria missed that. She missed that more than she missed Roland, who had always kept himself slightly apart. Craving distance because it felt safe to him. Big, powerful man— too frightened of his own mind and strength to do more than live behind glass windows, a cage he had put himself in. Just like Soria had. Until now.

Crazy woman. You're asking for trouble. You might die.

And she might leave this man and always wonder what happened.

What can you live with? Soria asked herself again.

Karr tilted his head, glancing sharply to his left. His eyes flared with light and more scales rippled across his skin. He twisted slightly, bending over as bones popped down his spine and across his shoulders, but the actual emergence of his wings was obscured by the glow that preceded them, spreading outward like tendrils of smoke. His arms and legs cracked new joints, his torso lengthening until he reminded her of some alien creature from the movies, caught between shifts; not human, not animal. It scared Soria, but she could not look away.

Until, finally, it was done. The golden light collapsed around him, revealing a sun-kissed creature that bore a closer resemblance to a sphinx than a dragon. His face remained vaguely human—leonine, rather than reptilian—while his limbs and the bulk of his body were covered in a variegated mix of scales and fur. Wings, folded along his back, were webbed and leathery like a bat. His shape-shifting was not consistent, she realized. Never the same body.

"Hurry," he said, holding out his arms.

She hesitated, memories crashing through her: that split-second choice on the mountain highway, stopping the car to help an old man she should have recognized. Trusting that she would be safe, because she always had been, in every war zone, in every city of the world, in the company of dictators and criminals. Never a scratch. Always able to handle herself.

Her stump throbbed. Soria stared deeply into Karr's eyes, wondering if she could trust herself this time, even after coming so far.

You could have walked away at the airport, but you didn't. So now you're here. Make it worth something.

She picked up the bloodstained sheet and pants, her movements slow and aching, and stepped into his embrace. His arms were stiff, as though it had occurred to him again that this might be a bad idea; but just before she could change her mind and bolt, he drew her close against his warm chest. Her fingers touched soft scales and fur, so very alien, and difficult to reconcile with his human body. She might know shape-shifters, but Karr was right: something *was* different about him, as though every time he shifted, his body was torn in three different directions.

And yet, she felt safe in his arms. Ridiculously so. It made no sense.

Karr hooked his arm under her legs, the other around her back. He lifted her easily, looking down for one brief moment. His eyes were the same, no matter what his body looked like.

"Strange woman," he murmured. And then, without warning, he took a running leap off the building.

Soria cried out, clutching at him as they dropped into freefall. Windows passed them in a blur, lights and concrete spinning, and just before they hit the ground, his wings snapped open. Winds howled around them, cutting through her clothing. Looking down made her breathless, but she tried anyway—watching the city in brief, dizzying patches of light. It was beautiful, un-earthly.

"We are being followed," Karr said, his voice nearly swept away by the wind.

A shape-shifter. She was certain that was what he meant. It made her think of Roland, and his secrets: his alliance with the organization that Serena worked for, his reluctance to talk about Long Nu. Little details that she picked over ruthlessly. All of it was bound to-gether because of Karr.

Whoever hired those men wanted him alive for a rea-son. Same reason they needed me, in order to translate. Which means they think he knows something or can be useful. Which means I won't be safe until he is.

Soria closed her eyes, trying to make sense of it all. A man—an inhuman man—resurrected after thousands of years. What could he possibly know that was worth killing for?

Lots of things, she decided. *Ask how he came back to life. Find that out, and you might have all the answers you need.*

Easier said than done.

CHAPTER NINE

THERE was a lake in the desert. Very small and isolated, though the waters smelled fresh, spring-fed. Karr also scented humans, goats, sheep, horses. Other creatures. None were there at the moment. He dipped his fingers into the lake, licked them, and found the taste cold and heavy with minerals.

Soria gave him a dubious look. "I will get sick. Maybe you can drink water from the wild, but my stomach is more sensitive."

"Then how do you survive?" Karr raised his brow. "You do drink water, do you not?"

"Purified. Boiled."

He shook his head. "We are in a desert. Drink this, or else nothing at all."

She frowned, but scuttled down the shore and knelt. Her frayed braids dipped into the water. Karr stood behind her, surveying the land.

He had flown for an hour before needing to stop, rested and then begun again—until he had seen this place in the distance. Human fires burned several ridges over, but the air was still and quiet. No sign of the shape-shifter who had followed them from the city. A body with wings, that much was certain. Karr had no doubt he or she was close enough to track them but not so close as to be detected.

He hoped the land and sky conspired to bring the shape-shifter discomfort. This was a cold desert, and not just because of the night. He could feel the elevation in his bones: the dry air, a bite in the wind that nipped at his human skin. Fur would be more comfortable, but Soria did not have the luxury. He did not want to be unfair.

Thick, scrubby grass grew around the water, but not a stone's throw away the landscape hardened into a rocky plain. He had flown over some areas of sand, but not many. Which was good. It was much harder to find prey among dunes. Not that he was planning on going very far.

Soria sat up, rubbing her mouth. "Do we stay or leave?"

"Stay. We both need rest." Karr walked away, claws surging through his fingernails. "Be mindful until I return."

"What?"

He glanced over his shoulder. "I smell goats."

She stared, until something passed through her gaze and a faint, wry smile touched her mouth. "For petting?"

It was such an unexpected thing to say—but so clearly in jest, he found himself smiling back. "I think not."

"Well," she said. "Good luck. I hear they are dangerous creatures."

"Ferocious," he replied, backing away. "But not nearly as intimidating as your knee."

She laughed, covering her mouth with her hand as though the sound startled her. It surprised him as well, though for a different reason. He liked her laughter.

Karr turned quickly away, breaking into a run. Golden light flowed over his skin, and he begged his body for a lion's touch, thinking briefly of his father. He desired speed as well, to put as much distance as possible between himself and the woman. He had been unnerved before by females, had suffered every emotion from lust to anger. But what she did, in the simplest terms, was make him feel things that were utterly unexpected.

Stop, whispered a small voice. *Stop now. There are weaknesses you cannot afford.* And even if he could, she was not the one to feel them with. She was not safe. *He* was not safe.

No sign of madness, he reassured himself. *You are fine. You will be fine. Long enough to see this through.*

To what end, he had no idea. He was a fool if he let himself imagine this adventure would have a happy end. All he was searching for were ghosts and chance, the faintest possibility of life. And Soria's motives were utterly a mystery.

Human scents grew stronger. Karr kept low to the ground. It was only hours before dawn. Most would be asleep, unless there was a guard watching over the livestock. A child, probably. Or dogs. He listened carefully as he approached the settlement, but heard nothing except the occasional soft bleat and the low, content sounds of horses. He was safely downwind.

He crept over the ridge, discovering a desert patchwork of rock and grassland, an immense plain that swallowed the small round tents arrayed less than half a mile in front of him. Tiny fires burned. He saw goats inside a loose pen made of rope tied around stakes in the ground. Horses grazed freely.

A tricky business, stealing from humans. Karr preferred a wild hunt, but there was no time—and he had been without meat since waking in the tomb. No wonder he was weak. He was starving.

He was careful to stay downwind, creeping close to the ground as he neared the settlement. The goats were very near. One strike was all he needed, and then speed would do the rest.

His scar tingled. Karr froze, listening to his body. Nothing more happened—no pain, no more sensation— but the warning was there. Whatever had brought him back from the dead was still running its course.

Magic. Blood arts. Someone had done this to him. He thought of Soria and her shape-shifter ally, but dismissed them both within moments. Soria had been too shaken. And the leopardess would have preferred to find his corpse in the tomb—of that he was quite certain.

And yet, she *had* unearthed him. Or had been directed to. And she had just so happened to know someone who could speak his language, however Soria managed that feat. Her explanation sounded like magic to him.

Goats, he told himself sternly, realizing that he had been crouched in the same place for too long. The winds were shifting.

He followed them carefully, focusing on the hunt. One thing at a time. Magic could wait.

HE RAN BACK TO THE LAKE AS A MAN, CARRYING THE WARM body of the dead goat on his shoulders, its broken neck flopping wildly. Stars glittered. At the top of the final ridge he stopped, searching for Soria. He found her kneeling by the water's edge. Her hair was free of its braids, hanging loose and wild down her back, nearly obscuring the pale line of naked flesh on her right side.

She had pulled up her shirt, the hem held between her teeth. Karr watched her scoop water into her hand, shake the drops loose, and then press her cold, damp palm over the stump jutting from her shoulder. Her arm ended well above where her elbow should be.

Such an odd, painful thing to see her disfigurement. He supposed, in a way, that she was lucky to be human and confined only to one body. For a chimera to lose a limb, especially those whose skins gave them wings, was a loss that could murder the second soul. He had counseled many who had lost parts of themselves in battle; limbs or otherwise. Some had recovered their minds. Others . . . not.

Karr tore his gaze away, and slowly, carefully, walked back down the ridge, just out of sight. He could hear water splashing, listened to the occasional hiss of her breath, as if she was in pain. He suddenly felt weary to the bone, and set down the goat, crouching beside its dead body. The scent of its flesh made him hollow with hunger, but he swallowed the ache and closed his eyes. Listening. Listening to her.

When finally the sounds of splashing water faded, he stood again, hefted the goat, and as loudly as he could, walked up to the top of the ridge. Soria still knelt by the water's edge, but her shirt was down, and she was awkwardly braiding her hair.

She gave him a little smile as he approached, and the weary ease of her regard made his breath catch. "Did it put up a fight?"

"She was old, and would have died soon on her own." Karr dropped the goat, claws emerging from his fingertips. "Would you like a piece of the heart?"

Soria hesitated. "Would you know how to start a fire?"

Karr stared. "Not at the moment, no."

She stared at the goat as though it might bite her. Or make her sick. He considered her water concerns, but there was little to be done about the matter. Fetid water could make anyone ill, but that was a risk one took—and rather unavoidable if the goal was to keep on living.

Karr knelt beside the dead animal, using his claws to cut open its belly. Guts spilled out, and the smell of fresh meat was so tantalizing he almost forgot himself and started eating. Instead, he gritted his teeth, reminded himself that he was in mixed company, and reached deep into the body. He pulled the heart free.

Still warm. He began to hand it to Soria, took one look at her face and used his claw to slice off a small piece. His stomach roared.

"Here," he said, almost sick with hunger. "Take it."

She looked quite pale, and not at all enthused. But she took the meat from his hand and without a word, shoved it into her mouth. Chewed hard, and swallowed. Karr had another piece ready. She did the same, making a face—holding very still for a moment like she would be sick. But she swallowed again, and nodded her head when he offered her more. Karr took a large bite out of the organ, closing his eyes to savor the bursting wild flavor. If anything, his stomach ached even more.

They ate in silence. Karr cut Soria small pieces of the goat, moving next to the liver. She stopped partaking at the eyes, and walked a short distance away when he started skinning the creature and pulled off its leg. He found himself shifting shape as he ate—in subtle ways, becoming more of a lion again. He could not help himself, nor did he want to; it was a pleasure to be free of the cage, free under the starry sky, free and alive. No matter his original reason for dying.

Soria busied herself with the bloodstained cloth, spreading it on the ground. He asked, "Why did you insist on bringing that?"

"I know it seems strange," she replied, glancing at him. "But my people have ways of . . . checking blood. Reading signs from it. Yours would tell them very different things. You do not want that."

"Would they make magic upon me?"

"No. But they would become aware that someone like you exists. There would be proof."

Karr set down the leg he had been chewing. "You say that as if no one already knows."

"Few do. I told you that. "

"What you told me is that if my people were alive, almost no one remembers them."

Soria sat down, rubbing her face. "No one remembers.

Almost no one knows. Or imagines. If they did, you and anyone like you—shape-shifters included—would become a spectacle. Your life would no longer be your own."

"We would be hunted?"

"In more ways than one." Soria gave him a deeply weary look. "So would I, for what I can do. What saves me—and others who are different—is that no one expects us to do the things we do. And what no one expects, no one sees. No one asks the crazy question: is it magic?"

Karr no longer felt hungry. "Has the world changed so much? What you are suggesting seems . . ."

"Impossible?"

"Impossible," he agreed. "And sad. That time can erase so many lives, until even the possibility of them becomes reduced to . . . nothing. What, then, is left?"

Soria opened her mouth, hesitated, and shook her head. She tapped the stained cloth. "We need to burn or bury this."

"If you bury it, animals will smell the blood and dig it up."

"So we wait for fire." She looked unhappy, and began rubbing her shoulder. A shiver raced through her. Karr set his jaw, glancing down at the goat carcass. He stood and walked to Soria.

"We should move away from the water before we rest," he said quietly. "Not far."

She nodded silently, and began gathering up the cloth and soft pants she had tried to give him earlier. The idea of clothing made his skin crawl. Too much like confinement.

But he took everything from her, ignoring her brief look of surprise as he tucked the bundle under his arm. He grabbed the remains of the goat—reduced to several legs and hide—and dragged it behind him. There was no use leaving more proof of their presence; the goat did not look as though it had been torn apart by an animal.

They walked along the water's edge, and over another ridge. Karr did not rush. Soria was much smaller than he, requiring two steps for every one of his. He stole glances at her face, and found her eyes hollow with exhaustion.

"The humans come often to this place," he told her. "Same path I took to find them. I could smell it on my way to their settlement. We are far less likely to encounter anyone on this side of the water. We will have some warning, if nothing else."

She nodded. "How do you know where you are going?"

"The stars have not changed," Karr said. "How far are we from where I was buried?"

"You were found southwest of here. Less than a thousand miles, I would guess. Does that make sense?"

He nodded, tight-lipped. "Those of us who could fly were returning from a trading mission. We had found a human settlement that was willing to deal with my kind."

"So what happened?"

Death. Insanity. "My life ended."

"Before, you used the word 'murdered.'"

Murdered. He remembered telling her that—even thinking it—but it was the wrong thing to say. He had committed suicide, and used his friends to take his life.

"It is complicated," he told her, far more sharply than he intended.

She gave him a hard look. "Death is never complicated. Just the how and why. Especially so in your case, Mr. Dead Man Walking."

Her phrasing was unfamiliar—one of the words foreign—but her meaning was perfectly clear. He looked around them, and found they had crossed the ridge. The lake was out of sight.

Karr tossed down the goat and the cloth bundle. "This is far enough."

Soria stood still, watching him. "The people who killed you. Were they capable of doing this? Bringing you back to life?"

"No."

"Someone is responsible. Unless your kind can—"

"No," he said again, interrupting her. "No."

"Fine," she said coldly. "But who, then?"

"One of you?" He stepped too close, deliberately using his height against her. She craned her neck but did not move. Her gaze was stubborn, defiant. "Are there any among your kind who could resurrect the dead?"

She hesitated. "I do not know."

That was not the answer he expected. "Really."

"I have heard stories, and seen strange things," she told him. "Stranger than you. But that does not explain motive. Who are you, Karr? Who *were* you?"

"And if I tell you?" he asked harshly, leaning over her. "What will you do with that information?"

She looked at him like he was an idiot. "I am in the middle of the fucking Gobi Desert. What do you think I am going to do? Run screaming for the first phone I can find?"

Not all of that was perfectly comprehensible, but her tone was. Karr forced himself to take a deep, careful breath. "Despite your . . . acts of kindness, we are on opposite sides. I forget that when I am around you, but your connection to the shape-shifters —"

A frustrated growl boiled out of her. "You are so one-track-minded."

"I am . . . not," he said, not quite sure what he was denying, but rather certain she had insulted him. "I am protecting myself."

Soria sat down on the ground, and then flopped backward, staring at the starlit sky. Her arm crossed over her stomach. She looked cold. Karr, after a moment, sat beside her.

"I am—was—a warlord," he told her quietly. "Though that is a human term, and does not describe the whole of it. I led my people. I protected them. It was my duty and honor to do so, because I was the strongest, in both heart and body."

"Were you born to the role?"

"Chosen." Karr lay down, watching the stars. "The elders appointed me."

"And was someone jealous of you? Is that why you were killed?"

He closed his eyes. "You ask too many questions."

"I think I have a right."

"I suppose, then, I have a right to know how you lost your arm."

Her answering silence was long and painful. Finally, she said, "I apologize."

"Do not," he whispered. "You have a reason for asking."

Soria sighed, holding the wrist of her empty sleeve. He thought, perhaps, that she was done with words; but then she said, "Thank you, for earlier. What you said about my arm. It helped."

"Are you in pain now?"

"A little." Soria spoke as though pain was something to be ashamed of. "Comes and goes. The more active I am, the more chances there are for my body to . . . imagine my arm is still there. When that happens . . . it hurts." She glanced sideways at him. "Your scar? More blood going to come gushing out of you?"

"I cannot say." He fingered the spot, trying not to think of the events that had preceded his death. "We should sleep."

"Sure," Soria muttered, still clutching her sleeve. "Easy."

"Are you cold?"

She gave him a long, steady look. "Yes."

Dangerous, whispered his mind. *You fool.* But that did not stop him from saying, "Roll over on your side."

Soria chewed the inside of her cheek, still staring at him, her expression utterly inscrutable. Finally, though, she sat up and grabbed the loose, soft pants she had brought with her. She threw them in his lap. "Put those on."

"I would rather—"

"Put. Them. On." Firm voice, unflinching stare. Cold as ice. Karr considered arguing. His skin crawled at the idea of cloth rubbing his skin, confining him to one body. But he thought about every other human he had seen, even the leopardess shape-shifter, and all of them had been clothed.

I would not expect you *to go naked simply to conform to* my *standards,* he told Soria silently. But it was an image that was far more intriguing than it should have been.

Gritting his teeth, he jammed his legs into the soft pants and pulled them up over his hips. They were too small. He hated the sensation. Soria, however, nodded at him with all the imperiousness of a queen, and rolled over. Karr briefly considered letting her freeze.

Instead, he curled close against her back, tucking her deep within the curve of his body. A perfect fit. He slid his arm under her head, draped his other arm over her waist, noticing that it was her empty sleeve that he touched. She stiffened but said nothing. He almost wished she would.

She smelled warm and sweet, and felt too good in his arms; small, astonishingly delicate. He had never noticed whether females were fine-boned or even feminine; the only qualities that ever mattered were integrity and strength. Nothing else could be counted on in battle, or in life. But he noticed now.

"Does that help?" he asked quietly, tasting tendrils of her hair against his lips.

She cleared her throat. "Yes."

"And this?" A golden glow spread over his skin, leaving a thick coat of fur in its place. He pulled her even closer, splaying his hand over her stomach. Her heart rate jumped. He could hear it, mirroring his own, though he wondered if she suffered the same powerful ache of loneliness that crawled from his heart into his throat, making it difficult to breathe.

"Yes," she whispered.

Karr swallowed hard, and closed his eyes. "Rest, then. Be at ease."

She made a barely audible sound of assent, but remained stiff in his arms. Karr calmed far more quickly. His stomach was full and his eyelids heavy. It seemed unfair to him that after being dead for thousands of years, he should still need slumber.

Just before he drifted off, Soria let out a quiet sigh and softened against him, finally relaxing. He was glad. He did not want her to be afraid of him.

She should be. You know what the risks are.

Yet he could not let go. He told himself it was because she was cold, but the truth was that he was just as cold—freezing and empty inside, and alone. The vastness of the sky frightened him. It was the same sky, and the same stars, just as he was the same man; but everything else had changed. He had nothing to hold on to anymore.

So he held on to Soria, and finally went to sleep.

CHAPTER TEN

K ISSES were unique as snowflakes, and so were a man's arms. No man had ever held Soria in the same way as another. Her boyfriend in high school had been too nervous to do more than pat her on the shoulder like one of the guys, while there had been a fellow in college who never held her at all, not unless he wanted something. Some men enjoyed groping when they got close, while others embraced like a cage.

Roland, who had been her last close relationship, had been tender and gruff, but even so—in something as simple as a hug—she had always felt the thinnest of walls between them. As though he was trying too hard; as though her presence, at times, made him uncomfortable.

The language of touch was just as sensitive and varied as words, full of nuance, personality, history. Soria had never been able to stop calculating the different sensations and what they meant. Always searching for the message. But she stopped thinking when Karr curled around her, his arm draped over her empty sleeve and waist, his body warm against her back. She quit analyzing, stopped conjugating every moment. She listened to other things, like her thunderous heart, and the tease of his deep, slow breathing, hot on her neck.

She got lost. Forgot why she was supposed to be afraid. In his arms, there was no fear; just warmth and safety, and comfort. Not that she could appreciate it at first. It was too new, too unexpected. She was not supposed to feel this way about him. Or anyone.

Half a woman. Half a good hump.

No. She did not believe that. Not really.

But it had been a long time since anyone had looked past the missing arm. Too long since she had been around anyone who could make her forget what she had lost. Who could just make her feel, utterly and completely, like herself.

Don't think about it. Don't you dare. Not the time, not the place, not the right man.

Yeah, well. It was kind of hard to ignore him.

Soria sank back against Karr's chest, pretending it was harmless to do so, that there would be no consequences. Just her and him. Drifting to sleep.

Which she did, finally. Blissfully. She was swallowed into darkness, where her aching stump could not follow, and where in dreams she had her arm again.

Near dawn she woke. Perhaps less than an hour asleep. Her eyes fluttered open just enough to reveal a faint light in the eastern horizon, and above it, a distant golden spark in the sky. A falling star, she thought sleepily. A floating, falling star.

Karr stirred restlessly, his arm tightening around her waist. She thought he might be awake, but he made a small sound that was both muffled and pained. Dreaming, she thought. Nightmares.

Soria rolled over, which was way more uncomfortable than she expected it to be. Rocks dug into her side, and her hip and neck ached. There was no way to prop herself up, either. She did not like lying down on her right side. Too much pressure on her stump.

She forgot her discomfort, however, when she saw Karr's face: contorted, bones shifting in random rippling waves, his features melting into a patchwork of scales and fur and human flesh. Golden light trickled from behind his closed eyes, his mouth hanging open in silent anguish.

Looking at him made her afraid. She knew what violence there could be in waking someone from a bad dream. She had hurt people in the beginning, those who got too close to her in sleep—her friends, parents. She had made Eddie's lip bleed during those first days in the hospital. But Karr's embrace was too tight to escape. Her hand hovered over his shifting face.

"Hey," she whispered, and grazed the tips of her fingers against his brow.

Pain pulsed through her head, followed by a shock of light as though thunderbolts were shooting from the sky into her skull. She glimpsed a battlefield littered with corpses, some of them animal, and standing among the bleeding dead was a small group of men and women who were animals themselves: Karr, larger than any of them, was wearing the form of a golden dragon. He was covered in blood, his claws gripping a sword. His eyes were profoundly grim. A wolf stood beside him, paw buried in the long hair of a golden-eyed man whose head he was yanking back—exposing his throat. The man was dying, not a threat, but the wolf's claws were raised for a kill, and there was no mercy in his eyes.

No, Karr whispered to him, reaching for his wrist—and then the vision dissolved into children—children screaming in the night, tumbling from humans into animals as they ran through a cool stone temple. Karr was behind them, eyes glowing, scooping up every one in his path, his arms full as small, clawed hands dug into his shoulders and neck, making him bleed. Other adults were with him, doing the same, but Soria could not see them well. Just Karr. Racing from the temple onto a narrow trail that led up a rocky cliff, shouts behind him, whistles and grunts. A blur, then a cave—a cave with a roughhewn statue in front—darkness full of weeping faces and Karr, shoving children inside, whispering, *Do not be afraid. Stay here. Be silent. I will protect you.*

But screams followed him as the night bled again, filled with the desperate high cries of those children, their faces lit by fire. Fire thrown at them. Fire blocking them. Fire destroying them.

It was the most horrible thing Soria had ever witnessed, and she battled to be free of it, fought with all her strength as Karr's mind boiled and burned through her, roiled with grief and rage and thunder.

At the last moment—on the very tip of escape—she felt a sword run through her body. Her hands touched the blade, and another dizzying light filled her mind, swallowed up by the image of the same weapon, but blackened with age, the metal corroded. It was displayed in a glass case, inside a room filled with armor and books.

There, whispered a voice inside her. *Go there.* A map flashed before her, a red dot with pulsing red lines that spiraled away across a golden plain, trailing into the gut of a rough cloth doll shaped like a man, golden eyes sewn into its head. *Follow the threads.*

Soria tore herself loose, and opened her eyes. She was blind at first, mind still lost in screams, and fire, and the image of a sword, but she blinked hard, fighting to be free, and when her vision cleared she found herself in the same position, as if no time had passed at all. Her hand was still pressed lightly on Karr's face, his arm snug around her waist. At some point, his features had stopped shifting; he looked like a man again.

But his eyes were open, and he was staring at her. His intensity was breathtaking, threatening. Soria felt an unaccountable stab of guilt, as though she had willfully pried open some secret diary and aired its pages to the world.

"You saw," he whispered. "I felt you in my head."

Her hand jerked away. "I was trying to wake you. You were having a nightmare."

Karr grabbed her wrist, pinning it behind her back as he dragged her under him, holding down her body with his hips and arms. Fury filled his glowing eyes. "Was that all you were trying to do?"

Soria lay very still, fighting back burning tears. "It was an accident."

"What kind of accident?" he snapped, grief replacing

fury. "Are you pleased with what you *accidentally* saw? Will you report back to you masters, your allies, with tales of children burning alive? I am certain they will be *completely* satisfied."

"Get off me," Soria growled, still lost in the memories of those small, frightened faces staring at Karr with trust. Tears slid free, rolling down her temples into her hair. "Get the fuck away."

"Not until you tell me what you were trying to discover."

"Nothing."

He shook her. "Do not lie."

"I am not!" she screamed at him, her throat aching, unable to stop her tears. "I would never want to see that."

Karr stared at her. His red-rimmed eyes were too bright—not with light, but with tears of his own. "Then why?"

All the fight went out of her, a vast and terrible weariness swallowing her aching heart. "I told you."

"An accident," he repeated, studying her face like it was an awful puzzle, with all the pieces scattered.

He released her, and threw himself sideways, flopping on his back. Digging his palms into his eyes. Soria lay very still, trying to catch her breath and not sob outright. It was impossible. She could not stop crying.

"You were dreaming," she said brokenly.

"Sometimes," he murmured hoarsely, "I feel as though I am always dreaming."

"Who—" She stopped, forced to take a deep, shuddering breath. "Who attacked?"

He grimaced. "You know the answer. I believe I have made it plain."

Shape-shifters. Burning children alive. A shudder raced through her. "Why? Why do such a terrible thing? You told me before that your kind were their mistakes, but I still do not—"

Karr help up his hand. "Stop."

Yes, stop. You should have stopped long ago, never come here, never left the airport, never left home, never stopped your goddamn car on that road. Maybe you should stop breathing while you're at it, too.

"No," Soria whispered. "No."

Karr tilted his head, staring at her. "We are the chimera. We are the broken breed."

She stared, uncomprehending. His jaw tightened, tears still rimming his hollow eyes. "My mother was a pure-blooded shape-shifter. As was my father. But they wore different skins. She was a dragon. He, a lion. They loved each other. They had me. It was forbidden."

"I still do not—"

"Our natures make us unstable," Karr said through gritted teeth. "We are constantly torn between three bodies, and the split can extend to our minds as well. We can . . . lose ourselves. When that happens, the results are often violent."

Soria closed her eyes, trying to make sense of what he was telling her, but all she could see were those small faces, those tiny hands clinging to Karr. "No one kills children because of that."

"You kill them before it is too late," he whispered. "You kill them before they grow large and strong, and can fight back. You kill them to teach others a lesson, to show them what will happen if they dare to place their hearts where they should not."

Soria stared, horrified. "That explains nothing!"

Karr squeezed shut his eyes, pain creasing his face. "Leave it be. Just . . . please."

She did not want to leave it. Not until she understood—if such a thing was possible. But she took one look at him and could not open her mouth. Not now.

The eastern horizon was growing lighter. Some distance away, Soria heard a bell tinkle, and the bleat of goats. She rubbed her eyes, grabbed the not-so-clean edge of the sheet crumpled beside her, and blew her nose.

Karr asked quietly, "Did I hurt you?"

Her entire shoulder ached. "A little."

He rolled to his feet and walked a short distance away, his back turned to her. He stood like that for a moment, staring at the ground and then the sky. Soria looked up again as well. The stars were fading.

Karr pushed down the jogging pants and tossed them aside. Soria was too wrung out to feel embarrassed. She stared, openly, and he turned to meet her gaze with a hollow grief that cut her to the quick. A golden glow shimmered down his chest. Scales rippled to the surface.

"I will take you back if you wish," he rumbled. "To the city where we came from."

She almost said yes, ready to go home and hide. But,

then: *There is nothing for you there.* It was a soft, insidious whisper, rising from her heart into her head. *Nothing that will warm you, heal you, nourish you.*

It was true, she realized. What was home for her? Just a job interview and a missing arm, and people who looked at her with pity—or people who did not look at her at all. She could return to Dirk & Steele, take up with her old friends, but it would never be the same. She would never forget those children screaming in her mind. She would never have the answers she now so desperately craved.

"Do you want me gone?" she asked him.

The sounds of bones cracking filled the air. Karr dropped to his knees, neck and torso elongating to inhuman lengths while his claws dug deeply into the dirt. "When it comes to you," he rumbled hoarsely, no longer looking at her, "I do not know what I want."

Soria stumbled to her feet, bundling up the bloodstained sheet against her chest. She walked on unsteady legs to where Karr knelt, bathed in gold, twice his human size now, and no longer just a man. He was a dragon with the legs of a lion, immense wings folded gracefully against his back. She thought she would never become accustomed to the sight, no matter how many times she saw him in all his varied bodies.

"I am sorry," she said. "I truly did not mean you any harm."

"We are both unpredictable," he murmured—and then, "It is not safe for you to stay with me."

She knelt to peer into his eyes, which glittered in a

long, delicate skull that was high-cheeked, fine-boned, and utterly alien. "So why are you letting me?"

He gave her a sharp look. "You do not wish to return to the city?"

"No. Are you going to accuse me of lying about that, too?"

Even dragons could grimace, she discovered; but his gaze turned suspicious as well, muscles flexing in his long throat, claws digging deeper into the dry soil. He began to speak, and Soria placed her hand over his mouth, which was little more than a beaked snout.

"Do not," she said quietly. "Not if you are going to ask me what my motives are. I understand why you want to ask those questions, but I am tired of them. I am here. Send me away if you want, or leave me with those people and their goats. But whatever you do, remember that it is *your* choice. You chose to let me come with you. The burden of that does not belong to me."

She removed her hand, heart beating a little too rapidly. Karr's eyes narrowed, but after a moment he inclined his head in a subtle nod. "Fair enough."

"Good," she said, tense. "Now tell me about the sword that killed you."

THEY WALKED THROUGH THE DESERT, AND THE PREDAWN air was cool and dry. Thirty minutes from the lake, grassland gave way to rock and sand, a flat plain that broke into sharp ridges resembling bony spurs in the early light. There was not a sign of life around them, but she knew how deceptive that was.

Karr did not revert to his human body. He stayed a dragon but moved like a lion in a cage, restless, graceful, every inch of him a breathtaking display of muscle, bone, and power. Traveling at his side made Soria feel like a princess in a fairy tale—the bedraggled kind, one-armed, hungry, and exhausted.

"The sword was forged by the Chalybes, who were of the Hittite people," Karr rumbled, as they walked. "Master craftsmen. Just one of their swords was worth a man's weight in silver. Most were made of iron, but the weapon that killed me was part of an experiment. Melting iron ore with charcoal and glass to make a new metal that could hold a finer edge than any other."

Steel, thought Soria. "How did it come into your possession?"

His tail lashed the air. "Chimera have always been skilled in war. We are stronger and faster than pureblooded shape-shifters, and there was a time when we were tolerated for our usefulness in such matters. In the case of the Hittites, there was a long history of alliance between my kind and their ruling family. When they required protection from invading northern tribesmen, we came to their aid. In return, we were gifted handsomely—and I was given the sword." He peered sideways at her. "You ask because of the dream we shared."

The wind blew, kicking up a small storm of fine yellow dust. Soria coughed, and rubbed her burning eyes. "The last image of the sword was no dream. Not your memories or mine. Something different."

"In my time," Karr said slowly, "those who found

power in dreams were either shamans, witches, or the insane."

"I am none of those things," she told him sharply. "Just a woman."

"And I am just a man." He tilted his head, staring at the glowing horizon. "Am I not?"

Soria gave him a dirty look. "It means something. Was the sword . . . special in any way?"

"I used it to kill. There is nothing special about that."

"Unless you consider that it killed *you*, or was supposed to have. And yet, here you are. Alive."

"You are grasping."

"At threads," she agreed, picturing the map again in her mind, red lines spreading like rivers or roads—or entrails—into the core of an odd little doll. A chill rushed through her. "Do you trust dreams?"

"I do not even trust my memories," he replied, glancing sharply over his shoulder. "We are being followed again."

"The shape-shifter?" Soria scanned the horizon but saw nothing. "If your parents were shape-shifters, then how is it you hate their kind so much? You are one of them, no matter what you say."

"You might love your parents," he rasped harshly, "but if their family exiled and murdered them—attempting to do the same to you—I suspect you would understand my feelings about the matter."

She stopped walking, and stared at him. "I know many shape-shifters, and they are good men and women. They would not do that."

"And your leopardess?" Karr shook his head. "You are not that blind. And neither am I. I know that the actions of one should not condemn the whole, but it is safer, in my experience, to assume the worst. Do otherwise . . . and you die."

"If I assumed the worst," Soria began to say, and then stopped, thinking, *If I assumed the worst, I would still have my arm.* But she swallowed that down, and continued, "I would never have freed you from that cage."

"You are too naive." Karr gave her missing arm a sidelong look. "Or perhaps you wish to prove something to yourself."

It took a strong effort not to grab her empty sleeve and give it a good tight twist. "Do you plan on wandering through this desert forever, or do you know where you are going?"

"It is not my custom to lead rats into my home." Karr sat up on his haunches, a golden glow shimmering over his skin. He studied the sky again and said, absently, "Was that a map in your dream?"

"Our dream," she said. "And yes, I think so. I may even recognize the location of where all those lines were streaming from."

Karr made a low grunting sound, still distracted. Soria saw nothing in the sky except fading stars, but moments later stood back as his wings unfurled. "Dreams," he muttered. "I do *not* trust them."

His wings thrust down, kicking up a whirlwind of dust. Soria turned to shield her face, and missed seeing him leap upward from the earth. She almost tumbled over, though, buffeted by the power of his beating wings.

He was well into the sky when she could finally see him through her watery eyes, and was hit again with a lurching sense of wonder and disbelief. It was one thing to see a woman turn into a leopard, but a *dragon* hit her in that place reserved for childhood fantasies, the kind that never died but just slept, waiting for moments like this: affirmation that the world was, indeed, a mysterious place.

Karr flew high into the dawn sky, obscured by lingering shadows. His body reminded her of a bird, though not nearly as graceful, and his wings seemed to labor so intensely it was difficult to imagine him carrying her.

Until, suddenly, he wove sideways in a tumbling roll that sent him into a steep dive. Quick, tight, his speed utterly punishing. Soria was so enthralled—and concerned—she almost missed the black speck in the sky that was twisting wildly to avoid him. A bird, she realized.

A crow.

She stood for long moment, stunned, unable to do anything but stare as her stomach filled with terrible, desperate dread. And then something broke inside her, and she started jumping up and down, waving her arms.

"No!" she screamed. *"Stop!"*

Too late. The dragon crashed into the bird, sending it spinning wildly toward the earth. Soria started running, well aware it was useless: no way was she going to catch him. At the last moment, though, Karr tucked his wings against his body and swooped low to snatch his victim from the sky.

Soria exhaled sharply, staggering to a stop, but her relief was short-lived. Karr landed roughly, hopping several steps before coming to a full stop. Whirlwinds of dust surrounded him, but this time Soria did not shy away. She dropped onto all fours, scrabbling beneath his belly, struggling to reach the crow he had pinned to the ground. Karr made a muffled sound of surprise but did not move, even when she slammed her fist against his chest.

"Let go," she snapped. The crow twitched, opening its shining golden eyes. Staring at her with familiar intelligence.

She hit Karr again. *"Let him go."*

He tossed the crow aside like a piece of trash. Soria threw herself across the small, feathered body. Karr snapped at her head, raking his claws through the rocky soil. Beneath her, the crow began to glow.

Soria sat back, breathing hard, and an immense clawed hand clasped her aching shoulder. Karr's touch was gentle but unmistakably firm. She did not think, simply reached up to grasp his hand, as much of it as she could. Her fingers traced the hard, cool curve of talons, as well as soft scales. He stiffened but did not pull away.

The crow transformed, lost within a well of light. In moments, feathers faded into flesh, and Soria leaned backward against Karr to make room as a man took the place of the bird. He was tall and lean, covered in tattoos. Long black hair, snarled and dirty, covered much of his handsome face. He looked as though he had not bathed in a week. Scratches covered his chest. Blood.

"Koni," Soria whispered.

He replied hoarsely, his gaze flickering to Karr. "Nice to see you again, Soria."

CHAPTER ELEVEN

Q UITE oddly, there was a moment when Karr felt certain he understood what the shape-shifter was saying. The words melted and reformed inside his brain, flowing from gibberish into something that was meaningful.

"Nice to see you," he heard, and then everything else faded into a puzzle, and he was lost once again; frustratingly so. He had never realized how isolating language could be—or how inclusive. He rather preferred the latter, though watching Soria's body language as she spoke to the crow was quite illuminating.

Clearly, she knew the shape-shifter—which at this point was hardly a surprise. She might very well be acquainted with every one of them in existence, and it would not be a discovery any less traumatizing than the one she had given him this morning, when he realized that she could see inside his mind.

There was, however, a level of comfort in her behavior around the crow that both fascinated and disturbed Karr. With the leopardess, there had been distance, anger, distrust. Here and now, only the anger was present, but it was an exasperated irritation, the kind born from long familiarity. She talked fast, her one hand gesturing wildly, occasionally making stabbing motions. Karr detected tension in her, even awkwardness, but not enough to consider worrisome.

And she hugged the shape-shifter. Which Karr found that he did not like at all.

The crow was nearly as agitated, and just as informal. He was a tall, lean man, quick in thought and movement. He spoke to Soria as though she was an equal, but unlike the leopardess there was no underlying threat. Karr could tell they were friends, even though his gaze kept flicking down to her empty sleeve. As though he was used to seeing her arm, and found its loss glaring.

It can be done, Karr remembered telling the children of his clan, *friendship between our kind and humans. The imbalance of power is not so great. The barrier is in how we are perceived—and in how much we dare trust those who might fear us.*

Fine words. But he had rarely seen the truth of it. Until now.

"We are all in deep shit," he heard, suddenly understanding every word the crow said; even the nuances. *"Soria, she's not making sense."*

He said more, but the words faded into nonsense, an incomprehensible riddle that was completely frustrating. Karr found himself wanting to squeeze his hands into fists, and remembered at the last moment that he was still holding Soria's shoulder.

He could not bring himself to release her, though he

had no good reason for his reluctance beyond some lingering distrust, some desire to give the shape-shifter a message, a warning: *I am guarding her back. Do not hurt her. Do not think dark thoughts of her. Be her friend or I will hurt you.*

Not that it seemed necessary. Karr reverted slowly into his human body, descending from his dragon height. He still dwarfed the other man. His wings receded, yet his scales remained, iridescent and golden beneath the rising sun, curved into soft plates like the skin of a snake. His right hand retained its claws, but Karr took care with his left, making certain it recovered its blunt human nails. He tightened his grip on Soria's shoulder.

The crow-man watched him transform with wariness but no fear. Curiosity, perhaps—a far odder reaction than what Karr was used to seeing in a shape-shifter. It was both annoying and intriguing.

"Tell me what was said," he rumbled. "Before I kill him."

"You will not," Soria replied. "He is a friend."

"Give me a better reason."

Soria looked as though she wanted to strangle him, which he continued to find refreshing. Perhaps more so than was healthy. "His name is Koni. We are part of the same group. Different from the one that Serena works for."

"The leopardess. How many of you are there?"

Koni rattled off a stream of words. Soria held up her hand, focusing on Karr. "I know it is complicated, but please, just once, believe me when I tell you that I am trying to help. As is he."

It was nearly impossible not to believe her when she stared at him so openly, with that weary annoyance lingering in her gaze. Such a natural expression, confident and utterly unaffected. As though she trusted him to listen and would set him straight if he did not. It made his heart ache with unsettled wonder to be looked at as a man and not just a monster.

You are such a fool, he told himself.

"Koni was sent here. Told to follow us," Soria said.

"And he obeyed." Karr stared into the shape-shifter's golden eyes. "Who sent him? Another of your . . . allies?"

She looked down, and then back at Koni. Spoke a long, soft sentence that flowed through his mind.

"This does not make sense," he imagined she said. *"Not even to me."*

"Join the club," replied Koni, his words trailing through Karr's head as gibberish, and then reforming into something understandable. A strange sensation, almost like listening to a conversation in a dream. The crow-man rubbed his tattooed arm as though it ached. *"I was in Russia on other business when she called and told me to get here. I haven't been able to speak to any of the other shifters, so I can't be certain she's been in contact with them. I must have arrived in Erenhot soon after you did."*

"You didn't let Roland know?"

"She told me she was speaking for him, which I didn't question closely enough at the time. When I did, finally, she made it very clear that if I wasn't with her,

I was against her. In that I'm-gonna-rip-off-your-dick-and-make-you-eat-it sort of way."

Karr squeezed Soria's shoulder again. "Who is this woman he keeps referring to? The leopardess?"

She gave him a startled look. "You understood all that?"

"Perhaps." He suddenly felt awkward. "But the meanings I heard inside my head might have been little more than my imagination."

"I . . ." Soria stopped, still staring. "The woman he was referring to is another shape-shifter, *not* Serena. A matriarch, of sorts. Unsurprisingly, she does not like you very much." She frowned at Koni and added, *"She should not have known about him in the first place."*

Koni shook his head. *"She has her ways."*

"Who?" Karr growled.

Soria made a low, frustrated sound. "Her name is Long Nu. She is a dragon."

"A dragon," he echoed, thinking of his own mother and how only the very stupid ever made the mistake of confronting her. "I assume she wants me dead?"

"She told Koni you had kidnapped me."

"Because that would be easy," he said dryly, which earned him a gleam in her eye. "What will he do now, knowing that you are alive and well?"

She translated. Koni narrowed his eyes. *"Are you sure you're safe with him?"*

"Yes," she replied firmly, but the shape-shifter shook his head.

"I'm not blind," he said, his voice raspy and melodic.

"I saw things in Erenhot, from a distance. I saw how you didn't run from him when you had the chance, and when I finally was able to contact Roland, he confirmed you had freed him. But that doesn't mean he's not dangerous."

A surprising amount of anger flashed through her eyes. *"Does it bother you, then, what he is? Is that the reason you think he's a threat?"*

Koni gave her a puzzled look. *"What's that supposed to mean? He's one of us."*

Soria hesitated. Karr studied the crow's face for lies, and murmured, "Ask him, then, what he thinks I am."

"I should be asking how you suddenly understand my language," she muttered, but translated.

Koni frowned, but now he looked wary. *"Dragon, of course. His scent is odd, but that's not why I think he's threatening. Am I missing something?"*

Yes, he was missing a great deal—and Karr believed him. He could not be that good of a liar. Even for a crow.

Karr's hand slipped off Soria's shoulder, and he walked away without a word. Behind him he heard a slither of voices, followed by the soft, quick tread of footsteps. He tried to ignore them, gazing at the crown of the rising sun. Finding it heartbreakingly familiar.

"He does not know," Soria said quietly, just behind his shoulder. "He has no idea what you are."

"Which means that the existence of the chimera has been wiped away."

"Not for everyone." Her fingers grazed his arm. "Serena knows. Long Nu."

"Enemies." Fear struck him, and terrible regret. The shape-shifters had won the war and wiped his kind away.

If you had only decided to live, perhaps you could have . . .

He stopped himself from finishing that thought. It was too painful. " If that one over there knew the truth, he would turn against you for helping me."

"No." Soria moved even closer, the heat of her body riding over his skin with distracting sweetness. "I trust him."

"Your trust is not the same as mine."

"Fine. But whatever you have planned, you will not be able to accomplish it on your own. Not if you want a life after this journey of yours is done. You need help."

"Not his. I can barely tolerate yours." Which was a lie. And it was something he regretted saying the moment it slipped from his mouth.

Soria gave him a long, steady look—her silence worse and more damning than any words. When she began to turn away, he grabbed her arm, his fingers loose, gliding down to her delicate wrist.

"You saved my life," he murmured. "But I ruined yours, I think."

"No," she whispered. "If mine could be ruined, it would have happened a long time ago. Nothing you do could be worse than that."

Soria pulled free. He did not watch her go, but listened to her feet scuff sand, each step loud as thunder in his head, echoing his heart.

"What's wrong?" Karr heard the shape-shifter ask,

his voice low and filled with concern. Easier to understand him now, with only a slight delay between hearing the words and feeling the meaning splash through his brain.

"Nothing," came her short reply. *"What's your plan?"*

"Don't know. Even when she said you had been taken, I could tell that wasn't her priority. She was only interested in him. *She wanted me to follow, find out where he ended up."*

"That's it? Nothing else?"

"Nothing. Just observation."

Karr was not surprised. It was a tactic that had been used before. During the war, he had kept survivors of the first massacre well hidden, on the move, until finally settling them in the mountains north of the great plains. Returning from trade missions and hunts had become a tiresome affair, always on the lookout for spies in the skies or forest. Discovering the location of his people had been the first priority of the old queens who had captured him.

Koni hesitated. *"As long as we're talking about Long Nu's behavior, I'm surprised that Roland sent you out this way alone. That doesn't make sense, either."*

Soria said nothing. Karr glanced over his shoulder, only to find her staring at her hand, frowning as if it were marked with blood.

"Soria," continued Koni, gently. *"There's something about that shape-shifter you're not telling me."*

"You need to contact Roland again," she said. *"Go back to Erenhot. Tell him what's going on. See what he can do."*

"There's nothing he can do. You don't get it. Long Nu doesn't answer to anyone. But all of us shifters? We answer to her, in one way or another."

"I don't give a damn. Something is happening here that I don't fully understand, and it's ugly and it's hateful."

"Soria—"

"We were attacked," she interrupted ruthlessly, her voice even more lethal because it was so quiet. *"By men with guns who had orders to take us both alive. And Serena Serena had him—Karr in a cage that would have killed him if he changed shape. Immobilized, hooded in iron, strapped to a floor wearing a goddamn diaper. Did Long Nu tell you that? Did Roland?"*

Stunned disbelief flickered through Koni's face. Karr finished turning, allowing his body to finish its final reversion into his human shape. Flesh absorbed scales, revealing the full extent of the sores and welts banded across his throat, chest, hips, and legs. His wrists were red, raw in some spots. Sore and seeping. He had ignored his injuries completely until now— even forgotten them—but he wanted the crow to see. He did not want to give the shifter the luxury of being blind to suffering.

But Soria looked at him sadly, with such weariness Karr found himself striding to her side. He did not touch her, but stood very close, giving her a little of himself. He had done the same for others before battle. Stood at their backs, being a wall. Extending his protection, if only for a moment.

He gave Soria more than a moment. He towered behind her, feet planted, feeling a great and terrible determination swell from his heart to his heels, as though he were growing roots in some invisible earth that was beyond sight, beyond this desert. He was rooting someplace deeper and wilder, where he could still be the man he had been, where he could still do good in honor of the dead . . . and where maybe, just maybe, it was permitted for him to care for this woman.

Soria's spine straightened, ever so slightly. Karr gazed over her head at Koni and said, "I am not afraid of his mistress. Tell him that. If this Long Nu wishes to fight me instead of sending her soldiers to spy, I will be happy to oblige."

"You are asking for trouble," she replied. "Fighting does not have to be your first choice."

"You say that now. When they come for you without mercy, you will change your mind."

Her expression hardened. "I know when to fight. But I believe in options. Right now, communication is your biggest enemy. Everyone had been told one thing or assumed another. No one knows the truth."

"And you are the master of mine?" Karr asked harshly. "You do not know—"

Soria placed her hand on his chest, stopping him in midsentence. Her touch burned him. Koni tensed.

"There is right and wrong," she said, holding his gaze with furious intensity. "And there are all the parts in between. I am certain Long Nu has a reason for why she thinks you are a threat. And I know you have good cause to feel the same about her—or any shape-shifter. *I know that.* But there has to be another way."

Karr covered her hand with his. "Tell him what I said."

"Soria," murmured Koni. *"Looking a little cozy."*

"Shut up," Soria replied, still staring at Karr. But, moments later, she translated his message.

Koni exhaled slowly. *"Brass balls, but not much brain."*

"Never stopped you," she retorted.

The crow-man gave her a dirty look. *"What has he done to deserve this shit?"*

I was born, thought Karr—and Soria said, *"Answer something: what would happen if you had a child with a different kind of shape-shifter? A dolphin, for example?"*

He blinked, staring. *"That would be one fucked-up kid."*

"I'm being serious."

"So was I. It's not done. The children don't survive. Too much stress on the body."

Soria's gaze grew cold. Karr remembered that she had shared his nightmare. Seen the fires. Heard the screams. Those children in his care had not survived being born as chimera, that was true. But not because of any sickness.

"Who told you that?" she asked, her voice deathly quiet.

Koni gave her a wary look. *"It's common knowledge."*

"Does it happen anyway?"

"No. I told you. No one would risk a child. So we keep to our own, or find mates with humans."

"This is a mistake," Karr rumbled, touching Soria's shoulder. "Do not."

But she ignored him, and he did not try to stop her. It was wrong, and not something he would have ever contemplated, this invitation to trouble—but he was, despite himself, curious about the shape-shifter's reaction. He wanted to see what would happen. It would be easy to kill the crow if things went poorly, no matter how much it might grieve Soria.

"This man behind me is a dragon," she said fiercely. *"But he's also part lion. His parents were different. You understand, Koni? Your common knowledge sucks."*

Koni stared at her, and then burst out laughing—a cold, hard sound that was stunned and disbelieving. *"You're shitting me."*

Karr had never heard so many creative expletives. He held up his arm, concentrating, and scales rippled over his flesh, replaced within moments by fur. He allowed the transformation to continue shifting between dragon and lion, but it took all his concentration to make certain the two parts of his nature remained distinct and recognizable. Sweat rolled down his back, and it became harder to breathe as a great yawning darkness filled his mind, the trembling edge of some chasm that was frighteningly familiar.

He stopped shifting, blood roaring in his ears, sparks in his eyes. Everything seemed too bright to look at, but he forced himself to study the crow's face, and saw the realization in the shifter's eyes, the soft horror.

"*Fuck,*" Koni whispered.

"Indeed," Karr replied, hoarse, drawing a worried glance from Soria, who then proceeded to snap her fingers in front of the other man's face.

Koni tore his gaze from Karr, staring at her, golden light gleaming in his eyes. There was no hate, no rage or disgust, instead only a stunned, careful reaction that was almost as dangerous.

"*This is impossible,*" he said.

"*You don't know the half of it,*" Soria replied. "*You need to talk to Roland. These are complicated issues. I don't think he's aware of what I just told you.*"

Koni wet his lips. "*Long Nu means business. She wouldn't have gone to all this trouble otherwise. If Roland tries to stop her, it's going to be war.*"

"*Just do it, please.*"

Koni gave Karr a distrustful look. "*What about you? How will I find you again?*"

"*Take care of your end. I'll contact the agency when I can.*" A furrow gathered between her eyes, as though she was in pain. "*Tell Roland I hate his guts, and that I hope he shits acid the next time he's on the toilet.*"

Karr raised his brow in surprise, uncertain whether he had translated correctly. Koni smiled. "*I think I missed you.*"

"*Right,*" Soria muttered, and kicked dust at him. "*Go on, get out of here. Maybe all Long Nu wants is to introduce herself and sing 'Kumbaya.'*"

"*Or maybe she hired the men who attacked you.*" Koni spread out his arms, tattoos flexing along his lean, hard muscles which were quickly obscured by the black feathers that rippled from his skin. Golden light rose from him like steam and he added, *"I'll find out what I can. Hopefully she won't catch up with me first. In the meantime, be careful. I don't like leaving you here with him."*

"I'll be fine." Soria's faint smile did not reach her eyes. *"And just so you know, I think he can understand every word you say."*

"That right?" Koni's gaze turned menacingly sharp.

Karr let him look. A crow was nothing to be feared—just bones and feathers, and too much talk. But the change in attitude bothered Karr. He could see it in the other man's eyes: a different kind of tension than before, as though now Karr was something new and strange, and a more dangerous threat because of it.

Well, he *was* a threat. But it was an odd irony. Soria was right: he was so close to the shape-shifters as to be one of them. But the differences were there. Especially if one looked at only the surface, the combined scales and fur, at the heritage perceived as *wrong*. It was a hard battle to win—impossible, maybe.

You look at them the same—as a threat, he reminded himself. *You give them no time to prove themselves. Kill first, ask their corpses later.*

Koni sidled close. *"I don't know you worth shit, but if you hurt her . . ."* He did not finish the threat. There was no need.

Nor did Karr respond, though he had all manner of comments running through his head, none of which would have been fair to make Soria translate. He wondered, specifically, at the honor of the man who had sent her to speak to a prisoner whom so many found dangerous. She was a strong woman, yes, but strength had limits.

And Karr wondered, too, where this shape-shifter or any of her allies had been when she lost her arm. Or whether they had taken the effort to punish the one who had stolen it from her, and to make her safe. It was a wonder that Soria had come this far with him: a stranger, dangerous, unknown to her. That hit him squarely in the gut.

Brave, mysterious woman, he thought, glancing down at her, watching how she clutched her empty sleeve, a peculiar mix of emotions in her eyes: a hint of sadness and something else that was distant and lost.

She pushed between them, her hand resting briefly on Karr's chest. Her gaze was not on either man, but at the ground. She did not have to say a word. Koni's jaw tightened, and golden light flooded his skin. He threw back his head and opened his mouth in a silent cry as long black hair melted into feathers. A ripple of energy rode over Karr's skin, the sensation bringing back unpleasant memories. He gritted his teeth, and bore it, watching as the shifter became a crow.

It happened in the blink of an eye. Wings fluttered wildly; then, with a sharp piercing caw the bird launched upward into the clear dry air. He circled once before gliding southeast. Karr wondered if he was making a terrible mistake by letting the shifter go, alive and in one piece. Crows had always been the most cunning of scouts used in the war.

"You keep strange friends," he said at last.

Soria pressed her palm against her right eye. "No stranger than you."

But we are not friends, he thought. "Are you in pain?"

"My head." She peered up at him, grimacing. "It will pass."

He began to touch her face, realized what he was doing and stopped. "Seeing him was difficult for you."

"No," she said, but he could taste the lie. He let it pass, and glanced again at the sky. Koni was merely a speck. Easy prey for eagles—or dragons.

"I think," he said slowly, "that you need rest."

She looked at him as though he was an idiot. "Rest where? Or better yet, where are we going? This is the Gobi Desert. We have no way to carry water or food. Maybe you can survive here, but not me. Not for long."

Humans of his time had been able to survive a great deal, in elements much harsher than this, but there was a physical softness to Soria and all the humans he had seen thus far in this new world that made him believe her. "We are going north," he said. "We will fly most of the way."

Soria shook her head. "This area is not that deserted. There are *tourists* and *fossil hunters*, not to mention the locals. They will see you for sure."

Unfamiliar words, but this time he was able to make sense of them. He saw in his mind an odd vision of men and women hammering the earth for bones; and in another, more humans in wagons, smiling and holding small black boxes to their eyes. He said, "You have given me your gift of languages."

"No," she replied, bowing her head as though it hurt to see the rising sun. "That is impossible."

Karr could think of several things a great deal more impossible. She might not call herself a witch, but that, he thought, was a bit of self-delusion.

"And do not change the subject," she continued, her words slurred with pain. "North is vague. North is a direction, nothing else. Do you know where you are going, or not?"

You could know for certain, came the unbidden thought. *If you are willing to take the risk.*

"There are landmarks," he began to say, but was cut off by her shaking head.

"Thousands of years and human progress might make your landmarks unreliable," she told him hoarsely, eyes squeezed shut as she kneaded her brow. "If there was time simply to go north—north of here, north of wherever—and explore what you find familiar, that would be one thing. But I think we are running out of time. You need specifics, now."

Karr took her hand. Soria flinched, opening her eyes with surprise, stiffening as he knelt and tried to draw her down in front of him. She followed, finally, and he made her face him, her shoulders slumped, eyes hollow.

"What . . . ?" she began to say, and then stopped when he placed his hands on either side of her head and began kneading her skull.

"There are places to touch that ease pain," he said softly. "It is the same for shape-shifter and human. I have some experience."

"Changing the subject again," she mumbled, closing her eyes. "Oh . . . *there*."

"Breathe," he whispered, watching her face relax. His fingers slid over her head in a pressure dance: behind her ears, at the base of her skull, spanning through her hair to knead spots that he knew would take the bite from her pain, and from the nausea she must surely be feeling. "Chimera often suffer such discomfort, especially the children who begin shifting at a young age. Physical stress is strongly entwined with the mind. Head pain is the most common result."

Soria made a small, incoherent sound, sagging closer to him, eyes shut. Karr told himself he needed to watch her face for fleeting changes in her expression, as a guide for his fingers, but that was a lie. He simply liked looking at her. Such a puzzle. Beautiful, yes, especially now with the first touch of morning light bathing her face in a glow as golden as his own; her skin was soft and flawless, her body full of curves.

But it was more than that. Her compassion fascinated him. As did her trust. She had placed herself in his hands, in more ways than one, without question. Surely she knew what he could do to her. She was not naive, or foolish. And yet, here she was, relaxing in his hands. His hands, which had killed so many.

"Does this help?" he asked, finding it difficult to speak.

Soria nodded. "You surprise me."

He wished that she would open her eyes. "No more than you."

Her mouth tilted, but with little humor. Her lashes suddenly looked wet. Tears.

She began to twist away, but his hand slid around to the back of her neck, holding her still. She finally opened her eyes. Red-rimmed, bright with terrible emotion: grief, perhaps, and something else he could not name.

"Enough," she whispered hoarsely. "Thank you."

He did not let go. "Did I—?"

"No. You did not hurt me." Soria carefully wiped her eyes. "Just . . . I had forgotten . . ." Her voice trailed into silence as she visibly tasted her words, refusing to meet his gaze. "I had forgotten what it felt like to be . . ."

"Touched," he said.

Soria still could not look at him. "Small things. Always the small things a person takes for granted. Like fastening your clothes or scratching an itch. Making more trips to carry bags. Small, stupid things." She swallowed hard, her fingers fidgeting with the hem of her shirt. "I lost my dominant hand. I had to relearn how to write. I got rid of mirrors in the beginning, too. I could not look at myself. Felt like I was staring at an alien. You know, chopped up. Not me."

Karr was not certain what *alien* meant, but he understood all too well what she was telling him. "How long has it been?"

She closed her eyes. "A year."

"Were you alone?"

"I had my father and mother."

"Friends?"

"At first. And then I stopped wanting to see them.

People remember what you lost, and then they try too hard. You have to reassure them. Comfort them. Tell *them* it is okay that *you* got hurt." Soria shook her head. "It was easier to be alone."

"I doubt that," he said quietly.

She finally looked at him. Her eyes were haunted. "I should not have told you this."

A massive stroke of heartache cut through him—shocking not for what he felt, but for the intensity, a power such that he could hardly breathe. "You do not speak your suffering often."

"I do not suffer—" she began to say, but he cut her off with a tiny shake.

"I am not one of your so-called friends who requires comforting," he replied roughly. "I speak the truth. You suffer. You *have* suffered. You do not have to make excuses or be ashamed of what you feel.

"And I do not pity you," he added, far more gently. "There is nothing to be pitied in a missing arm. You are more than that, and you know it. I am certain you do, or else you would not have come so far on this journey with me." He leaned in very close, holding her face once more between his hands. "You are brave—and I do not say that lightly."

Soria drew in a ragged breath, and then laid her hand on his chest. Her touch was simple and light, but he felt the press of her fingers as though they reached through skin, straight to his heart. Searing, aching hunger filled him, unlike any he had ever felt, born of a peculiar tenderness for this strange human woman. She had given him his freedom. His freedom, which was more important than life. No matter who her allies were.

Karr covered her hand with his, and it was suddenly his turn for awkwardness; his nerves were adrift in ways he had not felt since childhood. He could not look at her.

She whispered, "Thank you."

He removed her hand from his chest, but could not bring himself to completely let go. His other hand had slid down her slender throat, her pulse warm and quick against his palm. His thumb was touching the corner of her mouth. He did not remember doing that, but the realization sent another shock through him—lower, deeper, in his gut.

"I have forgotten, too," he murmured, staring at her mouth. "Even before I died, I think I had forgotten."

Her breath caught. Karr swallowed hard, and leaned in, slowly. Expecting her to pull away. But she stayed still, and he was the one who stopped, just at the last moment. He could taste her scent, warm as the new sun. Her lips were so close.

He pulled back, dropping her hand as though burned. He *felt* burned, a terrible heat washing through him, unrelenting and savage.

"I am sorry," he muttered, standing. Soria scrambled to her feet, and grabbed his arm. Her hand was tiny against him, her fingers hardly more than a patch on his dark golden skin. He made the mistake of looking into her eyes. Found nothing hidden, no walls or distance between them.

"What hurt you?" she asked. "Or who?"

He had never felt so exposed. "We should go."

Soria's expression did not change, though the flush in her cheeks seemed to deepen, as did the shadows in her eyes. "I . . . want to find the sword."

It was not what Karr expected her to say. He realized, with some shame, that he had wanted her to keep pressing, to not give up on him so easily.

Like you gave up. She should not have to beg for a kiss. Not her.

"The sword," he replied hoarsely. "You believe it still exists? You trust your dreams that much?"

Her fingers tightened against his arm. "I have to trust something."

I want to trust you. "You cannot truly believe one weapon holds those answers."

"I think that even if we find your homeland, we will still have to go after the sword. Anything related to your death is suspect. Something, *someone*, did this to you."

"Thousands of years ago, according to you. There is nothing left."

"Except the sword," she said. "Maybe."

"Maybe," Karr echoed, and covered her hand with his. "You recognized the location in our vision?"

She hesitated, frayed slips of her hair flowing around her face as the wind kicked up. "It looked like a map of this country, Mongolia, and the red dot seemed to align with what I know of its capital, Ulaanbataar. It should not be far from here."

His memory of squiggly red lines and a golden-eyed doll were crystalline and chilling, but he said, "I cannot see it clearly in my head. Can you draw the map for me in the sand?"

Soria knelt. Karr joined her, watching as her finger traced lines in the shallow sheet of loose dirt covering the rocky ground. He had thought that seeing her illustration would help orient him, but he realized his mistake in moments. She was right: he needed more. Simply journeying north was not enough.

The blood ritual would be all you need, if you had the courage.

"Enough," he said, touching her shoulder. "You are certain about the sword and its location?"

She smiled bitterly, which Karr took as a *no.*

He bowed his head, considering his options as his fingers traced lines through her map in the sand. Soria's hand lingered near his, and this time he did not fight his need as he grasped her wrist and kissed her palm. Soria went still.

Karr rumbled, "I cannot fault your strategy. If nothing else, it is worth a brief scouting mission. We can resume our path north, afterward."

His scar tingled as he spoke those words. As though invisible fingers teased the outer edges of the surrounding skin. He touched the spot, for a moment certain he would feel another hand there. He discovered nothing but air—a chill—and the sharp memory of a sword piercing his stomach, the tip of the blade touching his spine. Tau, staring at him.

No, he thought, fearing another rush of blood.

But nothing happened. Karr took a deep breath, then another, and the sensation began to fade. He looked up, and found Soria's gaze flickering between his face and the hand pressed to his side.

"We should hurry," she said.

"Agreed," he muttered, and pulled her onto her feet.

CHAPTER TWELVE

ULAANBATAAR was over four hundred miles north of Erenhot, and the easiest way to get there was by car, bus, or train. None of those was an option, especially the latter. Karr had no papers, no identification—something Roland should have considered before telling Soria to journey south to Beijing. Unless he had intended for her to leave Karr behind.

Leave him for Long Nu or Serena? Had Roland made a deal with one—or both—of them?

And where, Soria wondered, would loyalties rest in such matters? Even though Serena had her own employers, would she obey their wishes over those of Long Nu? Would blood trump reason?

Or maybe they're all working independently of each other, with separate motives. Face it, you know nothing.

Nothing except that she didn't hold high hopes for their safety if they returned to the border city. She had a bad feeling about who else might catch up with them.

But, walking was out of the question. So was hijacking a tour group, although she considered stealing a vehicle for all of ten minutes, until she remembered stories about an increased police and military presence along the major roads through the region. Concerns of terrorists coming down through Russia and using Mongolia as a bridge to China had sparked the change, and that meant more eyes, more chances of being stopped. Better not to take the risk.

"We could ride horses," Soria suggested flippantly, knowing full well what his response would be.

"I think not," Karr rasped, his voice barely comprehensible; a sandpaper growl, rough and quiet. It reminded her a little too much of all the Narnia novels she had read growing up, with Aslan stoically rumbling.

Karr was a lion now, mostly, but he was as huge as a dragon—what little she knew of them. The lower half of his body was covered in scales and hard ridges. He looked like a throwback to some prehistoric age, especially when he stretched his massive wings, which were golden, with webbing the color of a dawn blush.

"You know," she said, turning in a slow circle to scan the rocky horizon, "birds have hollow bones. Makes them light so that they can fly."

"Is that so," he replied. "I assure you, my bones are quite solid."

"Not my point. The ratio of your body mass to wing span . . ." She stopped, watching his feline mouth somehow manage a smile. *Magic*, she told herself, shaking her head. *Just tell yourself it's magic. He flew last night. He can do it again.*

Except that someone, eventually, was going to see them.

The morning sun was bright, blinding—or maybe that was the dust in Soria's eyes. Her nostrils ached, too, and her throat was patchy with thirst. Temperatures were comfortable, but it was only morning and late spring. She did not want to think about what it would be like here at the height of summer.

"Come," Karr said, sitting up on his haunches, holding out long arms huge with muscle, his skin covered in sleek tawny fur. Sunlight glimmered against his wings, which rested delicately around his shoulders. A long, scaled tail flopped restlessly in the sand.

Soria hesitated, staring, wishing despite her concerns that she had a camera, a piece of paper and pencil, something, anything to record him now, in this moment. She wasn't entirely certain that she hadn't lost her mind somewhere back in San Francisco—or her sense of wonder, long before that, whenever she had first started taking shape-shifters for granted. But she felt wonder, looking at Karr. He was beautiful, wild. Extraordinary.

And totally bizarre.

Dolphin and crow, she thought, remembering her question to Koni. She couldn't even begin to imagine what that would look like, given the way Karr seemed to mesh his different shapes, mixing fur and scales and abilities.

Soria walked over to him, holding the tightly folded bundle of cloth against her stomach. She held her breath as he picked her up, with such ease she felt light as a feather, floating in the hard confines of his arms. He cradled her close, tight against his warm chest. She knew what to expect.

But this time she felt a different energy between them, and she was not entirely certain whether that made her less comfortable with him or more. It was impossible to know how he felt, except through his actions. His eyes revealed nothing.

Except when you were kneeling in the sand and he was talking to you about your arm. Except when he leaned in to kiss you.

He had been vulnerable, then. He had looked young, the hard lines of his face softening with hunger and desire. There had been so much need in his eyes. Terrible loneliness. Things that were mirrored in herself.

Stop, she told herself. It was no good thinking about how much she had wanted him in that moment. Just one kiss, to see if his mouth felt as good as his hands, which had melted through her pain and filled her with a warm comfort that she had forgotten could exist. Comfort and safety. Not just locked doors and a fuzzy blanket, but that soul-deep conviction that nothing bad would happen to her ever again. Not with him. Not while he was close.

She felt it now in his arms, and it was an odd, frightening weight in her heart. She did not want to rely on anyone to make her feel safe. No one could be counted on—not even the people she had thought would always be there. Roland—she had been so sure about Roland, despite his occasional remoteness—but he had betrayed her in the end. That was how she saw it—a betrayal. Just one phone call at the hospital, filled with tense silence. Flowers, a few cards sent with computer-generated messages.

One year together, and nine years before that as simply friends. She had thought all that time would mean something. At least an effort. Some sign that he wanted to be the one who kept her heart safe as she healed.

He had told her later that he had been afraid. Guilt-ridden, unsure what to do. A powerful man who led psychics, shape-shifters, and other nonhumans—unsure what to do with one hurt woman he was supposed to love. And yet, Soria had believed him. She still did. His fear was real. She knew him too well. That was Roland. He could handle everyone's lives but his own.

Which had not been enough for her.

Karr, certainly, had his own agenda. She was useful to him for now, and she wanted to help, but after this was over, however that managed to come about, she had no illusions that he would—

Oh, God, she thought. *Don't go there. Have some self-respect.*

Right. Fuck romance.

"That's the spirit," she muttered, settling deeper into the crook of Karr's arms, feeling the muscles of his chest coil and heave as his wings began to beat. Dust kicked up, choking her, and through watery eyes she saw him give her a questioning look. His leonine features were far more expressive than his dragon visage.

Soria shook her head. "Just go."

THEY FLEW OUT OF THE DESERT LATE THAT AFTERNOON. Soria had no way of knowing how fast they were traveling, but the miles seemed to slip away, even though Karr was forced to stop every hour to rest. He did not say so, but as time went on it seemed to grow progressively harder for him to fly while carrying her. Just breathing seemed to take a great deal of effort.

Soria remained quiet for most of the journey. She was thirsty, and the one small lake they had found—hours after starting—was too salty for either of them. Not for camels, though. She saw them from a distance, long necks bowed. When Karr swooped close, they scattered and ran. Easy prey, she thought. Kill them, drink from the humps, eat their hearts, or fat. It was an option she supposed they were not desperate enough to take. Not yet.

Now, outside the desert—the change was marked only by the sustained presence of rock and withered grass, and not rock and sand—storm clouds were gathering, coiled into tumors the color of dirty snow, edges glowing silver from the late sun, and bleeding into a blue sky. The grassland stretched as far as the eye could see. No trees. No caves. No place to hide.

Lightning flashed. Karr made a hissing sound and descended sharply, chased by thunder. His arms tightened around Soria. Just before they hit the ground, a golden glow rose from his skin, so bright and warm it felt like being bathed in dawn light. He hit the ground running.

A gust of wind slammed into them, and then another: a continuous howling blast that stole Soria's breath and burned her eyes. Karr staggered, putting his head down, but he could not take another single step against its force. A haze filled the air, light at first, but filled with choking dust. Sand and other small particles hit

Soria's face, getting inside her mouth each time she coughed. Visibility worsened, and not because her eyes were watering. Dust blocked out the sky, the entire world, until she could see only several feet in front of them. It happened in moments.

"Give me that cloth," Karr said roughly, dropping to his knees and laying Soria down on the short grass. Before she could ask what he was doing, he dragged the sheet from her and shook it loose. It nearly ripped free of his hands, and Soria had to help him drag it down over them. They hooked one end under around their legs, and pulled the flapping, bloodstained fabric over their heads and bodies.

Karr curled around her, dragging her so tightly into the curve of his body she could barely breathe. His sleek, furred arm crossed her chest with his soft, pawlike hand cupping her cheek. His warm wing draped over her, and just before he enclosed them entirely in the sheet, Soria glimpsed the grassland beyond: black as night, cut with a flash of lightning that was faint through the dust storm haze.

"We are still too close to the desert," he rasped in her ear. "Not much rain, but a great deal of dust. This cloth should keep out the worst of it so we can breathe."

Soria tried to work some saliva around the inside of her mouth. Her teeth crunched on sand and grit. "You have experience with this?"

"Some. Never the luxury of a tent, however. We are fortunate."

Soria half laughed. "Really." Thunder cracked, so close it made the ground shake.

Karr pressed his mouth against her hair. "Rest, Soria. It will pass."

Like hell, she thought. And then she realized something odd about what he had just said to her. She chewed on it for a moment, wanting to make certain that she was right. "That is the first time you have ever said my name."

His arms tightened around her. Soria listened to the wind howl beyond the rippling confines of their cotton cocoon, flinched as lightning and thunder shook the air. *Hit and fried*, she thought—*someone will find our strange charred bodies, burned together, molded together: a winged lion and a human woman.*

Slowly, quietly, Karr said, "You are so loose with names. You speak them without thought."

"We were talking about you. Not me."

His voice was nearly drowned out by a ripple of thunder. "Names are reflections of bond, connection. To know another's name is to know part of them. To speak it is to tell the world that you have a connection."

"Is that a bad thing?"

"If you do not know one another. Or if you are enemies. It is a violation."

She tried to turn her head to look at him, but all she could see in the darkness was the fringe of golden mane. "You told me your name. Unless you lied about it."

"No." He sounded disgruntled. "I spoke true."

"Our customs are different. Names are important, but

not like that." Soria frowned. "So why *did* you tell me your name?"

"I thought you would not free me, otherwise," he said dryly. "Unless you have forgotten that part already."

She had, but was not convinced by his answer. "You could have lied."

"I would not lie about something so fundamental. Tell too many such lies, and they might come true." He hesitated. "I fear becoming someone else."

"I think we all do," she said, feeling the pressure of the ground against her stump. "Truth and honor. Means a lot to you."

"It is the root of what divides us from mere animals."

"And yet shape-shifters hunted you like animals." She paused. "Were all of them dedicated to that task, or just one group?"

"Enough were involved. It was war, after that night."

When the children died, he did not have to say. Soria could still hear their screams, and she shivered so violently her teeth chattered.

Karr held her closer. "I should have returned you to the city."

"No," she managed to say, though it took concentration. "Those children . . . were any of them yours?"

He was silent a long time. "All of them, and none. Most were abandoned by their parents. It was customary to do so. Ours was a temple dedicated to rearing the unwanted. Some of the children, though, belonged to chimeras themselves, those who took human mates."

"Not another chimera?"

"In the same way your crow would never dream of mixing blood with another outside his skin, a chimera would not take the risk of doing the same with another of our kind. Or a pure-blooded shape-shifter. That truly would be a disaster."

"You have seen this with your own eyes?"

"Yes," he rumbled. "The . . . baby died soon after birth. It was unrecognizable as anything that could be human or animal. Nor did the mother survive."

"I am so sorry."

Karr's chin pressed against the crown of her head, and he changed the subject. "This storm could last for hours. Best if we try to sleep."

"Right," Soria said, as the winds howled. "Dreamy atmosphere."

"Hush," he murmured. His voice was rumbling and soft, as if he was truly sleepy. "I will protect you."

He said it so simply, without hesitation or mockery. Soria shivered again, listening to her heartbeat, and the thunder roll through and around her. *I'll protect you, too*, she thought. Wishing she had the guts to say it out loud. Wondering what his reaction would be to a one-armed woman telling him—seven feet of pure animal muscle—that she would watch his back.

"So, you've made up your mind?" she asked softly.

Karr rumbled something incomprehensible, and she added, "About me. Being your enemy."

He sighed, and after a brief moment twisted her around until she lay on her back. He loomed over her. The huge naked man was pressed against her thigh—which seemed somehow more explicit than having him glued to her back. She didn't know whether to laugh, freeze, or grope him.

Karr held the top of the sheet with his fist, and reached over to tuck the rippling edges under Soria's body. Beyond their small cocoon the winds continued to scream, but the air inside was stuffy and growing hot. If it had not been for the faint glow of Karr's eyes, she would not have been able to see much of his face at all, despite the fact that he was leaning over her, close enough to rub noses. Or kiss.

His left hand lingered on her waist, touching her bare skin in a spot where her shirt had ridden up. She felt fur, and then a golden glow curled from his body like smoke and his sleek tawny coat faded into skin that was only a shade paler. His face shifted into his human visage, though the sharpness of his cheekbones remained, as did the leonine tilt of his eyes. His wings disappeared in a bone-cracking flash of light.

And all the while, he studied her face. His gaze never left her, and the intimacy of that scrutiny, his utter shamelessness, burned through her heart until she was afraid to breathe.

"In my other life," he said slowly, "few humans would interact with my kind—or with the shape-shifters. Those who did had power. They fancied themselves gods, or godlike, with a lineage beyond their own people. I saw this among the Hittites, and in the southern empires which existed from the edge of the great Nile, eastward to the sea. Vastly different worlds. But the roots of how power was perceived were always the same."

"I do not believe I am a god," she remarked dryly.

Karr smiled. "But you believe we are equals. You have never said so outright, but I know what it is to be treated high and low, as god or monster. When *you* look at me, though . . . when you speak to me . . ."

"I speak to the man," she said.

"As I have always been. Just . . . a man. No matter how my body shifts." His hand on her waist flexed, large and warm. "You are a perplexing woman."

She tried not to smile. "And?"

"And, nothing. You confuse me." Karr's hand trailed up her ribs, brushing against the side of her breast—by accident or on purpose, she did not know. But her heart lurched, and his eyes flared brighter. "Everything I thought I could trust is gone now, and there are . . . new complexities. Shape-shifters, humans, my own kind. The question of why I am alive. You."

Thunder boomed, but it sounded far away. Winds, however, still battered their tiny cocoon. Soria murmured, "I should be the least of your concerns."

"But you are not." Karr briefly closed his eyes. "I find it difficult to imagine existing in this new world without you, and that . . . troubles me."

She had to clear her throat, and even then her voice sounded awkward, strained. "I can teach you my language. Seems as though you are already on the way to learning it. The rest will come."

Karr hesitated, looking away from her. "Yes. Of course."

She stared at him, torn, unsure what to say or do. It would be so easy to just let this go. Better that way. Less complicated. Hiding was always safer.

She thought of Eddie, huddled in his glass cage. Roland, in his tower. The last painful year, hiding in her apartment: no mirrors, a grocery delivery service on speed dial, online shopping, the occasional walk at night through downtown Stillwater, when no one paid much attention to an empty sleeve. Slowly, painfully, entering the world again. Until here, in this tiny, flimsy, storm-ridden space, she felt more herself than she had in a long time.

Soria unclenched her fingers from where they were digging into her stomach. Tentatively, carefully, she touched the strong, lean line of Karr's shoulder, and then his neck. His expression instantly hardened, becoming almost cruel.

She froze, suddenly certain she had read him wrong. Heat flooded her cheeks: shame, embarrassment, the keen desire to curl into a ball and pretend she was invisible. She started to do just that, but Karr placed his hand against the side of her face. A firm, gentle touch; it was very warm, his fingers sinking into her hair. His expression, however, did not change, not even when his thumb grazed her mouth, slow and deliberate.

"This is a mistake," he rumbled softly—and then kissed her.

For a moment she barely felt his lips; her heart was hammering, making her dizzy; and a rush of tingling heat poured through every inch of her body. But his mouth pressed harder, his fingers dragging across her cheek, and Soria surged upward to kiss him with every ounce of strength in her body. He made a small, pained sound but did not break away, just met her with equal force, his hand grabbing her waist to pull her tight and close. There was not much between them. She could practically feel his pulse against her leg.

She broke off first, drowning for air, and the two of them lay together, cheek to cheek, breathing so ragged that the winds whipping around them sounded gentle in comparison. Karr was very nearly on top of her, his scent rich and warm with sweat. Every bit of her ached to feel more of his touch, but she held still, trying not to think, trying not to do anything except simply savor what she had been given—and what she had taken.

"Why," Karr asked slowly, his mouth pressed to her ear, "have you no mate?"

A thrill raced through her, followed by heartache. "What makes you think I do not?"

"You told me yourself that you have been alone."

Soria closed her eyes. "And you? Who did you leave behind?"

"Friends. I never took a mate. Some humans would have had me, but for the wrong reasons."

"Because you are so handsome?" she asked, smiling against his ear.

He made a small, strangled sound: laughter, she realized. His hand tightened around her waist. "No one ever said so. I believe it had to do with family desires for powerful alliances, or a belief that future generations would be enriched with the blood of gods."

"So you could have had a princess."

"Many," he said, and this time she felt *his* smile, which was warm on her cheek. "Several of my kind were not so circumspect. They took such offers seriously, though with humans of lesser status. I was a leader, and so those who ruled would deal only with me."

"Those humans never approached pure-blooded shape-shifters?"

"Few shape-shifters interacted with humans, unless it was to use them as slaves. Some felt we should do the same, to swell our numbers in battle. But it would not have . . . been right."

Soria had trouble imagining any of it. "Things have changed."

"So it seems." Karr pulled back, just enough to look into her eyes. "There can be nothing between us, Soria."

She studied him for a moment, trying to understand what was going through his mind, considering making a joke, as there was very little between them anyway—and something not so little. But she had a feeling any attempt at humor would not go over well.

"Because I am still your enemy," she said.

"No," he replied, closing his eyes.

Is it my arm? Soria wanted to ask, but she could not say those words. "Fine. A kiss is nothing, you know. Human women are very liberated nowadays."

Karr sighed, pressing his brow against hers—an intimate gesture that was not lost on Soria, and that only fueled the simmering quiet hunger she felt for him, which ran deeper and stronger than anything she had ever known. It was not just lust, but a sense of home-sickness that his presence eased; a comfort in being around him that she had only become conscious of at the lake, after leaving Erenhot. And even then she had not allowed herself to think much of it until now. No man, not even Roland, had ever felt like home—a better home than the one she had left.

Karr fingered one of her braids, staring at it with particular tenderness. "The storm is fading."

"Easier to talk about the weather than what just happened?"

"I cannot want you," he whispered, almost as if talking to himself. "It is too dangerous."

"For you or me?"

He met her gaze again, golden eyes glowing faintly. "I was not murdered. I asked to be killed. I committed suicide. My friend ran me through with my sword because I asked him to. Then I was buried alive, left to bleed out in the tomb where I was found."

Soria stared, unable to speak. Karr turned his head, looking away from her. "I lost my mind. It happens, among my kind. We lose ourselves, sometimes permanently. When that happens, we have two choices. Exile, or death."

She was still hung up on the part where he had committed suicide. "I think *I* just lost my mind. Exile or death? For going a little crazy? That makes no sense."

"We do it to save lives," he rumbled dangerously. "When we break, our animal natures overcome us. All instinct, no thought. We kill. We hurt those we love. And we are nearly impossible to stop once we start. That is why the shape-shifters fear us. We are . . . unpredictable."

She tried to respond, but nothing came out except a small choking sound. Words had fled her, utterly. Karr tightened his jaw and lifted the edge of the sheet. Silver light trickled in from the hazy sky. He had been right: the dust storm was losing strength. Soria, however, was not yet ready to face the world.

"You committed suicide," she managed to say, though the words cut her—the idea of this strong man, with his strict code of honor, taking his own life. "What did you do that you could not live with? Who did you hurt?"

He gave her a sharp look, and—

Whatever he was going to say was interrupted by a loud, piercing blast: a gunshot. Soria scrabbled for the edge of the sheet. Dust-heavy wind hit her face the moment she poked out her head, but she wiped her eyes and covered her mouth and nose, scanning what little of the grassland was still visible. Everything seemed covered in a yellow-gray sheet of dust. Even the sky was leeched of color.

"I do not see anything," she said, just as another gun blast rocked the air behind them. For a moment she froze, feeling like a little kid: pulling the blanket over her head to keep the demons out. But she flung back the sheet, keeping tight hold of it as the cloth rippled in the wind, and stood on shaky legs to look around.

Her eyes instantly burned with flying dust, and it was hard to breathe. Karr tore a strip from the sheet and tied it around her nose and mouth, standing in front of her to block the worst of the wind. Soria gathered the remains of the sheet against her chest, and did the same with the jogging pants.

She heard a third shot, but still could not see where the noise was coming from. Karr said, "Wait here."

"No—" She began to protest, but he had already

begun to run, dropping low to the ground in a burst of golden light. His body transformed as he moved, fur rippling over skin, and within moments a lion took the place of the man. He raced from her, surrounded by the thick, choking haze. Soria stumbled after him, unwilling to be left behind, flinching as the sky flickered with lightning. She did not call out to Karr, not even when he disappeared completely within the storm. Just kept pushing forward, hoping she was going in the right direction.

Within moments, though, she saw a shadowy figure loping toward her: a lion with glowing golden eyes. Relief poured through her heart, more than she expected. She had not realized in that moment how frightened she was of being left alone in this place.

Karr rubbed up against her left side. "Take hold of my mane. Do not let go."

Soria wrapped the sheet and pants loosely around her shoulders and chest; then she sank her fingers into the coarse hair surrounding his leonine face. *Sheena, queen of the jungle*, she thought, *eat your heart out.* "Thank you for coming back."

His tail lashed through the air. "I should not have let you out of my sight. All we have here is each other."

He said it so easily. Soria tightened her fingers in his mane, wishing she had her other hand to shield her eyes, and tried to keep pace as Karr began moving quickly across the dusty grass.

The storm had eased—the winds were weaker, the haze less blinding—but it was still treacherous and painful. Soria let go of Karr only once, and that was to pull the bloodstained sheet over her head, wrapping it securely until she felt like a character out of *Lawrence of Arabia*. The dust, however, was still alive, getting beneath the cloth into her mouth and nose, and beneath her clothing as well.

Another gunshot split the air, along with something else that could have been a voice but was ripped away by the wind before she could hear it completely. Karr tilted his head, staring, the muscles all along his body sliding lean and hard beneath his sleek fur.

"What is it?" Soria asked.

A growl rose from his throat. "I smell sheep. I will frighten them like this."

A golden glow spread over his body. Soria watched the transformation, trying to understand even a little how it was physically possible. She heard joints popping, but as with Koni, there was no accounting for the difference in mass, or a transition that was smooth as falling water—one minute one shape, one minute another— with nothing between but light. Until Karr stood beside her as a man.

"You are made of magic," she said, and then flushed, knowing how stupid that sounded.

But Karr seemed to treat her words seriously. "We are all made of magic. What else can account for life?"

Science. Molecules and electrical impulses, and a complex biological formula of *here and there*. Except, she thought, science might as well be magic. Just another word for invisible forces making things happen.

"Sheep," she said. "And who is with them?"

Karr bowed his head against the wind. "Let us find out."

"Wait." Soria grabbed his arm. "The gun."

"Gun," he echoed, tasting the unfamiliar word—which suddenly sounded unfamiliar to her as well. She had become too used to speaking his language. "In a storm like this, the only reason someone makes a loud noise is because they want to be found. Not because they intend to hurt anyone."

"I thought you were the paranoid one."

Karr took her hand and held it tightly. "I have been lost before in storms like this."

He took the lead, his grip on her hand never easing as he pulled her forward—more slowly now, with a great deal of caution. Her eyes were burning, watering, but after a minute of careful movement she glimpsed white blobs in the sandstorm haze; like ghosts, or very large cotton balls.

Sheep. Huddled against each other on the ground, heads tucked down. The right idea, she thought.

Karr said, "Call out. A woman's voice will be less frightening."

Less frightening to whom? Soria wanted to ask, but nodded her assent. It took her a moment, though; her gift for languages was an unconscious one. She rarely had to think about what she was doing: words and meanings, and their cultural significance usually entered her mind, no questions asked. But she was in the presence of Karr, who spoke one language; and the person in front of her, assuming he or she was Mongolian, spoke something radically different. She had to concentrate to filter out the variations . . . and it was a thornier problem than it should have been. She had become so immersed in Karr's language, it was difficult to separate herself.

Finally she did, and found a stream of Khalkha dialect flowing through her mind. Khalkha . . . and English. Which did not make sense.

"Hello?" she called out, tentatively. "Is anyone there?"

Winds howled. Karr held very still, head tilted, staring into the haze. He seemed unbothered by the dust, though his eyes were bloodshot, which made them appear even more alien than usual. Soria tried not to cough, but had to take a deep breath and found herself choking on the grit in her mouth.

She sensed movement among the huddled sheep. Called out again, between coughs, and finally saw a slender figure appear in the haze. A kid, maybe a teen. Hard to tell. Wearing goggles and a bandana, with a rifle in his hands that was almost as big as he. She could not see his expression, but from the way he stood so still, staring at them, she had a strong feeling that encountering a huge naked man and a woman with a sheet over her head was not what he had expected.

"Don't be afraid," she called out, which seemed rather laughable. "We're here to help you."

"Dude," said the kid, in both perfect English and an unmistakably female voice. "You need more help than I do."

CHAPTER THIRTEEN

Her name was Evie, which was the only thing that Karr truly understood, because the rest had to do with things called *exchange programs* and *cultural immersion*, and something else that was pronounced *an-thro-pol-o-gy*, which the young woman was quite excited about, given the spike of adrenaline in her scent when she started talking to Soria about why she was in the middle of the grassland, huddled with sheep, during a sandstorm.

"This is so frakkin' cool," said the girl, which Karr's mind could not quite translate. How he was able to understand anything at all remained a pleasant mystery, one that he hoped to discuss with Soria sooner rather than later. She might claim that it was impossible, but clearly *something* had happened. Perhaps when sharing his dream she had left part of herself behind. A bond, a link. Magic.

The storm had finally died down, and they were traveling across grassland that was yellow with soft dust that kicked up around them with each step. The girl rode a brown horse, a sturdy animal wearing a simple saddle, with red tassels dangling from its bridle. It was also covered in dust. All of them were filthy, and Karr kept fighting the urge to scratch his lower extremities. He was uncomfortably dressed in those soft, tight pants, which Soria had tossed to him at the very first moment the girl had turned her back. He felt as though sand was inside them, which was an unfortunate sensation.

Sheep were plodding along in front of them, sometimes exhibiting quick bursts of nervous movement, their eyes bulging and rolling whitely in their heads whenever the wind shifted and they caught Karr's scent. The little horse seemed equally displeased by his presence, but was more easily controlled. Karr lingered well behind to keep the animals calm; and to watch their surroundings without being watched in turn by the girl, who seemed to have an unholy fascination with him and his body.

Soria kept pace with the horse, her braids frayed, the folded sheet tucked under her left arm. Her shoulders were slumped but her stride was steady and long, and her voice did not slur with exhaustion. She was a strong woman. Despite the dust coating her hair, he could still see the hint of a glossy shine, and the rich olive tones of her skin were healthy and flushed with faint pink. He could still taste her lips. It took all his willpower not to allow his desire for her to manifest in a physical manner. Even among his kind that would have been cause for embarrassment.

But he did want her. He wanted her badly, and could not explain that need. It frightened him, because with Soria he felt things in his heart that had nothing to do with the heat of his body. He liked her. She might, in the end, be his enemy, but he admired her courage, her stubbornness, the intelligence in her eyes. He respected all those things, and more.

And even more after that.

Enough, Karr told himself, but he could not stop struggling over his feelings. He had always managed to control himself in such matters, regardless of who had been flung in his direction. Nubile women, naked, more than willing, with the power of empires behind them—he had been tempted, yes, but only by the protection that could be offered his people. Protection that some, including Tau, had argued was needed, no matter the cost.

That cost being the future life of any child Karr might have with his bargained mate. A child that would not be reared by him but suffer the influence of humans with their politics and strange ways. He could not imagine doing that to a son or daughter, having them locked up in the nebulous human cage of conformity and intrigue. Never.

With Soria, the problem was quite different. He was terrified of hurting her.

The girl, Evie, looked quite young, though certainly old enough to bear children. She handled her horse with surprising agility, even while continuing her animated discussion with Soria. Slender, short, with close-cropped blonde hair that suited the sharp lines of her freckled face, she was dressed in a soft blue wrap, and had loose pants tucked into tall boots.

"*It was dead back home,*" she said, talking fast. "*Seriously, seriously dead. Like, as far as studying this stuff goes. I mean, what—you're gonna get a PhD in nomadic cultures and not get your ass out here? Dude, my parents had a meltdown. Like, a 'You're-gonna-get-kidnapped-and-sold-into-white-slavery' meltdown. Ugly, man."*

Soria looked rather dazed. *"How long have you been out here?"*

Evie shrugged. *"Little over a year. Took me a while to find a family willing to put up with my weirdness, but you know, everyone is free-to-be-me out here anyway, so a little crazy goes a long way. I'm from Montana. I get the life."* She glanced over her shoulder at Karr, her gaze roving his body with an interest that made him feel a bit like a skewered lamb. She smiled, a devilish glint in her eyes. *"Guys like yours really should be clothing optional. Man, he is totally lickable."*

Soria made a choking sound. Evie gave her an innocent look. *"What? You said he doesn't understand English."*

"He understands some," she replied, also giving him a sidelong glance. *"He constantly surprises me with how much he knows."*

Karr almost smiled.

Evie said, *"Are you sure it was a local operator who stole your stuff? Crime hardly exists out here, unless you're in the cities. I mean, there's muggings, pickpockets, and prostitution . . . but full-scale robbery and abandonment?"*

"Shit happens," Soria said. Which was an apt turn of phrase Karr wished he'd had in his vocabulary during the war.

Ahead, the sheep began to scatter. Evie kicked her horse into a trot, herding them carefully. While she was distracted, Karr caught up with Soria and touched her elbow. It was brief contact, but it sent warmth through him and a sickness for home that made it difficult to breathe.

"I think we can trust the girl," she said immediately, softly. "She seems like a good kid. A student. Grew up on a ranch where she had to regularly work outside with animals. Made it easier for her to integrate with the nomads in this region, but I think she panicked a bit out in that sandstorm."

"She talks too much," Karr murmured.

Soria laughed quietly, shaking her head. "She's sharp. I'm worried about the story I told her."

"We will leave soon enough," he replied. "First, food and rest."

She nodded, watching the girl round up the sheep. Her smile turned painfully wistful. "I was like that once."

Karr did not have to ask what she meant. "You took the risk of coming with me, did you not? I would call that a far greater gamble than battling sheep."

"You certainly grumble a lot more." She gave him an amused look. " 'Enemy this, enemy that.' "

Again, he had to fight a smile, and ducked low to whisper in her ear: " 'Trust me,' she says. 'I am harmless.' "

Soria turned her head so their noses brushed. "I never said that."

"Not with so many words," he murmured. "And I still take issue with all the shape-shifters with whom you are acquainted."

"I think you always will," she replied.

Karr wanted to taste her lips again. "Always is a long time."

Amusement flickered through her eyes and then faded just as quickly into something quiet and pained. Soria stopped walking, and turned to face him. Her cloth bundle was held tight under her arm, which freed her left hand to clutch at her empty sleeve.

"Do not play games with me," she whispered — without anger, though the sadness in her voice was worse. Karr stared, and a crushing ache pushed through his heart.

A whistle split the air. Evie was waving at them.

"Hey!" she shouted, the accent of each word crisp and clear. *"It's just over the hill!"*

Sure enough, Karr glimpsed riders in the distance, cresting a low rise. He was reluctant to meet them, or to go anywhere near a human settlement. Not because he doubted their safety, but because he was not yet done with Soria.

THERE WAS A CREEK THAT HAD ONCE BEEN A RIVER, BUT the waters were little more than a snake trail at the base of the rocky bed. It was too early in the season for snow-melt from the distant mountains, but even then Karr suspected the waters would not rise far. A river this dry was a sign of more substantial problems.

It was enough, though. Four tents had been erected a short distance from the creek. Large, round, and white, they had domed roofs and colorful wooden doors painted in designs that resembled leaves and flowers.

Horses grazed nearby, alongside long-haired yak. Small, stocky goats, shaggy coats thick with dust, clustered near the creek; the air was thick with their musky scents. Dogs barked, surrounded by children who tried to hold their wildly wagging tails while staring at the procession of riders, livestock . . . and two strangers.

"There are three families here, all related by blood," Evie said. She waved at some women who were carrying buckets of water from the creek. *"I bought my own ger to live in—paid for all the wood pieces, and the felt to cover it. When I finally leave, I'll let Batukhan take it. He's the youngest son, around seventeen or so. Looking for a wife, so it'll be a good place for him to live, down the road."*

"We don't have much to offer," Soria said. *"But I still have some cash that was hidden on me."*

Karr watched the girl shake her head, studying her for any hint of malice or deception, but her eyes remained clear and her mouth tugged into a wry, amused smile. *"You can stay with me. As for the rest, don't worry about it. These folks aren't generous because they expect to receive things in return."*

But they *were* curious, Karr found. Not that he could blame them. The men on horseback who had appeared at the top of the hill were small and lithe, much like their horses—lean, muscled, quick to dart, spurring into graceful gallops that appeared natural as breathing. Lassos hung from the horns of their saddles, which were hardly more than pads of leather and cloth. They had no stirrups.

Seeing the men filled Karr with quiet pleasure: not

all things had changed. He remembered the horsemen of the plains: small, stocky men and women of fierce eyes and sharp wits, some of whom had acted as guides along the great trade routes that sprawled through their territories. The empires of the west and south had seen them as little more than barbarians, but Karr's dealings with the nomadic tribes had usually been fruitful, when he could find them. The nomads he remembered had understood survival and freedom.

The encampment was tidy, and smelled like roasted meat and smoke, undercut with the musk of livestock. Wagons were parked off to the side—real wagons, and not the odd, enclosed kind that Karr had seen in the city. The men wore simple clothing, while several young boys who rode up were dressed in a puzzling assortment of stripes and symbols that reminded him more of the clothing he had seen in the city.

Women put down their buckets and whistled, which seemed to be a call for more people to emerge from the white tents. Karr lost count. Most everyone came out smiling and laughing, pointing at him, which he endured with patience. He had suffered worse, and there was no maliciousness in their eyes. Just surprise at the giant half-naked man, and a friendly sort of humor.

When Evie shouted explanations, however, the laughter disappeared. Then Soria joined her, speaking the herders' language with an ease and fluidity that made them all blink in shock—and which caused Evie to give her a sharp, speculative look. Karr listened carefully. Oddly enough, some of the words sounded familiar to him. They should not have been.

He and Soria were led into one of the white tents, which was spacious on the inside and bursting with color. The beams above their heads had been painted bright red, a shade featured predominantly in the two beds arranged along the walls, also decorated with extravagantly embroidered rugs that had been hung like tapestries, and that also covered the hard wood planks that lined the floor. A long stuffed chair, large enough to seat three, took up space along the wall, along with a tall wooden cabinet that held bowls and pots, and other items for cooking. In the center of the tent was a stone and iron fire pit. A metal pot sat on top, and a pipe of the same material rose up through a small hole in the tent roof. Karr was fascinated with its design, and with the simple luxuries inside this home, many of which he would have considered unimaginable.

An old woman took his hand. Her brown face was leathery and wrinkled, and she wore a yellow kerchief around her hair that would have cost a fortune in Karr's time, simply for the rarity of the dye and quality of cloth. Her posture was slightly stooped, but her grip was firm, and she studied his face with a gentle warmth that twisted at him like a soft knife. A good pain, but pain nonetheless.

She rattled off a stream of words and patted his arm. Evie laughed outright, as did everyone else stuffed inside the tent. Karr raised his brow at Soria. She was biting her bottom lip, trying not to smile, but she gave up when he looked at her, and grinned. "She said that if she was just a little younger, she would tie you to the back of a horse and drag you off somewhere."

Karr tried to give the old woman a grave look, though it was difficult when she kept stroking his arm and pointing at his chest. He carefully picked up her hand, mindful of his strength, and kissed it—watched as her wrinkled face scrunched up with delight. She pulled away, patting her cheeks and muttering to herself. Everyone around her continued to laugh.

Only Soria remained silent, observing him with a peculiar look on her face that was hard to define, as he was certain no one had ever looked at him in quite the same way. Amusement, yes—but something else that seemed very much like quiet tenderness: warm and gentle, and weary. It moved so deeply through him that when he remembered to breathe, he felt as if he had been half-asleep this entire time, part of him left behind in that tomb. Only, now the missing part had been retrieved and it was quietly burning in the gaze of the woman in front of him.

Do not play games with me, he could still hear her saying, and all around them he felt their hosts taking surreptitious glances at her dangling, empty sleeve. Soria did not appear to notice, but he knew that was an act. When it came to her missing arm, she was aware of every detail, no matter how small. And yet she stood straight, proud, and tore her gaze from him to smile at the children who stared up at her with curiosity. When she spoke to them in their language, they beamed.

They were each given a bowl of sour-smelling white liquid. Karr drank it all, and then choked down some cheese curds. His stomach protested, and he struggled with his discomfort—made worse by the closed-in walls of the tent, and the thick air, which was very smoky, the fire occasionally fed by one of the small girls who tossed dried dung inside the metal chamber. The closed space had not bothered him at first, but the longer he remained indoors, the more he was reminded of the tomb. Of being buried alive.

He forced a smile on his face, nodded his thanks—which was all he could do, lost as he was in language—and made a swift retreat for the door. He practically had to bend in half and crawl to get out, but once he did, the cool swift breeze of evening poured over and through him with brisk, clean strength. He inhaled deeply, grateful for the privilege of breathing.

Goats scattered. Dogs started barking at him and then whining, backing away and then making small charges that only carried them a few feet. They were too scared to attack, too brave to let go.

Karr walked away from the beasts and down to the creek. Rocks shifted beneath his bare callused feet, and he allowed his skin to stretch in a soft haze of golden light that was quick and fleeting, and created a ripple of fur that shifted into scales. It was brief; he quickly resumed his mask of human flesh.

Is it truly a mask? Karr wondered, as the scar over his gut tingled ominously. *And why is it that we hold ourselves to standards of humanity? Why do we even resemble humans at all when we are not wearing our animal skins?*

These were questions that had plagued him before, and again now. Never had there been an answer, nor did he expect one. Perhaps in this new world people knew where stars came from, or the wind, or how shape-shifters and Karr's kind had sprung into existence . . . but Karr preferred the mystery. He crouched by the creek, dipping his fingers into the swift-moving water before tapping them on his tongue. Ice-cold, sweet. He bent and drank deeply, listening as a hum of music rose from the tents behind him: a thrilling trill of notes that shot chills down his spine. Humans had music, and shape-shifters did not. He could not explain that, either.

Tau filled his thoughts, memories of him standing in the old royal courts, listening to plucked strings and beating drums. Uncomfortable beneath the stares of the curious and awed; and yet hungry for such luxuries, and for the attention he received, which both repelled him, and made him feel strong. A false strength, Karr had tried to tell him, but Tau would flash that wolf's smile and say, *"Brother, they think we are gods, and there are few who can claim that privilege. You are both fire and king to these humans. Enjoy it. Savor it. A reward for what you—all of us—suffer."*

Karr had not found it to be much of a reward, and it seemed the world had changed to agree with him. His kind were merely phantoms in the wind. He wondered if Tau had found happiness, later; or had died in the war.

He sat for a long time before catching a familiar scent on the wind. Rocks crunched. He did not turn his head or say a word, and Soria sat down beside him.

"They saved you some more food," she said, after a moment of silence. "Whenever you feel like eating."

Karr glanced over, and found a small cloth bag in

Soria's lap. She followed his gaze and smiled. "Soap. According to Evie, a bath makes everything better. Even in freezing water."

"Sounds foolish. You will become ill."

"I am not going to go swimming," she said wryly. "Just wash my face."

Karr remembered her at the edge of the lake, her shirt pulled up and held in her teeth, soaking her stump in cold water as if seeking relief for pain. He glanced down at her empty sleeve. "How is your arm?"

"You say that like it is still there."

"Your mind thinks so. Until it stops, you have a limb. A ghost."

Soria touched her sleeve. "What are your ghosts like?"

He hesitated, and tapped his forehead. "You have seen some of them. The rest have been swallowed up."

"Is that why you wanted to die?"

Her words were softly spoken but blunt. Irritation sparked inside him, though it was quickly stamped down. He had started this by telling her the truth, and Soria was not a woman who let things go. Nor, he thought, was she a woman so weak as to take her own life simply out of guilt.

Shame dripped through him—for that, and for many things. "I killed my friend's wife."

Soria said nothing. He could not bring himself to look at her. "She was human, a priestess of some name- less goddess, who was not put off by my friend's ap- pearance. Tau . . . could not pass as human, though he was a man in every sense." Karr waved his hand over his face. "He had the face of a wolf, if that makes any sense. Wings of an eagle. It was easier for him to stay like that. It was his natural state."

"I have noticed a rather leonine aspect to your face," Soria said softly, but her face was solemn, as though she was speaking merely to show him that she still could, that his confession had not broken her voice.

"I would not know," he replied just as quietly. "But Tau was proud of his human woman, perhaps more than he should have been."

"You can be proud of the one you love."

"But he did not love her." Karr ran his hand once more through the cold water. "Or rather, he loved the idea of her—which was certainly enough for *her*. Yoana believed that she had given herself to a god, and he did not disabuse her of that notion."

Soria upended the bag, and a small pale brick fell into her lap. "Did they have a child?"

"No." Karr took the brick from her, running his fingers over the smooth, waxy surface, though where his hand was wet it became slick and soft. "I killed her soon after she learned that she was expecting."

Soria went still. So did Karr. He had never said those words out loud. He had hardly let himself think about the unborn child. Just the woman. The rest . . . was too much.

The waxy brick fell out of his hands onto the rocks. He did not pick it up. It was all he could do to lean forward, bowing his head between his legs. Forcing himself to breathe. His stomach hurt so badly he thought his scar had opened again, but there was no blood, and the flesh was whole. Just pain. Just memory.

Soria did not say a word, but instead inched closer until he could feel the heat of her body. Even her scent was warm. He was afraid to look at her. Behind them, he heard men laughing and the bleat of goats. Dogs still barked. The sun had set, and the darkness was falling thick and cool. The skies cleared of the storm.

"Yoana was not supposed to be with us," he said finally, quietly. "Our trade mission to the south was meant to be quick. But she was tired of living among chimera, without regular human contact. She wanted to be useful." Karr reached down and handed Soria her soap. "I was not supposed to lose my mind."

"How did it happen?"

"I do not know." He closed his eyes, trying to remember, but all that filled him was darkness. "The humans we traded with told stories that made us think that some of our kind could be hiding in nearby forests. So I attempted a . . . special ritual to try and find them. I remember nothing after that, until I woke covered in blood. Yoana was dead. Tau told me I had killed her." He scooped water from the creek and ran it over his face. "We cannot predict our triggers, but once we break, we do not risk it happening again."

"And yet you are here," Soria said softly. "Around people. Me. Searching for your kind."

"I know it is irresponsible—"

"It would be if you were really crazy," she interrupted, running a handful of water over her face. "Frankly, I cannot imagine what you went through, or what you are feeling now. But I *have* been around. Seen things. Made only one mistake in my life when it comes to judging character." Her jaw tightened, and her gaze ducked down to the soap in her hand. "I do not think I have made a mistake with you."

"Soria," he began, but she shook her head.

"It would be irresponsible of you to hide. Not the other way around. You are alive for a reason. A second chance. I think you know it, too."

"Easier said," he murmured.

"We all break," she replied, and the expression on her face was heartrending in its fullness of memory. Yet she said nothing else, and dipped the soap into the creek, turning it over and over, one-handed, until it began to foam. She dropped the bar on the cloth bag and rubbed her face, leaving white suds behind. Her eyes were closed.

When Soria bent to rinse her face, her braids fell into the water. Karr pulled them back. She gave him a startled look.

"Let me help you," he said. "No games, no regrets."

"I can do this."

"I know." He looked down, searching for a way to express the feelings that were bubbling inside his heart, boiling up his throat. He felt wounded with the things he wanted to say. "Let me anyway."

He did not expect to see such vulnerability in her eyes. Nor did he expect to feel the same defenselessness. He had battled, and bled, and been tortured. He had died at the end of his own sword. None of that made him feel as naked and small as standing here before this very human woman.

Soria said, quietly, "Just hold my hair, please."

So he did, observing the line of her throat in the shadows, and the flick of her delicate wrist as it splashed water on her face. He watched the tension melt from her, bit by bit, though it was not gone entirely when she finally sat back, sighing. Water dripped down her face, which she tried to dry with her dirty sleeve. Karr caught her hand. "Leave it."

Soria hesitated.

Karr asked, "Are you in pain?"

Again, that vulnerable flicker. He remembered what she had said about running from her friends. Which meant that, except for her parents, no one had cared for her at all since she lost her arm. She had done everything for herself. Lived alone. Healed alone.

Conflict filled her eyes. Even shame. "I am not used to this much activity."

"And so the left side of your body strains, trying to make up for the loss on your right." Karr released her hand. "May I see the injury?"

"No," she began, and then stopped. She held still, eyes distant, thoughtful. And pained.

Slowly, so slowly, almost rigid with tension, she turned and reached over her shoulder to hitch up her shirt. He followed her lead, carefully pushing up her clothing until most of her back was exposed. As well as the remains of her right arm.

Most of it was gone. Some withering had already occurred, and he could see that the skin was dry and flaking. No seepage, no bruises. Just a bony lump at the break. Her limb resembled a small, naked wing. It hurt to look at.

"Does it ache at the end?" he asked.

"Sometimes." Her voice sounded strained. "You going to stare or help?"

Karr dipped his hand into the water. "I am not staring. Just deciphering. Yours is not the first missing limb I have ever seen."

Some of the strain drained away from her. "I suppose they just endured."

"Not everyone was as strong as you." He placed his cold, wet hand on her stump, and she flinched, twisting away from him.

"No," she said. "Just . . . stop."

Karr released her, and she scrambled to her feet, pulling down her shirt. She stooped a moment later to pick up the soap and little cloth bag.

"I am sorry," Soria mumbled, and then glanced over her shoulder at him with dark eyes that seemed to swallow what little light was left in the night. "I am so . . ."

She stopped, jaw tight, and shook her head.

"Sorry," she said again, and walked off toward the encampment.

CHAPTER FOURTEEN

B Y the time Soria reached Evie's *ger*, she had managed to steady herself into some semblance of calm
and dignity. Not easy. Too much had just happened.
From Karr's confession, to his touch on the remains of
her arm—both things had seared her in different ways.

Stupid, she told herself angrily. *You should have
known that would be your reaction.*

But she had not known. She had thought she could
handle having someone—having *Karr*—touch her there.
It should not have been a big deal. It was just a goddamn
part of her mangled arm, and nothing he hadn't seen before if he was to be believed. And she did believe him.

Of course, she had only just begun to have the stomach to look at herself again in the mirror. Mirrors, which
always made everything feel real. She could hardly
expect to feel comfortable with anyone else getting an
up-close look, not to mention touching her injury.

Music drifted from Evie's *ger*—nothing local, if the
English lyrics were any indication; electronic and melodic, and effortlessly moody. Soria paused outside the

door and took one last deep breath of the cool night wind.
The sky was clearing, stars coming out. She could hear
the soft murmur of voices in the camp, and goats making
quiet chewing sounds. Lost and found, she thought, marveling at where she had ended up.

She could not help but look back, to see if Karr had
followed. She did not see him.

*I killed her soon after she learned that she was ex-
pecting.*

Horrible, horrible words. Heartrending, terrifying.
She had watched him break a little, making that confession. Watched a part of him fade that she hadn't
even known was there. And there was not a thing she
could do about it.

She could hardly even remember now what she had
said to him. It was all a blur, based on instinct. She'd
been driven not to make him feel better about the past,
because nothing was going to do that, but to keep him
from wanting to kill himself again. Soria had never been
tempted to take her own life, but she knew all about hiding so deeply that her life hardly existed. Now was not
the time for any of that crap.

*How do you lose your mind so completely that you
kill without realizing it?* Soria wondered. She did not
doubt the truth of his story as he knew it, but it just
seemed such an odd thing that a strong mind could
break so easily. For this to be common . . . And for Karr
to be prone to it?

*He might kill you. If he could snap and kill a preg-
nant woman, he sure as hell can murder you.*

Right. And back home she could be shot at the gas

station, lost in a plane crash, have a lightning bolt explode her into a thousand charred bits—or stop to help an old man at the side of the road and have her life turned upside down forever and ever.

Her stump ached. So did her neck. Ghost fingers tingled. Soria shook her head, smiling bitterly, and went inside the *ger*.

It was well lit with oil lamps and candles. Evie sat at a fold-up card table with a laptop in front of her. Several little girls and boys were spread out on the floor, resting on their stomachs with workbooks before them, pencils in hand. All looked at Soria, but only Evie smiled. The kids had deep concentration lines in their brows, and appeared as though they were either in the throes of some horrible math problem, or trying to excrete a bucketful of prunes.

"I teach in the evenings," Evie said, as Soria returned the little bag of soap. "English, math, whatever they want to learn. I had my parents send me a boxful of study materials. Nothing you can't find at Barnes & Noble."

Soria looked around. Besides the laptop, she saw a bed covered in soft, thick blankets, and another desk that held a surprising amount of electronic equipment, along with several half-full jars of candy. The walls were somewhat plain, with the *ger's* lattice frame clearly visible, but the wood floor was covered in bright rugs, and the heat emanating from the central stove was fierce and sank pleasantly to the bone.

"Is this really immersion?" Soria asked, trying not to smile.

Evie grinned. "Sure. Nomads can be modern, too.

I've got a solar panel rigged on the side of this sucker, along with a satellite. Not for television, but communications. I won a grant to pay for most of it. I blog, write reports back to my thesis adviser, make sure my parents know I'm alive."

"I love technology," Soria said.

"I bought the T-shirt," Evie replied, whipping open her sweater to reveal a faded flimsy tee underneath that was covered in dancing robots.

Soria had to laugh, and plopped herself down on the floor near the children. Evie joined her, bringing along a jar of candy. The kids put their pencils down, staring, and the young woman heaved a highly dramatic sigh before chucking peppermints and chocolate in their direction. Squeals filled the air, and just as quickly descended into contented silence as the girls and boys began studying again, this time with their mouths full.

"Amazing work ethic," said Evie. "I'm probably ruining their teeth."

There were tiny Snickers bars. Soria drooled a little on herself and took one, wrestling one-handed with the wrapper. Finally, she gave up and delicately put one end in her teeth, tugging until she tore a hole large enough to squeeze the chocolate through. She looked up, and found Evie dragging down her laptop to place it on the floor beside them.

"Is there anyone you want to contact?" asked the young woman.

"Yes," Soria replied. "I don't suppose you have a phone?"

"Ham radio. But the signal won't carry all the way to the States." Evie smiled wryly. "I wish."

"You're homesick."

"A little. I love it here, though. You come to this place and you're judged by your actions and what you contribute. Nothing else matters." Evie ran her finger along the bottom of the keyboard. "You know, I read once that some Greek philosopher—at least, I think he was Greek—was told that *so-and-so* is a good person. His name was probably Bob, right? And this philosopher's response was, *'Bob is good for what?'* That always stuck with me. What am *I* good for? But suddenly I come here, and all those weird little things about me that never seemed to fit are suddenly good for something. I feel as though I make sense for the first time in my life."

"I felt like that once. And then, like you, I got lucky. Found my place." Soria said the words, but they sounded hollow in her ears. She had found her place for a while, and while a piece of her felt good to be part of Dirk & Steele again, the baggage that went with it, her self-imposed exile, made it hard not to feel as though she was telling a small lie. She took a bite of chocolate and closed her eyes. "You certainly speak the language like a native."

"I knew someone when I very young who was from this part of the world. She taught me. Started my fascination." Evie hesitated. "You, though, are something else. I thought your name sounded familiar, so I did a search. Found out quite a bit about this prodigy in linguistics who just . . . disappeared about ten, fifteen years ago."

"Really? Do tell."

"She was hot stuff, man. And just hot." Evie turned

the computer around and Soria saw a familiar picture of herself as a teen, standing beside some professor at Harvard whose name she couldn't remember, but whose garlicky breath would be forever embedded in her mind.

It hurt a little to see that photo. There was a look in her eyes that was very young and happy, carefree, not a real stress in the world. Plus, she had two arms.

Maybe regret showed on her face. Evie's smile faded, as if she suddenly realized she had made a mistake, that Soria would take all this the wrong way. But before the girl could stammer out an apology, Soria said, "My mom loves that picture. I haven't seen it in a while. That was a good summer."

Evie looked down, still a bit pale. "Is it true, that you can speak any language in the world?"

"I haven't been everywhere in the world. But . . . I seem to pick things up."

Evie nodded, ready to ask another question, and then seemed to think better of it. Her mouth snapped shut, and she pulled up an empty browser screen. "I hope you have a Yahoo or Google account for your e-mail."

Soria did, and took the computer from her. Evie stood immediately, and began moving to each child, checking their studies and murmuring in their ears.

The Internet connection was slow, but it worked—a small miracle, given where she was. She tapped out a short message to Roland.

Alive. Hope Koni was able to contact you. Heading to Ulaanbataar to follow a lead. I want to

*know what's going on with Long Nu. Next time I
call, don't hold back or else I will sink you.*

*Up yours,
Soria*

She was finishing a note to her parents when the door
opened and Karr peered inside. Her heart gave a deadly
little twist. He looked at nothing, and no one else, but her.

Evie waved at him. "About time you showed up."

Soria could not tell whether he understood—it made
no sense that he should—but after a brief moment of
hesitation, he squeezed himself through the door into
the *ger.* Near the center, where the roof sloped upward,
he could stand at his full height; but he stooped nonetheless, as though he felt the walls touching him. Certainly, the entire space felt smaller with him in it; and it
was not just his size, but the energy of his presence.
When he stood beside her, Soria felt lightning race over
her skin: charged, wild, dangerous.

The children all sat up, staring at him with huge eyes.
Evie held out the jar of candy. He gave it a curious look.

"Take one of the brown ones," Soria said. "Remove
the wrapper. I think you might like it."

He raised his brow, and tried to reach inside the jar.
His hand was too large. Evie laughed, and shook some
out into his palm. "Dude. I think you must be a football
player." Karr gave her a quizzical look, but she had already turned to face Soria.

"What language was that?" the girl asked. "What

you were just using with him? I've never heard anything like it."

Soria hesitated. "It's a rare dialect. Karr is from northern Russia. Very northern. Way out there."

"Huh." Evie's eyes narrowed. "How'd you meet?"

"Fate," she said, hoping the young woman would leave it at that.

She did, but not before giving them a speculative look that made Soria uneasy. Evie was a smart girl. Too smart to spend much time around, no matter how enjoyable her company.

"I'm going to see about finding him some clothes," she said, gathering up the children. "You guys can stay here tonight. I've already radioed someone I know who has a truck. He'll be here tomorrow to take you to the nearest town. It's not too far. Twenty miles or so. You'll probably have to pay for gas, that's all."

"That was kind of you," Soria replied, meaning every word, even though the idea of being driven to a populated area filled her with peculiar dread. But there was no way to simply disappear in the night. Not really. Evie knew her real identity, and she had contact with the outside world. It wouldn't take too much to raise an alert that would bring way too much attention to Soria—and to Karr.

Of course, she could just tell Evie that they wanted to walk, but she doubted that would go over well, either.

I should have lied and given her a different name. Except, she hadn't expected that anyone would recognize her. It had been over a decade. This girl would hardly have been out of diapers at the beginning of all that hoopla.

Evie left with the children. Soria placed the laptop back on the card table. When she turned around, Karr was standing directly behind her, so close she ran into him. His hand grazed her waist but she stepped out of his reach. Bumped into the table behind her. Had to crane her neck to meet his gaze.

"I am sorry," he said. "About earlier."

"You were trying to help." Soria swallowed hard, and nodded to the chocolate in his hand. "You ought to try that."

Karr frowned. "I did not mean to frighten you."

She fidgeted, desperate not to have this conversation. "You did not."

"I was referring to the things I told you, about me and what I did." He swayed closer, but there was nowhere for her to go. "I could expect no one to—"

He never finished. Soria took the Snickers bar from him, bit down on the corner of the wrapper and tore it open. She handed back the chocolate, and he stared at it—and her—for one startled moment. Then he said, the corner of his mouth tilting ever so slightly, "Let me guess. Poison."

"You wish," she replied, glad to have changed the subject. "But no. There are some things we take for granted in this world, at least where I am from. *That* is one of them."

Karr gave the chocolate a tentative sniff, and then his tongue darted against it. He savored the taste for a moment but did not look impressed. Indeed, after a nearly nonexistent nibble, he handed the whole thing back.

"You," she said slowly, "have just committed an act of sacrilege against my people."

"If that is sacrilege," he replied, with a faint smile, "then I want nothing to do with your people."

Soria finished off the tiny Snickers bar in two bites, and wiped her hand against her thigh. "Did you understand what Evie said?"

"Not everything. The terms she used . . ." Karr reached out and rubbed his thumb against the corner of her mouth. "Unfamiliar."

Soria's breath caught. He held up his hand, and she saw a spot of chocolate on his finger. His gaze was intense, dark, and held a hint of pain that was not her imagination. It was hard to think when he looked at her like that. Bits and pieces of her body that she had forgotten existed began tingling, and a flush of heat rode over her skin in a slow wave that made it impossible to start breathing properly again.

"She hired transportation," Soria finally managed to say. "I am afraid we may need to take it in order not to draw attention to ourselves."

"Too late," he rumbled—and then, even softer, "I do not want to hurt you."

"I know."

"I am afraid," he said. "What I did was unforgivable."

Soria closed her eyes, briefly; then she pushed away from the table, craning her neck to stare into his face. "No time for that. Life is too short. I wasted the past year of mine on idiot things. Like, being afraid of how people would see me. Or worse, being afraid of myself. Not being able to *forgive* myself." She yanked on her empty sleeve. "I still have not. This is my fault. Right here. I was stupid."

"I doubt that."

She shook her head, on the verge of telling him what had happened, how she had lost her arm. "I am still afraid of making mistakes. I may never forgive myself. But I suppose I will just have to keep on living. Same as you."

"I murdered—"

Her hand took on a life of its own, covering his mouth before he could finish. He was very tall, and it was quite a stretch. Miles of muscle that she had to lean on to reach his mouth. His lips were firm against her palm, and his hand rose slowly to encircle her wrist. His other hand touched her waist. All the while, his gaze never left hers, and the longer she stared at him, the more she felt herself drifting, as if her feet were floating off the ground and she was made of air.

"I should not feel the way I do about you," he murmured against her palm. "I should be stronger than what I feel."

"Whatever," she said in English, touching his lips with her fingers, marveling at the pure masculine heat of his eyes and body. "I think you should kiss me."

Golden light flared in his eyes, and in moments all that quiet thoughtfulness was consumed by hunger. Karr bent low, grabbing Soria around the waist, pulling her off the ground until her feet dangled. He bowed his head and kissed her so hard she could not breathe. She had never been held so tightly, with such strength, but rather than feeling trapped she felt as though she fit for the first time in her life; that if humans could be puzzle pieces, then she was matched perfectly with this man.

His mouth was hot, relentless, and when his hand grazed her breast the pleasure that rocked through her was so fierce she gasped, squirming closer and forcefully rubbing against his growing hardness. Karr broke off the kiss, a low growl rumbling from his throat. His eyes were glowing, his mouth wet. He licked his lips, and she darted in for another kiss that ended with a long, slow tease of his bottom lip. He made a startled sound, his hands sliding up her back with possessive force, snaking beneath her shirt to touch bare skin.

Control, she told herself, dazed; but she was wet and aching, and it was difficult to think when for the first time in a long while she wanted to reach inside a man's pants and ride him full and flush. She cupped him over the outside of his clothing, her thumb sliding, stroking, savoring the feeling of his straining body. Karr hissed through gritted teeth, muscles straining in his neck.

Soria suddenly found herself sitting on the edge of the table, placed there by Karr. He leaned over, massive, a giant, his large hands braced on either side of her, and lowered his head until their brows brushed. She stayed still, trying to catch her breath, listening to her thundering heartbeat. Every part of her body was tingling, and she suffered the startling, overwhelming urge to laugh.

"Forget science," she muttered in English. "I'm donating my body to magic."

"What?" he breathed.

Just saw it on a T-shirt once, she wanted to tell him, but shook her head, biting her bottom lip—which felt deliciously swollen. "I want to do more of that."

His laugh was quiet and ragged. "I am not certain I would be able to stop."

Soria pressed her cheek against his, closing her eyes. "I would never dream of asking you to."

His breath caught, and she felt something unfurl inside her mind: a sweet light that was small but warm. She did not know what it meant, but moments later she sensed another tickle, and suffered a sensation of falling, down and down, into the rough edges of Karr's mind. She saw no memories, but felt his emotions—raw, wild, aching with loneliness and desire. All of which her presence eased, like that sweet warm light.

A light he was afraid of crushing.

His fear cut her loose, and she tumbled back into herself, flinching as she suffered the same plummeting sensation as in a dream—waking just before impact. She opened her eyes and found Karr watching, his face slightly more leonine, his skin radiant with golden tones. He still looked like a man, but an extraordinary one, breathtakingly striking. Not made from any modern mold, but something far more primal and dangerous.

Soria heard a shuffling sound outside the tent. Karr straightened smoothly, moving with liquid grace, and was standing over by the stove by the time Evie poked her head in. The girl's gaze was sharp, knowing, as she glanced between them, but her focus settled on Soria and was not entirely friendly.

"What kind of e-mail did you send?" she asked.

Soria blinked. "Just letting people know we were okay. Why?"

Evie frowned. "You better come with me."

Dread filled her. She glanced at Karr, and found him looking troubled. His hands were curled into fists.

Outside, the night air was cool. Soria stood braced against the wind, but did not see anything out of the ordinary. Karr said, "I hear something."

After a moment, so did she. A chop-chop sound. A helicopter.

"If you go to the other side of the camp, you can see the lights," Evie said, beside her. "You're not really tourists, are you." It wasn't a question.

Soria gave her a sharp glance. "What?"

But the young woman continued on as if she had said nothing strange. "I need to warn the others. We have to lock down the livestock, or else those choppers will frighten them into running."

Soria grabbed her arm. "We have to go before they get here. Thank you for your help. Please, tell the others how much we appreciated it."

Evie hesitated, and then hugged her hard—a surprising gesture that brought equally unexpected tears to Soria's eyes. "Don't be a stranger," whispered the young blonde woman, who then turned quickly on her heel and began running through the camp, shouting.

Karr's hand clasped Soria's shoulder. "What is that sound?"

"Trouble," she said, craning her neck to look up at him. "Or help. But either way, I do not want to find out here, with these people around."

It was too late. Somewhere close, a woman cried out. It was a muffled sound, choked off at the end, distinctly startled and afraid.

Soria flinched. Karr took off running. She tried to follow, but he moved like a ghost, hardly seeming to touch the ground as he flowed through the air. Golden light flickered over his skin, scales flowing like pearls. And then the light went out and he vanished in the darkness.

Soria staggered to a stop, her eyes unable to adjust. Except for bare glimmers from the pale *gers*, she felt blind. She heard goats bleating on her left, and Evie's voice ahead, on her right, movement inside the tents—but all those were safe sounds, and she had the sudden chilling sense that she was not alone with anyone, or anything, that was safe.

She took several tentative steps, mouth shut tight, willing her eyes to adjust to nothing but starlight. There had been campfires earlier—she had burned that damned bloodstained sheet in one of them, much to the consternation of all who watched—but she saw no hint of flames now. Everything had been stamped out.

Air whispered across the back of her neck, replaced by something cold and hard. Soria resisted the urge to clutch her chest, and took a deep breath. "Who sent you?"

The gun barrel pressed harder—and then she sensed rather than saw a ghost fly out of the darkness. She heard a whuffing sound behind her, and the gun disappeared.

She heard a loud crack, like that of a breaking bone, and she turned and found Karr—naked again—

towering over the crumpled body of a man. *Dead*, she thought, and felt no twinge of remorse.

He reached for her hand, but just before his fingers closed around her wrist, Soria heard a popping sound. Karr staggered sideways, grunting. More pops filled the air, small impacts thudding against him. He dragged Soria into his arms, and began running. She yelped as something hard and painful hit her back. A rubber bullet.

For a moment, all she could hear was the harsh rasp of Karr's breathing; and then shouts trickled through, and screams. Dogs started barking, drowning out the frightened wails of children.

A loud whistle cut through it all. Karr went down. Soria flew out of his arms, rolling over rocks and grass. It seemed to take forever to stop, and another eternity to move again. After an intense, dazed struggle, all she managed to do was prop herself up on her hand and knees, ready to vomit.

She crawled to Karr, who was struggling with the tangled netting wrapped around his legs. His claws were out, but that seemed to be doing him little good. *Metal wire*, Soria thought. Almost thin as thread, cutting into his skin.

He saw her coming, and snarled. "Soria, *go*. Run."

She ignored him, just kept struggling to reach his side. She got to Karr just as men came racing from the shadows, and threw herself over his body—thinking, maybe, that might protect him. He tried to push her away, but she wrapped her arm around his neck with suffocating strength.

"Soria," he rasped.

"Shut up," she muttered. "All we have here is each other, remember?"

His gaze blazed golden hot, and in one quick move he rolled over, pinning her to the ground, shielding her with his massive frame. He stared at the men surrounding them, and a snarl tore free of his throat—which was shimmering, shifting, fur chasing scales over his skin as his muscles contorted. Fangs appeared inside his mouth.

It was hard to breathe with him on top of her. Soria craned her neck, trying to see what was going on, and saw two bare feet step close. A moment later those feet were joined by a hand, knees, and a familiar sharp face, eye patch neatly in place. Serena peered at them, crouched low, dressed in a seamless black body suit. She held a cattle prod.

"Still alive. And looking cozy," she remarked.

"Fuck you," Soria replied. "He's not what you think."

"You don't know what I think," Serena said, and stood. "Get them in the helicopter."

CHAPTER FIFTEEN

Karr could not fight them. He tried, but the leopardess stabbed him in the back with a long rod,
sending a paralyzing jolt through his body. He collapsed,
twitching, choking on his own spit and fury as his hands
were bound behind his back with the same thin metal
wire that had become tangled around his legs.

Soria was dragged away from him. The men were
rough with her. Karr could see little of their expressions,
but their scents were acrid, angry. One of them—bald,
pale, and hard-jawed—grabbed her braids and yanked
back her head so far and with such strength that Karr
thought her neck would break. Soria's breath rattled, but
she reached up, clawing at his eyes. He raised his fist—

The leopardess barked out a single word.

The bald man shot the shifter a cold and deadly
look, still ready to punch Soria. *"I lost friends because
of them,"* he growled.

"Your friends were stupid and careless," Serena replied. *"If you continue showing the same traits, I'll kill*

you myself—and then pay the rest of your men triple for the privilege."

Hate filled his eyes, but the bald man let Soria go. She staggered, and the leopardess caught her arm. Soria did not fight her, but looked down at Karr with unflinching determination. Serena yanked her away.

Karr tried to watch, but the bald man and several others hooked a thick rope to the bindings around his legs and began dragging him across the grass. Metal wire cut into his flesh, as did rocks. The pain burned through him, but he clamped his mouth shut and did not make a sound. The men kept watching him, smiling grimly whenever they thought he would break. Frowning when he did not.

Easy enough. All he could think of was Soria and the look in that man's eyes, the thick strength of his raised fist.

Dead, Karr thought, staring at the back of that pale, hairless head. *You are dead. Even if Soria is your ally.*

Although maybe she was not an ally anymore, he realized, watching as she was unceremoniously shoved into a dark hole cut into the side of a remarkably odd object: sleek and rounded on one end, sharp on the other; black as night, with long dark blades sprouting from its roof. Karr felt a quick stab of uneasiness when he saw the thing: too strange, its purpose was not easily divined.

He was tossed in after her. Behind him, he heard continuing sounds of disturbance in the nomad encampment. It wasn't violence, exactly, but there were shouts of anger, fear, and confusion.

Soria reached for him, sliding her arm around his

chest. Her touch was warm and solid, and unexpectedly soothing. This was not the first time he had ever
been bound and captive, but he had always been alone
in such moments. No kind touches. No compassion. It
made a difference . . . and he wished that were not so.
It meant weakness. It meant he had something to lose.

Soria glared at the leopardess. *"They're good people.
If you hurt them—"*

*"These men are not interested in terrorizing goats
and their keepers,"* replied the shape-shifter, sitting
down on a small leather bench. *"Just the job. You. Him."*

Soria glanced at the dark-clothed men climbing in
after them. *Mercenaries,* Karr thought, following her
gaze. He could see it in their eyes, which were hard,
steady, accustomed to death. A regular soldier might
be all those things, but men who fought and killed for
money were a different breed entirely.

The bald man climbed in, staring. The area they filled
was crowded. Men squeezed together on low benches.
Soria tore her gaze away, and looked again at Serena.

*"These are the same kind of men who came for us
back at the beginning,"* she pointed out. *"You sent them.
You double-crossed your own people."*

"No," Serena replied, her golden eye glittering. *"But
circumstances have changed. I was forced to make a
choice."*

Karr nudged Soria with his shoulder. "She has allied
herself with the dragon," he guessed.

Serena gave him a sharp look. *"What did he say?"*

Soria hesitated. Karr understood why: reveal too much,
and the leopardess would guess that he comprehended

her language. Better to maintain that secret for as long as possible.

You trust Soria to protect you, he realized then, with some shock. *You trust her to lie to her own people for you.*

It was a revelation. For all the connection he felt toward her, all those deep feelings he could not name but that twisted him like a knotty riddle, this was something he had not considered. But considering it now made him feel like a blind man able to see—not the world, but inside himself. He trusted her. Apparently, he trusted her with his life.

"He wants to know why you're doing this," Soria said, confirming his feelings with a lie. *"And I want to know how Long Nu got you under her thumb."*

Serena's face hardened, and she snapped her fingers at someone behind Karr. He heard a loud, screeching whine that made him wince, followed by a deafening roar and an unholy wind that felt like the spine of a storm. He tried to move closer to Soria, and the leopardess slammed her foot down on his shoulder. Claws poked from her toes, digging into his flesh.

Everything lurched. Karr glanced over his shoulder and watched in amazement as they floated off the ground. He tried to see more, but a wall slid between him and the night, cutting off the roaring wind.

Soria grabbed Serena's foot and shoved it off Karr's shoulder. *"Where are you taking us?"*

"Someplace productive." Displeasure twisted the shape-shifter's mouth. *"What have you learned from him?"*

"What does Long Nu want?"

Serena eyed her, and then eyed Karr. *"He does not understand us, does he?"*

The incredulity that passed over Soria's face was so convincing, he very nearly found himself believing that he *was* imagining all those words. Except, while he might have lost his mind once before, no hallucinations had ever been involved. Just a blackout. Darkness, swallowing him. Spitting him out into a sunlit morning where he was covered in blood, and there was a woman's body nearby. And his friends—Tau, in particular— staring at him as though he were a monster.

A wave of nausea passed through him. He swallowed hard, focusing on a spot on Soria's foot. Her shoes were odd. He had not noticed until now. Scuffed leather that had once been white, they were laced with delicate white string. Seeing such a simple yet alien article of clothing, combined with every other little and not-so-little thing— enclosed wagons moving of their own accord, lights that burned without flames, the prevalence of metal, and the fine delicate substance that those children had been reading (reading!) in that nomad tent—combined once again to hammer home his displacement. Karr had no home. He had no one.

Except Soria, he thought.

Yet he could not be certain if his feelings toward her were genuine or due more to the fact that he was utterly, magnificently alone. Alone, with only one person in the world who could understand him. Desperation could make a heart feel many strange things, attachment toward a captor included. Even if that was something that had never happened to him before.

You think too much about the wrong things. Focus on now, he told himself sternly, studying the men and Serena. *Sort out the rest when you have the luxury of knowing you will survive.*

The air was bumpy, and the metal box in which they traveled—a flying wagon, Karr thought—rattled too much for comfort. But they were not in it long before he felt the beginnings of a slow descent. Soria tensed, and Karr rumbled, softly, "Stay with the shape-shifter. She will protect you from the men." That was all he cared about.

"I am not leaving you," she muttered.

"This has happened before. I was caught several times during the war. Caught and tortured." He held her gaze, feeling the scrutiny of everyone seated around them. "I have always escaped. Stay alive. I will find you."

Soria's jaw tightened. One of the men said, *"Sounds rabid. All that fucking growling."*

"Sex talk," said another, and laughed.

The shape-shifter gave her men a cold stare, which she then pinned on Soria and Karr. Disturbingly thoughtful, her one good eye narrowed, glinting sharp as the light on a blade. Karr stared back, unflinching. Finally, she looked away.

The structure around them shuddered and then went still. The surrounding roar quieted to a whine and then an odd rhythmic sound that was just beginning to die when the men slid the vehicle open and began jumping out. Karr's leg restraints were hooked again, and he was dragged out, falling several feet. It knocked the breath out of his lungs. Soria scrambled after him, shouting at

the men. No one paid attention. Karr wanted to tell her
to save her voice, but could not find his own.

He smelled another shape-shifter. A new scent. Wild
and old, and full of ash, like the remains of a burned forest. Except, the scent was cut with a spice that reminded
him of a hot jungle: warm, wet, verdant. He craned his
neck, trying to see.

Finally, he did. It was an old woman wearing a human
form, golden eyes glowing faintly. Her hair was silver,
mixed with strains of black, and she was small, slightly
hunched, clad in a glossy dark coat of fine cloth and loose
pants. She was barefoot, like Serena. Her hands were
hidden, but Karr would not have been surprised to see
claws pressing into her palms. She radiated an unusual
energy, like the edges of a storm gathering lightning.

The old shifter ignored everyone but Karr. When he
was tossed at her feet, a rattling cough escaped her, as
if her lungs were being squeezed with a fist. He met
her gaze, but unlike Serena she did not back down.
She showed no fear, no hate, no compassion. Nothing
but emptiness.

Soria was brought close. Spine straight, left hand curled
into a loose fist. Her empty sleeve twisted in the wind.
Around them, a short distance away, he saw the sharp
edges of a human settlement. Few lights, no people.

The woman spoke to Soria. She used an incomprehensible melodic language, one that reminded him of
the words his caretaker had uttered back in his cell.
Same rolling tones and sharp accents. Her voice was
smoother than her skin, soft and compelling—but not
in a gentle way. Listening to her reminded Karr of the

old shifter queens and human royalty, men and women of such power and authority that they found it unseemly to raise their voices.

Soria remained silent, jaw tight, staring back with disgust and fury infusing her scent. Utterly, carelessly defiant.

Serena walked up behind her, graceful and swaying. *"She has formed an attachment to him. I doubt she will help you."*

"You bet your ass I won't," Soria snapped, not once taking her gaze off the old woman. *"Who the fuck do you think you are, pulling this shit? Kidnapping, imprisonment, torture? What has he done to you?"*

"He exists," said the old woman, a hint of weariness in her voice that was utterly at odds with her steely demeanor.

Soria dragged in a deep breath. *"He can't tell you why he's alive. He doesn't know."*

"You misunderstand me," she replied, weariness bleeding into malice. *"I do not care why he is alive. Resurrection and immortality are the least of my concerns. What I want to know is where the others of his kind are hiding."*

Soria stared in disbelief, but Karr was not surprised. Thousands of years had changed nothing. He could not hide his contempt as the old woman met his gaze, studying him with cold, hard, unbending strength.

I am stronger than you, he thought. *Let me go and I will show you.*

Her eyes narrowed, almost as if she heard him. Karr

clamped down immediately on his thoughts, tightening his focus. His mother had been born with limited mind-gifts. Magic. Karr had shown little talent for it; his attempt at mentally searching for others of his kind being a prime example of just how disastrous his efforts could be. But pure-blooded dragons were never to be underestimated. And though no one had said so, he was quite certain he knew who this old woman was.

She turned and walked away, a slow shuffling motion that kicked dust from the grass. Soria lunged, but Serena grabbed her arm, holding her back. Soria tried to shake her off, but when it did no good, she looked at the retreating old woman, and shouted, *"What will you do, Long Nu? What will you do when you find them?"*

Long Nu said nothing, though her pace briefly faltered. Karr tugged on the metal wire binding his wrists and said, "She will kill us all."

"Yes," Soria muttered in his language, glancing at Serena. "I figured."

No one eased the tightness of the wires cutting into his skin. No one took care as he was hauled another long distance across open ground. Rocks cut his face and chest, and bruised his genitals, and he felt the wet heat of blood running down his legs. He was dragged the entire way, suffering in silence, wondering if he would find himself crippled by night's end.

Soria could do nothing to help him. Serena hauled her out of sight into the human settlement, which consisted of wooden structures, a street, and little else. No people. No signs of life. Even the scent of the place was dull and dead, in the same way as a corpse: something vital was missing; a spark was gone.

The mercenaries spoke to each other as they dragged Karr. He could not understand them, even though the sounds of the words were familiar. Not being near Soria made the difference, he decided. Somehow, he truly was absorbing her gift for language. Or rather, *her* language.

He found her again when he was finally dumped inside the front room of a small brown structure. She was seated in a chair—tied down to it, her left arm bound behind. Her braids were even more frayed, and the flush that filled her olive cheeks was deep and rich. Her eyes were wild with anger, lips clamped so tightly they disappeared into a thin line. She rocked forward when she saw him, the back of her chair rising off the floor and then falling so hard he thought it would break.

Long Nu stood behind Soria, her hands still clasped behind her back. Serena was nowhere in sight, though her scent lingered. The old shifter ignored the mercenaries as they left, though the bald-headed man took the longest to go. His gaze lingered on Soria with thoughtful menace, and after he shut the door, he loitered outside, his gear shifting, rubbing, every time he moved. Karr could hear this, though he barely had the strength to lift his head.

Karr lay on his back, savoring being still. Fighting not to show his pain, or wince every time he breathed. It took all his willpower, but when he glanced at Soria and saw the tears in her eyes, he knew what he looked like, and no amount of hiding was going to change that.

Long Nu drew near. Karr watched her, studying the lines of her face, the emptiness of her eyes. A careful blankness, he thought. She was trying hard not to show him her true feelings.

"I know you understand me," she said quietly to him. *"Do not waste your energy trying to pretend otherwise."*

She glanced over her shoulder at Soria. *"You did something to him."*

"No," Soria replied, tugging on her restraints. *"You're mistaken."*

The old shifter gave her a grim look. *"Try all you like, but you won't free yourself. I have heard how savage you are when cornered. I took precautions."*

Soria froze. Karr murmured, "Tell her I do not know the answer to what she wants. She can ask me all that she pleases, but I am alone in this world. If there are others, they are as unknown to me as how to speak your tongue."

Soria gave him a long look, wetted her lips, and then translated. Long Nu watched him all the while, her gaze piercing, sharp. *Reading my mind,* he thought, scrambling to remember more of what his mother had tried to teach him of such things. Some he had put into place the moment he sensed that the old dragon was a mind reader. But on the surface of his thoughts, all he could think of was the stretch of his mother's powerful wings, and the golden light of her gaze, which was warm and soft and utterly the opposite of the old woman who stood before him.

Long Nu shut her eyes, drawing in a deep, hissed breath. *"Your mother was a dragon."*

"And she was murdered by one," Karr replied, in his own language. "My parents were killed by those they thought were their friends."

"For having you," Long Nu breathed, as if she understood his every word. *"Making certain they could not have another."*

Soria made a low sound. Karr could not look at her. "You can read my mind. You know I am telling you the truth. I cannot tell you whether there are more."

"But you know how to find them," she said, her voice deathly quiet.

Karr's breath caught. "No."

Soria hopped in her chair, dragging it toward Long Nu. *"Stop this."*

"I cannot," whispered Long Nu, still staring at Karr. *"There are things you do not understand."*

His scar tingled. Fury rose through him, and grief. Now was his chance to ask how the war had ended, and what had happened to his people—but he suddenly could not bear to hear what she would tell him. "I counseled mercy during the war, though we were shown none. I was called a fool for it, but I believed in being better than your kind." He lurched upward, growling against the pain. "I am not the same man. I will not make that mistake again."

Long Nu glanced at Soria. *"You already did."*

Soria rocked violently forward. *"You had an alliance with Dirk and Steele. We trusted you!"*

"I know what I am sacrificing. I do this for the good of my people. They cannot be allowed to know what he is. What any of them are."

"Or what is possible," Karr rumbled, tearing his gaze

from Long Nu to look at Soria. "The crow did not know. He did not believe such a thing as me could exist. Our history has been murdered. But if that changed—"

Long Nu's hands flashed golden as the sun, claws sprouting like hooked daggers from her wrinkled fingers. Scales burst over her skin, and her slow movements suddenly quickened as though her joints were made of hot oil. She did not hit him. He thought she would, and braced himself—

He was still bracing himself when she turned and lashed out at Soria. Time slowed down. Karr could not think, could not react. All he could do was stare in horror as the old shifter razored her claws through the air, straight for Soria's throat.

But Long Nu stopped, perfectly still, just before making the killing blow. Her claws were pressed so tightly against the human woman's skin that blood welled under each sharp point. Soria sat frozen, eyes huge. Her breathing was ragged. So was Karr's. He had never been so frightened in all his life— a shocking, nauseating fear that put such pressure on his chest that he thought he might suffocate.

"I will kill her if you do not do as I ask," whispered Long Nu, though there was a tremor in her voice, and her hand shook, ever so slightly. All that emptiness in her eyes was faltering now, flickering with heat and pain; but Karr was not reassured. He was quite certain she would do as promised. Dragons never lied.

"Coward," he breathed. "You are nothing but an old bitch queen. Using pain and tricks to get your way. Too afraid to stand against me with honor."

"There is no honor in survival," Long Nu said. *"Survival demands sacrifice. And to live, sometimes it means being the monster. You should ask* her *about that."*

Karr glanced at Soria, and found her staring up at Long Nu. She was rigid, trembling—but not with fear, just anger. And a stupendous stubbornness that bled into her scent like smoke. The resolve in her eyes was frightening, almost as if he were looking at a different woman.

"Do not help her," Soria whispered, her accent thick as it choked on the growling tones of his language. "Karr. Do not dare help her."

Do not. Do not break, he told himself. Not now, when he had already endured so much. He had suffered worse pain, more terrible conditions than this . . . and had never found himself so close to the precipice as he was now.

It was not even the threat to Soria that made him falter. Looking at her made him feel stronger, the resolve in her eyes as rock solid as anything he had ever known. It made his heart burn with passion for her, even then, in that moment.

Instead, what cut him deeply, and made him question himself, was the endless cycle of it all: that this should be happening again, after so much time, even when it appeared that few shifters were left and perhaps no chimeras at all. He could not fathom the stupidity and uselessness of the old vendetta.

And yet, here he was. Trapped. Karr had once thought that death was preordained, and he had taken his own life; he had removed himself from fate. Or so he had thought. Now, thousands of years later, he was set for death once again. This shifter would murder him no matter what he did. She would likely murder Soria, simply for knowing the truth.

If he found others of his kind, he would be condemning them as well. If he did not first lose his mind.

You are bound. You can do no harm except to yourself. You will not kill Soria. You will not hurt her. But the idea of losing his mind terrified him more than death. Death was easy. He knew that firsthand. Just darkness and nightmares. But to live, to live with the actions one committed, whether conscious or not . . .

Memories swelled inside him. His scar tingled, and he felt a brief pressure around his throat like fingers. Those fingers were sliding up his neck, were in his gut, probing his flesh. He gritted his teeth.

Long Nu narrowed her eyes and said cryptically, *"There is something about you. Something more than your blood. How did you survive?"*

Soria bared her teeth. *"I thought you didn't care."*

"She cares about power," Karr remarked. "Resurrection is a great magic. Controlling and killing my kind is power. She is a queen, and cares for nothing else."

Long Nu's eyes flared hot with light. *"I care for my people. I do this for them."*

"You murder for them. For what? To keep them ignorant and pure?"

Soria blew out her breath. "Heil, *Hitler.*"

Karr did know who Hitler was, but Long Nu gave her a hateful look. Murderous, even. Whatever was driving the shifter ran deeper than the threats of the old queens with whom Karr had dealt. Those female shape-shifters had considered chimeras to be a very real threat: volatile, unpredictable, far too potent to be trusted. Karr could not always disagree.

But there was a dark river running through the old woman in front of him, dark and pained and deadly, and it made her more dangerous than the past queens. Emotions were running her actions. Not calculation. Not just survival.

"Does your word mean anything?" Karr asked, his voice strained, barely recognizable. He was wondering if she translated his words directly from his mind, or Soria's. "Or have you lost all your dignity?"

Her gaze did not flinch, nor did her hand slip one fraction from Soria's throat. *"I keep my promises. Always. That is no lie."*

Dragons do not lie, Karr told himself again, and he believed her. He could see the truth in her eyes, in her scent. So, oaths still meant something.

"Promise there will be no death," he said roughly. "Kill me if you like, but no other. Not Soria, not anyone I might find. They are innocent in this matter. If they have survived this long unknown to you and yours, they can have no interest in causing the trouble you seem so eager to avoid."

"Karr, no!" Soria snapped, leaning forward against Long Nu's claws, cutting herself more deeply upon them. Blood trickled down her throat, and the sight of it made him ill. It reminded him too much of Tau's wife, Yoana, dead on the shore of the river with her neck torn out, her expression frozen in horror.

He controlled himself, though. He watched the old

shifter, and caught the moment when something changed in her eyes.

"I promise," she whispered. *"I give you my word."*

A great and terrible fear swallowed Karr's heart, but he washed it down with resolve, along with the realization that part of him had given up hope that his kind still existed. He had succumbed, on a primal level, to the idea that he was utterly alone, with nothing to lose.

You do *have something to lose*, he reminded himself.

But the attempt would keep Soria safe, so it was right. There was honor in it.

As for the rest, he could very well be wrong that there were no chimeras left in the world. If that was the case, then it was good that he still remembered some of his mother's lessons. Like how to fool a mind reader. Assuming he still had a mind when this was over.

CHAPTER SIXTEEN

SOMETHING was wrong. Besides the obvious, something was very wrong with Karr.

Soria felt safe harboring that thought. Long Nu was obviously telepathic, but she was not as strong as Roland, and he had taught Soria some things over the years. Here and there, bits and pieces. Languages might be all her mind seemed capable of handling, but both she and Roland had always known that the root of that gift lay in the ability to read another person's mind. And a mind reader was just as vulnerable as normal people to being scanned.

Roland had taught Soria how to partition her mind. How to create blocks of safe space. It was an odd and difficult thing to do, but she'd had years to practice, and not just with Roland. There were others at Dirk & Steele who could play mind games. She had gotten very good at keeping things private.

Something is wrong, she thought again, disturbed that Karr had acquiesced so easily—not just to selling out his kind, but attempting *this*, whatever it was. It sounded like the same thing that had caused him to lose his mind all those years before, and his grief and horror at that still rocked inside her, relentless and searing. She doubted he would ever forgive himself, though he might learn to live with the hole in his spirit, just as she had learned—was still learning—to live without her arm.

Because of that, however, Soria felt confident Karr would rather rip out his own heart than risk murdering an innocent, or before condemning anyone to being murdered. No matter what Long Nu promised.

The old shifter backed away from her, and stood beside Karr with her hands clasped behind her back. "If you trick me, I will know," Long Nu told him. "And I will kill Soria."

Betrayer, betrayer, Soria projected at the old woman, knowing that much would be heard. *Dirk & Steele helped you, offered safe haven to your shape-shifters. We have kept your secrets, and this is what you do. You're nothing but a self-interested murderer, a piece of trash. You think that any of us are going to let you—*

Long Nu shot her a deadly look. Soria did not stop. She let her thoughts run wild, thinking of the most disgusting, hateful insults she could imagine, savoring the faint flush that appeared in the old woman's cheeks and the glitter of her golden eyes.

Hit me, she pushed. *Go ahead, do it. Show how tough you are, bitch, threatening a cripple tied to a chair.*

The old woman's mouth became a hard line. "I could have had you killed, had I wanted. Don't make me change my mind."

"Why didn't you?" Soria pressed, leaning against

her restraints and trying to ignore the narrow look that Karr gave her. "Because you needed a translator?"

"I thought I did." Long Nu glanced grimly at Karr. "He has an interesting mind—more so than I imagined when I learned of his existence." She held out her hand, scaled and clawed. The very tips of her fingers, little more than black hooks, were still wet with Soria's blood. She held them over Karr's mouth. "Taste her blood, chimera. Maybe it will help you concentrate."

"You know better than that," Karr growled. And then his jaw clenched, and Soria heard an odd crunching sound. Blood seeped over his bottom lip. He had bitten his tongue.

"Blood calls to blood," whispered Long Nu, watching him intently, head tilted as if she were listening for something.

Karr ignored her, looking straight into Soria's eyes. *"Maybe I* will *take some of her blood. If I have her permission."*

"You do," Soria said without thinking. She trusted that glint in his eye, which she felt as though she had known forever.

Long Nu hesitated, and again clasped her hands behind her back. "You're wasting time. Call to your people. Find them, if they exist."

Karr fixed his gaze on her. *"Remember your promise."*

Long Nu said nothing. Soria did not trust her. Karr was going to die here tonight, and so was she. No one was going to help or spare them.

No one helped you the last time you were tied up,

she thought, battling the same unholy urge to scream
that had hit her when Serena first started binding her to
the chair. There were so many memories, so much that
swelled and burned inside her, leaving nothing but
white rage. But, better rage than fear. Better rage than
tears and helplessness.

She jerked against her bonds and felt the phantom
presence of her arm swinging free. It was a useless
little ghost making pain in her head. Soria bit the inside of her cheek, tasting blood and wanting more.

Karr gave her one last look and closed his eyes. Soria
hoped he knew what he was doing. She hoped to God
that it would get them out of here—untied, or whatever,
because when and if she found herself free again, she
was going to take care of this. She was going to rip apart
Long Nu and anyone else who got in her way.

Horror crept through at the violence of her thoughts,
and yet she could not shake them. It made her want to
hide for another year in the dark.

Long Nu stood near Karr, her back slightly turned.
Soria tried to scoot her chair closer to him, ignoring the
look the old woman gave as she did. Karr looked terrible,
covered in deep, oozing cuts and bruises, but he began to
hum to himself, a low, sonorous sound that was more a
purr than a melody. Golden light trickled from beneath
his closed eyelids, seeped down his face, and left behind
a trail of fur and golden scales. His cheekbones shifted,
growing wider and more pronounced, while his hair
thickened, roots spreading down the sides of his neck.
Muscles bunched in his already impressive chest, expanding and thickening . . . and she watched his limbs

with concern: the wire was already cutting into his skin, a simple but effective trap.

Karr did not transform all the way, simply lingered in a half state, more human than animal. The low purr that rumbled from his chest gained strength until the sound felt like thunder rolling through Soria's bones. She remembered what he had told her about losing his mind: the nothing, the emptiness, followed by the realization that he had murdered. He had no memories of the event, except the testimony of his friends.

His eyes began moving beneath his eyelids. Long Nu watched without blinking, still as stone and tense. This made Soria angry all over again, afraid for him. She scooted forward until she was so close that the tips of her shoes could touch his leg—and they did, just a brush.

And Soria got sucked into his mind.

The sensation was twisting and violent, almost as if she were swirling down a drain. But when it stopped, unlike her past encounters with his thoughts, she was not bombarded with memories. There was just darkness, still and quiet. She did not feel Karr there, but sensed a great eye in the distance, unblinking and golden: Long Nu. Spying.

But just as suddenly as she arrived, she was yanked away—cut sideways through a sticky veil that Soria could feel on her mind like gum—until she was through, free, and warm inside familiar arms.

"I did not expect that," Karr rumbled.

Soria shuddered. "You are crazy."

"Yes," he replied, and turned her around so that they faced each other. Even in this place that was not real, she had to crane her neck to look up into his eyes; and each movement seemed magnified as though physical action were an echo felt again and again, until dying into some lost place inside her dreaming muscles.

But what a dream. Karr was made of golden light, glowing and radiant as though every perfect dawn were burning under his skin. Flames flickered inside his eyes, licks of shimmering heat streaming down his tawny hair. He was otherworldly—an Adonis, an Apollo, something so beyond her imagination that she could barely see past the shine. And yet, there was something about him that still retained humanity: blazing, indefinable, and raw. Karr might not be human, not by any stretch of the imagination, and yet he was *more* human than many who bore the name.

"Is this what losing your mind feels like?" Soria asked. "Because I think I just did, quite literally."

He squeezed her shoulders. His hands were large and warm, even here. "I found something."

"You found something," she echoed. "I thought you were afraid of doing this."

"I am." Karr's eyes blazed more brightly. "I suppose I could be afraid of everything, as anything could be a trigger. But I am still me. If that changes, my body is bound. I might cripple myself if I lose control, but I am prepared for that. I would only hurt me."

"You did not have to do this," Soria remarked, feeling the echo of each word sink through her. "Can Long Nu hear us?"

"No." Karr tugged her, gently. "Not here. Close your eyes and then open them."

She did as he asked, suffering the disconcerting sensation of floating—and when she could see again, it seemed as though she were. The world was spread beneath her; or rather, an abstract view of it. There was nothing but an impression of shapes bound by dips and curves, and scattered among them were lights. Tiny stars.

"You see?" he murmured, his voice filled with awe. "They exist."

"How . . . ?" Soria meant to ask, *How do you know, how did you do this*? But before she could utter the words, a boom smashed through their small cocoon, and Soria was flung back into her body. Her chest ached and it was hard to breathe. Sharp pain lanced through her skull, and she sagged forward, hardly strong enough to keep from pitching sideways and knocking herself and the chair to the floor.

Someone grabbed her braids, yanking back her head. Soria tried to open her eyes, but they felt glued shut. Even getting slapped hard enough to make her ears ring did little to help, though the pain was enough to pull her back into true consciousness. She got hit again, on the other cheek, and the sting made her angry.

She cracked open her eyes, found herself staring at Serena. "Hit me harder," she muttered. "It's just getting good."

Serena slapped her so hard the front feet of the chair lifted off the ground. "How's that?"

Soria spat blood on the floor—and became dimly aware of someone behind her, fiddling with the handcuff on her left wrist. Her vision was a bit blurred, but there was another person in front of her, cutting at the wire binding Karr's legs. Karr's arms were already free, and his eyes were just beginning to flutter open.

Beside him lay Long Nu, limbs askew, mouth slightly open. She was not dead, just unconscious. Something sharp and dartlike, jutted from her shoulder.

"No one's ever going to trust you," Soria said to Serena, realizing that a double-cross had taken place. "What now? You change your mind?"

Serena gave her an icy smile that would have frozen blood had Soria's not already been flowing cold. "Whoever said it needed to be changed?"

Her handcuff snapped open. Soria flipped the shapeshifter a one-finger salute, then craned around to look at the person who had freed her. Red hair filled her vision, along with the familiar lean line of a pale jaw.

"Yo," she muttered, rubbing her sore wrist against her thigh.

"Greetings," Robert replied, speaking an archaic form of Arabic. He glanced sideways, and said in slightly accented Taiwanese, "Ku-Ku. Go check the perimeter."

The person who had been using wire cutters to free Karr stood gracefully and turned. It was the girl, though Soria had not recognized her from the back. She wore a black body suit much like Serena's, except that her feet were clad in black high-top sneakers decorated with sparkling pink laces. Ku-Ku's glossy back hair was pulled up high, and she blew a pink gum bubble at Soria's face before reaching down and picking up a machine gun that she slung over her shoulder. Her eyes were still cold and empty, and ringed in glittering black liner. Soria felt properly intimidated.

Ku-Ku slipped silently out the door, and shut it behind her. Serena said, "You do know she's too young for you, Rob."

"Everyone is too young for me," he replied, taking the cutters to clip at the wire embedded in Karr's flesh. "But I assure you, our relationship is strictly professional. I had to regenerate my testicles once, and that is not something I want to repeat."

Soria rubbed her aching head. She was very ill, and it was affecting her hearing.

Slowly, carefully—because her knees were quite wobbly—she slid out of her chair and crawled to Karr's side. His hands had been freed but were a bloody mess, much like the rest of him. She patted his face, very gently, and his eyes opened for a brief moment. He stared at her, but she was certain he wasn't really seeing her. His lips moved soundlessly.

Serena said, "He needs to move. Now. Wake him up, or I will."

Soria gave her a dirty look. "You'll probably give him a concussion. Why don't you mind your own—?"

Robert reached out, grabbed Karr's balls, and twisted. Karr's eyes shot open, and a loud grunt of pain passed his lips as he jerked upward, swaying and furious. He tried to lunge at Robert, but was too weak to hit him before the man moved smoothly out of arm's reach, wiping his hand on his pants, and saying in the click language of the San Bushman of the Kalahari, "Soria, make him start wearing pants."

Soria stared, even as she tried to steady Karr. "One

of these days you're going to tell me how you know all these languages."

"I get around," Robert said dryly, in Russian. "But you're the only person I can practice on all at once."

Soria frowned at him, then said nothing more as Karr exhaled slowly and gave her a bleary, pained look. *"Are you well?"* he asked her.

"Better than you," she replied, brushing her thumb across his cheek. "Can you walk?"

"I do not imagine there is an alternative."

Robert raised his brow, not understanding Karr's language. "Was that a yes?"

"He'll need help," Soria suggested, and glanced at Serena. "What about Long Nu?"

"We leave her. She has done nothing wrong."

"You're crazy. Kidnapping, torture, death threats—"

The shape-shifter held up her hand, her single eye glinting dangerously. "She is one of us. I will not restrain or harm her. Not for doing what she thinks is right. Drugging her pushes the limits."

"She won't feel the same about you, not for helping us."

"You assume I'll be around when she wakes up." Serena studied the unconscious shape-shifter, and her expression softened with compassion. "She is the oldest of us now, and the most powerful. And she cares. She cares a great deal about our survival. She has suffered for it."

Serena looked at Karr, and the compassion disappeared; everything in her features hardened. "There are so few of us left. We must breed if we are to live. And so, what if everyone learned that we can take mates from other shifters? It would be tempting, easier, because of our secrets. But those children from such unions? How would they live and survive? Chimera require special rearing, with control over their abilities more difficult to learn. They are violent by nature. They are made for war. There is no place for such instincts in this new, modern age."

Soria narrowed her eyes. "You seem to know a great deal about his kind. I wonder why that is."

Robert laughed quietly to himself. It was an unpleasant sound. Serena backed away, looking toward the door. "We must go."

Soria stood. "You know something. What are you hiding?"

Serena peered out the door. "Come. Hurry."

Robert grabbed Karr's arm and slung it over his shoulder. "I knew a giant once," he muttered, wincing. "He was always drunk. But I think you're heavier."

Karr's eyes flashed golden. *"I am going to bite off your hands for touching my balls."*

Soria bit back a smile, opened her mouth to translate— only to have Robert shake his head. "I can guess what he said."

"No," she replied mildly, slinging Karr's other arm around her waist. "I really don't think you can."

It was cold outside, and the stars glittered. There was a smooth breeze carrying the faint scent of smoke. It was perfectly quiet, eerily so. No one spoke as Serena led them quickly across town, back toward the helicopters. Soria glimpsed movement on her right—almost

cried out and then swallowed her voice when she saw
Ku-Ku looking back from the shadows, gliding alongside them like a specter.

Soria kept expecting to be shot at, and the anticipa-
tion was almost worse than an actual bullet. When the
helicopters were finally in sight—or rather, just one of
them, as the other seemed to be missing—she murmured, "Where are the men?"

"Fool's errand," Robert muttered, as Karr's breath
whistled quietly with pain. "Serena sent them away. Said
there was a package—the human kind—that needed to
be retrieved at a certain set of coordinates. They'll be
there soon. I suspect they will wait for quite some time
before realizing they've been duped."

"Will they hurt Long Nu when they return?"

Robert exhaled sharply, but with cold laughter.
"Doubtful."

Serena climbed into the pilot's seat and began prep-
ping the helicopter. Ku-Ku slid up front beside her, while
Robert helped Soria ease Karr into the back. She grabbed
a first-aid kit that was belted to the wall, turned on a
flashlight which she held her in teeth, and began trying to
clean up the mess that the wire had made of his legs.

It was awful. Karr glanced down, and tightened his
jaw. Soria hardly knew where to begin, and spit the
flashlight into her hand. "Robert, can you get him some
antibiotics to prevent an infection?"

"I have some. But first, the hard part." He took the
gauze from her, along with a bottle of peroxide, and began swabbing at the long, serrated cuts. The peroxide
foamed. Karr hissed.

Soria could not hold his hand—not while handling the flashlight—but she sat close, nudging his elbow with her thigh, and a moment later he reached out, grasped her leg in one huge hand, and squeezed gently. His grip was warm, firm . . . and very much alive.

Relief hit her so hard that her eyes burned with tears. They were out of there. She was loose, free with him. The importance of that, and how much it meant to her that he was safe, was staggering. Soria struggled with herself, finally gaining control over her emotions, but not before sharing a long look with Karr that said more than anything that language alone could have conjured.

The helicopter roared to life. Serena shouted, "Where am I taking you?"

"Ulaanbataar!" Robert called back, before Soria uttered a word. When she stared at him, brow raised, he shrugged. "Roland said you had a lead there."

"He said that, did he? What else?"

"That I am not to leave your side."

"So why did you the last time?"

"Because some things you can handle yourself. And others"—he glanced up front at Serena—"require a different kind of touch."

Soria shook her head. "I do not want to know."

"I'm certain that's a lie," Robert replied, "but it's the results that count."

IT TOOK THEM TWO HOURS TO FLY TO ULAANBATAAR. Serena landed on the outskirts of the city, almost ten miles away. It was still night. A Land Cruiser was parked nearby. Soria heard the heavy rush of water: a river was close, though she could not see it in the darkness.

Karr's legs had been bandaged as well as possible, and he had choked down a first round of amoxicillin. Robert and Soria helped him walk to the Land Cruiser. Ku-Ku followed, as did Serena more slowly, her one good eye faintly glowing.

"I won't be traveling on with you," she said quietly. "I'll take the chopper south, as far as it will go, and then leave it. I can find my way back to civilization more quickly on my own."

Soria hesitated. "Thank you."

Serena looked like she couldn't care less. Tilting her head, she leaned in toward Karr, who was perched on the edge of the Land Cruiser's backseat. He was almost too large for the vehicle, especially with his wounds. Soria suspected they would have to put down the back seats so that he could use the trunk space as well.

Karr watched Serena warily. Golden light flickered dangerously in his eyes.

"I am not changed in my opinion of you," she told him quietly. "I think you are dangerous. To believe otherwise is naive."

"Then we feel the same," Karr rumbled, and Soria translated.

A cold, almost seductive smile passed over Serena's mouth. "I will take that as a compliment."

Soria had the uncomfortable feeling that Serena would take a great deal more than that, if she had the chance. Even Karr narrowed his eyes. He did not look amused.

Serena inclined her head toward Robert. "Don't be a stranger, old man. I have a grandchild to show you."

"A grandchild," he said, gently mocking. "You must have been birthing babies when you were a baby."

Warmth touched her gaze, but it was so fleeting as to have been imagined. Serena turned, nodded at Ku-Ku—who was watching her with those empty, dead eyes—and began striding back to the helicopter.

Soria hesitated, glanced at Karr and then ran after her. Serena must have been moving more quickly than she looked, because she was already climbing into the machine when Soria caught up. The shape-shifter paused, one foot raised, lean with muscle and sharp angles. Her blonde hair seemed spikier than usual, her cheekbones higher and more feline. Feral, dangerous, and deadly.

"Why did you help us?" Soria asked, breathless from running. "Back in the village, and now?"

Serena hesitated and looked away. "I thought of my daughter. Kidnapped, strapped down. For nothing but experimentation. We shifters hide because humans would find us freakish and dangerous. We would be hunted without mercy, without a chance to prove ourselves. It was only fair to give your chimera *his* chance."

"And yet?"

"I meant what I said. His kind . . ." She stopped, looking down at her hands. "There are none like him. He comes from an age when the chimera were still powerful. When they meant something. His presence alone could bring those days back. We cannot afford that." Her voice dropped to a whisper. "He is living proof of a time better left forgotten."

Soria wished she had more time, but she felt the pressure of those waiting behind her, as well as the tenseness of Serena's posture, swaying deeper into the helicopter. "I still don't understand. The chimera are part of you. You can't deny your children."

"Children grow up," Serena replied bluntly. "And then, sometimes, they kill you."

She climbed into the helicopter, and slid the door shut in Soria's face.

CHAPTER SEVENTEEN

THE wagon—or *car*, as Soria called it—was too small for his body, though after they folded down the soft leather seats to reveal a rather more spacious area (a marvel of human ingenuity that he would be most pleased to investigate at a later date) Karr was able to rest on his back with more comfort—meaning that he could lie down with his knees up so that his calves and ankles did not rub or bounce against the hard surface beneath him.

The pain was relentless; nauseating, strength-sapping, almost worse than a stab wound because it was spread over a much wider area. Those wires had cut him deeply; and the lacerations were rubbed full of dirt. Even though he had suffered terrible, life-threatening wounds in the past, pain was pain. It always felt like the first time.

The man, Robert, was up front behind the wheel used as the car's steering mechanism. Beside him sat his youthful companion, with her eyes like a cobra's, her personality just as lethal. He had never seen such an odd pair.

Soria rested close, on her side, facing him, his right

hand in her left. Her cheek pressed against his shoulder, and occasionally her mouth touched the same spot. The comfort he took from her presence ignited a heat inside him that he had never felt or considered. Such a simple thing—having her lie beside him in this strange dark wagon, in this even stranger world—and yet, being near her was like resting in the presence of a great and wondrous mystery, the kind that had no answer but existed solely as a delight of magic, proof that the wondrous did indeed happen.

He could not say any of that, though. Not simply because they were in the company of others, and not because he was shy around her, for he was not. Saying certain words cheapened them. Feelings were not words. Actions were not words. Words were fleeting. It was the look in the eye that lingered, or a touch, or moments such as this that he would always remember: in pain, fearful . . . but oddly content.

"They are alive," he whispered to Soria, as he watched lights pass in a blur beyond the glass of the wagon, lights that reminded him of lives. "Not many, and they are scattered. But they are alive. The chimera exist."

"How do you know?" she asked softly, her voicing of his language little more than a purr. "What I saw . . . I did not know you could do that."

"Blood calls," Karr said quietly, his scar aching. "Not many were capable of that magic, but my mother had certain gifts that she passed on to me. I used it, sometimes, to find lost children." He hesitated. "Maybe I should not have taken the risk. In hindsight, I cannot believe that I did. But it was worth it, just to know."

"Are any close?"

"I think so, yes. But I have only a vague sense of where they might be. There was a cluster to the north-west, and one very far from here, in the heart of the land south of the Nile."

Soria tensed. "Really."

"You know something?"

"No," she said, and then hesitated again. "A little over a year ago, right around the time I was hurt, a place was found where shape-shifters had been imprisoned. Taken by humans for experiments in breeding. The people I work for managed to free them, but there were pregnancies involving many human women. Given the nature of the experiments, I suppose it's possible that some chimeras were made. On purpose. Just to see what would happen."

"Humans hurting shape-shifters?" Karr exhaled slowly. "Controlling them? Using them in such ways? I cannot imagine."

"They hide for a reason," Soria answered, her hand tightening around his. "You will have to do the same, or else live where there are no humans."

"Do such places exist?"

"They are rare." Soria smiled against his shoulder. "You might have to compromise."

Will you *be there*? Karr wanted to ask, shutting his eyes against the lights and passing buildings, trying not to listen to the roar that the wagon made around him. Dizzying sights and sounds. This was a world Soria had been born to, and took for granted. She had a life here. He had nothing but himself.

So, nothing has changed. All you ever had was

yourself. You can still be useful. Perhaps you are no longer a warlord, but you know things that no one else does. You know of a world and life that has been dead for thousands of years. That is worth something.

The wagon made a sharp turn and then slowed. Soria struggled to sit up. *"Where are we?"*

"I had a contact set up a safe house for us," Robert said, turning in the seat to look at them. *"My people can be trusted."*

"Your people," she said dryly. *"I thought you were a mercenary."*

"I am." Robert smiled, though it did not reach his eyes. *"And I am very good at what I do."*

Soria gave him a sour look. Karr glanced at the girl seated up front, and found her staring back with eyes so flat that he seriously considered killing her just to be on the safe side. Instead, he held himself still as she slid gracefully from the wagon, taking with her a large black bag into which she had slid her sticklike weapon. Robert opened the side door and offered a pale, sinewy hand.

Karr took it. He did not want the man's help, but his pride had limits and his legs felt as though they were still being sawed with wire. Gritting his teeth, squeezing Soria's hand, he hobbled from the wagon toward a door that the girl held open some short distance away. The city was quiet in this district, though Karr heard the distant buzz of voices and strange music. The buildings reminded him of what he had seen in Erenhot: windows covered in bars, smooth pale stone, simple flameless lights. These were functional in ways that should have dazzled him but that did not. There was no loveliness in the stone here, nothing that begged the eternal, as had the temples in the Nile kingdoms or near the dark seas of the Hittites. Even the nomads had kept about them a warm, living lushness.

It was cold inside the building they entered, but quiet. The air smelled clean. Not much to see except a table and chairs. Robert led them into another room where there was a large bed pushed against the wall beneath a startling painting of a naked woman. Karr stared for a moment, tore his gaze away, and eased himself onto the bed. He was accustomed to sleeping on the ground, but the padding was soft and felt good on his aching body. He tried not to sigh, and closed his eyes.

"Interesting," he heard Soria say. *"You decorate this yourself?"*

"I leave that to experts," Robert replied. *"Make yourself comfortable, if possible. Ku-Ku will be nearby."*

"Leaving already?"

"Research. We need to learn who in town might have an ancient sword collection. There can't be many."

Soria was silent a moment. Karr cracked open one eye and saw her giving the man a pensive look. *"Where did Roland find you?"*

Robert smiled. *"Maybe I found him."*

He turned and left the room. Karr muttered, "You are surrounded by strange people."

Soria shot him a wry look, and shut the door before coming back to sit on the edge of the bed. "It's just me now. If you want to scream from the pain, I promise not to tell."

Karr could not help but smile, though that hurt as

well. "Come. Rest beside me. Perhaps I will scream very quietly in your ear."

"Exactly what a girl wants to hear." Soria curled on the bed, angling her body away from his so that her legs would not accidentally brush against him. Her distance—when she was so close—was as frustrating as the pain. He wanted to feel her body pressed tight against him.

He settled for holding her small hand, savoring the press of her head against his shoulder and the rare sense of place and time he felt in her presence: not displaced, not lost in another world but anchored here and now, because he knew her. Because, miracle upon miracle, he trusted her. This woman—his enemy, his friend, his mystery.

"When I died," he said quietly, after a long silence, "this is not what I expected."

Soria exhaled sharply. "What was it like?"

Karr closed his eyes. "A long nightmare. Darkness and dreams. Memories that never ceased. I was always battling, always in blood, with brief moments of peace that never lasted. But I always believed we become in death what we were in life, so I suppose I should have expected nothing less than what I received."

"That is horrible," Soria replied. "Are you sure you were dead?"

"Maybe I am not alive even now. Perhaps this is part of the vast dream, and I have simply moved from one state of sleep to another. It would make more sense than all the wonders and tragedy I have seen since opening my eyes."

"I do not feel like a dream," Soria murmured.

"You do to me," he replied gently—and, feeling bold, kissed the top of her head.

She scooted closer and brushed her mouth against his. Her touch was exquisitely tender. No one had ever been so careful with him.

"You touch me as though you are afraid I will break."

"Maybe I am," she whispered, her eyes like dark honey. "You are not invincible."

"Simply hard to kill."

She smiled, but it was strained. "Just once. I would rather not tempt fate again."

"Really." Karr swallowed hard, his heart aching. "Would you grieve for me?"

Soria looked away, but not before he caught a glint in her eyes that was bright and pained. Tears?

The sight stole his breath, his voice. He let his hands play at words: dragging her close, ignoring the pain that caused, caring only that he could touch her face, brush his thumb over her soft lips. Her face was hot and flushed, and he breathed, "Look at me."

She did, reluctantly, and it was almost too much to see the expression in her eyes, her weariness and grief, the pain of loss.

"I think you might miss me," he whispered. "But I am not gone yet."

"Why would you stay? After all this is done, why—?" Soria stopped herself, jaw clenched tight. She looked ashamed, maybe even disgusted, and stared down at her empty sleeve. At first he thought she might believe he cared about her disfigurement, but memories passed through him, insight trickling into instinct, and he grasped at a possible truth, one that grew stronger the longer he studied her face.

"You had no one after you lost your arm," he said carefully. "No one but family. But there was more than that, I think. Someone abandoned you."

"He had his reasons," she said. "Reasons that were important to him, though that did not make it right."

Not right at all. To be hurt in such a violent way, and then be abandoned, heartbroken . . . it was more than most would be able to bear. Anger rose through him, but there was nothing he could do except transform his emotions into furious tenderness. The past was never entirely dead, but it did not have to poison the present, or future. He was beginning to see that now.

"So you left and cared for yourself alone." His hand tightened against her face, his voice dropping to a whisper. "And you are used to that. You think it makes you strong. And it does. But there is no shame in saying that is not enough. That you . . . need."

Soria shook her head, still not looking at him, and gave a halfhearted chuckle. "And who, or what, have you ever needed? You—warlord, prince. Going to battle, living your epic life."

"I needed no one," he said truthfully. "And I lived as I believed. I needed no one, because no one suited me— and I was not cheap with my heart, even if my body wanted to be otherwise at times. Princesses, you remember. Many princesses, tossed at my feet."

That made her laugh fully, which was what he had intended. Karr smiled, running his hands down her braids, loosening the cords that bound them. Her hair, thick and heavy, unfurled in his hands. "And then I woke from death. I found myself in the presence of my enemy—my lovely, brave enemy—who I found suits me, curiously and unexpectedly."

Warmth replaced the shadows in her eyes. "How do I suit you? My skill with words? I think that might be the only reason you like me. *If* you like me."

"I like you," Karr breathed. "And I am not ashamed to say I need you. Not simply for your words or your knowledge, but because . . ."

He stopped, searching his mind and memory, thinking of all his years on the move, serving those he loved, fighting endlessly to protect and feed them, searching for alliances that would strengthen, always strengthen, those generations yet to come. He had not been alone, but he had stood alone. It had seemed necessary.

With anyone else, he would have still felt alone. Here, in this city, on a battlefield, with other chimera, in a wagon crammed with bodies—he would have been alone in his heart. But not anymore.

"I need you," he finished simply, unable to find better, stronger words. He picked up her hand and placed it over his chest. "You are here, inside me. Part of me. And I need you."

Soria stared at their joined hands and then met his gaze with a heat that he felt down to his bones. And then the way she looked at him shifted again, with uneasiness and pain.

"My arm," she said hesitantly. "Do you want to know?"

"Yes," he said, afraid of what he saw in her eyes.

"It was someone I knew." Soria smiled, but there was no humor; just a grim, almost gruesome incredulousness as though she still could not believe what had happened. "I did not know it, though. He had changed, aged. An uncle I never much saw. But he and I had a history from when I was little. Not a good one."

Karr tensed and she shook her head. "Nothing ever happened back then. But he tried and I told, and I never saw him again. I forgot him. But he did not forget me. I think he wanted to punish me for how my father and the rest of the family threw him away."

Soria closed her eyes. "He knew my schedule. I was going home and saw an old man at the side of the road who needed help. So I stopped. He . . . drugged me. Put me in the trunk of his car. Took me to his home, locked me in the basement. He told me who he was, and when he did . . . I knew. I knew that was it. I was not the first girl he had done this to, either. He had pictures. A system. He liked them to fight him. It turned him on." She drew in a ragged breath, trembling. "So I woke up with my right arm in chains, all the way up near my shoulder, and lower, at my wrist. A knife at my side. He said that I had a choice. Fight him in the morning or kill myself."

Karr shook with rage. "Soria."

"It was not a big knife," she whispered. "I knew he would rig the fight. My good old uncle."

"Soria," he said again, but her face twisted in a grimace, and she tucked her chin down against her chest, huddling closer.

"I did not want to die. I did not want him to—" She stopped, then, for a long moment. "The cuff on my upper arm was too tight to move down past my elbow. That is why I lost so much. I had a shoelace I managed to tie around . . . you know, up high. To help with the blood. But the pain . . ."

Her voice was suddenly too hoarse to go on. Karr dragged her deep into his arms, horrified for her, wishing he could be in her memories to ease her pain—to move through time and stop it all before it had happened. Magic had brought him back to life. There had to be magic for time, as well.

And suddenly, as though someone had heard him, he found himself in her thoughts. He saw—he saw the flash of the knife, and the splitting of flesh beneath it. Listened to her strangled screams and felt the bite of tears. He felt her resolve. He suffocated on her determination. Her fury. Her fury, which ran so deep, so bitter and powerful, that he felt frightened for her, of her, what slept inside her.

So much like the fury sleeping inside him, as well.

Memories flashed, blurring, seen through her eyes. Movement, light, a sense of stillness and quiet, and difficulty breathing. Slick knife still tightly held, barely able to stand, dragging herself through strange rooms, trailing blood. Seeing on a table—*a gun*—which was suddenly warm in her left hand.

Then, an old man sleeping in a darkened room. So normal and mundane. Opening his bleary pale eyes just as she pressed the barrel to his head and pulled the trigger.

Karr found himself flung out of her mind. Soria gasped just as he opened his eyes. Staring at him in horror, mouth still open, contorted, as though silently screaming. He covered her mouth with his fingers, lightly, his eyes burning with tears that he had not known he possessed. Emotions raged through him, none he could name except that they were primal and hateful, grieved and tender; and full of the endless, unwavering desire to protect this woman so thoroughly that she would never, in dream or waking, ever suffer so much again.

"You saw," she breathed. "Oh, God."

"I am glad," he said huskily, hardly able to make his voice work. "What you did—"

"I killed my uncle."

"He deserved it. I was speaking of your arm."

"My arm," she breathed. "I was crazy. Only a crazy person does that. Like an animal chewing off a limb."

"You wanted to survive." Karr pressed his lips to her brow, quite certain he would never in this life have her strength.

"My uncle," Soria said again. "He deserved to die. I know that. But he was family. I still have not told my parents. I never will. They think I lost my arm in an accident. Only my friends know. They covered up the evidence that I was there. Found a private doctor, people who would not talk . . ."

"Soria," he whispered. "Soria, be at peace."

She fixed him with a tear-stained gaze. "Peace is hard to come by. You have to fight for it. No giving up."

Karr knew she was not just talking about herself.

"I was a coward," he said quietly. "But I am ready to fight."

"Good," she whispered, tears spilling over her eyes.

"It is worth it, you know. Even if it does not feel like it at the time."

Karr leaned in, quivering, and pressed his mouth to her ear. "I wish you had been alive then, to tell me such things. I wish I could have been alive in your past, to spare you your pain. I wish so many things, Soria."

The door to the bedroom opened, making both of them flinch. The girl Ku-Ku strode inside, carrying two clear bottles of liquid and a flimsy white satchel that fluttered and made crackling sounds. She hardly looked at them, nor made a sound, just dumped everything on the edge of the bed and then left.

"You thirsty?" Soria asked, hoarse. She fumbled, rubbing at her face, and handed a bottle to him. He was not thirsty, but he understood her need to make something light and new. She had to show him how to open the thing, and once the lid was off, he smelled liquid. Water. He tested it with his tongue and found the taste strange—but not enough to spit it out. It felt good to have something cold running down his throat.

Soria dumped the contents of the bag onto the bed. Karr saw boxes and oddly shaped materials, small containers that defied explanation and a number of other objects that he was sure were very useful but could not possibly be much help in healing his wounds unless they were magical.

He watched, though, and braced himself as Soria began fussing with the bandages that had been placed over his legs. Blood was beginning to seep through some of them. She hissed to herself, anger simmering in her red-rimmed eyes, and glanced to her right at another door. She saw a strange white chair that from a distance appeared to be made of gleaming white marble.

"Can you walk?" she asked, her voice still rough with tears. She pointed at the chair. "Just over there."

Karr gritted his teeth and swung his legs off the bed. It hurt so badly he thought he would be sick on himself, but he swallowed down the pain and with Soria's help stumbled across the room. He hated his body for betraying him, for making him feel so weak. He could not control the injuries that others inflicted on him, but there was a part of Karr that had always believed he should be stronger.

The room with the white chair was extremely tiny, and filled with odd structures that bore only a limited familiarity to things he had seen before in the pavilions of the Nile royalty. There was a small basin for washing one's hands, and a shallow white pool for bathing; though in the past he had seen spouts made of clay, while these were iron. For water, Karr thought. Water for bathing, brought inside a home. Soria seemed to take it for granted.

"What is considered luxury among your people?" Karr asked, sitting heavily upon the white chair, the top of which sagged slightly. "What is solely the domain of royalty?"

Soria smiled to herself, though it was still fraught with emotion—as was his own voice and heart, his body weak with what he had just seen and heard, and the feelings that had overwhelmed him. "There are few royal families left in the world, and they are largely ineffectual. Some humans are governed by collective bodies of their peers, chosen by a majority, while others are ruled by groups that consolidate power among a minority. That is the simple explanation. The reality is far more complex. But luxury . . . it depends on what you are used to. There are some who would consider this place a dream come true. Others would find it a hovel. I suspect it was the same in your day, just with different fixtures."

"Yes." Karr followed her hand gestures and swung his legs over the edge of the bathing basin. "Some of my people were envious of the fine things the royal families had in their possession. We could have lived there among them, but I feared becoming too dependent on their well wishes. Or, that time would make us little better than slaves."

"Familiarity breeds contempt," she muttered, and poured a dark yellow substance over his legs. He hissed with pain, flinching, but except for a tight-lipped glance that could have been an apology, she showed nothing except deep concentration.

"You already cleaned my wounds," he said tightly. "If you do this much longer, I will not have any legs left to heal."

"Big baby," she accused. "Cry me a river when all these cuts become infected and you rot from the inside out." She froze, then, staring at the crisscrossed wounds. "Damn it. You need a tetanus shot."

Karr had no idea what that meant, but he was tired, in pain, and the scar in his gut was beginning to tingle again, rather violently. He touched Soria's shoulder, sliding his hand around the back of her neck—and savored the quick flush of her cheeks and the hesitant, breathless way she glanced up at him.

"Clean my wounds if you must," he said softly, "and bandage me. But do not put so much on yourself. I am strong. Indeed, I am so magnificently mighty, I came back from the dead. This will not kill me."

A faint smile touched her mouth. "Now you are a braggart."

He wanted to be clever for her, to say something that would make her laugh, but all he could think of was the loveliness of her smile and how much he wanted to taste it. He had not tasted nearly enough of her. Crazy. He was a crazy man, and would pay.

Karr leaned forward and kissed her. He tried to be gentle, but the moment their mouths touched, he lost himself to a jolt of raw, hot pleasure that sank from his heart into his groin. Everything quickened—his heart, his blood—and the ache below his waist as his body reacted with desire made his leg wounds feel mild. Her tongue darted between his lips and then sank deeper, and his hand roved down her throat, falling lightly upon her breast. She gasped against his mouth, arching deeper into his touch, and it took all his willpower not to rip her tattered shirt right off her body. He had never wanted a woman as badly as he wanted her, never dreamed that one single presence could collapse so deeply into his own psyche until inhaling her scent and tasting her lips felt as urgent to him as breathing.

"Take off your shirt," he commanded, his voice barely more than a growl. "I want to see you."

Soria hesitated, stiffening. "My arm."

"I want to see you," he said roughly. "*You*, Soria. You are not your arm. Indeed, your arm is a badge of honor. You should wear it more proudly than you do."

Karr could see her uncertainty, and he remembered what had happened the last time he touched her. But a deeper hunger was riding him now, and he was not going to let her pull away. Not for *this* reason. Not after seeing what he had.

He did not help her. His patience fraying, he watched in utter silence as she slowly pulled her shirt over her head. Underneath, she wore a cream-colored band of cloth that clung like a second skin to her full and heavy breasts. He could see no way to undo it, except to pull it up—and as she reached behind her, his patience finally snapped. He leaned forward, placing his mouth over her nipple, sucking on it through the thin material.

Soria cried out, throwing back her head as Karr pushed his fingers under the garment's curved, hard band, pulling upward until her breasts were free and soft in his palms, his thumb dancing over one nipple while he sucked and nibbled hard on the other. Soria writhed, eyes closed, and when he raised his head to kiss her, she met him halfway, driving him backward with dizzying force. Her mouth was hungry and hot, and her left hand drifted down into his lap, brushing over the head of his penis with a deftness that made him wild.

The pain in his legs momentarily cut through his pleasure, but not enough to stop him. Soria, however, broke off the kiss and tried to stand. She wobbled on unsteady legs, and his hands snared her waist.

"I'll hurt you," she gasped in her own language, but her gaze flicked down to her right, to the stump of her arm.

Karr drew her back gently, forcing himself to stay steady and calm. It was difficult. All he wanted was to tear off the rest of her clothing and have her sit hot, wet, and naked in his lap.

She sat in his lap, but her legs were still clothed. Very carefully, with desire burning through him, he leaned over and kissed the disfigured remains of her arm. Soria shuddered, but he did not stop or look at her face. He was relentless in his caresses, running his hands up her back as he buried himself in her scent, spreading slow, careful kisses over the scarred, bumpy skin.

Soria touched his face, fingers sliding under his jaw so that he was forced to look at her. She was smiling wryly, but there were tears in her eyes.

"I get it," she said. "You are not turned off."

"I did not notice until you did," he said truthfully. "You forgot, did you not?"

"Yes. Until that side of my body tried to reach for you."

"Then let it reach," he whispered, sliding his hands beneath the soft waist of her pants. "If your body wants something, let it have it."

She laughed. "Oh, really?"

He tried to smile, but it felt like a grimace. "Will you have me, Soria?"

Her breath caught, but in a different way. "There might be consequences."

You might kill her, whispered an insidious little voice. *And you* will *break. It is only a matter of time. It happened once, it will happen again.*

He went cold. Desire fled him, though his body stayed hard for her. Soria, who had been staring into his eyes, frowned. "I meant babies. Not you. I do not believe you will hurt me."

"Believe it," he murmured, closing his eyes so that he would not be tempted by her breasts or the lean, lithe lines of her body. He heard her move away, which filled him with an unexpected pang—and then gasped out loud as her mouth unexpectedly touched his penis.

He was so stunned he could not move; he could just feel, riding a wave of pleasure so violent he almost climaxed in her mouth. Which seemed to be exactly what she wanted, given the way her tongue stroked him, hard and soft, striking a rhythm that made his hips buck against her.

"What does *your* body want?" she murmured against him, staring up with eyes that were heavy-lidded with desire.

Seeing himself half in her mouth was enough to send him over the edge. A growl snapped free of his throat, and a golden haze fell across his vision until he went almost blind. He grabbed Soria's arm, hauling her up on her feet, and before she could protest he turned her around and forced her to straddle his lap with her back against his chest. His right hand slid down the front of her pants, searching for her slick heat, and with his other hand he drew her back until she leaned against him, panting with pleasure.

He pushed his fingers deep inside her body, craning to see her expression, loving how she bit her bottom lip, whimpering and shaking. He pulled out and then slid his fingers back in, deeper and harder, grinding his hips against her back as she let out a long, ragged cry. He bit the nape of her neck, fur shimmering over his body before receding into flesh, flesh becoming scales and back again, dragging his left hand across her breasts to squeeze her nipples in the same hard rhythm of his stroking fingers. He inserted another finger, and she moved against him, bracing her feet against the side of the washbasin. Her left hand reached behind her back, trying to touch him, and he briefly stopped caressing her breasts to guide her fingers to the right spot.

Pleasure cut straight through him, so hard and fast he hardly knew he was coming until her back was suddenly wet, his hips jerking hard against her. Soria let out her own low cry, leaning forward as her body spasmed around his fingers. He tried to withdraw his hand, but she caught his wrist with tight fingers and held him in place.

"Stay there," she breathed raggedly. "I like how it feels."

So did he. But as his fingers began to move again, very gently inside her, he felt that tingle in his gut. He remembered the sword, and Tau's face, and felt something else that was hot and wet against his stomach.

Blood.

CHAPTER EIGHTEEN

I would make a terrible nurse, Soria thought, standing in the shower.

Karr was, or had been, bleeding from the scar in his side. She had no idea how to help him. And while it would be interesting to have a reputation for being so wild in bed that a man's guts spilled open, she knew that was not the case here—and if it were, it would be entirely too gross and frightening to ever attempt an encore.

"How is your stomach?" Soria called out to him, rinsing away the last of the soapsuds. She turned off the water and peered around the curtain at Karr, awkwardly trying to towel off, and watched him pull his own formerly white towel away from his bloodstained gut.

Her knees wobbled, and she tried not to think about how it had felt to turn around and see that scar gaping again, with blood oozing free like a running faucet. It was so horrifying and otherworldly that she had almost burst out laughing in that way people do at funerals or especially tragic events. It was too ridiculous. Life was too strange to bring one moment of bliss and then another of chaos. Life had allowed her almost thirty years of innocence, and then in one night stolen it away. Life had given her a gift for languages, and brought her to this odd man who seemed made of magic more than flesh. And life had let her love again.

Soria loved him. Not in some cheap attached way, but down in her bones, with a quiet certainty that felt like the same love she had for being alive. And it terrified her, though she was done allowing fear to ruin the gift she had been given when she had survived that long night, one year past. She had been resurrected in her own way, and had not realized it then. Not until now.

"Karr?" she asked, when he said nothing.

He frowned. "I have seen far too much of my blood lately."

"But it stopped."

"It appears so."

For now, she wanted to add. There was blood on the floor and toilet. Red, smeared, disgusting. It looked as though someone had been murdered and the evidence poorly concealed.

Karr was murdered, came the unbidden thought. Murdered. She kept hearing it over and over in her mind, and the longer she did, the more right it felt. Murdered.

But he had committed suicide. He had told her that himself. He'd said that he made the choice, asked for the deed to be done: a sword run through him. And now, thousands of years later, that same spot kept opening and bleeding. Almost like a message, his body's way of crying out.

Karr began wiping at himself, trying to clean his

body. Soria tried not to look at all the blood, but the moment her gaze fell down on that drying crusty floor, a wave of nausea rolled over her that was so powerful it took all her strength not to bend and gag. She gritted her teeth, waiting for it to pass, and found Karr watching her with concern.

"You have this reaction to blood," he said. "Everyone has some disgust, but you . . ."

"There was a lot of it when I lost my arm," she found herself saying—not meaning to, though after the words came out she did not regret them. It felt right, and safe, to tell Karr that much. He had seen. He knew the truth. He had not judged her, or pitied her. Just looked at her like she was a good, strong human being who needed tenderness and love. Just that, to make the pain begin to fade.

Without her right arm, Soria had no easy way to wrap a towel around her body. She didn't bother trying, stepping lightly from the tub with just one end held over her breasts, while the rest of the towel draped around her like some long loincloth. Karr stared, his eyes flaring golden hot, jaw clenched so tight she thought some of his teeth might crack.

"If I was not in a great deal more discomfort now than I was earlier," he said grimly, "you would be on the floor with me inside you."

"Wuss," Soria said in English, though the thought made her breathless.

She wondered if she was not just a little insane. She had not felt so *right* in years, nor had she imagined she would ever feel this way again. As she turned, Soria caught a glimpse of her reflection in the mirror, her stump front and center, a disfigured little wing that she'd rarely had the stomach to examine so closely, especially under bright lights.

But there was no twist in her gut, no disgust when she looked at herself. She was not so far gone as to say that she felt nothing, because she did suffer one small pang, but she was not afraid to see herself. She was not afraid of what she would feel. And that acceptance, that peace, however small, was such a burden lifted that she could not imagine how she had lived this past year, hating her body as she had.

She turned on the water again, feeling for the temperature, and glanced over her shoulder at Karr. His hand was raised to touch her back, hard-jawed wonder in his eyes, though he hesitated when she looked at him.

"Climb in," she said gently. "We need to wash all that off."

"My legs," he said, and smiled. "I have accomplished a great deal sitting down, but standing will be another matter."

"Good thing you do not have to." Soria locked the drain, and the tub began filling. "Come on, a bath after a couple thousand years will certainly not kill you."

Karr grunted, but stood slowly with a wince, transferring himself the short distance into the tub. He sat awkwardly, far too large for the small space, and gave her an incredulous look.

"Hey," she said, trying not to look at the awful wounds on his legs. "This cannot be worse than having a sword run through you."

Again, he said nothing. But his gaze darkened, and he tugged hard on her towel. She let him have it, and laughed quietly when he dipped it into the rising hot water and began scrubbing the blood and dirt off his body. The water quickly turned pink, and then brown.

She heard a knocking sound outside the bathroom, and poked her head around the door. Robert stood just inside the bedroom, holding a large shopping bag.

"I found something," he said. He was all business, with not even a glint of humor in his eyes. "There's an old man in town who owns several ancient artifacts. Swords, included. He teaches history and archaeology at the local university, though my understanding is that he's here on loan from Oxford."

"Oxford? Here, in Mongolia? That's an odd jump, unless he's doing research." Soria frowned, thinking hard. "It's also strange to travel with a personal collection— especially one that's valuable."

"Either way, it's a start." Robert tossed down the bag. "There are clothes in there for the both of you. If you can . . . tear yourselves away, we'll drive over there and see what we find."

She almost told him about the blood and the mysterious case of the opening and closing gut wound. She decided on, "I hope you're not planning on breaking in."

"My dear lady. I am a professional." He held up his cell phone. "I called ahead. We have an appointment. Though, if behaving in a law-abiding and civilized fashion is too much of an affront, I'm sure Ku-Ku would be more than happy to kick in the door and make Mr. Mul-

raney her bitch." Robert finally smiled. "As the young
people say."

"Young people," Soria repeated sarcastically, as from
behind she sensed Karr struggling with the faucet, the
bathwater about to overflow. "You don't look any older
than me."

Robert's smile widened, and it was not particularly
pleasant. "Get dressed."

ULAANBAATAR DID NOT WEAR ITS RUSSIAN INFLUENCES
well. Soviet-style flats—blocks and blocks of them—
ranged over wide swathes of city land like gray decay-
ing fortresses, utterly at odds with the piercing blue sky
and unrelenting cheerfulness of the morning sun. Even
the government buildings, while impressive, were solid
and heavy, so ponderous that they seemed almost like
an affront to the nomadic spirit of "here and there."

Robert drove the Land Cruiser into the south side of
the sprawling city. On a faraway hill Soria could see
among the green grass and shrubbery the pale stone
spire of Zaisan Memorial that honored the deaths of
Russian soldiers in World War II.

Karr studied the structure—the entire city—with a
grave curiosity that was both serious and thoughtful. Perhaps he was uneasy, as well. His face was hard to read,
and he looked uncomfortable—all that raw, muscled
strength crammed into a tight space. His legs were probably killing him, though he did not complain.

Nor did he give her any indication that he was thinking about what had passed between them. Except for

once, when she caught him staring at her instead of the city, a golden glimmer in his eyes that was full of such tender heat she could feel his fingers inside of her again, pushing and stretching. Her thighs shifted, unable to ease the ache that rippled briefly through her.

Karr noticed, though she tried to mask the movement with a stretch. A faint smile touched his mouth—and it was thoughtful enough to make her uneasy. She knew he had concerns. She supposed that she should, as well, though having already faced attempted murder seemed to have put some perspective in her life. It was all about choices. Karr was dangerous, but there was good in him, too.

And she wanted to be naive for a little while. She wanted to trust herself and others again.

Professor Tom Mulraney lived on the outskirts of the city in a *ger*. He was not alone. Several other families were nearby in their own tents, some with cars parked out front and others with horses and livestock bleating inside rough pens. It was a semipermanent settlement for those who could not stand the crush of the city, with a creek running a short distance away for water. Soria thought of Evie and the other good people who had helped them—those children, the old woman—and a swift pain throbbed through her stump into her head. She was going to make it up, somehow. And if any of them had been hurt . . .

She did not let herself finish that thought.

Ku-Ku stayed with the Land Cruiser, her window rolled down and her headphones sitting heavy over her ears. There was a motorcycle parked in front of Professor Mulraney's *ger*, which was larger than the others and had two smaller secondary structures attached in the back. His home resembled a clump of very large white mushrooms.

Women were washing clothes in the river, and they stood to stare as Soria and the others walked up to the professor's painted red door. Winds whipped at her new long dress: red, with an easy cut that could slip easily over the head. Robert, thankfully, had not provided her with anything that required buttoning or zipping. A long cashmere sweater kept her warm. It was a dowdy though comfortable outfit.

Karr wore loose pants and a short-sleeved shirt. He moved uneasily in clothing, shrugging slightly as though trying to adjust the weight of the material on his back. Shoes had been provided, but that was beyond his limit. Like Serena had done, he went barefoot. He also limped heavily. Robert had given him a cane to lean on, and much to Soria's surprise, he was using it. She had wondered if he would. Some men would have had too much pride.

A woman answered the door, wearing a long blue robe with a high collar and a silk sash tied around her plump waist. She appeared to be in her forties, and had the look of the steppes about her: a multiethnic hodge-podge of freckles, blondish hair and Asian features. She smiled, and it was friendly, even sweet.

"Welcome," she said in accented English. "Tom will be here soon. He went for a walk."

Robert entered first, and then Soria, but Karr froze on the threshold, frowning.

"What is it?" she asked.

"I do not know," he said, the muscles in his throat flexing convulsively. "I think—"

He stopped, placing his hand over his stomach. No blood seeped through his white shirt, but Soria held her breath for one long moment, waiting. Nothing happened, though, and after a moment he relaxed. Not much, though. Tension still rolled off him, and there was an uneasiness in his eyes that made her afraid.

"The sword?" she asked him. "Do you feel something?"

"Not just that," he replied, and shut his mouth as the woman approached. Robert stood behind the woman, watching with empty inscrutability. Soria wondered if he had taught Ku-Ku that expression, or if it was the other way around.

"Please," said the woman gently, "don't be shy."

"Thank you," said Soria. "You have a beautiful home."

And it was lovely. Clearly, this was a *ger* not meant to be moved very often, because its amenities were rich and tailored, and looked quite expensive. Thick tapestries hung all along the wall, and there were several long couches that looked well used, but also as if they had come out of the showroom of a very expensive store. Hardwood floors, soft rugs, some rosewood benches scattered here and there; and there were porcelain vases filled with flowers. Music played softly—surprisingly, a Chinese pop song—and a large-screen flat-paneled television sat dark near a small, richly carved eating table. Soria had not seen a satellite or solar panels, but she supposed they must be somewhere outside. The air smelled like garlic.

"Tom said to show you into his study if you arrived early," the woman told them, pointing to another red door set in the wall of the *ger*. "Would you like tea?"

"That would be lovely," Robert replied. "And you are?"

The woman smiled. "Betty. That is my English name. But I was born Bayarmaa."

"Bayarmaa," Robert repeated, speaking it perfectly, without accent. He held out his arm. "Lead us to the study, my lady."

Soria shook her head at him, and turned to find Karr standing still, his eyes squeezed shut. He looked as though he was in pain or concentrating very hard. Golden light trickled from beneath his eyelids, which would not do for Bayarmaa to see.

"Karr," she whispered urgently.

His eyes shot open. "I think I am losing my mind."

"Well, wait," Soria replied tersely, and grabbed his hand. "Unless you think it is too dangerous to stay here?"

"Not dangerous. Just . . . strange." His eyes were wild. "I do not even know how to describe what I am sensing."

Soria chewed on her bottom lip, ghost arm aching. "Come on, then. One thing at a time. Let's see if this professor has a sword you recognize."

But it was not a question for long. Within the study, rows of dark wooden shelves lined every inch of wall space, crammed and heavy with books; and there was a large mahogany desk in the center of the room, across from a tiny dung-burning stove that was laden with papers, candles, and pens. Soft leather chairs dotted the room, placed on thick Turkish rugs, and there, nearby, Soria saw a wooden pedestal; and on it, placed in a case, was the sword.

Soria recognized the weapon like the face of a friend after years of absence. Karr, too, walked toward the blade as though moving in a dream, staring with a lost, stunned expression. She watched him, feeling a tingle in her own gut, and held her stomach at the same moment he did, his fingers tracing a line over the scar that was hidden beneath his shirt.

She joined him, brushing up against his arm. He flinched, and then relaxed when he saw it was her. She had not imagined that he could look so startled, or flustered.

"I did not believe it," he murmured to her. "Though we saw it in our minds, I did not truly believe."

"You are sure?"

"I would stake my life on . . ." Karr stopped, shaking his head. "Yes, I am sure. I held that sword when I was last alive. I used it to fight, and kill. I wore it on my hip here"—he touched his side—"and if you turned it over, you would see an inscription on the back in a language that is probably as dead now as mine, but that spells the name of the king who placed it in my hands."

The metal had corroded, and hardly looked capable of killing—not without snapping in two—but there was a grace to its construction that she would not have envisioned for a weapon thousands of years old. Of course, archaeologists and historians were always finding themselves surprised by innovations and technologies of the past, things done then that were not possible today, even with modern gadgets and gizmos.

The weapon was beautiful. Soria could imagine it in Karr's hand.

Bayarmaa swayed close, flicking hair out of her eyes. "You like? My husband is especially proud of that sword. It is his favorite thing."

"Where did he get it?" Soria asked.

The woman shrugged. "He had it when we met, but I have only been with him for several years, and he is older and has traveled all over the world. A man can live through a great deal that others cannot know."

"Yes," Soria said solemnly. "I understand what you mean."

She heard a shuffling sound from the other room. Robert turned to face the door. Karr did not, still engrossed with the sword.

An old man entered. He was bigger than Soria would have imagined, broad and tall, with a grizzled strength that reminded her of how the movie actor Clint Eastwood had aged. He had short gray hair that was thick and bristly, and there was an angular quality to his wrinkled face that reminded her, for a moment, of Karr.

He wore sunglasses, and stood very still, watching them. Soria suffered a chill as she stared back. Bayarmaa glided up to him, and slung her arm around his waist with genuine affection. He relaxed, but only slightly.

"Tom," she said. "Here are the guests you were expecting."

Soria heard a sharp sound behind her. She turned

and found Karr staring at the professor with a look on his face that made her think he might faint. He was pale, stricken.

"Oh," Robert said. Soria glanced back, and found that the professor had taken off his sunglasses. He had golden eyes—and appeared just as shocked.

"Tau," whispered Karr.

CHAPTER NINETEEN

K ARR stared, numb. He had sensed his friend as soon as he entered this place, found himself washed in that old familiar scent that he could not believe. Not here, not now. *I'm losing my mind*, he had told himself.

But that face—human somehow, no longer that of a wolf—was recognizable to Karr. It only felt like days since he had last seen Tau. Days, across thousands of years. He knew his friend.

This was impossible.

"*Baya,*" Tau said hoarsely, in Soria's native language. "*Would you leave us?*"

The woman blinked, surprised, but after a moment gave a curt nod. Quietly, quickly, she exited the room and shut the door behind her. Robert went to stand in front of it. Soria stayed by Karr's side. He could feel her concern but did not look at her. All he could see was Tau. He was afraid that if he looked away, his friend would disappear.

"How?" whispered Karr. "How is this possible?"

Tau opened his mouth, then shut it with a snap. "I need to sit."

So did Karr. His legs were throbbing, and each step rolled agony through him. Soria took his hand and led him to a nearby chair. Her expression was closed, thoughtful; but just before she let go he felt a brief flash of connection between them, and saw Tau through her eyes: with suspicion.

Tau began to sit in a chair opposite him, and then paused, staring, rocking on his toes. He took a step, and then another, until he stood close to Karr. His golden eyes were still the same—sharp and hard, and so familiar. Karr forced himself to breathe, but it was difficult. The room suddenly felt small and dark.

He let Tau touch his face, though. He closed his eyes as the man's fingers lingered on his brow, and trembled. Both of them, shaking. Memories burned through Karr, a lifetime through childhood—Tau, close as a brother, playing, fighting, bleeding, killing—until now, here, in this moment . . .

"It *is* you," breathed the other chimera. "I never thought . . ." Again, Tau stopped. Backing away, he dropped into a chair with a thud. "I buried you myself. Three thousand years ago."

"And you are still alive." Karr gripped the arm of the chair so hard his fingers tore through the leather; his claws were out, and he had not realized it. "How?"

Tau hesitated, and it was so strange—seeing him here, seeing that look on his face that Karr knew so well—that he wanted to scream.

"He killed you," Soria said quietly, staring at the other

chimera. "He killed you, and you are alive, and he is alive, and the two must be connected. He did something to you, Karr. And it affected him, too."

Tau gave her a sharp look. "How do you speak our language?"

"How do you remember it so well after three thousand years?" Soria replied, just as sharply. "You must practice a lot."

Karr touched her hand. "She is a friend, Tau."

The other chimera's nostrils flared. "A friend? Your scent is all over her. I think she is your mate."

Soria narrowed her eyes. Karr struggled with his patience—and his nerves. It was so difficult to speak. "She is right. Answer the question. Why are we both alive?"

Tau looked down at his hands, golden light flaring briefly over his skin. Silver fur rippled free of flesh, black claws replacing his nails, followed by a trail of dark golden feathers. Eagle and wolf, bound in one man. His control had improved. Karr had never seen him look human, except once in their childhood.

Strange, he thought, suffering nausea from the pain in his legs—and from this shock. *Stay calm.*

"We are alive," Tau said slowly, still not looking at him, "because I did something terrible to you. Unforgivable. And seeing you here now, like this . . . I think it must be my punishment. My nightmare."

"Those are not the words of a friend," Karr said, feeling as though he were in another man's body, floating beyond himself. This was not happening. This was a dream.

Grief crumpled Tau's face, raw and wild. "I was not your friend after you killed my wife and child. I have had years to regret that." He hesitated, slumped in his chair, looking every inch an old and broken man. "But you are here. And you look . . . exactly the same."

Soria made a small, frustrated sound. "What did you do?"

Tau shook his head, closing his eyes; shame and despair rippled through the grief etched deep in his wrinkled brow. "I buried him alive. And I made sure he would stay alive in that darkness. Forever."

THE CREEK WATER WAS COLD. KARR SPLASHED A HANDFUL over his face, gritting his teeth against the chill and the throbbing ache in his legs. His heart hurt, too, in a thousand different ways. Tau sat nearby, drinking from a long-necked brown vessel. They had relocated outside and now talked a short distance away from the others.

"I went back to look for you," his friend was saying. "To set you free, if I could. But when I opened your tomb, you seemed truly dead. No heartbeat, cold to the touch. You had not begun to decay, but I blamed magic for that. There was nothing I could do for you."

"And you were still angry," Karr said heavily, remembering Yoana in her husband's arms, smiling slyly, with that cold look in her eyes that had warmed only for Tau. He glanced over his shoulder and found Soria watching him. She stood by the black metal wagon, with Robert at her side and Ku-Ku leaning out the window, playing with a large knife. None of them looked particularly pleased.

"I had stopped being angry by then," Tau said quietly. "But I was afraid, and ashamed. You being dead was easier than the alternative. I knew that if I had found you alive, you would never forgive me. Rightly so."

"And your immortality?"

"Linked to yours, I suppose. I have aged, obviously, a bit at a time. But death has eluded me. I did not know that would happen. I was not thinking. Just . . . reacting to an opportunity to take revenge." Tau looked ill. "I am sorry, Karr. I am . . . I am filled with words that have no meaning. What I did is beyond apologies."

Karr finally met Tau's gaze, searching for lies, for history, for anything that could tell him the story of this man's life, this onetime friend whom he did not know anymore. All he had was the past, and that could no longer be counted on. Strange enough to be sitting here in the grass, dripping wet, with someone Karr had assumed was long dead. Worse, to find out he was alive because that friend had wanted him to be tortured for all eternity. Buried alive. Conscious. Clawing at stone, trapped in darkness, in filth. The idea made him ill. Every memory he had of Tau suddenly seemed tainted with the rage that had driven his friend to harm him. A desire for revenge that Karr had expected then, and that he still understood.

"I forgive you," Karr said, wondering if that was true. "I hope you forgive me for taking your family from you."

"I forgave you for that a long time ago." Tau looked back at Soria. "Is she the one who found you?"

"No. But she saved me."

"Saved you." Tau gave him a sharp look. "From what?"

"Old feelings die hard." Karr smiled grimly. "Shape-shifters. Some of them still remember the old ways."

For a moment, pure hate filled Tau's eyes. He took a long drink. "They are not so mighty now."

Karr disagreed, but did not want to discuss the matter. "Other chimeras still live. You know that?"

"There is a group of them near here, less than a day's travel. They live in the mountains, very isolated. I go there sometimes, just to visit." Tau smiled sadly. "The world has changed, my friend. In so many ways. You cannot imagine the things I have seen. Humans have risen in ways we could never have believed. Their power is deep. And their lack of belief even deeper. I have hidden among them, pretending to *be* one of them, for more years than I can count. And still, they do not see the wolf among the sheep."

Karr imagined a hint of disdain in his friend's voice. "How were you not hunted by shape-shifters? How did the war end?"

Tau shook his head. "Badly, as you can guess. Your death . . . changed everything."

Karr looked down, wanting to ask more, but he did not have the strength to make those words. He had not fought for his people. He had left them, killed himself, rather than fight his own nature and make amends with action. A coward's choice.

Not one he would make again, no matter what.

Karr said, "You have a human wife. Another one."

Tau shrugged. "There have been many. Women are

easy to find, and when they are gone, there are others. To have someone to take care of me is not such a bad thing. Like Baya. She is a good woman, though she does not know my secret. You cannot trust most humans with such things."

"Not even the ones who love you?"

Tau clapped his hand on Karr's shoulder. "Does *she*? That woman who speaks our language?"

"Love me?" Karr looked back at Soria again, and met her gaze. She looked worried, and her concern was a twist in his guts. "I do not know. But she is my friend, and I trust her with my heart."

"Imagine that," Tau whispered. "You, who could have had anyone . . . after all these years, finding trust with a cripple."

Anger filled Karr's throat. His vision blurred with golden light, but even as he turned, Tau held up his hands. "I always spoke the truth as I saw it. I still do. I apologize if I was insulting. But you know my meaning."

"She has more courage, more heart, than any one skin can contain," Karr whispered dangerously. "We are in an odd place, you and I. If we are to be friends again, do not insult her."

Tau bowed his head. "My apologies."

Karr gritted his teeth, digging his cane into the ground to help him stand. "I would like to meet these other chimera. When can we go?"

"Now," Tau said. "But we should go alone. They will not take kindly to strangers."

"I will not leave Soria or her companions behind."

Tau hesitated. "How long have you been free, Karr?"

"Only days."

"Then you know nothing of how this world works, or who you can trust. Humans are not like they used to be. There is no awe left in them. They do not respect our kind, only fear us."

"Soria knows what I am," Karr replied. *And much more than that.*

Displeasure flickered over Tau's face. "You did not used to be naive."

"No," Karr agreed, a cold edge creeping into his voice. "I was the one our people trusted with their lives. I am still that man."

Tau's mouth tightened, but after a moment he nodded. "I think, perhaps, I will be apologizing to you for the rest of our lives."

Karr hoped not. Weariness filled him. Still, he hid it as he had done many times before, forcing himself to stand straight and tall. "If you do not wish to take us—"

Tau waved a hand and shook his head. "No. Let me tell Baya that I am going with you. She will pack us things to eat."

He walked ahead, back toward the tent. Graceful, quick on his feet—he did not move like an old man, and Karr realized he had forgotten to ask his friend an important question, one of many. *Will I ever die? Why have I not aged like you? You look old, but you are not three thousand years older. We are the same.*

Soria and Robert met him halfway to the wagon. Her braids were frayed again, and the wind tugged her long dress tight against her legs. Faint worry lines creased her brow, and her eyes were dark with shadows.

"You do not care for Tau," Karr said, not needing to be told.

"Neither of us trusts him," Soria replied in her own language, presumably so that Robert could understand. *"Anyone who condemns another to be buried alive is not all there in the heart or head. I don't care how much time has passed."*

Karr could not disagree. He felt many things seeing Tau again, including excitement and a stunned, careful happiness. But there was grief, too, and distrust. A sense that this was *too much.* He had not survived in battle, or human politics, or led his people for years without listening to his instincts. Even when those instincts railed against his very best friend in life.

"He is taking us to a group of chimera who live in the mountains near here," he explained.

Soria translated for Robert. Tau emerged from the tent holding a loose blue bag, and a red canister. Bayarmaa clung to his side, and when he bent to whisper in her ear, she smiled—but not with happiness. Her eyes held a sad acceptance, as though she was used to her husband taking unexpected excursions without her. It could not be an easy thing, especially as Tau had not told her what he was. Karr could not imagine keeping such a secret. To shift his shape—to live in another skin—was too much a part of him. To live under the same roof and be a mate to one who so obviously loved him, and yet hide that . . .

Perhaps Tau was afraid of frightening the woman. He obviously did not trust her. But if either of those things was true, then Karr thought it more merciful for Tau to be alone. More merciful for both sides.

"Let us play at being gods," he remembered Tau saying, more than once. *"Let us play, when we have so little. The humans are begging for it."*

"No one begs for deception," Karr had replied, always.

And like always, as though part of a game, Tau would whisper, *"But lies can ease the pain of living."*

He could hear those words ringing through him as he watched Tau load his bag and the sloshing red container into the back of their wagon, and then hop onto the two-wheeled transport sitting upright outside his home. He made a kicking motion and it roared to life, spewing a dark fume that made Karr's nose itch and burn. Odd, seeing his friend so well adapted to this modern world, moving through it with ease and grace. It rubbed at Karr, making him uneasy. Like seeing the sun in place of the moon. Felt wrong.

Tau drove ahead, taking a road that led them north of the human capital and then west toward the mountains. Their wagon bumped and bounced over a dirty track that led across the rocky plain, passing men on horseback driving sheep beneath a sky that yawned blue and brilliant. Sunlight was constant, pressing warm through the window on Karr's skin. Soria sat close beside him, also warm.

No one talked, though Soria began tugging on her empty sleeve. A sign of nerves, Karr thought. He needed a sleeve to twist, himself.

"I do not understand any of this," he said quietly. "I trusted him with my life."

"Trust is difficult," Soria replied, just as softly. "It is a leap of faith."

"Sometimes you fall."

"Hard." Soria smiled bitterly. "I used to have a lot of trust."

She said nothing else. Her silence was heavy and solemn, lost; and Karr did not want to press. Not here, where there was nowhere for her to run. Karr wanted to protect her from pain, not cause it.

I trust her with my heart, he had said to Tau.

He had trusted Tau, as well. From childhood unto death. And now he knew that trust had been misplaced. His friend had confessed to betraying him. *Betraying* him, and sentencing him to an eternity of torture.

A numb horror filled him. He could not have imagined resurrection all those years ago, nor Soria. And not this. Not *this*. He did not know how to reconcile the discovery, except to treat it as part of the surreal dream his life had become.

Tau had become his enemy. Once, long ago, without him realizing it. Was he still?

Was Soria, for that matter?

He glanced down at her, and she met his gaze. There was nothing hidden—not her concern, and not the tender heat that made his heartbeat quicken. He had been inside her mind; he had felt some of what had shaped her, and it was powerful, and tragic, and wildly fierce. He could not deny that. He could not convince himself that it was untrue. It felt natural as breathing, to trust her. He was simply worried that she should not trust him.

Especially when he was still here, risking her life. Selfish, stupid. Yet he was burdened by a tiny voice in his head that was certain he would never allow her to be hurt—not by any enemies, not by himself. It was that sense of self, that little voice, which had allowed him to make excuses and ignore the danger, that little voice that had allowed him to keep her by his side.

No, it made no sense, his feeling of security around her. And if it was true, that made it almost worse that he had killed Yoana and her unborn child: the idea that somehow he had been conscious enough to stop himself, had he wanted.

They reached the foothills of the mountain late that afternoon, a forested area of large rock formations and distant snowcapped peaks. They pushed their self-propelled wagons along yet another rough trail, bumping and sliding through with bone-jarring strength until, finally, neither Tau's two wheels nor their four could take them any farther. Ahead was a small footpath that led upward into the forest. Karr's legs throbbed just looking at it.

"This is another reason why I thought they should not come," Tau said. "We must fly the rest of the way."

"Fly," Soria repeated.

"You can walk, if you like." Tau smiled. "It will take longer."

"I will carry her," Karr rumbled, disliking the way his old friend looked at her. As though a mask was slipping from his eyes, revealing a hungry wolf.

Soria translated for Robert and Ku-Ku. Robert stared directly into the sun for one long moment, and then glanced away. *"My little friend and I will wait here for you. I think, perhaps, that would be the best."*

"Indeed," Tau replied, in the same language.

Robert smiled, but the expression was icy. *"Tell me something, Professor Mulraney. Who taught you how to live forever?"*

Tau gave him a sharp look, as though he was seeing the man truly for the first time. *"You would not understand such things."*

Ku-Ku made a small sound, picking at her nails with the tip of her long knife. Robert's smile grew *"I might not be a professor, but I am a curious man, and what you are and what you did are no secret. I don't think how should be, either."*

Tau's eyes narrowed, and he looked at Karr. "My wife," he rumbled, in the language of the chimera. "You know she was a priestess. She was also aware of magic. She hid it well from everyone else, though she taught me some things before her death."

Soria translated. Robert looked thoughtful, as if he did not entirely believe the chimera. He opened up the back of the wagon, and took out the blue cloth bag that Tau had brought. He tossed it at Tau's feet and it made a clanking sound. Karr did not think it sounded like food.

"You brought the sword," Soria said tightly. *"Didn't you?"*

Tau began to strip off his clothes. Golden light seared his skin, feathers erupting in long, rippling waves. He bent to pick up the bag, and Karr saw his shoulders bulging with wing buds.

"I seldom go anywhere without it," he rasped, his voice thickening, deep and sharp. "It is too precious."

Too precious to leave behind—especially if you are never going back.

Karr slowly took off his shirt and pants, leaning close to Soria. In her ear he whispered, "Stay. Something is going to happen."

"I know," she breathed, brushing her lips over his ear. He pulled back, staring into her eyes. No fear. No doubt. Just trust and determination, wild stubbornness.

"My dangerous woman," he murmured. "How I love you."

He did not expect to say those words, but he felt no shame afterward, nothing but heat as her gaze turned liquid. A tentative smile touched her mouth and then shifted into something fierce. She grabbed his hand as golden scales rippled over his skin, and squeezed hard.

"Do not dare leave me here," she said. "Promise me that I will face this with you."

"I promise," he agreed, closing his eyes as bones broke inside of him, expanding and growing, muscles churning. His haunches slipped into the form of a lion, and his neck stretched, mouth hooking into a short, draconic beak. Talons curled through his shifting hands but he was careful; Soria still held on to him, and her touch was an anchor. He could feel nothing else, not even the ground beneath his feet.

When Karr could see again, Tau had also finished transforming. His friend crouched on all fours, wearing the body of a wolf and the wings of an eagle. He clutched the satchel in his hands, which were still humanoid, though covered in thick silver fur. His eyes glowed, trailing light down lupine cheeks.

"Brother. It is good to see your face again," Karr whispered. Heartache filled him—and anger at himself, for not forgiving and trusting Tau—but before he could say a word, the chimera leaped into the air, wings beating furiously.

Soria stepped back, shielding her eyes, and looked at Robert. *"Are you going to surprise us?"*

"Oh," he said, as Ku-Ku tossed him something that resembled a black brick covered in tiny red squares. *"I'm sure I'll catch up somehow."*

Karr was not entirely comforted.

He picked Soria up, holding her tightly in his arms. His legs still ached, but not nearly as much. It had always been thus with his wounds: he was stronger in this other body; faster, tougher, harder to injure. Pain had always slipped away, as it did now.

His wings thrust down hard, and he leaped high into the path of a strong breeze. Slowly, painstakingly, he gained altitude, and then he followed Tau as quickly as he could.

The air was cold, and the winds gained strength. The world was vast beneath them, lush forests tumbling down rocky hillsides that were cut with frothing rivers. Light dazzled, and each breath was labored but sweet. Tau drew alongside him for a short time, and Karr could almost forget where they were and what had happened. It was good to be in the air again with his friend. Good to be himself with someone who remembered the old times.

He lost track of distance, only the changing shape and lushness of the land. Until Soria shouted, "I saw something glitter!"

Karr saw it as well: a reflective surface, shiny against the side of the mountain, there and gone in the blink of an eye. It was an odd place to see something like that: a sheer cliff face, just stone and nothing else. Except, as he drew closer he picked out small dark spots, like caves, and when he was closer still, some of the lines in the stones looked structured, as though cut by hand, shaped and molded into something that resembled a small, perfectly camouflaged city. Several narrow trails led up the cliff face, and Karr saw people on them. Men and women who wore loose robes buffeted by the wind.

Tau did not seem unnerved in the slightest to fly toward them. Karr followed his lead, noting uneasily how several of the humans pointed and started running.

They landed on a narrow ledge beside a rough-hewn staircase that wound against the rock face toward the open mouth of a cave. Karr heard a soft babble of voices above him, and smelled rich, smoky scents that he had not encountered since visiting the Nile kingdoms. Incense, thick and lush. Several men poked their heads out of the cave—just one of many caves, Karr realized. Their heads were shaved, skin dark and leathery, and they wore dark robes.

Soria sounded faintly stunned as she said, "They are monks. I have heard of remote monasteries, but this . . ."

Her voice trailed away. Karr understood why, also losing the ability to speak or think. Above him appeared a tall, pale woman, silver hair hanging loose down her back. She was very old, but her eyes were golden, and Karr knew her face.

"Althea," he whispered.

She stared at him like he was a ghost or a demon, and staggered backward, clutching her chest. "No!"

"Althea," he said again.

"You are dead," she breathed, eyes large with disbelief. And then she looked past him and saw Tau, and her expression hardened with hate. "You. What have you done?"

"I do not yet know," whispered Tau, staring at Karr. "I have not decided."

CHAPTER TWENTY

THE woman named Althea leaned hard against the side of the cave entrance. She was striking, more than six feet tall and lean as a cat. She was clearly old, with pale, fine skin drawn tight over her bones, but she also had a grace that reminded Soria of a dancer. Despite her aged appearance, she would have put most supermodels to shame.

She was not happy to see Tau. In fact, Soria had the strong feeling that if Althea could have punched a hole through the chimera's chest, she would have. Karr, however, was another matter. Soria could not quite judge Althea's reaction to him, other than complete and utter shock. Which she supposed was natural after thousands of years thinking someone was dead. She could only assume this ancient beauty was a chimera from Karr's past: if Tau, then why not more?

But why aren't you *dead*? Soria wondered, a chill stirring over her skin. *And did you participate in betraying Karr?*

All around them, human monks leaned out of caves,

or stood lightly upon uneven steps that had been carved and hacked from the mountainside, precariously narrow, bordered by thick ropes used as handrails—not much protection against the stiff winds and dizzying drop that had to be well over a thousand feet. It reminded her of the cliff dwellings of the American Southwest, or of those in Afghanistan's Bamyan valley, where the two giant Buddhas had stood before being dynamited by the Taliban. Those mountains were full of caves where people still lived, as were parts of China. And also, apparently, here.

"Althea," Karr rasped again; and Soria felt a tremor race through him, held as she was against his chest. "What has happened?"

What have you done? Soria looked at Tau, and found him staring back at her, golden eyes glittering in his wolfish face. She did not like the way he held her gaze, as though she was a challenge, one that he already felt he'd bested. *Dangerous*, she thought. *He's dangerous.*

Yet she did not disagree with Karr's handling of the situation. Tau was dangerous, but in the same way a family member might be. Like her uncle. Someone you trusted who betrayed you.

Tau was like her uncle, except on a far more extreme scale. He had committed a terrible act, but had explained it away with a reason that Soria knew Karr would find compelling. In this case, revenge. Revenge followed by contrition. Which Soria totally did not buy.

"What happened is that you are alive," murmured Althea, closing her glowing golden eyes. "Alive, after all these years. And, oh . . . if only you had stayed dead."

Karr went very still. Soria tapped his broad, scaled chest with her palm, and he let her down slowly, carefully. When her feet were firmly on the ground, he shifted into a humanoid shape, his face becoming more leonine while scales and fur lingered over his powerful, naked body. Soria felt very small beside him; small yet fierce.

"You want to explain that?" Soria asked.

Althea blinked hard, staring down at her. "You speak our language. How is that possible? None but a handful of chimera understand our tongue."

Soria tilted her head, jaw tight. "I asked you a question."

Karr's hand fell gently on her shoulder. "Althea. I was awakened from my tomb. I found the world quite changed. But I was *not* expecting to discover that any of you were still alive. Tau has offered some explanation, but he did not mention you."

"And why would he?" Althea inhaled a shuddering breath, and ran long, elegant fingers through her silver hair. "We exiled him. For murdering you—and for other crimes."

Soria turned to stare at Tau, even as Karr murmured, "Murder? But I asked him to—"

"Because you thought—" Althea interrupted, taking a step toward the edge of the cave. But she stopped, head tilted, listening. Soria tried to listen, as well.

Karr's hand tightened on her shoulder. "Those . . . sky wagons," he murmured. "I hear the blades."

"No," Althea breathed, covering her mouth. "No. Not now. Not again."

"Who is here?" Karr limped up the stone steps toward her, golden light trailing across his shoulders. His voice shook with anger. "If you are alive, who else?"

"Dozens," she whispered, staring at him as though he were both ghost and nightmare. "All of us who were your strongest warriors. After you died, we were changed. *He* changed us. And the things we did—"

She did not finish, and the expression on Karr's face was horrible to look at. "Who is here now?"

"Just three of us," Althea breathed. "And some children. Shape-shifters still mate across different breeds. This is one of several sanctuaries."

Karr's jaw tightened. Tau said, "I told you this would happen. I warned you he had come back to life. *I felt it.*"

His voice was closer than it should have been. Soria flinched, turning, and found Tau looming over her. He was almost human, though more animal than man. Standing upright, covered in fur; his face very much resembled a wolf.

Werewolf, she thought, thinking that she finally understood the origin of the legend.

The duffel bag at Tau's feet was open, and in his hands he held something both strange and familiar: a small brown doll with two gold beads sewn into its head, and a sliver of corroded metal that was larger than a needle but sharp on one end. Soria had seen that doll in a vision, red threads pouring from its gut. Dread filled her. She tried to grab, but he knocked her aside. Karr lunged, and Tau slammed the needle into the doll's gut.

Karr folded over, grunting. Soria, sprawled on the ground with her ears ringing, saw blood pour down the front of his legs.

"Tau," Althea said, voice choked. "Stop this."

But Tau did not. His eyes were glowing. There was no madness in them, no delusion; just simple calculation. Three thousand years, Soria thought. He had been alive all that time, making a life for himself while knowing—believing—that Karr was buried alive. And he had thrived.

The heart that could do that was beyond cold. It was dead. It had been cut out, along with whatever soul Tau had possessed all those millennia ago. Soria suddenly felt as though she was looking at a burned-out shell.

"Because of you we were losing the war," Tau whispered, bending low to stare into Karr's face. "Hiding, when it was our right to fight. Our right to take their children, as they had taken ours. Our right to *destroy* them, without mercy, as they were trying to do to us. And you . . . with your honor. With your rules. There are no rules in war, my friend. And after you were gone, we beat them. We won."

"No," Althea breathed, digging at her face with long nails that shimmered into claws. Blood welled. "We lost everything."

"What," Karr rasped, eyes glowing with fury and pain, "did you do?"

Tau's wolfish jaw twisted into a grimace, and he dug the needle deeper into the doll's guts. "You had no stomach."

Soria gritted her teeth. It was difficult to imagine she was a match for this creature—this monster of myth who had betrayed his friend—especially when she had only one arm. Nonetheless, anger carried her forward.

She lunged, taking with her a loose rock near her hand. She slammed that into Tau's elbow with all her strength, and the doll tumbled from the chimera's grip, needle still stuck inside.

Tau snarled, whirling on her, but Soria was too furious to back down. She had been this angry only once before, and a man had died. She had been afraid to ever feel that way again, but the rage was inside her, flowing through her blood, and it felt good and strong.

Karr was still bent over, blood gushing through his fingers, but he met her gaze and began hobbling toward the doll. Althea pushed away from the wall and leaped forward, landing light on her feet. She was also looking at the doll—but not, Soria sensed, to keep it from Karr.

Tau did not seem to notice. He was staring at Soria, and she spat at him, desperate to keep his attention. "*Coward*. Crippling a man you are too afraid to fight."

Behind him, Althea reached the doll and pulled out the needle. Tau began to look over his shoulder, but Soria darted in, ready to smash her rock against his testicles. Instead, she found herself hit so hard that she flew off her feet—and right over the edge of the mountain ledge into cool, empty air.

For one moment Soria felt as though she were floating, the blue sky blazing above and surrounding her in soft light. She heard Karr howl her name. And then she plummeted toward the ground.

She had time to think, which was awful. There was time for her life to flash before her eyes—no joke, because she saw *everything*, including Karr—

Strong arms caught her. The impact was so jolting,

Soria's head snapped back and made a cracking noise. There was nothing broken, but Soria was so stunned that she could hardly muster the emotional energy for relief. She looked up, expecting to see Karr . . . and found herself staring into the angular face of another dragon entirely.

"I should drop you," Long Nu rasped, her voice nearly lost beneath the roar of the wind.

"So drop me!" Soria shouted back, heart hammering. "You've come here to kill, haven't you?"

The dragon-woman's eyes glittered, and she twisted sideways. Soria saw two helicopters behind her in the distance. "I have come to end this. Whatever it takes," she agreed.

KARR WATCHED SORIA SPIN OFF THE LEDGE AND TRIED TO follow her. He tried with all his power, blood still trickling from his closing wound—closing, he imagined, because the needle had been plucked from the doll— but Tau got in his way, slamming claws into his gut, grappling and holding him until Karr knew it was too late: he would never catch her.

She was dead.

"You see how it feels now?" Tau hissed in his ear, hot spittle flying across his cheek. "I never loved Yoana, but I loved my child. How does it feel, Karr? Tell me."

Karr screamed, throwing back his head in agony. Golden light blurred his vision, then darkness as well, churning and rolling inside of him like a storm. His heart cracked—with grief, and also with something pure and cold and primal.

Rage. Blinding, soul-killing rage.

He threw himself away. His mind was swallowed in golden light as his body transformed, thickening and breaking itself as his claws erupted and wings unfurled from his aching back. He felt his father in him, and his mother, and embraced every deadly aspect of his nature, lost in his desire to rip apart the thing in front of him.

Tau stumbled backward and then braced himself, snarling. His eyes also flashed, but the light was tinged with red: gold rimmed in crimson, bloodshot with hate and fury.

Karr threw himself at Tau and took them both over the ledge. He did not try to fly. The two chimeras spun wildly, snapping at each other's throats, punching and raking with their claws. Karr closed his teeth over Tau's ear and ripped it off, taking bone and brain. Tau screamed.

Karr broke away, twisting as the ground raced toward him. His wings beat furiously, but only enough to slow him down. His back feet hit rock, almost pitching him forward on his face in a devastating fall, but the strength of his wings was enough to save him. He tumbled, but not hard enough to crush bone.

He searched for Tau and found him nearby, sprawled on his back. Still breathing. Eyes open. Drool and blood flowed from his mouth, and his limbs were twisted at odd, broken angles. But there was defiance in his eyes. Satisfaction.

Tau laughed when he looked up at Karr; a cold, empty sound. "You cannot kill me," he breathed. "You cannot kill any of us. I made the bargain. I sealed it with the sacrifice. Blood of my child, blood of the mother, blood of the friend . . ." Tears leaked from the corners of his eyes—suddenly pain or grief, Karr could not tell. "I told myself I could make another baby. A better world for a new life, when the war was over."

"Sacrifice," Karr repeated, his enemy's words cutting through his desperate fury.

"I found something," Tau breathed, his gaze briefly turning inward. "Something came to me, and it was powerful, and it breathed inside my heart. Taught me dreams and possibilities. It was not my wife who gave me the ability to kill you, but another. I never saw its face."

And then Tau's expression hardened, and he tilted his head sideways to spit blood and teeth. "I knew you would never break. Never lose your mind. You were too strong. So, I drugged you. It was easy to do. I killed Yoana myself, and covered you in her blood."

"Tau," Karr breathed.

"You made me do it," he hissed. "If you had been stronger, if you had listened to me, I would not have been forced to take such measures. It was your fault. You *did* deserve to die. The rest . . . torturing you . . . was for me. My child. All our children who you lost through your weakness. *You were never supposed to wake.*"

"I see," Karr said. And he ripped off Tau's head with his bare hands.

THE HELICOPTERS LANDED IN A PASTURE ON TOP OF THE mountain, located just above the cliff face where the monastery had been built into the rock. Except for a rather noticeable trail that led to the edge, along with several small *gers* and milling livestock, Soria would never have guessed that there could be such activity directly below, in such an improbable place.

Long Nu dropped her on the ground, hard. Men poured out of the helicopters. None seemed shocked by the sight of a dragon, which raised all sorts of questions for Soria, despite the fact that these were Long Nu's mercenaries. Of the men, it was Baldy—the mercenary who had raised his fist to her—who led the charge.

"Make sure she doesn't go anywhere," Long Nu rasped to him. "And I want her unharmed. If there is so much as a tear in her eye when I return, you will die."

Baldy's jaw tightened, but he gave a curt nod. Grabbing Soria's arm with bruising strength, he dragged her past the gathered men, all of whom looked at her as though she might have an Uzi stuffed up her dress.

If only, she thought, imagining a machine gun strapped to her missing arm, just like in the movies. Bang, bang.

But then memories filled her—her finger pulling the trigger, the two bangs, the shots in the head—and she pitched forward, almost stumbling as the nausea, fear, and stress of the last ten minutes rolled right up her throat. She gagged, and Baldy cursed, grabbing at her braids to haul her backward into the helicopter. He threw her down inside, and she heard a loud protest beside her—a familiar voice.

Evie.

Soria was stunned to see the girl. She had a bruise forming under her eye, and her bottom lip was split. Her cheeks were flushed, her gaze sharp and furious. Her hands were bound behind her back.

"What the fuck?" Soria snapped, rolling over to stare at Baldy. "What is she doing here?"

Baldy smiled grimly. "Apparently, she started poking around, all worried about you. Started calling people, asking the wrong questions. Brought attention to herself. We had to control the situation."

"Screw you," Evie snarled.

"'Screw you,'" he mocked. "Say *fuck* like a real woman, and maybe you'll luck into some."

Soria sat up, crouching in front of the girl. "You try, you die. I *will* kill you."

Baldly bit his bottom lip, speculation heavy in his gaze. "I'd like to see that. The one-armed woman against me." He tapped his chest. "Special Forces, darlin'. I ain't no pussy."

"You look like one," Evie snapped. "Bet you have a big old rug under those pants."

Soria gave her a dirty look, and the girl cringed. Baldy just roared with laughter and pulled a large knife from the sheath at his waist. He tossed it at Soria, and the blade landed hard, skittering across the helicopter floor.

"Go on," he said. "I don't care what the old bitch says. This'll be worth it. I owe you a little something."

Full circle, Soria thought, staring at the knife with creeping quiet horror. She could hear her uncle's whispers in the darkness, telling her to fight—fight or kill herself. She could see him flicking that little blade in the beam of the flashlight he carried, that he had shone over the disgusting photographs strewn at her feet.

"Fight or die," her uncle had whispered, crouched just out of reach. "But I hope you fight. If you do, I'll know that deep down, *deep, deep down*, part of you still wants me. Like they all wanted me." And he had kicked the photographs closer, showing terrified hollow faces, naked women in chains.

Soria looked up now and saw her uncle—and then the image faded and it was Baldy again. Slick with sweat, his eyes gleaming. Made of the same stuff, she thought, rage hard in her throat.

"Little's the word, all right," Soria muttered, gritting her teeth as she picked up the knife. It felt heavy in her hand. The last time she'd held something this heavy, it had been in darkness and she'd been lost, a chain around her arm. Touching the knife made her almost as sick as holding a gun, but not quite. This surprised her, but there was no accounting for memories.

She had been right-handed before, always bad with her left, but her grip was strong. She could do this.

"Outside," she said. "Back up."

"Marko," called a low male voice. It was the helicopter pilot. Soria had not noticed him, but he was staring at Baldy with a look of extreme displeasure. "Cut it out."

"Nah," said the man. "Nothing's going to happen. Look at her, she's shaking. I'll have my knife back in two seconds."

"That's not the point," groused the pilot. Soria thought about trying to take him hostage. His back was turned. It would be easy. But after she had him . . . that would be the tough part. Hostages were hard work.

She looked back at Evie and tried to smile. "Hang tight, kiddo."

The young woman gave a tight nod, but she looked

ill and afraid. And yet, there was a continued hint of defiance in her eyes that was all Soria needed to get her ass in gear. She had survived worse creeps than this. Gone to extremes to survive. This would be nothing.

The mercenaries that Long Nu had taken with her were out of sight. Soria heard scattered gunfire and shouts, but no screams of fear or pain. That could not last. Perhaps the monks would be safe, but not Karr. Not Althea or any chimera.

"Come on, baby," said Baldy, his hands in his pockets, backing around the chopper and away, clearly expecting her to rush him and not at all concerned. "Show me what you got. And then I'll show you what *I* got."

"Okay," Soria said, when they were far enough away. She looked at him, and again saw her uncle. A ghost in her mind. Baldy swam back into focus.

She threw the knife at his face.

Not for nothing had she spent ten years working with a bunch of men and women who liked playing with sharp objects. But her aim was off. The blade sank into the meaty part of Baldy's arm. He stared for a moment, stunned, and then the pain caught up with him and he howled.

"Damn," Soria muttered, and Baldy ripped the knife out of his arm and charged toward her, red faced, eyes bulging with pain and fury.

She ran back toward the helicopter, and jumped inside. The pilot was swearing, trying to unbuckle himself from his seat. Soria grabbed Evie and looked at the restraints around her wrists. Thick plastic wire. She was going to need something sharp.

"Give me a knife," she barked at the pilot. "Or shoot him. He's going to kill us!"

"Fuck," muttered the pilot, as Baldy reached the helicopter. He stood outside, staring at Soria like a zombie: hungry, mindless, hateful. Blood gushed down his arm. He held the bloody knife. Soria, crouched low, moved in front of Evie.

"Marko!" shouted the pilot.

"I don't care," rasped the other mercenary, and began to climb into the helicopter. But, halfway in, a shadow moved behind him and something long and sharp slid between his legs, angling upwards to press against his crotch. Baldy froze.

So did the pilot, raising his hands as Robert peered around the edge of the door, holding a gun. "Finally, some ladies in distress. Makes me feel like a man again."

"Yes," Soria said shakily, glimpsing glossy black pigtails and Hello Kitty sunglasses behind Baldy's ass. "I'm certain you get tired of Ku-Ku having more testosterone than you."

Robert's lips quirked up. "I see you've forgotten the arm."

"It's just an arm," Soria replied, and let him help her out.

CHAPTER TWENTY-ONE

K ARR did not sit with Tau's body; he tossed aside the grisly head and went looking for Soria's remains.

He did not find her. Not anywhere. Which meant that someone had already carried off her corpse—unlikely—or she had come back to life—given his own situation, not impossible, but still unlikely.

Or she had never hit the ground.

Hope sprang wild. He turned in a wide circle, staring up at the sky, and glimpsed flying wagons descending on top of the cliff. *There.* He had to get there.

"Karr."

Karr turned, and found Althea behind him. She was accompanied by two other familiar faces, men whom he had last seen in their prime, young and strong and healthy. These two chimeras who stood before him now still looked strong, but the physical effects of age had appeared, shriveling their flesh, hollowing out their cheeks and eyes.

"Bax. Cruno," Karr said, shocked to discover that

their existence was not exhilarating as once it would
have been.

Truth had torn out a piece of his heart. Loyalty and
family meant nothing. He had found his people—found
more than he could have hoped of what he'd known—
and instead of joy and comfort, he had discovered
strangers and deception. He had no home.

There was only Soria—if he could find her.

"It is true," Bax whispered, swaying. He had always
been the shortest of the chimeras, a squat, solid fighter
who wore the skins of the crocodile and wolf. Fur rippled
over him, followed by a rough, dark hide that shimmered
like a river over his body. Beside him, Cruno slouched,
becoming more bear than man, though in moments he
shifted into the slender body of a hawk.

Althea herself wore white fur dressed in leopard
spots, silver wings clasped over her shoulders. Her face
was feline, though she stood upright like a woman. Her
golden eyes were glowing, her face contorted with grief.

"You were my friends," Karr said quietly. "And you
betrayed me."

"No," breathed Althea, tears glimmering in her eyes.
"It was we who were betrayed. Tau made all your warriors immortal. He did not tell us. We discovered only
through accident."

"But we did betray you," Cruno growled. "Your
memory."

"We let him lead us. Tau was always your second,"
Bax rumbled. He glanced down at the decapitated body.
"This is not over."

Karr shook his head, backing away. "I do not . . . I have no time for this. I . . ." He stopped short as shots filled the air far above. The other chimeras flinched.

"Hunters," Althea whispered. "It has been fifty years, but I knew they would come again. It happens, sometimes, when we have not been careful. Not all shape-shifters know of our existence, but those who do keep a watchful eye for any who might be chimeras. Or those who might be making them. It is not an easy thing to hide if two shape-shifters of different breeds fall in love, especially if they do not know that what they are doing is truly forbidden, and punishable."

Karr gave her a sharp look. "You said there were children."

"Hidden." Bax gave the others a worried look. "Deep in the caves. If we go back, we might guide the humans straight to them."

"They are led by a shape-shifter," Karr said. "A dragon. She will smell them."

He did not wait to see if they followed. He leaped into the air, wings beating hard, fighting for a sharp ascent back to the caves. He thought of Soria and died a little, but if there were chimera children in hiding, with a dragon hunting them . . .

Screams filled his memories—small faces and smaller hands gripping his shoulders and hair, his name called out by terrified voices. And those nets, the nets and hands that had held him down as he watched those children burn.

Karr felt movement behind him. Althea and Cruno were flying swiftly at his back. Near the caves, he saw monks running down the precarious stone steps, and close behind them were those dark-clothed men with their strange modern weapons. Their task seemed to be fear, chaos; they were aiming at the sky and shooting.

Karr looked for Soria but saw no sign of her. But he felt a chill against the base of his neck, and Althea suddenly shouted. He twisted to the right just as a dark green body plummeted past with crushing speed. The dragon immediately halted, and swerved to the left, screaming in rage.

"Get the children!" he shouted at the others, and then folded his wings against his back, diving toward Long Nu.

She was old but fast, and neatly evaded his first charge—but Karr shifted his lower limbs in midflight, forcing his arms to lengthen into a lion's reach, and when Long Nu made another pass, he grabbed her around the neck and raked talons down her chest. She cried out, eyes glowing, and he dug his lower feet into her spine, fighting to break her back.

Long Nu made her wings go limp and she dropped through the air like a stone, taking Karr with her. The two spun, rolling wildly. The moment his grip loosened, the old dragon curled around herself in a tiny ball. Karr had no choice but to let go.

The moment he released her, Long Nu flared her wings, catching him in the face. He grunted, tumbling backward through the air, and she dropped again, feet first into his gut. Karr grabbed her ankles, but that only anchored her close enough to swipe at his face. At the last moment, he twisted so that she caught his shoulder instead—but the pain was sharp and the ground very close.

He flung her away, straightening out before impact, his belly skimming tree tops. High up, he heard a familiar shout.

It was Soria. She stood on the ledge that she had fallen from. She was not alone. Robert and Ku-Ku were on her right, shooting at the mercenaries streaming down the stairs. Much to his surprise, the blonde girl Evie was close by, huddled low with her hands over her head.

Long Nu saw Soria, too. Karr felt the change in the old dragon, knew what she was going to do before she began her ascent. He screamed at her, enraged and terrified. But despite his brute strength, Long Nu was faster. She flew straight toward Soria, and he could not catch up.

IT WAS A MIRACLE—AND A LOT OF BULLETS—THAT HAD gotten them this far, but Soria had insisted on coming back to look for Karr and those children that Althea had mentioned. If Long Nu was hunting chimera, she would not stop at adults.

But now they were stuck, and Long Nu was headed straight for her. Karr was close behind, but Soria knew he was not going to be fast enough. Perhaps Long Nu did not intend to kill her, but one thing was certain: the dragon-woman was going to use Soria against Karr, and she could not let that happen.

She turned, and found Evie staring at the dragons with huge eyes.

"No way," the girl muttered, and then, again.

"Way," Soria replied, desperately casting around for

a weapon, anything that she could use to fight Long Nu. Robert and Ku-Ku were armed, but she didn't want to distract them. The mercenaries had them pinned and knew it. It was just a matter of time before the pair ran out of bullets.

And then it happened. Robert's gun clicked. Ku-Ku shook her head, and he held out his hand. She gave him her knife, and Soria watched in horror as he left safe cover and charged up the steps toward the men who had been shooting at them. Ku-Ku blasted away at anyone who raised a gun, but there were too many.

Soria watched Robert get shot . . . but not before he reached the first man, made a quick, lethal motion with his knife, and wrested the mercenary's gun away.

He was shot again, and staggered, but at this new angle he had a cleaner view of the men, and took out another before being hammered a third time in the chest. Again, he made a clean shot—again, another bullet entered his body—and Robert pitched forward off the edge of the cliff. Soria clapped her hand over her mouth, gasping. Ku-Ku showed nothing. She just kept shooting.

Evie squeezed Soria's arm and pointed. Long Nu was almost on top of them. They had run out of time.

But just before the dragon made contact, a small mass of black feathers plummeted from above and slammed into her head. Long Nu jerked, and the distraction—and the dragon's incautious speed—sent her crashing narrowly past. Her wing struck rock. Soria heard bone break.

A crow circled and landed lightly beside Soria on the stone ledge. His golden eyes gleamed. Off to Soria's right, the mercenaries started shouting, dropping their guns and shaking their hands. The metal glowed red-hot. Ku-Ku rose from her hiding place, gun aimed. The men reached for other weapons, but started screaming again, holding their hands. Smoke curled from gloved palms.

"Eddie," Soria whispered, glimpsing the young man at the top of the stone steps, wind blowing his tousled hair over his eyes. Serena was with him, and she held small guns in each hand. Light trailed over her shoulders, and she slid around Eddie to take the lead.

Karr arrived at the ledge, shifting as he drew near. He was almost human again when his feet touched the stone—as was Long Nu, whose draconic body morphed within a sheet of heavy golden light into a naked, wrinkled woman lying upon the stone and cradling her ribs.

Silence, all of them staring at each other. Long Nu's expression was bitter and twisted. She looked past Karr to Serena, and then Koni, who still wore the skin of a crow, and her mouth tensed even more. "So. What now?"

Karr hesitated, glancing at Soria, who stared back. Time stretched between them—time and heartstrings, which tugged so fiercely that she found herself stepping toward him before she could stop herself.

She loved him, she realized. It was simple as that. No explosions, no thunderous applause. She loved him. A tighter, stronger, cleaner love than any she had ever felt, burning straight through her to the bone. No rhyme or reason. Just *this*. She had come searching for truth, and found it—and though it was not what she had expected, she knew that she would give her life to keep it safe.

Fierce warmth filled Karr's eyes, as though he could read her mind. He looked down at Long Nu. *"I do not want to fight. Not anymore. There must be another way."*

Soria translated. Long Nu stared up at him, her gaze hollow and old. "If you only knew—"

A single shot rang out. The bullet slammed into the rock beside Long Nu. In one smooth movement, Karr stepped in front of the old shape-shifter just as another shot sounded. The bullet skimmed his shoulder, spinning him to his knees.

Soria spun. Althea stood on another ledge above them, a gun in her shaking hand. She was staring with horror at Karr. Soria sensed movement on her right: Ku-Ku, gun raised.

"No," Karr gasped, holding his hand out to the young woman. *"No!"*

Soria shouted the same thing, though she didn't give a rat's ass whether Ku-Ku played target practice with the female chimera. She ran to Karr, falling down beside him. His shoulder was bleeding, but the injury was not terrible.

Long Nu stared at him, and reached out, tentatively. Soria did not want her touching him, and batted away the old woman's hand. The moment she made contact, though, rough sparks buried her mind. She lost herself in memories, flashes of light and darkness.

She saw Long Nu, much younger, kissing a man with golden eyes.

Shadows shifted, revealing the tall lean figure curled around her. It was Tau, she realized with shock. *Tau.* Smiling down, but with a coldness in his eyes that

Long Nu did not seem to see—or care about. It was clear that she was enthralled, and hopelessly in love.

The vision shifted again. Soria saw Long Nu holding a baby. It had just been born—or rather, Long Nu was in a bed, with a human woman at her side, and she was covered in sweat and was naked beneath her blankets. The baby was very small, but horribly disfigured, with limbs covered in scales and silver tufts of fur, its face not recognizable as human or animal, just a mash of bone and features crushed together. Long Nu was rocking her dead baby against her chest, choking out deep, guttural sobs—a terrible, aching sorrow that sank hooks into Soria's heart and would not let go.

Tau stood in the doorway, watching. Coldness in his eyes. Smiling cruelly.

The vision collapsed again, but this time Long Nu was alone, no baby—standing over the corpses of two shape-shifters, caught between human and animal, bodies so ravaged it was impossible to know if they had been male or female. Long Nu still wept, but there was a fury in her heart that invaded Soria, a rage so deep that it burned with its own terrible life.

A scent covered those corpses. It belonged to Tau.

He had used Long Nu. Killed those closest to her. Made a baby with her that he had known would not survive. Tau had continued his war, long after it had ended. Soria could only guess at how many other lives he had destroyed through the centuries.

Soria swayed into Karr's arms, tears racing down her cheeks. Long Nu was also weeping, but silently, anger and grief mixed hard in her eyes.

"You will not say a word," she hissed, staring at them. "Neither of you. That is mine. What you saw is *mine*."

"Yes," Karr breathed, holding Soria tightly against him. *"Yes, but surely you know that you are not alone."*

Soria did not translate. She felt the dragon knew what Karr had said.

Long Nu squeezed shut her eyes, and snapped her fingers at Koni. "You, crow. Help me stand."

Koni's wings fluttered nervously, but moments later he stood on two feet, all arms and tattoos and long black hair. His sharp face was creased with uneasiness, but he extended his hand and helped Long Nu to her feet.

"We're done here," the old woman snapped at her mercenaries. "Go back to the helicopter and leave."

The men looked at each other. Soria was certain they would disobey. But whatever their experience was with Long Nu, it held true. In a dazzling display of obedience, they turned and marched up the stone stairs. Serena watched them carefully as Eddie jogged down the steps, skirting abandoned weapons, and Evie stood as he reached them, hugging herself, trembling. He hesitated, staring at the girl.

"Please," Soria said to Long Nu. "Let it go."

"I want to see the children." She stared down at the stone, her cheeks still wet with tears. "I can smell them. I want . . . I want to see."

"Karr," Althea called out. *"You cannot."*

Karr ignored her, giving Long Nu a careful look. *"It is interesting the lengths that some will go to in order to harm that which they once loved."* Long Nu frowned, but he stood slowly, leaning heavily on Soria. *"Honor your word, dragon. Or I will honor it for you."*

She gave him a hateful, weary look. "My honor is my life. I promise I will not harm them."

Karr's jaw tightened. Soria knew how much this was costing him. What plagued his nightmares.

Althea was still protesting when the small group entered the caves. Karr gave her a look—just one—and she closed her mouth with a snap. Grief and weariness, and fear, filled her eyes, but she turned and led them into narrow darkness. Evie stayed behind, Eddie with her, his one hand tentatively reaching toward her. His soulful brown eyes were full of the compassion that Soria remembered so well. Evie would be safe with him. And where they were going was not something the girl needed to see. She had been exposed to too much already.

"Were any of the monks hurt?" Soria asked Althea.

"Just frightened." The chimera's golden eyes glimmered. "Their order has kept our secret for hundreds of years. This was a sanctuary for our kind. But not, I think, anymore."

Two more chimeras waited ahead of them, bearing old rusty swords. When they saw the three shapeshifters, their snarls rent the air.

Hate, Soria thought. *So much hate.*

Karr held up his hand. *"No more. If you ever trusted me, do so now. No more. Let us through."*

"Do it," Althea said, when they did not move. *"Fate has brought us here."*

The chimera wanted to fight, that was clear. Soria could not tell what their ancestors had been, except they were covered in fur and feathers and scales. Long Nu and Serena ignored the chimeras' disgust, but Koni could not stop studying them as he passed; there was confusion and dismay in his gaze.

Soria heard snuffling sounds the moment they entered the chamber. Long Nu stopped, frozen. Serena did as well, staring into the darkness. Several pairs of golden eyes gleamed, and Karr tensed beneath Soria's hand. She could see little of them but their eyes, but there was enough light to glimpse fur and human skin, and round little bodies huddled together on blankets.

"Oh, my God," Koni breathed, his voice stricken. "Were you coming here to kill them?"

Long Nu closed her eyes, swaying. Serena grabbed the older woman's arm. "We do not murder children."

"Once we did," replied the dragon, pressing her hands to her belly. "Thousands of years ago. There were prophecies. Prophecies that foretold that the chimera, our half-breed children, would destroy us all. There were already those who saw them as aberrations. They struck first."

"But in doing so, they caused the war," Karr said hoarsely.

"And it was a war that destroyed *us*," Long Nu agreed. "The chimera ruined us as we ruined them. Murdered entire families, children, enslaved human women to make more of their kind. They could not be stopped."

She gave him a hard look. "Their warriors had become immortal."

Karr exhaled slowly, and Soria clutched his arm as tightly as she could. Holding him steady, giving him strength.

"I remember," Althea whispered brokenly. "The memories are always with us. Karr had led us to believe in mercy, but once he—you—were gone, Tau changed everything. And we followed. We followed, because we wanted revenge; and to taste our success and see the shifters bleed and run while we stood unharmed was . . . intoxicating. And then it stopped feeling right. It became uglier than we could conceive."

"And by killing us, you killed yourselves," Serena said quietly. "For there are no chimeras without shape-shifters. You can breed with humans, but the children are diluted. Without your true power."

"Without our power, but stable and whole," Althea replied. "But no. They are not us."

Karr studied the chimera. "You left Tau?"

"After a hundred years, yes. By then, the damage was done. We scattered across the world. We lived with our shame. Some of us tried to make amends. And now you are here, to remind us of our sins."

"All our sins," Long Nu murmured. "I wanted you dead for that. You are proof of past crimes. You are truth." She fixed Althea with an icy stare. "And I wanted the rest of you . . . The moment I heard that a shape-shifter had been found alive in an ancient tomb, one who could take on both fur and scales, I knew he was one of you. I thought it might lead me to Tau. But if not, I was certain the chimera would take me to where you all were hiding. So I could end it. And *him*."

"And now?" Soria asked.

"It is ended," Long Nu said, and left the chamber.

CHAPTER TWENTY-TWO

A LTHEA insisted that they find Tau's remains. Evie stayed with the monks, no longer looking quite as frightened. Just thoughtful. Which was almost as worrisome. Soria suggested that Eddie remain with her. He did not protest, except to pull her aside.

"I came for you," he said, with a gentle shyness that was undercut with determination. "I didn't tell Roland. I saw the e-mail you sent him and just walked out."

Hacker, she thought, wondering how he had managed to get here so quickly. Remembering, too, how he had curled on the floor of a fireproof cage, frightened of losing control. Scared to step outside among normal people. She could only imagine what it had cost him to do this. Or what the risk might be.

Soria flung her arm around his neck, and found him warm—warmer than any human had a right to be. "Thank you."

"We're your friends," he whispered against her hair. "All of us at the agency. We missed you. I didn't want you to be alone again. I had to try."

Soria dragged in a deep breath and nodded. "Eddie . . ."

"I know what Roland did to you," he said, his eyes very old despite his youthful face. "Back then, a year ago. I know how much it hurt you. I didn't want to be like him. Too afraid to help the people you care about because you don't trust yourself not to hurt them. I think . . . that's another kind of death."

Soria was going to cry if she didn't get away from him. She stood on her toes and kissed his cheek. "Right. Go and live, then. Go on and enjoy that girl's company. I saw how you looked at her. And you can do damage control while you're at it. She's nice and smart. I think you'll do fine."

Eddie blushed. Soria turned and found Karr watching her with weary compassion. He said nothing, though. Merely held out his hand.

Everything stopped inside her. All the pain, all the loneliness and grief of the past year, rising for one suffocating moment—right before it was swept away in a rush of profound, tender warmth. Soria stared at Karr, unable to move, too stirred with wonder to do more than breathe him in.

He limped to her. The bullet had skimmed his shoulder, taking a chunk of flesh. Soria did not want to think about how much pain he was in.

"Your eyes," he said quietly. "The way you look at me."

"Because I love you," she said, meaning those words with a ferocity she had never felt for any other, gritting her teeth as tears burned her eyes.

Karr said nothing, but there were words in his silence, in the way his thumb brushed against her mouth with gentleness and awe. She leaned forward as his hand slid around the back of her neck, warm and strong, until she was buried against his chest, engulfed within the strength of his arms.

"For you," he murmured. "For you I would suffer another three thousand years, just for this."

They flew down. Long Nu insisted on joining them, and was carried by Althea—a leap of faith that Soria would not have taken. Serena said she would find her own way to the base of the cliff, while Koni soared in ever-descending circles through the late evening air.

Soria received a shock when they landed. Robert was there, sitting up, looking slightly scuffed but very much alive. He was drinking a bottle of water. Ku-Ku sat beside him, painting her nails with a machine gun tucked under her skinny legs. The blue duffel bag sat beside her on the ground. She looked up briefly when they arrived, but shape-shifters flying through the sky were clearly not as interesting as pink polish.

"You need to do something about that," Robert said, pointing to a very decapitated body that was sprawled less than twenty feet away. "Burning him and scattering the ashes might work. Or"—Ku-Ku stopped painting her nails long enough to kick over the duffel bag—"you could try stabbing him with the sword used to kill you. Hard to say what will work. Magic is fickle."

"I suppose you would know," Soria said, suddenly too weary to do more than throw in the towel of disbelief and simply accept that her life had room for one more oddity.

"Oh," Robert replied, in Greek, "I'm familiar with the concept."

"Stab him," Long Nu said, staring at Tau's head with bitter hate. "And then burn him. Or let him find his way back to life, and then do it."

Prolong the pain. Soria remembered what she had seen of Long Nu's memories, and could not fault the old shape-shifter for her rage. Part of her felt the same. But Karr stared at Tau's corpse with peculiar compassion and sadness.

"My brother," he breathed, so quietly that Soria was not entirely certain anyone else heard. And then he gave Long Nu a sharp look. *"And now? We have peace, but is it dependent on my kind remaining in the shadows? Will we always be outcasts?"*

"No," Soria said fiercely, squeezing his hand and staring at the old shape-shifter. "You have a home with us. All of you. Dirk and Steele will not turn you away."

"You cannot speak for them," Long Nu said.

"I can speak for what's right," she replied coldly. "You made a deal with Roland, didn't you? That's why he didn't involve the rest of the agency. Why he told no one but me about Karr."

The old woman's eyes narrowed. "I acted on my own. What he did was done to preserve the peace. In case Karr had to be killed."

Koni made a disgusted sound. "You won't be able to hide this. I won't let you."

"Little bird," whispered Long Nu. "You forget yourself."

"No." He met her gaze. *"You* forgot."

Displeasure flickered. Behind Long Nu a leopard glided free of the shadows and made her way to Robert's side. Robert glanced down and rested his hand briefly upon Serena's furred shoulders. He smiled tightly. "You cannot bury history. But you can bury *him*. So do it now. Cut that tie, at least."

Soria almost suggested they burn the voodoo doll, as well, but she was afraid of what would happen to Karr. She leaned down to poke around the bag, and found the doll in moments. Maybe she would keep the damn thing, lock it up. Something. Karr watched her tuck the doll into the pocket of her dress, but except for a tightening of his jaw, said nothing.

"What about the rest of us?" Althea asked, stroking the long white tail that curled around her waist. "Not everyone wants to die. If you break the magic . . ."

Karr peered at Tau's head, and kicked it with his foot. *"Are you certain this is necessary?"*

Soria translated. Robert raised his brow. "Do you want to take the risk that he'll haunt you, your children, your grandchildren—"

Karr held up his hand. *"What of me? Will I die?"*

Soria's heart lurched with fear, but she shared the message. Robert shrugged. "Of course you will. You're not immortal."

"But he's three thousand years old," Soria said.

"And he can barely stand after suffering injuries he received *yesterday*. For the truly immortal, that doesn't happen." Robert pointed at himself. "I would still be dead, otherwise."

"Oh, for God's sake," Koni muttered, dragging over the duffel bag. "Stab the fucker already, and then burn his ass. You've got your own living matchstick up there on the mountain, and plenty of room to scatter him. Worry about the voodoo later."

Karr gave him a long look, shook his head and then picked up the sword. A faint tremor raced through him when he held the blade. Uneasiness pricked at Soria. Second thoughts. But before she could tell him to stop, he buried the sword in Tau's heart.

The corpse jerked, almost as if it was alive. Silence descended. Everyone stared at each other.

Althea said, "I do not feel any different."

"Nor do I," Karr added, staring at Soria.

"Well, then," Robert said. "Ku-Ku brought marshmallows."

ESCAPE.

That was all Karr wanted. All these people, most of them strangers, and now that the fighting was done, he had nothing left. Just his wounds and a sore heart—which eased considerably when Soria found him.

He was on the edge of the cliff, amongst the rocks. It was night, and fires burned around the tents behind him. Long Nu had gone with her soldiers. Althea and the others were down in the caves, tending to the chimera children and monks. As for the whereabouts of the rest, that was a mystery he was content not to solve. He had mysteries enough in his own heart.

Soria sat down beside him, their shoulders rubbing tight and warm, and, there was such effortlessness in the way she touched him, such comfort, that he found himself smiling again, and kissed the top of her head.

Soria closed her eyes, leaning her brow against his

chin—so close to him, closer than any other, in body and heart. She *was* his body and heart. And it was as miraculous as the circulation of his blood and the breath in his lungs. Karr remembered briefly how it had been to stand under the night sky for the first time after his resurrection, knowing he had been born anew. Feeling new. It was happening again. He was shedding something of himself. Pain, betrayal, becoming nothing but dust in his heart. Ghosts were dying. There was no room for shadows. Not with her.

"Nice night," she said softly. "Stars."

"Yes," he said.

"Right there." Soria pointed. "North."

"North," he echoed. "My homeland. I doubt it exists anymore."

"It does not mean you stop looking."

He smiled faintly, sliding his arm around her and leaning back until she sprawled warm and soft across his chest. "And if I have found home? Some measure of peace? What if all I wanted was to stay here in this spot, with you? Or perhaps journey south, or across the oceans? What if I wanted to simply live, without fighting, without war? With you?"

"That is a long trip," she said, brushing her lips against his mouth. "You think you can stand me for as long as it takes?"

"Only if it takes all my life," he murmured. "There is no journey without you."

Soria stared into his eyes, defiant and brave, and unafraid.

"Let's get started," she whispered.

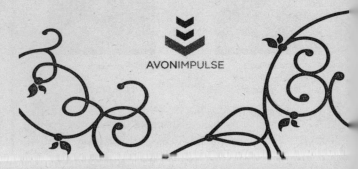